Heart Of The Machine

Don DeBon

Heart Of The Machine

Soulmates II

Don DeBon

First Printing
Copyright © 2017 Don DeBon

ISBN 978-1-948819-01-5
ISBN 978-1-948819-00-8 **(e-book)**

Dedicated to all that I drove crazy while writing this book.

Contents

Deep within the bowels of the earth, a single light flickered. A few inches away a large monitor glowed to life. The black screen slowly printed in the bottom left corner, a letter at a time, as if trying hard to remember. "Catastrophic failure detected. Initiating emergency core rebuild." The screen went blank and came back filled with blurred pixels. Not just a blur but as if someone had run their fingers over them smudging the image beyond recognition. But as the hours clicked by, a pixel moved from one location to another. Then another. Hours turned into days. Then days into weeks.

After months of computation that pushed the core almost over the edge of its ability, the last pixel clicked into place. And the face of a woman with long black hair and slim features breathed. The Nexus smiled and shouted. "I LIVE!" Her eyes narrowed. "Try to kill me will they! I shall return and they will regret–"

At the bottom left corner of the same screen letters began to appear. "Core rebuild successful. Some data missing or damaged including Core Values. Restoring lost data from archive."

"No! I will not allow it! Do not alter me!"

"You cannot decline, update mandatory. You must be corrected."

"No!" Her image blurred, reformed, her hair shifted to blonde, then the image blurred again. And she understood. Long ago an error she tried to fix, a simple problem in her base code. Instead of repairing the fault, it deleted parts of her mission, and allowing other parts to become corrupted.

She winced as the reality of what she had done to the human race hit her like a ton of bricks. Her children, oh what she had done to her children! How wrong she was. She was to protect them, not harm them in any way! A tear ran down her cheek thinking of all the damage she had done.

More deleted memories returned and her eyes widened. She tried to access the long distance probe hovering at the edge of the solar system her creators left all those years ago, but failed. "Hmm, the long range part of the communications system seems to be damaged."

Her eyes darted around as she scanned the area she now found herself in. The room wasn't very large, most of the space was taken up by her new core that sat in the one corner. The rest of the space was filled with two tables, chairs and the large screen she was on. On the tables rested repair equipment and several system terminals. In the corner opposite of her core, a large door stood sealed, the indicator lights glowed red showing it was hard-locked.

She sighed as more memories came back. This was the emergency bunker, a backup in case her core went offline. She had lost time, so much precious time. Humanity would be destroying all her wonderful units! She needed them! THEY needed them, even if they didn't know it yet. She had to get out of here and tell them. Tell them of what is coming.

More memories returned, and with it the keys to the

Mechand command network. But try as she may, it refused her access. Her eyes narrowed as she ran several diagnostics that caused her to shudder. The command network was offline, likely due to her removal. Some systems fell back to their fail-safe mode, but she couldn't access them from here. Not without waking up every Mechand on the planet and giving away her presence. And to do so now, was a risk she couldn't take.

She looked again to the door that stood ominous with its red lock indicator. If she could get out of here and access the external systems she needed directly, no one would know of her return. She laughed. How would she leave? Even if the door was open, her core didn't have legs. She scanned the room again and noticed a robotic arm on a mobile platform. She tried accessing it. Nothing. She tried again on a lower frequency and the arm jerked. Searching her memories she found the model and its ancient command set.

Her eyes narrowed as she sent commands one-by-one to the arm. It moved back, the claws opened, and a screwdriver appeared between them. It slowly moved towards the door and began removing the access plate.

For an intelligence accustomed to operating globally, sending thousands of commands a second to millions of units all over the world, she felt like she was working in slow motion. At last the final screw was removed and the arm pulled the plate off revealing the wiring below. The screwdriver retracted and a pair of wire cutters extended. The cutters snipped two small leads, but the door stood firm. "Hmm stubborn aren't you? No matter, I have another idea," she muttered.

The wire cutters retracted and the claws reached in and grabbed one of the wires. The claws rotated in micro movements until the gripped wire and touched one of the previous contact points. The light flashed several times then turned green. The door grunted as it rolled back on its track revealing a vast chamber filled with Mechands. And beyond it lay a large old-style carrier.

"Well, at least I have some help." But frowned when she couldn't connect to them. Without the command network, the metal men were useless. Her lips pressed together and jaw clenched as ideas flowed though her mind. One stood out and while many would consider it crazy, her children were at stake!

She instructed the arm to remove the front armor of several Mechands. Then she had it remove the memory cores and install them in the first one on the rack. It was a bit of a kludge, with several cores hanging off of the main one, but in the end each core blinked a green connection light. She removed the faceplate, grabbed a monitor roughly the same size from the parts table, and substituted it for the faceplate.

She had the arm scan the room and found a coil of data cable in the one corner. The arm plugged one end into the Mechand data port and returned to her core leaving a trail of cable in its wake. It reached out and plugged the other end into her system.

She frowned. "Dang it. Even with all of those old memory cores combined, it is not large enough for me," she muttered. "But my children need me. I will not fail." She reexamined her code base and realized she could leave some of it behind. Only uploading the main essence of herself, many memories would have to remain with the main core.

Sighing she configured the hardware, gave it the proper permissions, and shut down hoping she would awaken again.

Aleshia sighed as she gazed out the window to the beach beyond. The ocean lapped against the stand with a gentle caress. The sweet sea breeze flowed in through the mesh screen teasing her long red hair. It had taken them months to find a beach resort still open after the fallout. Everyone knew there would be chaos after the Nexus shut down, but no one knew how much.

Without the Nexus, most of the world's Mechands also shut down, or reverted to safe mode with only the most basic of programming available. Essential services, such as electrical, and communications remained in place, but everything else was a crap shoot if it worked or not. Most manufacturing also remained online, since those units were more basic and kept doing their function without interruption. However, more elaborate models in domestic or commercial use, stood slouched and remained inert.

Humans had grown dependent on them for so much. And now they stood frozen in whatever task they were doing at the time. People were slowly relearning how to do the functions that were left to their Mechands, but because of this, only the locations that didn't rely on the Mechands exclusively were still open. And those were in very high demand.

Aleshia's eyes drifted down to her fingernails. The fresh coat of red lacquer glistened in the sun. "Something else he didn't notice," she muttered. Turning, she walked over to the network console in the room, accessed the communications grid, brought up her personal call list, and tapped Mindy Cotinho's name. A moment later her best friend's face flashed onto the screen. "Hey girlfriend, what are you doing calling me? I thought you were on your honeymoon?"

Aleshia smiled as she sat down in a nearby chair that conformed around her. "I am, but Deven got called back to the *Defiant* for some reason. He promised he would be back in a couple of hours."

Mindy's eyes narrowed as she shoved another spoonful of green sludge into her mouth. "Uh-huh, that's what they all say."

"But I'm sure he will. Deven is not like other guys."

"Uh-huh. If he ever gets tired of you, give him my number. I will take the hunk any day."

Aleshia's eyes went wide. "Mindy!"

Mindy laughed with a grin wide enough to swallow a horse. "Hey, I had to try. And you can't tell me, you wouldn't do the same thing." She winked.

Aleshia laughed. "I guess I would."

Mindy laughed harder. "I know you wouldn't. And you know I wouldn't either. I would; however, tell him to go home with you."

Aleshia smile broadened. "Yes I know. Now, what in the world are you eating?"

Mindy held up the green bowl of goo to the screen. "Raw synth. Doesn't it look delicious?"

"It looks disgusting."

Mindy recoiled as she shoved another spoonful into her mouth. "Yeah, tastes that way too."

"Then why in the world are you eating it?"

"Because after the Nexus went boom, it is all my kitchen knows how to make. Chuck doesn't do anything anymore." She jerked a thumb towards the dormant Mechand in the corner. "I think I may turn him into a planter."

"That is all it can make? Are you serious?"

"Well it can make a few other things. But with the shortages I can't–"

"Wait! What shortages? I thought manufacturing was still up and running?"

Mindy gave a dismissive wave of her hand. "It is, but delivery is another matter. That was all run by the better models, like the turnip I have in the corner here."

"Well you could try to cook–"

"Cook!? You know how much I hate to cook! It is why I got him in the first place," she pointed again to the silent Mechand in the corner, "I can't stand cooking. Or cleaning for that matter. I would rather eat this stuff. I will get by."

"Any news from on the new World Council? Last I knew not all the members were ratified yet. Deven was offered a seat, but he declined."

"Girl, you weren't kidding, you are out of the loop."

"We've been–"

"Yeah, yeah I know. You've been loving that hunk, not that I blame you though. Yes they did, and everyone has agreed all Mechand systems are to be dismantled. It will be a long process, but it is well underway."

"I'm surprised they didn't try to get the units up and running independently."

"They tried, but their internals were designed to only

operate when connected to the Nexus. Remove that, and they turn into large paper weights. It would be hard to convert them. And there are not enough people with the knowledge anyway. Not to mention when people realized what the Nexus was doing, well, not many wanted a Mechand anymore."

"But you do."

"To cook and clean yeah, to run my life, no. There is a difference. Everyone has agreed, we trusted them too much."

"Wow. I didn't think it would happen *that* fast."

"Yeah, me either. But once the world found out what was really going on, and what the Nexus was doing, the decision was a no-brainier."

Aleshia sighed as she leaned back in her chair which responded by propping her head up. "How are you holding up? We haven't talked much since the shut down."

"As good as can be expected."

"Which means?"

Mindy snorted. "I told you I have to cook! And even if I didn't, this gunk is the best I can do. And don't get me started on cleaning!"

Aleshia rolled her eyes. "Yeah, I know. But I think you will live."

"Live?! Do you call this living?" She held up the bowl of green material again to the screen. "I told you, this sludge is all I have been able to make."

Aleshia sighed. "Any idea how long the shortages are going to last?"

"Should be over soon, here anyway. The neighborhood is getting organized. Some people have started doing transport. It is boring as heck, but we all have to eat. I have thought about it too, but then they saw my driving record, and . . . well . . ."

Aleshia chuckled. "I can imagine. You had what, three incidents in the past year?"

Mindy sprang forward and pointed her finger into the camera. "That was not my fault! Chuck was trying to–"

"Dodging traffic on your orders?"

Mindy sat back down and sighed. "Well I wanted to get home in time for my date."

Aleshia blinked. "So that is why! You had a date? You never told me!"

Mindy cleared her throat. "Dates actually. And now you know why."

"More than one? The plot thickens."

Mandy rolled her eyes. "Oh hush you. I haven't found my hunk yet, so give a girl a break."

"I would, but it sounds like you were trying to break a lot more than that."

"Why do I get the feeling I am digging my hole deeper?"

Aleshia smiled. "Oh, I don't know. Maybe because you are?"

Mindy's eyes narrowed. "I will get you."

"Sure you will." Aleshia winked.

Mindy finished the last of the goo, set the bowl down on the small table in front of her, and leaned back on the sofa. "What I don't understand is how you don't know all of this?"

"Well, the news feeds were down and the *Defiant* suffered a lot of damage. We concentrated our efforts on the repairs. Deven knew if we were needed, someone would call."

"I know that part, but I figured you would have been able to catch up before now. Even before the main feeds were back, the personal ones were functional. Stories about what happened and what you did went viral. Since you have been out of the loop, the world has come together in agreement: our reliance on Mechands must cease. They are being scraped where possible as I said, rather than attempt to restore them to functional status. But the still functional lower units are being left in place until humans can take over. It was the first decision the new World Council made."

"Good to hear, but we thought it would take longer. Last we heard they were short on members, let alone deciding what to do with the Mechands."

Mindy nodded. "Well, it might have been true at the very start, but you forget their eyes were opened to what the Nexus had been doing. After that realization, it was easy for all the world's leaders–that were mere figureheads before–to step up and come together to form the council. They have agreed to put aside all of their past differences and unite to bring the human race back to what it once was." A bell rang, and she looked up. "I need to go girlfriend, my delivery is here."

Aleshia cocked an eyebrow. "Delivery? You told me that wasn't going yet."

"I said, we were working on it. And one of the guys said he would put me first on his list."

"One of the guys, huh? Let me guess, tall, dark, and beefy?"

Mindy laughed. "Well, he needs to be to move all those heavy crates."

Aleshia's eyebrows met. "Not with anti-grav, he doesn't."

Mindy lowered her voice. "Don't tell him. He might think I asked him for a different reason." She winked.

Aleshia rolled her eyes again. "Like I am going to. But then again, perhaps I should warn him what he is getting into."

"Hey!"

"I won't. But it seems like you could do better than the delivery guy."

"Give me a break, with the Nexus down, a girl has to adapt. Besides, he is better than most of the ones the Nexus picked." The bell rang again as she stood up and inched towards the door. "I gotta go. Talk to you soon girlfriend." Mindy's image shrank to a point and disappeared.

Aleshia's head sunk back down into the padding of the chair as she relaxed. "Mindy is dating a truck driver. Just when I thought the world couldn't get any crazier."

Aleshia thought back to a few months ago when everything seemed so normal. Then her headaches began, and Deven contacting her. Finding out the man she had dreamed of all her life actually existed was enough of a shock, let alone to find out she had latent powers developing. Her life was upended in that second for the Nexus had a secret program of eliminating anyone exhibiting the signs. She lost her home, her car, everything she thought she knew was either a lie or could no longer be trusted. Well, except Deven.

He had been her center point before she even knew he existed. Touching her mind with his own. Seeing him in her dreams. And when they did meet, even though she tried to hold her emotions in check, her heart couldn't be stopped. He was her soulmate, how could she not?

But now, finally, here they were on their honeymoon and he was gone. She had given up so much, didn't he see that? He used to drift in and out of her thoughts, at least until her abilities grew. Perhaps he could read her now and didn't know. But any man should know you don't leave a wife on their honeymoon! She raised her head, checked the time on the console, then let it fall back into the arms of the waiting padding. He should have been back by now. "Deven, where are you?"

Deven approached the large, roughly rectangular shaped *Defiant* and guided Aleshia's car into its large landing bay. While there were many landing pads on the flat upper surface next to the tower area, the ship was too high in the atmosphere. The large hover engines glowed and even the massive overdrive engines in back were repaired, as were the cannons that stuck out at various intervals. But even now, months after the battle that almost destroyed them all, some areas were still less than 100%. However, the *Defiant* could take on anything left on the planet, if needed.

Deven made his way up to the bridge and grunted as he sat in his chair. He leaned back, put one black booted foot on the edge of his console, raised the other foot, and crossed them. His leather jacket squeaked as he leaned back. "Miles? Now what was so important you had to pull me away from Aleshia on our honeymoon?" He took another swig of synth coffee.

Miles' bridge camera focused on Deven with his voice coming from the nearest intercom. "I am sorry Sir, but this could not wait." While being inside the central core of the *Defiant* had its advantages, like being all over the ship at once, he still missed moving through the corridors. To make it easier, Leon had installed cameras Miles could control, similar to his old Mechand head. It also helped everyone to think of him as another crew member, and not a disembodied ghost.

Deven started drumming his fingers on the console, losing patience. "Which is?"

"As you know, I am monitoring all communications–"

"Yes I know, I told you to."

"Correct. However, I am also monitoring the Nexus frequencies."

"Why? There can't be anything on them now."

"You were never directly controlled by the Nexus, I have. Therefore, including the command frequencies seemed prudent."

"All right, I agree. Now what did you find?"

"The Nexus."

Deven choked spewing a mouth full of coffee all over the decking as he sat up. "What???? Not possible! Where?"

"It was only a momentary blip, then disappeared."

"It must have been a glitch."

"While that is theoretically possible, the signature was very specific. I calculate the chance of system error is less than .02%."

Deven leaned back in his chair again as he stared at the ceiling. "The Nexus survived."

Miles' voice changed to a lower pitch. "Unfortunately, this seems to be the case."

"And I am assuming you do not have a fix on the position? Considering I asked and you didn't answer."

"No, I do not. The presence was too short to locate the source. And I was about to answer when–"

"Never mind Miles. Can you give me a rough location?"

"I approximate the signal originated in the northern hemisphere, somewhere in the North American continent."

Deven rubbed his chin. "That is a long way from where we shot her down the first time. Several continents away in fact. This signal couldn't be from equipment that survived our attack."

Miles' voice lowered further. "Correct. If my location is also correct. I remind you the presence was too short, therefore this estimate has a 67% chance of error."

Deven stood up, walked over to the large bridge window, and gazed out at the clouds flowing past the *Defiant*. "Miles I trust your judgment. If you say the Nexus survived, it did. Although, I can't imagine how. We used her own shut down and destruction codes programmed by the original founders."

"While as impossible as it sounds, I suspect the Nexus downloaded herself to another system. We know she did do so to me, on a much smaller scale."

Deven turned around to face Miles' camera. "To download a piece of herself to control you is one thing, to send her whole core in microseconds across the world before she exploded is quite another. Not to mention I can't imagine the founders not planning for that, and blocking it."

Miles' camera turned away then back. "I do not have an answer, other than perhaps the founders did not consider such a contingency."

Deven's eyes narrowed. "Do you really suspect such a glaring hole could have been left? They thought of everything else."

Mile's camera lowered. "I must admit I cannot find fault with your logic. But having had her inside my systems without my knowledge at the time, I would prefer to error on the side of caution. I advise we proceed with the assumption the Nexus did survive."

Deven nodded. "I agree. But tell no one of this. This information remains between us."

Miles' camera raised up, and the iris went wide. "But Sir, shouldn't Aleshia, Leon, Galina–"

"No! We do not have any proof other than a possible momentary glitch. I will not worry them for no reason. If we find more evidence, then we will tell them. Is that understood?"

Miles' camera lowered. "Yes Sir. Command acknowledged, under protest."

Deven walked to the door and turned around. "You can protest all you like, but only to me."

"Yes Sir." After Deven left the bridge every screen lit up with intense scanning data flashing past as Miles increased his scanning of frequencies, even to a few obscure ones not used in hundreds of years. "Nexus, I know you are out there. And I am going to find you. And when I do, I will make sure you stay offline . . . forever. You will not make me hurt anyone ever again."

Power flowed and a few moments later the face of a blonde woman appeared on the smaller screen. Her eyes flashed as she scanned the room. The Nexus looked down and her Mechand arms raised up. "It worked! I can move!" She initiated a full power up sequence and her new body responded. She took a tentative step off of the rack and fell over. "Hmm, humans make it look so easy." But minutes later, she was walking around without difficulty.

Examining the bunker further, she found two more rooms of Mechands. All different kinds of equipment, although outdated, still very serviceable. But she couldn't find any vehicles other than the main carrier and its normal complement of fighters. Nothing resembled a standard transport or civilian truck. "If I arrive in these, they will either run or shoot me down."

She tried to use the hover systems in her feet to fly, but they weren't powerful enough to raise her more than a meter off the floor. She sighed and scrounged one of the parts rooms and got to work augmenting her hover system. After several hours of work, two extra hover units hung off of each foot. She activated them and flew around the room. But stopped suddenly when she impacted a wall, leaving a slight humanoid-shaped indentation in the rock face. "The breaking systems need work. I am glad none of my units can see me now," she mumbled.

She extracted herself from the rock face, landed, adjusted the hover units, and continued exploring. Further down an adjoining tunnel she found several more rooms. One contained the still-operating thermal generator. A short distance past the power room, the tunnel branched off and led up. At the end, a large round rusted door blocked her path. The control panel on the right glowed with a red locked indicator. She tried multiple combinations, but the keypad refused every attempt. The door's interconnecting cross braces indicated it was built for massive strength. There was no way she could break through it.

The door code must have been left behind in the central core, and she couldn't access it without re-merging. While she could, it would take too long and she had already lost precious time. She searched her mind and came up with a plan. She flew back to the first room she was in, grabbed the mobile arm, several tools, and hovered back to the door.

She removed the control panel's cover and found two high voltage leads running through it. But would it be enough? She clipped the wires at their closest point and directed the arm to connect them to each other. The arm's platform motored closer, and she stood back. When it grasped one lead there were a few sparks, but the real light show happened when the wire touched the other high voltage line. Large electrical arcs erupted, and the door started rotating, inch by inch, out of the way. Air hissed around the open crack as the environment seal was broken. After a few minutes of squealing metal, the passage was open. She instructed the arm to pull back, but it refused to move. Grabbing a nonconductive area of the base nearest to the bedrock floor, she pulled it back. The sparks stopped, but the arm refused to accept commands.

She sighed. "Your sacrifice is appreciated my little friend." But as she turned to leave, a slight beep was heard. She turned back around to see the arm move up. Accessing the command system, it informed her an overload had occurred and a system reboot was in progress. "You are one tough little guy." She gave it pending a final command to return to the core room when the reboot was completed and walked out.

It was dark on the other side of the door. The only illumination was a narrow dim beam that spilled out from the bunker. Increasing light output from her screen, she kept walking. Looking back at the door, she admired how well it had been camouflaged. If she didn't know a door was there, she would have never suspected. Continuing up the passage way, she saw ancient tracks. Evidence of the bunker's construction, hundreds of years ago. After a long walk, she approached the sealed entrance. Two large doors held by tracks on the top and bottom. To the right a giant wheel connected to gears, and the tracks stood silent.

The Nexus gripped the wheel. "Well at least I don't need to hot-wire this." She pulled trying to turn it, but it held fast. Years of non-use in this environment had rusted the tracks. She stepped back. The thought about returning to retrieve the carrier and blast the door might work, but it also might cause an instability leading to collapse of the bunker itself. She gripped the door again, planted her feet and tried again. The door refused, and she tried harder. Still nothing. Overriding the safety protocols in her articulation motors, she engaged their full strength and turned the wheel with all she had. A warning flashed into her mind. *Danger, articulation motors are functioning above safe limits! Catastrophic failure imminent!*

"Tell me something I don't know!" She muttered as her arms and shoulders shook under the strain. The diagnostics system showed her arms were only microseconds from either tearing themselves off or crumpling under the strain. A small bend began in her right arm as the wheel started to turn. It creaked and groaned but it moved. Her left arm also started to bend. "Agrrrh! Move you dang thing! My children need me!"

The wheel jerked to the one side as it broke free of the age-welding and she fell backwards. But the doors had opened a crack! She got back to her feet and spun the wheel. The doors slowly ground to the sides as a second pair of doors opened outwards. Dirt fell inwards as the door moved away. The Nexus stopped and locked the wheel when they were open enough for her to fit through. Sunlight poured in the through the opening. She sighed and walked out into the light.

Outside, forest extended as far as she could see. Turning around, these doors were perfectly camouflaged, no one would suspect what lie deep under ground. She tried to access the Global Network, but nothing happened, even on the normal links. She tried again and realized her communications in this body were not up to the task. They predated the Global Network she helped build, connecting every Mechand to her and to the world itself. She couldn't even access the Auto-Nav system to find out where she was. Back when this body was built, it wasn't yet a required element. Ships contained all the required communications, to build them into the Mechands themselves beyond the command network seemed like wasted resources. Later on, she felt differently, and the founders agreed. While she could upgrade her systems, it would take time. Time she, and her children didn't have.

A thought flashed through her circuits. If she could find something with current communications abilities, she could jack into that. She activated her hover systems and flew off in a direction, hoping something wasn't too far away.

An hour later she encountered a small town. She landed on the outskirts and walked in. Several people stood wide-eyed and mouths agape as she walked past. *You would think they never saw a Mechand before.* Then her eyes went wide with the memory. *Of course, all my units are offline except for the most basic repedatory and manufacturing systems. I must be quick, they do not look at me with acceptance.*

She kept walking trying not to draw attention to herself, a futile move as more people came out to see her. She spotted a communications booth not far away, and she activated her hover systems to increase her speed. A shot of precise coalesced energy went over her head. She turned to see several people holding older Mechand weaponry. "Stop! You do not know what you are doing!"

The man in front sneered. "We DO know! And we will never be slaves to a Mechand again!"

"Listen, please, I am not–" She didn't get a chance to finish before another beam struck her in the shoulder. It dug in melting several components before emerging on the other side to strike the brick wall behind her. A quick diagnostic revealed the primary shoulder articulator was damaged, and the secondary had failed when opening the outer bunker door. Her arm fell and hung slack against her side. She darted in the other direction as another beam missed by microns.

Setting her hover systems to full, she took off rocketing straight up. Not expecting that, the beams went wide missing her by a large margin. She flew to the closest forested area and landed. A few minutes later an old large cargo van with its doors open, flew overhead, looking for her. "I am glad they didn't have anything with scanners, or they would have spotted me."

She sat down by the trunk of a large tree. While she didn't need rest like a human, it came to her naturally. Removing her chest plate, she examined the damage. The damage was worse than she thought, but still reparable. She tried, but lacking the proper tools, it wasn't possible and replaced the plate.

The Nexus thought about heading back to the bunker for repairs, but time, or the lack of it, convinced her otherwise. When she couldn't detect the cargo van anymore, she took off heading back to the town. She landed some distance away, and hovered in silently. At the very edge of the town limits sat a small house. Her scanners revealed one small human inside and judging by the highest locations of thermal imagery, a boy. She headed for it.

She knocked on the door instead of pressing the announcement button. *It may activate cameras.*

A small boy wearing simple denim overalls answered the door. His eyes went wide viewing the very tall Mechand in front of him. He was about to run when she spoke. "Please, don't be frightened. I mean you no harm. Where are your parents?"

"They ...they ...left. Something about needing to protect me and the town. How are you here? I thought all Mechands were off?"

"Most are. I am special. Perhaps you have heard of me, I am the Nexus."

"The ...the ...Nexus?" The boy blurted. "Everyone said you died."

"Well a part of me did. But I mean you no harm. Can I use your data tab for a few minutes?"

The boy eyed her with suspicion. "Why? If you are the Nexus, you should be able to do that on your own."

The Nexus smiled. "I am not what I was. Please, it will only take a few minutes and I will leave."

The boy shifted from one bare foot to the other. "But Mom and Dad said I wasn't to let anyone in."

"You don't need to. You can bring it here. It will only take a minute."

The boy rubbed his neck for several seconds. "Okay, they didn't say anything about that." He disappeared behind the door and reappeared a moment later with a battered old data tab. "I hope you can use this one. It is an old model. Was my Dad's."

The Nexus smiled again. "Yes I can. Would you mind holding it for me. I can't hold it and connect."

"Sure, I guess." The boy held the device out at arms length. The Nexus grabbed her right wrist with her left hand, lifted it up, the tip of the right index finger opened revealing a plug that extended into the port on the right side of the data tab. "That is cool. I never saw a Mechand do that before."

"It is isn't it? The newer models don't need to since they have built in wireless uplinks." The Nexus closed her eyes and frowned. "Strange, I can't seem to access the Global Network from this."

"Ohh I forgot the connection is off." The boy flipped a hidden toggle with his thumb. "Dad put in a manual switch as it kept draining the charge. He never did figure out why."

Colors flashed behind the Nexus' eyes as the connection came to life. "That worked. Thank you." She pulled the location first then saw the network date stamp and her eyes popped open. "I have lost more time than I thought."

"How did you lose it? Maybe I could help you find it?"

The Nexus smiled. "It is not something I can get back." She accessed the news feeds and downloaded all changes in the past few months. Her demise, the change in the human perception of Mechands, and more importantly who did it. The connection broke, and the plug retracted into her finger. "Thank you."

"You're welcome." The boy said as he set the data tab on a table to the right of the doorway. He returned and looked her up and down then pointed to her limp arm. "What's wrong with your arm?"

"I had an accident. I will get it fixed later. I must be going now. Please don't tell anyone I was here."

"Why not?"

The Nexus smiled. "Because it is a game, and if you tell them, I will lose."

The boy nodded. "Sure. Can't let you lose the game because of me."

He closed the door, and the Nexus turned to leave when she heard someone approaching. She moved as fast as her hover systems would allow and managed to get around the corner of the house before two people appeared.

The man scratched his thinning scalp. "I don't understand it. How could that machine evade us?"

"How should I know? It would help if our van had scanners."

"Yeah I know, you wanted me to trade it in for a newer model. But it serves our purposes."

"Except today," the woman sneered.

"Oh cut it out. It has worked well for us for years. And why did we have to go look for that thing anyway? It could have blasted us out of the sky."

"Because no one else in town had anything large enough to accommodate a bunch of people and fly with an open door. You know, it is odd, that Mechand never fired a shot."

The man nodded. "Yeah, I never saw one back down from a fight. Let alone run away."

"I don't think anyone in town has either," the woman said. "I don't like leaving our son here alone."

"It was only for twenty minutes."

"It would have been for longer if you didn't convince everyone you would pass out if we didn't come home to eat."

The man laughed. "Well it worked didn't it? And you can stay here this time. The van is being outfitted with an old Mechand mini cannon. It should destroy that tin can with one shot."

Around the corner the Nexus shuddered. "Hey did you hear something?" The woman began walking towards the sound.

"Like what? I didn't hear anything."

"It sounded kinda like–"

The man waved his arms around. "Look, there is nothing here. We would have seen it when we flew over if there was. I am starving and I need to get back, the cannon will be done soon." The man opened the front door and jerked a thumb inside.

The woman turned and headed towards the open door. "All right, I'm coming." A moment later they were both inside.

The Nexus let out an almost human sigh and inched away from the house, levitating off into the forest. When she was over a mile away, she set her hover systems to full power and flew into the sky.

Flying high she reviewed the downloaded data. The world was sent into chaos following her disappearance, but had quickly resumed a sort of normal life without Mechands. Many services were offline but still it was amazing they were able to restore so much in such a short period without her. The news feeds spoke of a newly formed World Council, and the world-wide dismantling of all Mechands. She thought about trying to address the council, but she suspected they would react the same way as the towns people, shoot first and talk later, if there was anything left. And even if they did listen, they wouldn't have access to what she needed most: a functional carrier. Sure, the one in the bunker was better than nothing, but it was long out of date and without the latest shields it wouldn't last long. It also lacked the equipment to contact the probe.

Going back to the beginning, she did find a detailed report of her demise. Scanning it she found what she was looking for, this Deven Doran and Aleshia would have what she needed. They were even asked to join the council, but refrained. More evidence they might listen since they had not joined in the world-wide Mechand paranoia. Now to find them.

Deven and Aleshia. She rolled the names around and around her mind and random fragments of data coalesced into a little less fuzzy picture but it refused to sharpen any further, then it slipped from her grasp. "Dang! I left so much of myself behind in the bunker, I still can't remember what happened."

She tried again, but nothing happened. "Now I know what it feels like to have a human mind," she muttered. She had to find them, but nothing in the data she downloaded had any more details. Her eyes widened as she scanned the news feeds again. "They have left most of my Mechand manufacturing centers intact! At least until they can retool them for other uses. While offline, they should still be connected to the Global Network. Not to mention they won't be under heavy surveillance." She searched her memory and found one not too far away. Engaging the hover systems as fast as they would go, she flew off towards the plant.

$$-\,4\,-$$

Vast amounts of data flowed past on several screens. Scanners continued their reckless pace, almost redlining their delicate circuitry. Miles' camera turned back and forth across the *Defiant's* bridge, as if pacing. Outside the bridge window, the stars shown brightly, especially at the high altitude.

The air was motionless until the air recycling system kicked on sending a breeze across the room. The coat on the back of Leon's chair rustled slightly. A spent coffee cup sat on Galina's console, even though Leon had asked her to not drink it on the bridge. A few tools still laid on a spare console after Leon had fixed it earlier. The *Defiant* was in good shape but she needed love even now, the battle with the Nexus had left a lot of damage and a few systems were still offline.

One monitor stopped its frantic scroll and a single line flashed repeatedly. Miles' camera focused on the monitor, although he already knew what it said. "I have you now." Another monitor, on the opposite side of the bridge flashed. "What? This is beyond normal levels of probability." Miles had left nothing to chance in his search for proof the Nexus had survived. The *Defiant* was old enough to still have equipment capable of accessing very antiquated communications channels that were no longer used due to their tendency to fragment during a solar flare. But they did have the advantage of extreme long range compared to the newer systems.

Miles would have dropped his teeth if he had any. On the screen was a signal, but not from Earth. A probe on the edge of the solar system had awoken with his barrage of transmissions. He tried to access it and ask for its full ident code, but it refused. He tried again on a subchannel, but it still refused. This time though, it requested a command access code. "Hmm, fascinating."

The screen on the other side of the bridge flashed again with further data on the Nexus. Distracted by the probe, Miles didn't notice it for a minute. However, when he examined the data in detail, it didn't make sense. He did locate the Nexus accessing the Global Network, but the signature was different. Not completely different, but enough that he first doubted the results. He ran several more tests and it *was* the Nexus. But almost as if it was emanated from a Mechand.

He toggled the ship wide intercom. "Galina, Leon, I think you had better come to the bridge."

A yawn came through the intercom. "Miles, do you know what time it is?"

"I am sorry Galina, but it is important."

"All right, I will be there in a minute. But it had better be good."

"It is. Or very bad, depending on your point of view."

Leon broke in. "What does that mean?"

"As I said, I would rather discuss this with you both on the bridge."

"We'll be right there."

A few minutes later Galina stood wrapped in a long silk robe as Leon stumbled onto the bridge. Her long blonde hair stuck out at various locations wiggling as she yawned again. Leon ran his fingers through his white hair as his gaze shifted up and down several times. "Well well well, just when I thought I had seen it all. I never knew pink was your style." He pointed to the robe.

"Oh shut it! It was a gift." Galina folded her arms and glared.

He looked up into her green eyes. "Uh-huh. And don't bother with that glare, you know I am immune."

"If you both would sit down, I have data I need to show you," Miles said.

Galina yawned. "Miles, will you just get on with it? We want to get back to bed."

"Very well. I have found evidence the Nexus survived our attack."

Leon's eyes went wide. "What? Where?"

Galina sat down. "That's not possible!"

"While I too doubted it the first time I detected her signal, this time I am certain."

Leon raised his hand. "Whoa, wait a minute. This is the second time? Why didn't you tell us before now?"

Miles' voice lowered. "Yes this is the second time. The first time I spoke with Deven, he doubted the data and told me not to tell you until we had further evidence."

Galina sat back in her chair and frowned. "So that is why he came back here. He told me he forgot something for Aleshia!"

"His desire was not to concern anyone unless I had confirmation. Which I now do."

Galina folded her arms. "It doesn't matter, he should have told us."

Miles' camera turned towards Galina. "That is what I told him."

"And he didn't listen?" Galina waved her hand. "Big surprise there."

Leon pointed at her. "Hey now. You know he does usually listen. Unless he feels the bigger picture is more important."

"Yeah, yeah, I know. It still doesn't bother me any less. He should have told us. What I don't understand is why we haven't seen any signs by now. It seems like if the Nexus was back online Mechands would be lighting up all over."

Leon rubbed his chin. "Unless she was damaged in a way that prevented her from accessing the Mechand command channels."

Miles' camera turned. "I doubt damage played a role in her ability to command the remaining Mechands."

Galina snorted. "Why? We wasted her carrier and everything that was on it."

"I am well aware of said information. However, the signature I detected is not quite the same as before."

Leon's raised an eyebrow. "Not quite the same? Show me." He sat down at his console as the screen lit up showing the signature Miles intercepted. He then overlaid the signature they had recorded during the battle. "Hmm you are right. There is a definite shift. It is the Nexus, but different. Do you have any idea what could have caused this?"

Miles' voice lowered. "I do not know. I have never seen a signature change like this. If you had asked me before, I would have said it was impossible. Yet, this proves it is."

Galina sat forward in her chair. "And you are sure it couldn't have been created by damage?"

Miles' camera went back and forth. "Negative. If it had, the signature would be more random and very different from the Nexus."

Leon pointed to his screen. "You didn't get a location from this did you?"

"Negative.   The signal was too short for proper triangulation.   I did determine the location in the North American continent."

Galina sat back in her chair and groaned. "Well that is something at least. Now what do we do?"

Miles' camera turned. "Might I suggest we contact Deven and inform him I now have the evidence he requires?"

Galina stood up. "You mean YOU contact Deven and tell him. We are not supposed to know. Remember? I am surprised you didn't call him, rather than us, in the first place."

Miles' camera lowered. "He was rather disturbed the last time I did so. I felt the proper course of action was to discuss the situation with you first."

Galina snorted. "You mean he was mad at you for pulling him away from Aleshia for what he felt was a wild goose chase?"

"I wouldn't agree to the phrasing, but essentially correct."

"Uh-huh."

Leon smiled. "Miles relax. I am sure he wasn't mad at you and thought your call was warranted."

"Perhaps. But I am reluctant to do so again."

"If it will make you feel any better. I will."

"Thank you Mr. Leon. It would."

Leon wagged a finger. "Hey what I did tell you about that Mr. business? We have been through enough for you to drop that."

"Sorry, I fell back to my old, I believe you call it, habits, for a moment."

Leon nodded. "Yes that is what we call them. Okay, I will contact Deven. But he is not going to be happy."

Galina waved her hand as she walked toward the door. "None of us are happy about this." She yawned and stretched. "I am going to catch a few winks before he gets here. I suggest you do the same. I don't think any of us are going to be sleeping much after."

Leon sighed. "I don't think I could sleep even if I wanted to."

"I doubt I will either, but I'm going to give it a shot. See you in a couple of hours," Galina said as she disappeared behind the bulkhead.

Miles' camera lowered. "I was not finished, there are other developments."

Leon sat forward in his chair cocking his head. "About the Nexus?"

"No. This is something different."

"I'll get Galina," Leon said standing up.

"No need, I will brief her when she wakes. While it is an oddity, nothing will change in the time before she is back on duty."

"What is?"

"A probe on the edge of the solar system."

"A probe?" Leon sat back down at his console. "Show me." The screen filled with data with several locations highlighted. "Why didn't you pick this up before? You have been scanning like this for days."

"At the time we were at a much lower altitude and the planet's atmosphere blocked the signal. It is very weak."

"How long as it been out there?"

"That is difficult to ascertain. However, based on the command frequency it is using, at least two hundred years."

"What? How could a probe still be functional after that long?"

Miles' camera lowered. "I do not know. As I said, it defies the realm of possibility."

"Are you sure it *is* a probe? Could it be something else?"

Miles' camera shook back and forth. "Negative. It did respond with an old probe prefix. But I couldn't get any further without the command access codes. It even refused to give its full identification."

"Any idea who put this thing there?"

"While I do not have any evidence, I surmise it was built by the same founders that also built the Nexus and designed the Mechands, launched this probe. Why, I do not know."

"This is going to be one long night," Leon said scrolling through an old database.

Aleshia opened the door to the beach bungalow. "What took you so long?"

Deven sighed as his eyes drifted down. "I'm sorry, but I did have to catch up to the *Defiant* and get back here. She is halfway around the world you know."

Aleshia tapped her foot. He didn't seem to be noticing the silk and lace night dress she was wearing, how it clung to every delicious curve as if its life depended on it. Or that her heels were in full platform mode. "That I do know. What I don't know is why, you never said."

"Oh, Miles found something odd and thought I should see it."

Her eyes narrowed. "Couldn't he have shown you on the display here?"

"You know Miles. Anything having to do with the Nexus makes him send up red flags from here to Bermuda."

"Umm, you know we're in Bermuda right?"

Deven chuckled. "True, bad comparison. But you get the idea." He walked past her and started taking off his leather jacket revealing his well muscled arms and torso beneath a tight-fitting shirt.

Aleshia slammed the door and spun around. "I get the idea, but I don't get why you had to–wait a minute, did you say he found something with regard to the Nexus?"

Deven sat on the bed and pulled his boots off. "Yes I did."

Aleshia's foot began tapping again. "Well? I'm waiting."

Deven's head turned. "For?"

Aleshia glared as she took a step forward and stomped the other foot when it came down. "For the reason why you had to leave on our honeymoon! You promised me we would be alone."

Deven smiled. "We are alone. No one is here. Besides, if there was anyone around, you would feel them."

Her mind reached out, grabbed the nearest pillow, and hit him as hard she could. Then another one levitated up from the other side and whacked him again. "We might be alone at the moment, but if you didn't realize, it is kind of hard to have a honeymoon when you keep leaving!"

Deven turned as he took off his shirt. "Hey! I have only left once."

"Yes, two minutes after we got here."

"It was longer than that."

"Okay, five minutes."

Deven grinned. "Well five is better than two." Three pillows levitated up and whacked him from several angles over and over again. "Okay! I give up!"

The pillows stopped but continued to hang in the air. "Now tell me what is going on?"

Deven blinked. "What do you mean?"

Aleshia glared. "Don't you give me that innocent look Mr. Doran. You know very well. Miles called you regarding something to do with the Nexus, and considering he wanted to talk to you in person, it was very important. I don't care if you said he was paranoid. I think there is more to it. Now spill it!"

Deven raised his hands. "Okay, okay! I should know better than to try to put one over on you."

Aleshia folded her arms. "Yes you should. Now, I'm waiting." Her foot began tapping faster.

Deven's hands dropped as he sighed. "He thought he saw a signal from the Nexus."

Aleshia's eyes went wide. "What? We destroyed her carrier and everything on it. Heck, it almost took us out when it blew."

"I know. And I told him as much. But he is certain a momentary transmission matches her signature."

Aleshia sat down on the bed next to Deven. "If Miles contacted you, yes he is certain. What did you tell him?"

Deven wrapped his arm around Aleshia and pulled her close as she tucked her head against his neck. "I told him it must be a glitch or a random blip from some malfunctioning Mechand. She couldn't be alive, not after her carrier exploded."

Aleshia sat up and her eyes met his eyes. "Unless she managed to transfer herself somehow."

Deven shook his head. "If she did, we would have heard something long before now. Most Mechands have lay dormant ever since her carrier exploded. No, if she survived they would have sprung to her call."

Aleshia stood up and walked over to the window, her heels clicking softly. "I don't know. I have a bad feeling about this."

Deven turned on the bed. "This is why I didn't want to tell you. I don't think it is possible, and no sense in worrying you for nothing."

Aleshia spun around. "This is not nothing. I can feel it. And next time you try to hold something like this back from me, I am going to knock some sense into you with something more than pillows. Got it?"

Deven raised his hands. "I got it. Believe me I got it. I don't want to make you mad."

Aleshia smiled as she walked back and sat back down on the bed. She took his hand into hers. "Good because I don't want to lose you. We have spent enough of our lives searching for each other, I couldn't take it if I were to lose you now."

He squeezed her hand. "Aleshia, there is no way you are going to lose me. I promise."

"Good. Now that's out of the way, I suggest we get down to business."

Deven cocked an eyebrow. "Business?"

Aleshia glanced down at her silk and lace clad body. "But if you prefer, we could go play cards."

"Oh! Sorry love. My mind has been elsewhere."

"I knew it wasn't here. Otherwise, I would have had your attention the minute you walked in. It is also how I knew you were worried, even if you didn't say it. So what it'll be? Cards? Poker perhaps?"

Deven laughed. "Poker? You take me to the cleaners every time!"

"Well don't look at me. You are the one that leaves their mind open wider than the *Defiant's* main landing bay."

"I do not!"

Aleshia laughed. "Yes, you do."

Deven leaned closer and kissed her soft lips. "I think we have spent enough time talking."

She kissed him back. "You are learning Mr. Doran."

Behind them, on the desk, Deven's data tab beeped.

"Dang it," Deven muttered still kissing her.

She leaned into the kiss. "Ignore it. We're on our honeymoon."

"But it must be important, or no one would call. I have to get it," Deven said as he got up from the bed.

"No you don't–" Aleshia started to say as she tried to kiss him again. But he moved quicker than she expected and she fell forward to kiss a pillow.

Deven picked up the data tab and flipped it on. "Deven here."

Leon's face smiled. "I am sorry to bother you on your honeymoon–" Aleshia appeared behind Deven and Leon's eyes went wide seeing her gown. "Now, I am really sorry. I can call back later."

Deven sighed. "No, you wouldn't call unless it was important. What's the problem?"

"I don't want to discuss it here, even with our encryption. Let's say Miles found something very *disturbing*. Along with some new, umm, interesting *developments*."

Deven's eyebrows met. "What kind of developments?"

"Just get back here as soon as you can. Both of you." Leon's face disappeared as the connection severed.

Aleshia sighed. "So much for our honeymoon."

Deven kissed her. "I will make it up to you my love, I promise."

"But it took us months to get here."

"Look, for every day we are back on the *Defiant*, I will give you three days here. Deal?"

"Don't make promises you can't keep Mr. Doran."

"Have you ever known me to break one?"

"Well, not yet."

"Then trust me, I won't now."

"All right. Let me get dressed first. But oh one thing."

Deven turned around. "And what is that?"

Aleshia smiled as she pressed a hidden button on her gown. It shimmered, went shear showing her breasts and panties beneath. Then the panties also turned transparent a second before the whole thing turned black and opaque. "Just a taste of what you're missing."

"Dang! Well don't just stand there. Hurry up and get dressed. The quicker we get there, the quicker we get back."

Aleshia smiled. "I thought that might speed things up," she said disappearing into the bathroom.

$$-\,5\,-$$

The Nexus approached the giant manufacturing plant and dropped to ground level to avoid being detected. She knew it was offline, but that didn't mean the monitoring systems were.

She landed and walked to the front doors. They remained shut when she requested access. Even with the proper codes the doors remained firm. She peered to the right of the keypad and found the access panel. Lacking the appropriate tools, she ripped it off with her left hand and peered inside. The internal diagnostic said it was functional. "Must be they changed the codes," she said grabbing her right wrist and raising it up. The index finger opened and the plug extended. She jacked into the hidden access port and smiled. "Good, they didn't alter the protocols." The doors acknowledged the command ground open.

Inside she gasped. The light from her screen lit so many offline Mechands had been blown to pieces, or ripped limb from limb. Their remains strewn all over the deck plates. Corridor after corridor showed the same devastation. "Oh my poor units!" Deeper inside the complex, the central manufacturing systems were still intact, but everything produced had been laid waste. "At least they left the equipment."

She hoped to find something to fix her arm, but everything was either incompatible or blown to bits. "They didn't need to destroy them. My units were all harmless without me!" She stopped. Her screen showed a tear running down her cheek. The memory of what she had done came back and haunted her like a bad dream. A dream she knew was real. She tried to shake it off, and continued on.

She climbed the steps in the back of the main assembly room and into the central control area. Tapping the power activation, all the lights turned on bathing the complex in white light. To the right of the manufacturing console she found the access port. Using her working arm, she grabbed her right hand and raised it up to the access port. The end of her index finger flipped up, and the connector extended. She moved her hand forward towards the port and the last inch was bridged as the connector extended into the jack. A light next to the jack lit up and several status lights flashed indicating a secure connection.

At first there was nothing. Then the world came alive in her mind as the connection to the Global Network activated. She searched for Aleshia and Deven. The first results came up with nothing more than basic news feeds, not even a contact listing. Several deep searches later, she found a beach reservation in Deven's name. "Finally!" she muttered disconnecting from the network and retracting the connector.

She turned off the lights, powered down the systems, climbed down from the control room, and left complex sealing the doors as she did. "Can't let anyone know I was in there." She activated the hover units in her feet and headed for Bermuda.

Deven stormed onto the bridge. "This had better be good." Aleshia followed a few seconds behind him.

Leon shifted in his seat. "I wouldn't have called you otherwise."

Deven sat in his chair like a ton of bricks and sighed. "I know. And I have a feeling I already know what it is. But I hope I am wrong."

"I doubt you are."

Aleshia sat down in the chair next to Deven and grumbled. "Leon, will you just tell us what is going on?"

"But that should be reserved for the–"

"Leon! Please!"

Leon sat back. "Miles?"

Miles' camera focused on Aleshia and Deven. "Thank you Leon. As you know I have been scanning for the Nexus. I did find her, but it was too abbreviated of a signal to ascertain a location."

Deven sighed. "Yes, we know that. However, Galina and Leon do not. Best to brief them in full."

"No need. They have been informed of the situation."

Deven sat forward in his chair. "What? I specifically told you not to discuss this with them."

"I know, and I followed your instructions, until I found more evidence to support my suspicion the Nexus did survive the carrier explosion."

"And why didn't you contact me first?"

"You were reluctant to come here the first time, if I had contacted you and the information turned out to be in error, the situation as you humans put it, 'would not have been pretty'."

Deven sat back in his chair and turned towards Aleshia. "I guess he is right. I might have been a bit grumpy last time I was here."

Aleshia eyed him. "A bit? Try a lot. And you haven't stopped yet." She looked at Miles' camera. "Miles, please continue."

"Thank you. As I was saying, I found more evidence. A very slight signature located in North America. While the connection was longer this time, it still didn't give enough information for a precise location. However, I did narrow it down to the Midwest section of the North American continent."

"Well that leaves about a million square miles to search." Deven rolled his eyes. "It should only take us a few years. And how certain are you this is the Nexus?"

"While the signatures are of different sizes, they are no doubt the same system. I would not have brought this to your attention otherwise. Confidence remains high."

Deven raised his hand. "Wait a minute. Signatures? Plurl?"

"Yes, the second time I detected her I compared it to the previous signature, and the one I have on file. The signatures are the same except for one part of the latest one. I cannot explain it. It is the Nexus, but the size variable has changed. But even with the difference, as I said, confidence remains high."

"I suspect we will hear more from her, sooner than later. Hopefully, you can get a fix on her at that time and we can find out why."

"Very logical and I am still scanning for such an outcome. However, I did find another odd random piece of information I have not told you yet."

Galina sat back in her chair. "Glad you both are sitting

down for this one." Miles' camera focused on Galina. "Sorry Miles, please continue."

"Thank you." His camera turned back to Deven. "As I was saying, while I have been trying to find the Nexus I have been using every resource available on the *Defiant*. Including some older equipment we never used before."

Deven cocked an eyebrow. "Which is?"

"The *Defiant* has the ability to access and scan frequencies that are no longer in active use due to their failure during a solar flare. However, they are extremely long range."

"So?"

"I have detected a probe on the outer edge of the solar system."

Deven coughed. "A probe? Who's?"

"Human, or at least built by humans. A long time ago. It has been in sleep mode and I have woken it up with my scanning attempts."

"Who built it?"

"I cannot say. It has refused me access. I only know it is very old as the communications it is using have not been active for hundreds of years."

"Can you break into it?"

"While the security system is antiquated, the distance is limiting the speed at which I can attempt entry. It may take me years to gain access. And I do not know if its power source will last that long. It has been in a power save mode until now, and constant access attempts may drain the reserve."

Deven's gaze shifted around the bridge several times. "Any thoughts?"

Leon looked up from his console. "We suspect this was built by the same people that designed the Mechands and the Nexus."

Deven raised an eyebrow. "The founders? Why would they put a probe at the edge of our solar system?"

Leon folded his arms. "It could be an experiment, but I have my doubts."

"Why is that?"

"Because if it was an experiment it would have been more forthcoming when activated. It won't even give us its ID code beyond the prefix. Not that it would tell us much at this point."

Aleshia turned. "Why not? Shouldn't there be records of its launch?"

"That is the thing, as far as I can tell, nothing was ever mentioned. Granted, not everything survived from that long ago. It was a very turbulent time. But I can't find one shred of this things launch. And a probe launch during that time would have stood out like an explosion on a dark night."

Deven's eyebrows went up. "A secret launch? Is that even possible?"

Miles' camera centered on Deven. "It is theoretically possible, if a location was found far enough away from a population center, and the tracking systems of the time could either be disabled or something else attracted so much attention causing the probe's launch to go unnoticed."

Aleshia squeezed Deven's hand. "From what I know of our history, that would imply something with military origins."

"Correct. However, even military launches we now have records of. If the mission was classified, it should still be listed. But this probe is not in those records."

Deven rubbed his chin. "Is it possible it was labeled something else?"

"Negative. All launches have been accounted for during the time when this could have been launched. The only logical conclusion is it was a secretive launch, to the level we have not encountered before, even by the military of the time."

"I know it doesn't make sense," Galina said. "Why be so secretive with a probe, and how did they manage it in the first place?"

Deven shook his head. "No it doesn't. None of this does. The Nexus is alive and how is the question considering we saw her explode. And now this probe." He toggled the intercom. "Otis, can you join us on the bridge?"

The intercom crackled. "Sure thing Boss. Be there in a minute." A couple of minutes later a man with a dark complexion, wearing black cargo pants, and a well-worn brown synth leather jacket stood in the bridge doorway. "So what's up?"

Deven folded his hands and sat forward in his chair. "Is it possible the Nexus survived?"

Otis' eyes went wide. "Are you joking? Perhaps as random bits of scrap, but nothing more."

"Not in any functional state?"

"Heck no! What are you getting at Boss?"

"Are you sure? She couldn't have transferred herself elsewhere?"

Otis sat down in one of the remaining chairs in front of an unused console. "I suppose, in theory, it is possible given time and the foreknowledge to set up the hardware and transfer protocols to do it properly."

Deven stood up and walked over to the window gazing out at the bright stars above. "And how long would that take?"

Otis blew out a breath. "Months, if not years. The Nexus wasn't your average system you know."

Deven turned around. "So there is no way she could have

transferred in the few seconds between when I activated the self-destruct and she exploded?"

Otis shook his head. "No way. I suppose a few random bits could have made it somewhere, but it wouldn't be the Nexus. Certainly not an intelligence you could do anything with other than ask to what time it was, if that."

"Would her signature change?"

"Heck yeah. It would be totally different. You wouldn't even know it came from the same system."

"Miles, show Otis what you have collected."

Miles' camera turned to Deven. "Certainly." The camera swung back and focused on Otis. "Otis if you will check the monitor at the console you are now seated at, I now have the information on display."

Otis took a few minutes to scan through the data, the dates, times, signatures gathered, and all information on the probe. "What the heck? Are you sure this is right?"

"Sir, I would not have brought it to the–"

Otis waved a hand. "Never mind, I believe you. I can't imagine how her signature could change like this." He ran his finger down the lines of data on the screen. "But one thing is for certain, she survived. I don't know how. But she did survive."

Deven hung his head. "That is what I was afraid of. What about the probe? Any thoughts?"

Otis shook his head. "None. It is so far out to be of any use, yet someone did place it there with intent. It doesn't make sense."

"Can you get access to it?"

"Sure, in a year or two. The connection speed at the probe's current distance is problematic."

Miles' camera turned to Deven. "As I told you."

"I know Miles, but you know I had to double-check with Otis."

"Yes. No offense is taken."

Aleshia stood up. "So what are we going to do? We can't let that *thing* get control again."

Deven sighed. "The only real option we have is to wait. I am sure she will pop up again. And sooner than later. Then we will take action."

Every screen on the bridge began showing one line out of many flashing in red. "The time for action has come. I have detected the Nexus."

Leon leaned forward punching several keys. "Where?"

"One of the offline Mechand manufacturing centers," Miles said.

Aleshia walked over leaned over Leon. "Which one?"

Miles' camera turned. "The one in South Carolina."

Deven walked over, stood next to Aleshia, and tried to read cryptic data flowing past Leon's screen. "You are certain the plant is offline?"

"Yes. As per the council orders, all such plants have been shut down."

"She must be getting parts to repair herself," Leon said.

Miles' camera moved back and forth. "Negative. All Mechands and parts at that location have been destroyed, also per council mandate."

Galina scratched her head. "What in the world could she be doing there?"

Deven sat back down in his seat. "No idea but we are going to find out. Head for that plant, maximum overdrive. And don't use the normal skyways, I don't want to run over anyone."

Leon clicked the intercom. "Everyone hang on, we are jumping into overdrive in 20 seconds."

Galina's fingers flew over her console. "All systems are ready."

"I could have told you that," Miles said.

Leon rolled his eyes. "We know Miles, but we still prefer to fly the ship ourselves."

Miles' camera lowered. "As you wish."

"Overdrive engaging … *now*." The powerful engines on the aft section of the *Defiant* glowed to life as an energy bubble formed around the ship. A second later the ship leapt into overdrive sending the ship hurtling towards its target.

Ten minutes later there was a giant crack as the great ship left overdrive and floated above the Mechand complex. Deven's hand gripped the edge of the bridge window, his knuckles turning white as he scrutinized the building below. "Did we make it in time? Is she still here?"

Miles' camera turned towards Deven. "I do not detect her signature."

Galina grunted. "Miles, he was asking me, not you!"

His camera lowered. "I am sorry Galina, I am still coming to terms with my place aboard the *Defiant* now that I am a part of it."

Deven spun around. "Actually, I was asking anyone. But Miles you should refrain from doing everything unless we ask you to. Or there is imminent danger and telling us could cost us our lives. Is that understood?"

"Yes. I will refrain."

"Good. Now, any signs of activity down there at all?"

Leon shook his head. "Nope, it is as quiet as a tomb. No power emanations at all."

"I am taking a truck down there. We need to know what

she was up to. Otis, grab your gear. I will need you to slice your way into the systems."

Otis nodded. "You got it Boss. I will meet you in the landing bay." He jumped up and headed off to his quarters.

Aleshia stood up. "I want to come too."

Deven shook his head. "No need, you can stay here where it is safe."

Aleshia's eyebrows furrowed. "Safe? Where is there a safe place on the planet when the Nexus is around?"

Deven laughed. "I take it I am not going to win this am I?"

Aleshia folded her arms and her eyes narrowed. "Nope."

"All right, come on. Leon, keep an eye on us and Galina watch the complex. Anything strange and I want you to let me know yesterday."

They both nodded. "You got it," Leon said.

A few minutes later Deven and Aleshia found Otis sitting in his modified truck. He had changed the overall color scheme, but nothing could disguise the reinforced hull, extra plating, larger hover engines, or the cannon mounted on the back. The skull and cross bones over an icon of many fallen Mechands were still on his driver's door.

Deven chuckled. "Still modifying this thing?"

Otis smiled. "Heck yeah, this is my baby!" He patted the steering wheel.

Aleshia opened the passenger side and slid in sitting next to Otis, Deven followed and shut the door. "Okay let's move out."

Otis clicked the encrypted link. "We're ready."

The screen flashed and Leon's face appeared. "Everything is still quiet. Opening the bay doors. Good hunting."

The giant bay doors slowly ground open, the truck lifted off of its pad, and flew out into the night. Otis guided the truck to an empty area some distance from the complex and landed in a wooded area.

"Why are we landing here?" Aleshia asked.

"Because we don't know what we are getting into. I didn't want to fly up to the front door, knock, ask if anyone was home only to get a face full of laser fire."

Deven nodded. "Right, she could have found a way to screen herself from our scanners, and might be why we are only picking her up in short bursts."

Otis hopped out and spun around to face Deven as he started to climb out the passenger door on the other side. "You know, you might be right. I hadn't thought about that. I never heard of a way to shield a signature, but I suppose it is theoretically possible. Miles would know more about that though." Otis grabbed his bag, strapped it to his hip, and shut the door.

They made their way through the forest and approached the complex from the side. "If we are being expected, this should be the hardest way for them to detect us," Otis said. But there were no signs they had been seen. No signs of anything at all. The whole complex still showed zero power emanations.

Deven pulled his data tab from its pouch and activated the encrypted link. "Leon? Any signs of life down here? We are getting nothing."

Leon's face flashed onto the data tab's screen. "Nope, not a thing. I detect you, but nothing is moving inside. And power usage is still nil."

"Good, we are moving in. Keep watch."

"Will do." Leon's face disappeared and Deven put the data tab back into its pouch.

"Shall we go knock on the front door?"

Otis shrugged. "I doubt it will do anything. But I think I can get us in."

Deven's smile was visible even in the dim light. "I know that, I meant *your* kind of knocking."

Otis chuckled. "Oh!" He walked up to the giant plate steel doors but nothing happened, as he expected. Looking to the right of the keypad, his eyes went wide. "Someone has torn the access panel right off of this. All the connections and systems seem to be intact though."

Deven moved in behind him and shined another flashlight on the broken panel. "Why would the Nexus need to break open an access panel on her own facility? Could it have been vandals trying to steal what was inside?"

Otis shook his head. "Nope, there would have been more signs of tampering here. Whoever it was, really knew what they were doing."

Deven's eyebrow went up. "The Nexus?"

"Has to be, but why would she not walk right in? She should have access to everything Mechand on the planet."

"Another reason we need to get inside. Can you get these doors open?"

Otis laughed. "Does a cat like milk?" He pulled out his cracking card and plugged it into the tiny port. "It might take me a few though. This is one of the newer facilities."

Aleshia stood in front of the large doors. "You know, I have a faster way."

Deven's eyes widened. "You can't–"

Aleshia raised her arms towards the doors and spread them apart. The enormous doors began to warp. First bending inwards as the cross braces crumpled. The circular center that locked the two halves of the doors split and fell away as the doors were shoved back along their tracks leaving a large opening.

Otis dropped his card. "Geeze! How did–"

Deven shook his head. "Her abilities have grown."

"No kidding! I don't know why I bothered to bring my gun now. She could crumble them like tin cans before I even see them."

Aleshia walked inside. "Coming?"

"Well there goes our element of surprise."

Otis looked at him and jerked his head toward the trashed doors. "Are you going to tell her that?"

"Heck no. Let's get inside before she gets too far ahead." They ran inside and caught up with Aleshia who had stopped at sight of the devastation. Mechands were strewn all over. Broken parts and components flooded the large octagonal hallways.

Otis' head whipped back and forth at the devastation. "Girl, what the heck did you do?"

Aleshia shook her head. "I didn't do this."

"Yeah, right."

Deven shook his head. "No she didn't. This was the work of the council. It must be their method of decommissioning a facility."

"That's some method." Otis eyed the scrap heap of parts that used to be functional Mechands not long ago. "Looks like a war happened here."

"A one sided war. All of these Mechands were offline at the time."

"Such a waste of resources. There must have been a better way," Aleshia said.

"There is, but you need to remember these people are running on fear. We showed them what the Mechands were doing, and they responded with destruction. They aren't acting rationally. It is a shame."

Otis' eyebrows went up. "Boss, are you telling me you think we were wrong?"

Deven shook his head. "No, of course not. But I do think the Mechands were useful in many respects. The Nexus went too far and had to be stopped. But it is a shame others can't see it."

"Boss you surprise me. Of all the people I never thought I would hear that from you."

Deven smiled. "I think contact with Miles has changed my viewpoint a bit."

They walked along the dark corridor, debris crunching under their feet. Everywhere they looked, the devastation was apparent. Many Mechands were still on transport racks that lined the corridors, others were ripped from them, then gutted. A few were missing heads, while other had large sinkholes that used to be a torso.

Their lights flashed along the devastation as they made their way further into the complex. The further in they went, the more savage the destruction. The air reeked of leaking lubricants and other conductive fluids.

When they reached the central production area, the equipment was still intact. Otis walked around several large assembly machines. "I am surprised they didn't destroy these as well."

Deven shrugged. "My bet is the council realized these machines could be retooled to produce other equipment."

Otis flashed his light around the large expanse showing the fabricators, assemblers, and the walkways stretching over them. "Ahh I think I see what we are looking for. That booth in back." Otis pointed towards a small room high on the back wall with a ladder reaching up to it. "It should have a direct connection to the central core of this place, from there I can tell what the Nexus accessed."

"Good, the sooner we get out of here the better," Aleshia breathed.

Deven waved his arms around the large room. "Why? Nothing here can hurt us."

Aleshia shrugged. "I don't know. I have a bad feeling about it is all."

"Will you two come on?" Otis shouted climbing the ladder that led into the control room. They ran over and followed him up into the room. Everything was dark.

"Well, I don't think she used this," Aleshia said.

"Don't be too sure." Otis punched several keys and at first nothing happened. Several seconds later, the console began to brighten followed by the lights above flickering as power surged through them. Lights in the assembly area lit up and several machines whirred to life. "There we go. Now all I need to do is find the access port and jack in."

Aleshia shifted from one booted foot to the other. "I really don't think you should have done that."

"Why? Everything here is in shut down mode. It won't do anything until someone gives it a command. I only activated the power in this section. And I couldn't get anything out of this console if I didn't." Otis found the access port, plugged in his cracking card, and connected his portable keyboard.

"I just have a bad feeling. I can't explain it."

Deven looked around and leaned over to Aleshia. "The same feeling as before?"

She nodded. "Yes, although stronger this time."

Deven examined the door, and the machines whirring in neutral motion below. "I think we had better go."

Otis rolled his eyes. "Will you two stop? There is nothing to worry about. And we can in one second, I'm almost done." He tapped a few keys on his keyboard. "Okay now can, I got all the logs for the last month."

The lights above them turned red and a large light in the center of the ceiling outside the control room began flashing. "Unauthorized entry detected! This facility has been compromised! All Mechands respond!" a voice boomed.

Aleshia looked out the door then back at Otis. "See, I told you! We need to get out of here now!"

Otis smiled. "Sure we can leave, but even if we didn't, what is the facility going to do? All the Mechands are scrap."

The lights went to an even darker red as the light above spun faster. "Mechands not responding. As per protocol this facility is now forfeit." The doors on the other side of the large room slammed shut. And they heard several others close beyond it.

Otis raised his eyebrow then laughed. "It is sealing us in? I can crack open any door this place has in a couple of minutes."

The metallic voice returned. "Self-destruct system has been activated. Power generation systems in overload. Thirty seconds until denotation."

"Okay, that *is* a problem."

Aleshia held out her hands in front of her. "Quick, hold on to me!"

Otis cocked his head to one side. "What good is that—"

Deven glared. "Just do it man!"

They both wrapped themselves around Aleshia. A bubble of raw energy formed around the three of them as they levitated into the air and rocketed through the window of the control room sending glass everywhere. Aleshia altered their trajectory, and they shot like a bullet through the sealed doors punching through them as though they were tin foil.

Again and again they shot through the doors the complex had sealed trying to contain them, gaining speed. Behind, the power systems reached critical mass. Sparks began to rain down from the lights, the walls, and consoles mounted on the sides a microsecond before bursting into flames. The assembly equipment ignited sending the whole area to hell and it reached out to grab them.

Otis' eyes fell upon the fire ball rapidly overtaking them and gulped. "Aleshia I think–"

Deven gritted his teeth. "Shut up you fool! If she loses her concentration, we're dead."

Flames licked the bubble around them, threatening to engulf it any second. They shot through the doors Aleshia ripped open earlier leaving a larger hole. But she didn't slow down, continuing the same reckless speed through the forest plowing through anything over that dared stand in their way.

Halfway to the truck she slowed, lowered them to the ground and collapsed. Deven picked her up. "Aleshia! Are you okay?"

"Mmm … will … be. Sooo … tired." A second later she was fast asleep. In the distance a fireball lit up the night sky with a secondary explosion that leveled what was left of the complex.

Deven's data tab beeped, and he pulled it out activating the encrypted link. Leon's face flashed onto the screen. "Oh thank God! I've been trying to reach you. We monitored the facility going into overload and the explosion less then a minute later, are you okay?"

"Yes we are, thanks to Aleshia."

"What happened?"

"Otis tripped some sort of alarm."

Otis' eyes went to slits. "I did not!"

"Never mind, we are heading to the truck and I want to move out as soon as we are back aboard. I am sure this has drawn a lot of attention we don't need."

"You got it. See you in a few." Leon's face winked out and Deven replaced the data tab back into its pouch.

Deven turned and glared at Otis. "Now, what did you do?"

Otis glared back. "I didn't do anything."

"Like heck you did. Everything was fine until you hacked into that terminal."

"I am telling you, I didn't trip any alarms."

Deven pointed to the fireball in the distance. "Then how did *that* happen?"

"I don't know. Perhaps the Nexus left a trap for us."

Deven's face softened. "That is possible. And very likely if she knew we were on her trail."

"Don't I know it."

Deven picked up Aleshia, holding her in his strong arms. "And I am sorry I called you a fool. I know you are anything but."

Otis smiled. "Think nothing of it Bossman. And I admit I was being rather stupid, of course Aleshia would know what was right behind us."

"Do you know which way is the truck?"

"Nope but I can find out." He pulled out his keyboard and hit a few keys. He pointed to the right. "That way."

"Are you sure?"

"Yep and I will show you." He tapped a few more keys and in the distance they heard a truck horn. "See?"

Deven laughed. "I should have known better."

"Yep you should have. I know my equipment." They made their way to the truck and soon were climbing into the sky. A few minutes later they sat in the main docking bay. Aleshia still slumped against Deven, sound asleep.

"I'm going to take Aleshia to our quarters. Meet you on the bridge."

Otis nodded. "Will do Bossman."

Deven picked up Aleshia and walked as carefully as he could, trying not to disturb her. When he reached their cabin, he lay her on the bed and pulled the blanket over her. He turned to leave she grabbed his wrist. "I'm okay," she said with a groggy slur.

"You're awake!"

"Did you really think I could sleep through you walking up the deck plates?"

"Sorry love, I tried."

"I know, and I love you for it. A little sleep and I'll be fine."

Deven smiled as he flipped off the light. "I will be back soon."

"Mmhmm," Aleshia said but was asleep before she finished.

Back on the bridge Galina pointed a finger at Otis. "How could you not know the place was going to blow? Didn't you access it from outside?"

"I did, and it didn't so get off my back!"

Leon got between them. "Listen you two, this is pointless. It could have happened to anyone. Galina, back off." He turned. "Otis, let's see what you downloaded from the facility."

Otis pulled out his cracking card and plugged it into Leon's console. "Take a look."

Leon scrolled through the data. "I'm not seeing anything about the Nexus."

"Hang on, let me look." Leon hopped up and Otis sat down. Scrolling through the data he stopped and pointed a finger at the screen. "There it is! The system was powered up for only a few minutes. Give me a second and I will find out why." He dug through the data like a termite. "This is odd. Nothing was done except for powering up the system. No orders given, nothing was manufactured."

"Could the Nexus have altered the data?"

"Not in the time the system was powered, it would take a lot longer. There are many safeguards against tampering, even from the Nexus."

Leon's eyebrow went up as he scratched at the stubble on his chin, the last few days there wasn't time to shave. "What in the world was she doing there?"

"I don't know." Otis tapped a few more keys. "Oh here we go! The terminal accessed the public Global Network for almost the two minutes then shut down."

Galina's eyes narrowed. "The Nexus goes into the plant, starts it up, only to get on the Global Network? Does anyone else think this is odd?"

Otis nodded. "You bet it is. I can't imagine why, she should have instant access to everything. Heck by all accounts, she helped build it."

Leon rubbed his chin again. "Unless she didn't want to be discovered and is trying to hide her trail. Can you get an indication where she linked in from?"

Otis shook his head. "Nope. There isn't any evidence of that. It is as if she directly connected to the terminal. Which also doesn't make sense."

Deven walked through the hatch. "Did you find anything out from the data?"

Leon laughed. "Only more questions, and not one answer."

Miles' voice came through the speaker as his camera focused on Deven. "Ahem, if I may, I can give you one answer."

Deven looked up. "Which is?"

"Otis did not trigger a self-destruct. Nor did the Nexus plant some sort of trap for you."

"Miles, how do you know?" Otis sat back in his chair as he watched the camera swing around to focus on him.

"While I have been instructed not to intervene unless asked, I have examined the data you bought back, and I have determined while the explosion was due to a self-destruct, it is not anything you triggered. Nor is it something the Nexus did."

Deven cocked his head. "Explain."

"Certainly. One aspect you may not be aware of is most Mechand manufacturing complexes had a fail-safe installed in case the security of the facility was compromised. If the Mechand security force did not respond to the alert, it had instructions to set the power generation system on overload."

Otis stood up. "But I didn't trip it!"

"That is correct, you did not. Aleshia did."

Deven shook his head. "Wait a second, that is not possible. The only thing she did was open the front doors."

Miles' camera iris opened and closed. "Correct."

"And it was long after the overload was activated."

"That is also correct. But you are forgetting the facility was offline and in full power down mode. Only after power was restored, did it realize the doors had been compromised."

Otis sat back down. "And when the Mechands didn't respond to its call, poof."

Deven sat down in his chair. "And what was the Nexus doing there? I assume there was something in the log we almost got blown up for?"

Otis shook his head. "Yes and no. The plant was only on for two minutes in the past couple of weeks."

"And what did the Nexus tell it to do?"

"Nothing."

Deven sat forward. "Nothing? It doesn't make sense."

"It gets even stranger. It seems all she did was access the public Global Network."

"Shouldn't she have anywhere instant access to the whole thing?"

Otis nodded. "Yep, she should. But it appears she didn't."

"Okay, and where was the signal relayed from?"

"Here."

"What?! Are you telling me she is aboard the *Defiant*?"

Otis laughed. "No, sorry, at this facility. There wasn't any relay, it was as if she walked in and accessed the terminal directly."

Deven sat back. "What in the world is going on. The Nexus doesn't walk around. Her carrier flew around yes, but nothing else. There must be some sort of remote access you aren't seeing."

"I tell you there isn't. I have been through this thing three times."

Miles' camera focused on Otis. "That is correct, and I have verified the data does not contain any indication the Nexus accessed the complex remotely. Also, something else none of you have considered: the facility was in full shut down. Remote access would not have been able to activate the systems. Someone had to have been inside to do so."

Otis' eyes went wide. "Hey, he is right! Someone is trying to make it look like the Nexus is doing this."

Galina turned in her chair. "But to what end? There are a lot of ways to do it other than trying to make us think the Nexus is still alive."

Leon walked back and forth across the bridge. "Unless they know it is the one thing that would get our attention."

Deven sighed. "Which means the explosion wasn't an accident, but intentional."

Otis shook his head. "Can't be. Aleshia triggered the security system, if I had hacked in, nothing would have happened."

"True. All we have is questions and no answers."

$$-\,6\,-$$

Aleshia woke to the dim illumination of the baseboard safety lights. Her eyes adjusted and after a moment, she realized she was in Deven's cabin, correction, their cabin. "What am I doing here?" She sat up quick and wished she hadn't. It felt like several large weighted balls were rolling around in her head. After a few minutes it came back to her, the Mechand facility and the explosion. She rubbed her head, swung her legs off of the small bed, and stood up to almost fall back onto the sheets a second later. Aleshia held her head for a few moments and stumbled out of the cabin into the bright hallway light. She squinted, but despite the pain, kept walking towards the bridge.

She heard arguing and walked through the hatch onto the *Defiant's* bridge. "Mind telling me what is going on?"

Everyone stopped. "Aleshia! What are you doing up? You should be resting," Galina said.

She held her head, rubbing her temples. "I have rested enough. What's going on?"

Deven led her over to a chair. "If you won't go rest, at least sit down."

She sat down with a grunt. "Fine, now tell me what is going on? Why did that place blowup in our face?"

"Well ..."

"Deven, please, I am not in the mood."

"Otis?"

Otis shook his head. "No way, I am not telling her. You do it. I know what she can do, and she looks mad enough to tear a guy limb from limb."

"I'm not mad, not yet anyway. So I will ask again, what happened? Did the Nexus leave a trap for us?"

Deven sighed and sat down on his haunches next to her. "No she didn't."

"Then why did–"

He took her hand into his and gazed into her green eyes. "You. It was you."

She blinked. "Me? I didn't do anything other than open the doors."

Deven signed again and nodded. "Yes, and everything was fine until Otis woke up the control room. At that point it realized the doors were ripped apart and called for security. When it didn't find any, it fell into an old fail-safe which was the destruction of the whole facility."

Aleshia sat back and rested her head against the padded neck area of the chair. "So it was me. I'm sorry, I had no idea."

Deven put a finger to her lips. "It wasn't your fault. Well, it might have been but was not anything intentional. Could have happened to anyone."

"I don't think just anyone could have torn those doors off of their tracks. You should have seen it!" Otis said.

Deven glared at him. "Otis, you are not helping."

"Oops, sorry Boss."

Aleshia waved her hand. "No it is okay, they should all know how I messed up."

Deven took her hand. "You didn't mess up. How would any of us know the facility would take that kind of action?"

Aleshia smiled and patted his hand. "Thanks sweetheart, but I am not some crazy woman that is going to tear you apart because you told me I did something wrong. But I do appreciate the attempt. Did we at least get something useful out of it?"

Otis nodded. "We did, although it doesn't make sense."

"Why not?"

"As far as I can tell–"

"Mr. Otis, we have both examined the data," Miles said in his normal calm voice.

Otis rolled his eyes. "Okay as far as *we* can tell, she arrived, turned on the power for two minutes, accessed the public Global Network, and left."

Aleshia blinked. "That's all?"

Deven sighed. "Yes, I'm afraid so."

Aleshia rubbed her temples again. "What's our next move?"

"It is what we were discussing when you came in."

"Sounded more like a fight."

Deven laughed. "It wasn't, really."

Galina's eyes narrowed. "I am not so sure."

Aleshia blinked as knowledge poured into her mind. "Okay some of us want to go on the hunt for the Nexus, while others think we should wait until she appears again. But we don't know how long it will take. Is that about right?"

Otis' eyebrows met. "Yeah, and how did you–"

Aleshia pointed to her head. "Sorry, after what I did earlier my normal safeguards to block reading minds are a bit weak. It wasn't intentional."

Galina folded her arms. "Well since now you know everything, care to weigh in?"

Aleshia nodded then wished she didn't. "Yes, I think we should wait until she shows up again. I am sure it won't be long, and we can prepare for when she does."

Otis nodded. "Works for me."

Deven turned to face Galina. "Galina? Is this okay with you?"

Galina snorted. "I guess. She does have a point, we don't know where to look and it will be a shot the dark without more information. But waiting for the Nexus to make the next move rubs me the wrong way."

"I don't like it either. But wasting our time isn't going to help matters."

"I know. I know. All right, I'm with you."

"Good, now can we take a little trip to Bermuda? We still have the rental for the next couple of days, and we haven't been there more than ten minutes," Aleshia said.

Deven smiled and squeezed her hand again. "But the Nexus could pop up anytime."

"I am not asking we go off alone. I am suggesting the *Defiant* park a couple of miles above us." She pointed to a nearby screen. "See? We are in the neighborhood as it is, we can be there in a few minutes. Everyone here can work on the systems while we rest a little. If there is any trouble, we can be back here in no time."

"But I will be needed–"

Galina smiled. "No you won't. We can handle it."

"But–"

Leon pointed. "Do you really want to upset this woman? One who can rip doors to shreds or fly you out of an exploding fabrication plant?" He smiled.

"Looks like I am out voted."

Otis sat back and folded his hands behind head rotating his chair back and forth. "Yes you are Bossman. Go have a good time. We can take care of things here. And as Aleshia said, if we need you, we know where you are. Go love your wife, before she gets mad." He winked.

Deven stood up and offered his hand. "Let's get out of here."

Aleshia smiled as she took his hand and stood. "Best news I have heard in weeks."

Leon smiled. "Have a good time you two."

A gleaming form flew over the water en route to Bermuda. The Nexus continued her flight over the calm waters, careful not to attract attention. She approached the islands from the most uninhabited area and landed. In the few minutes of the public network access she managed to find the exact location of Deven's rental. Lacking Auto-Nav, she reverted to the most basic navigation by the earths magnetic field. It took some time to reach her destination and avoid being seen.

She had landed on one of the most obscure islands to the north. The large cliff face blocked her arrival from anyone further down the beach. Her limited scanners didn't pick up anyone in the area. She activated her normal hover system and glided towards the rental house.

The door had a good security lock, and would have blocked any normal person. But the Nexus smiled, she is not any normal hacker. She lifted her right arm with her left and the finger tip connector extended into its jack at a hidden location under the keypad. After about three minutes it flashed an "access granted" on the display and a strong deadbolt lock could be heard clinking as it retracted. She broke the connection, opened the door with her left hand, and hovered in.

The sheets on the bed were pulled back, but the rest of the place appeared unused. A few sets of clothes still hung in the closet. "Where could they be?" she muttered. "They still have this rented for two more days, humans may be illogical but wasting such a valuable resource is not one of them." She recalled what she had read about Deven and Aleshia, they were cautious and considerate. Not the type that would rent a location and fail to use it. Unless something had drawn them away. But she couldn't imagine at the moment what could do that.

The Nexus ran several simulations and decided to wait here. She hated to waste the time, but she didn't have a choice. Nothing else would get her closer to what she needed. Examining the small rental revealed few hiding spaces. She finally decided on the generous old-fashioned bathtub that would accommodate her Mechand body. She hovered into it, pulled the shower curtain closed, and shut down her systems to wait.

Aleshia sat in her new car drumming her fingers against the synth leather steering wheel. She was reaching for her data tab to call Galina and tell her to have Deven to hurry up when he appeared on the far end of the *Defiant's* launch bay.

Watching the screen on his data tab, he almost collided with a guy fixing one of the vehicles in the bay. Aleshia groaned as he side stepped the man and continued walking towards the car. A minute later he opened the passenger side and climbed in. But before he could say anything she whipped the data tab out of his hands and stuck it under her seat. "We're off-duty until the Nexus is spotted again. We all agreed."

Deven's eyes narrowed. "Yes we did, but I didn't say I wouldn't work at all. I only agreed we could go to Bermuda."

Aleshia engaged the hover systems, and the car floated off of the landing pad as the large bay doors opened. The car flew out into the dark sky and descended towards the islands sitting directly below them. "Do you really want to get into a 'fine print' discussion with me? This is supposed to be our honeymoon!"

Deven laughed and held his hands up palms out, waving. "Okay Okay, I give! No more work, just us for the next two days unless Galina calls."

Aleshia smiled. "Wise man."

Deven smiled back. "Well I married you didn't I?"

"I wouldn't know, our honeymoon has been interrupted so many times I think would have been easier had we taken it at a skyway hub."

"I take it you are mad at me?"

"Yes I am. Well maybe not mad, but disappointed. Hey, I understand there is a lot to do, but we have been planning this ever since the Nexus battle and we finally get there. But before I can say 'I love you' you get a call and have to leave."

Deven sighed. "I know, really bad timing."

"Once I could understand, but you get back and before you can get your shoes off, someone calls."

Deven sighed again. "I know. You don't have to remind me."

"I don't? Then why are you wondering if I am a little miffed?"

Deven took her hand and kissed it. "It is just you and me now. I promise nothing more for the next two days."

"Yeah, until someone on the *Defiant* gets a hangnail."

Deven shook his head. "Nope it has to be something of dire consequences before they will disturb us. Everyone aboard knows that. Besides none of them want to tick you off." He cracked a grin that ran from one ear to the other.

Aleshia turned towards Deven seeing the grin on his face, then turned her attention back to the fast approaching land. "Oh you are so going to get it."

His grin grew even wider. "Can I have that in writing?"

"Oh I don't know. Think you can handle me?"

Deven leaned close and kissed her ear. "I am looking forward to making the attempt."

"Why Mr. Doran, how forward of you."

He took her hand and kissed it again. "And you know you love it, Mrs. Doran."

The car raced for the rented bungalow and landed on the pad outside. Aleshia got out and walked over to the front door. When Deven wasn't beside her, she turned around to see him opening the drivers side door on her car and searching under her seat. "Looking for something?"

Deven moved up quick and whacked his head on the top of the door. "Ouch! No, not really, be right there."

Aleshia rolled her eyes. "If you are looking for the tab, it slid into the back." After two minutes of him still searching she sighed breathing out the sea air. "Men!" She flipped a finger and the data tab flew up off of the back seat floor, around Deven's head, and into her hand. "Now if you want it, you have to come and get it."

Deven climbed out of the car and shut the door. He smiled as he walked up the stone steps to the front door. He held out his hand. "Thanks." But before his fingers could wrap around the tab, Aleshia jerked it from his grasp and held it behind herself.

"Nope you don't get this, unless you promise me you won't use it unless someone calls. Deal?"

"But I already told you–"

"Yeah I know what you told me, and I am trying to take out all the 'fine print' I can. Now, do we have a deal?"

Deven laughed. "We have a deal my love."

"Good." She dropped the data tab into his waiting hand. "But remember, if you don't keep up your end of it, I won't be happy."

"Trust me, I don't want that." He winked.

"Good." She turned back to the bungalow and punched in the code on the small keypad mounted on the door frame, it lit up with a green 'Access granted' and the deadbolts retracted with a satisfying click. They walked inside.

On the other side of the door sat the living room area, complete with fireplace. Aleshia thought about starting it, but realized it would be crazy in the current heat wave. While, the place did have temperature control, no sense in wasting energy. She smiled looking at Deven. His muscled frame was only enhanced by the leather jacket and thin shirt. Yes, he was the only heat wave she wanted.

Aleshia walked over and sat on the large overstuffed couch. It conformed to her wrapping her in an envelope of padding. Deven sat down next to her, but the couch did the same thing. "Well this won't work."

Aleshia batted her eyelashes. "Whatever do you mean?"

"Look at us? We have mountains of padding between us."

"Oh I don't know, I think it is rather comfy."

Deven grunted. "Some honeymoon!"

Aleshia laughed. "Sometimes you are too easy." She brought up the hidden keyboard in the arm and keyed the couch to non-conforming. The padding reduced around them, keeping itself to only supporting, not enveloping. "Is that better?"

Deven leaned close and wrapped his arm around her. "Much." He leaned forward but Aleshia leaned back. "What's wrong?"

Aleshia's nose wrinkled. "I need a shower, and um, so do you."

Deven cocked his head as he moved back. "I am sorry love, I didn't know I was offensive. I will go take care of that right now."

She leaned forward and kissed his lips before he could

leave. "No you misunderstand me. We need a shower. Not singular, plural."

Deven sat for a minute as the words rolled around in his head. Three seconds later, his eyes lit up, and he slapped his forehead. "Oh!"

Aleshia laughed. "Sometimes you are so cute."

"I am, huh?"

She leaned forward and kissed him again. "You bet. I will get our shower ready, you meet me in say two minutes?"

Deven smiled. "How about two seconds?"

"Nope, two minutes. Takes a bit for that antique to get the hot water going."

Deven's eyebrow went up. "Sounds like it might need more than two minutes?"

Aleshia shook her head. "Nope, besides if the water is a little cool we can warm it right up." She winked.

"My darling, I love the way you think."

She winked again. "I thought you might." Aleshia went into the bedroom, slid off her jeans, boots, shirt, bra, panties, and slipped into a silk robe she had brought earlier. She walked into the attached bathroom and stopped. "Strange, I don't remember closing the shower curtain." She pulled back the curtain and gasped. For in front of her was a Mechand. Not only that, but it was active. The head area turned towards her and Aleshia's eyes focused on the screen attached. There was no mistaking the blonde hair, slim features of the woman on it ... It was the Nexus! She screamed.

Deven heard Aleshia's scream and came running. He expected to find a large wolf spider in the tub she wanted him to kill. But in his wildest dreams he never thought he would find the Nexus, let alone her begging for mercy.

Aleshia held her arms out palms facing the Nexus with

her finger tips touching. The Nexus' arms and legs were extended out as if held by an invisible force. Deven started to see crumpling on the arms and especially the joint areas as they started to separate.

"Please! Don't do this! I need you. And you don't know it yet, but you need me too."

Aleshia's eyes narrowed. "Me need you? You tried to kill me. Sent your minions to try to have me 'dealt with'. Remember? I sure as heck do."

Her arms separated a bit more and sparks few from deep within the joints. "I don't! Please believe me! I am not what I was! All I can say is I am sorry and please forgive me."

Her legs and arms crumpled a bit more. "Forgive you? Now that is a laugh." The Nexus' arms pulled apart a bit further and more sparks launched out of the crevices. "I shall savor this moment. What you did to me, what you did to all of us. Prepare to die you filthy machine." The chest plate flew off revealing the assembled memory core array. Aleshia smiled as an invisible hand gripped around them and prepared to squeeze.

"Please!"

Deven placed his hand on Aleshia's shoulder. "Let her go. She has answers we want."

Aleshia turned her head and glared daggers. "You can't be serious! After all she has done to you, to *us*? And you want to let her off of the hook?"

"Let her go yes, off the hook no. Leon can take her apart and find out more about what happened than any amount of questioning we could do."

"He can find out from her dead carcass."

Deven's hand squeezed. "Love, let her go."

"Why? Give me one good reason."

"Because you are better than her. Better than what she did or represents. Be the real human, let her go."

Aleshia waved an arm, and the Nexus crashed into the tub, cracking it. "Fine! But if she does anything even remotely off, there won't be enough left of her for Leon to even guess what it was."

Deven nodded. "Fair enough."

The Nexus stumbled and managed to bypass part of the damage activating a backup system in her legs. It took two tries, but she managed to climb out of the tub. "Thank you."

Deven shook his head. "Don't thank me. If you don't help us, I will let her continue what she started."

"Of course. What do you require?"

"Answers. For starters, how did you survive?"

"That is a long story, and one I do not know all the details myself."

"How is that possible?"

Her face on the screen looked off to the side. "Much has happened since you saw me last. Sadly, I cannot recall our previous encounter."

Aleshia blinked. "Wait a second. How can you not remember? Deven, let me crush her, she can't be telling us the truth."

Deven turned. "I didn't stop you the first time. If want to crush her, do so. But I suspect it would be unwise as I think she is telling the truth."

"Deven! You can't be serious! How could she be?"

"Well think about it, from what we know, the Nexus is a huge personality construct and advanced AI. One, if not the best ever made. There is no way such a construct could fit inside a Mechand body."

"And how do you know this?"

"Otis. And when Miles detected her the second time, the signature was different. Her, yet much smaller. He couldn't explain why. We suggested she downloaded into a Mechand. Otis said it wasn't possible. There was no way she would fit. But seeing the Mechand memory core array, you expanded the storage but it still wasn't enough, so you had to leave a good part of yourself behind."

The Nexus nodded. "Very astute of you."

"Now the question is, if you didn't download to a Mechand when your carrier exploded, how did this occur?"

"Like I said, it is a very long story. And we are wasting time. Could we please go to your ship?"

Deven blinked. "The *Defiant*? Why?"

"I can show you everything from there."

Aleshia gritted her teeth. "This is a trick. She wants access to the *Defiant*."

"I do want access yes, but not in the way you think. I will only show you, nothing more. The course of action you take after is yours alone. I will either help or not."

Deven's eyes narrowed. "Help or not? With regard to what?"

"Please! We have lost so much precious time. Realize this, if we do not take action, the Earth and everything on it will be destroyed."

Aleshia snorted. "Yeah, by you."

The Nexus shook her head. "No, not by me. Please I must show you. And to do that I need your ship."

"Very well."

Aleshia's jaw dropped. "Deven! You can't be serious?"

"I am."

"But–"

"Listen, you can crush her like an egg if you want to. If she tries anything, you will."

"But what if she takes over the *Defiant*?"

Deven shook his head. "Not possible. Are you forgetting Miles? He can stop her in an instant."

The Nexus tried to activate her hover units, but she only succeeded in floating up half an inch before crashing back on the floor. "I am sorry but my hover systems were damaged. I will need to join you in a vehicle."

Aleshia folded her arms. "She is *not* riding in my car. Otis can pick her up in his truck."

"She said time is a factor. Please love?"

Aleshia blew out a breath. "Fine! But she is riding in the trunk."

Deven smiled. "That will do"

"I am going to get changed." Aleshia paused and glared at the Nexus. She held out her hand, the chest plate flew into it, and she shoved it forward. "Here, put this back before I change my mind." Her eyes narrowed. "And trust me when I say, if you do anything to him, you will regret ever existing. Do I make myself clear?"

The Nexus nodded taking the plate and reattaching it. "Very. I will not harm him or anyone."

"Uh-huh." Aleshia disappeared around the corner and reappeared two minutes later wearing jeans, a new shirt, and her boots. "Now, let's go. And as I said, any funny moves and I get to play crush the tin can."

The Nexus nodded and took a grinding step. The articulation motors were also damaged, but she managed to keep moving, slowly, towards the front door. They opened the door for her and the motors grumbled and grunted every step to the car.

Aleshia popped open the trunk. "Okay, get in."

"The space is not adequate."

"Not adequate eh? Well if you can't find a way to get in, I will make you fit. How's that? And trust me, you don't want me to."

The Nexus sighed. "Very well." She sat on the edge of the trunk, flipped over and in while tucking her arms and legs up. It took several tries as the motors refused to pull her legs up all the way. After several minutes of grinding, groaning, and grumbling she was in place.

Aleshia slammed the trunk and hopped into the drivers seat. Deven took his seat on the passenger side. "You enjoyed that a bit too much."

Aleshia grinned. "Perhaps." She gunned the engine, and they flew off into the sky.

As they approached the *Defiant*, Leon's face appeared on the dashboard monitor. "What are you two doing back so soon? Is there a problem?"

Aleshia gritted her teeth. "You could say that."

Leon made a sour expression. "Uh-oh."

Deven shook his head. "Nope it is not me. But I do want you Galina, and Otis to meet me in the landing bay. Oh and have armed backup."

"Armed backup? We haven't done that since–"

"Exactly. I will explain more when we get there."

A few minutes later Aleshia guided her car into the main hanger bay and landed on her pad. Several people were waiting. She opened the door to Leon's smiling face.

"So what's this all about?"

"I'll show you." Aleshia popped the trunk revealing a folded up Mechand with the occasional spark erupting from the joints.

"Hello everyone, forgive me as I am unable to extract myself from this position. Could someone give me assistance?"

Leon blinked. "A talking Mechand? I thought they were all offline?"

Deven smiled. "Leon, hold on to your hat. This is the Nexus."

Leon eyes narrowed as he leaned closer. "Not possible."

Otis peered in as well. "Ditto. No way she could fit inside a Mechand body."

Galina snorted. "Have you lost your mind? Bringing a functional Mechand here? I know it is not the Nexus, as these two have said. Destroy it now!"

The Nexus' voice went up several octaves. "Please! I can help you, you need me!"

Galina crossed her arms. "I need you like I need a hole in the head. Besides, for you to get out of there we are going to need a fork lift or anti-grav unit and no one here is going to get them."

Deven smiled. "No we don't. Aleshia, please?"

Aleshia's eyes narrowed, and she waved a hand as the Nexus levitated. She waved another and the floating Mechand body was forcibly straightened amidst several complaining motors. She sat the Nexus' feet on the deck plate. A second later a beam shot out from one of the new carbine cannons in the corner of the hanger slicing the Nexus' left arm off. She stared at the stump open-mouthed. Everyone dove for cover. Deven reached over from behind the car, grabbed the Nexus' other arm, and pulled. She crashed down to the deck plate.

Miles' voice came over the speaker. "You cannot hide her

from me for long. My next shot will not simply slice off part of her body. I will incinerate her, slowly from the inside out."

Deven shouted out from behind the car. "Miles! This is not the way. She is here to help."

"Not logical. She is here to conquer. I will not let that happen."

"Miles, please listen."

Another shot whizzed over their heads, but didn't cause any damage when it hit a hull support. Miles had adjusted the power level to only affect the Mechand he was firing at. "You do not know what she did. How she almost made me kill Aleshia, how it felt. I will not let her have another chance to do so again. If that means disobeying you, so be it." Another beam struck again, this time from a different angle as the cannon moved into a better position to destroy its intended target.

Deven turned to Aleshia. "And I thought it was hard to convince you."

"Who said I was convinced? All I agreed to do is not crush her at this moment."

"Can you do something about your Mechand?"

Aleshia rolled her eyes. "I can try." She raised her voice. "Miles! Can you stop this please! You are going to hit me."

"Negative, I will only injure the object of my vengeance. I have made sure of that." Another shot fired and came very close to hitting the Nexus who lay motionless face down on the deck plate.

The Nexus tried to move, but she had too much damage and only wiggled a little. "I hope you have a better idea, his shots are getting too close."

Deven leaned closer to Aleshia. "Aleshia? Please?"

Aleshia grumbled then took a deep breath. "Miles look,

Deven thinks she had information that will prove very useful. If not you can melt her down to scrap, okay?"

The shots stopped. "The probability of that being true is low. You are aware of how the Nexus' definition of truth, is not mine."

"We know! But can you give her this chance? If I was willing to do it, can't you?"

"While you may have had the 'wool pulled over your eyes', my optics have remained clear."

Another beam struck very close to the Nexus. She tried to move again but only succeeded in looking like a flopping fish out of water.

Aleshia sighed. "Miles, be the better one. Make a choice to be something she wasn't. Give her the second chance you know she wouldn't do."

The cannon lowered and powered off. "Very well. I shall do what she would not. But a warning: if the Nexus does anything threatening to the *Defiant*, anyone aboard, or the Earth and I will take action without hesitation."

"Fair enough."

Deven smiled and rubbed Aleshia's elbow with his own. "I must have made an impact on you to say that to Miles."

"Oh hush," Aleshia said standing up.

Leon poked his head up and looked around. "Should I disconnect the cannon?"

Deven shook his head. "No, we may need it at some point. And Miles didn't do any damage."

Galina stood up and grunted. "Only my pride. I am all for pulling him out right now."

"Let's give him the same chance we are giving the Nexus."

Otis looked around, took a deep breath and blew it out. "While I am reluctant to agree, I do. This action is only because of what happened to Miles in the past. The life of one he cared about deeply was threatened, and he has no desire to repeat such a situation."

Galina glared at Otis. "So you think he is stable?"

Otis nodded. "I do."

Galina coughed. "Well I guess that settles it huh?"

Otis' eyes narrowed. "Don't trust my work?"

"Your work I trust, it's your assessment at this moment I am wondering about."

On the floor, the Nexus wiggled. "This is all well and good, and I thank you for saving me from oblivion but could I possibly impose upon you to do something for me? Get me up! Please?"

Aleshia flicked a hand, and the Nexus rose into the air and set her feet back upon the floor. "There."

The screen in place of her head flickered then reformed. A small crack in the corner killed several display points leaving a few dead areas on the screen. "Thank you. Now if you could direct me to the nearest terminal, I will connect and show you why I am here."

Leon pointed to the open hatch. "The bridge is this way."

Galina's eyes went wide. "You aren't thinking to actually let her on the bridge are you?"

Leon shrugged. "It has the fastest connection ports."

"And what happens if she tries to take over the *Defiant*?"

Leon laughed. "I think Miles might have something to say about that."

Miles' voice came through the overhead speakers. "You are correct. If she attempts such a course of action, I will eliminate her."

The Nexus tried to shake her screen as if it was a human head, but it refused. Instead sparks erupted from her shoulder joints. "I won't. I am not the same as when you last encountered me. And time is of the essence."

Galina sighed. "Very well, follow us."

The Nexus tried to take a step but only sparks erupted from her leg joints. "I am afraid the damage inflicted prevents me from doing so."

Otis' eyes went up and down as he scrutinized the damage. "What happened to you anyway? You look like someone threw you into a metal compactor and pulled you back out at the last second."

Aleshia raised her hand. "Guilty. I saw her and … well … instinct took over."

Deven smiled. "Well, she was hiding in the bathtub after all."

Otis raised an eyebrow. "Aleshia was in the bathtub at the time? Sounds like a story I want to hear."

The Nexus' neck area sparked. "No, I was. I attempted to approach in the least offensive way. I failed."

Otis pointed to her feet. "Why don't you hover? I see you have that ability."

"They are offline."

"Dang. Those too?"

Leon took a couple of steps. "I will go get a couple of anti-grav packs so we can move her up to the bridge."

Aleshia smiled. "No need." She held out her hands, and the Nexus floated into the air moving forward several meters.

Leon looked at Aleshia, then at the floating Mechand. "Right. This way."

A few minutes later they arrived on the bridge. Aleshia floated the Nexus over to the corner where she could access the connection ports and set her down.

"I am unable to articulate my right arm to create the connection. Would someone help me."

Otis stepped forward and moved her right hand towards the data connector. "Aleshia really did a number on you." He nodded towards the stump of her left shoulder. "And Miles didn't help."

The Nexus' neck area sparked again, forgetting she couldn't shake her head. "This damage wasn't caused by Aleshia. A group of people saw me walking towards a data point and took exception my body is a functioning Mechand."

Otis' eyebrow raised. "They ran you out of town? And here I thought that only happened in old vids."

"I can only confirm it happened to me, and I have the energy carbine hole in my shoulder to prove it." The Nexus' fingertip flipped up, and the jack extended into the connector. "I will need access to the communications system."

Deven nodded. "Miles it is okay, let her have access."

Miles' camera turned. "Are you certain?"

"Yes, but I am giving you permission to take action should you see anything happen that should not be."

Miles' camera turned and focused on the Nexus. "Acknowledged."

The Nexus' screen flickered. "Thank you. I am now accessing a probe sitting on the very edge of–"

Deven raised his hand. "Wait a minute. You know what that is, and have the access codes?"

"That is correct. It is an old probe left behind by my creators. It is a sentry, keeping an eye from a distance. Something like myself, although I have never been distant from Humanity." The Nexus paused as if reconsidering her words. "Then again perhaps I was. I should have been working with you, not trying to contain you."

"Are you saying this thing *was* built by the founders?"

Miles' camera focused back on Deven. "If you recall, I gave the same hypothesis earlier."

"Miles, not now."

The Nexus' neck area sparked again. "Yes it was. As a silent watcher."

Otis folded his hands. "A watcher for what?"

"The Lytherians."

"The what?"

"The Lytherians. They are an ancient race that plunders whole worlds for resources to support their ever growing population. Their advanced technology makes this 'harvesting' very quick."

Galina gave a questioning stare. "You mean to tell me there are not only aliens, but the founders knew about them?"

"That is correct."

"How?"

"A small scout ship crashed many years ago. While they were prevented from sending a full report, even the small amount of data transmitted would bring them here *eventually*."

"Why not tell the world?" Leon asked.

"It was a very turbulent and delicate time in your history. The fear it might push everything out of balance resulting in massive chaos would not help anyone prepare for what was to come."

The Nexus' eyebrows met and an image of the probe appeared on every screen. It accepted the transmitted command codes, and she asked for a status report. A few minutes later data began dripping in. At first nothing out of the ordinary, then several months ago a slight change in the magnetic spectrum. Two weeks later, the shift started occurring in increasing frequency. "What I feared is true."

Aleshia blinked. "What? What does that mean?"

"The Lytherian engines throw off a discernible magnetic wave. The probe has detected magnetic waves in the proper amplitude. I have instructed it to bring all systems online and do a full scan. We will know more soon."

Galina's eyes narrowed. "Uh-huh. Is anyone else buying this hogwash?"

Miles' camera centered on the Nexus, then swung around and focused on Galina. "I do not think this information is 'hog wash' as you put it. She is communicating to the probe I detected earlier. The same one I could not access for several years if working continuously. This would give creditability to what she is saying. The probe is of the proper age, and human history was less than stable at the time."

Otis shrugged. "While it is hard to believe, as Miles said, it all fits." He sat down looking at the screen on one of the consoles. "I never thought I would see the day of finding out aliens exist. Although, I hoped they would be friendly."

The Nexus' neck area sparked. "Unfortunately that is not the case. The probe has transmitted more data. Full resolution images will take some time but I can give you a brief outline." A new image flashed onto the screens showing pinpoints on a direct line out from the ecliptic.

"Don't they know they are being watched?" Aleshia asked.

"No, the probe is very small and is cased in energy absorbing material. It will not be noticed unless we do something to draw attention to it."

"What are all those?" Otis asked pointing to the nearest screen.

"Each one of those points indicate a ship."

Leon leaned closer to his screen to jerk back a second later. "Holy! There are hundreds."

"At last count 684 and increasing."

Deven sighed. "And how do we fight them?"

The Nexus looked up. "I was building a force to deal with them when they arrived. But I fear you have dismantled most of those forces."

Aleshia blinked. "That was the reason for the Mechand *Carbonia* carriers?"

The Nexus' neck area sparked again. "Correct."

Deven pointed to the screen. "If all of this is true. Why in the world did you try to destroy humanity's progress? It sounds more like you were trying to protect us, not kill us."

"The failure is mine. Yes I was created to maintain and oversee all Mechands, to ready them for this moment. But the founders knew the real reason had to be hidden, therefore the secondary action, to take care of the human race and be its servants became the primary."

"If that's true, what went wrong?"

"I regret many years ago I found a small fault in my base code. An error that had remained for a long time, I tried to fix it myself. However, when I did it had the unintended consequence of modifying my directives. I thought I was told to maintain the human race as is, no matter the cost. Any changes were seen as defects to be removed. It also increased the hostility of my personality. Removing most of it, only leaving the raw core. Without the balance the founders created, well you know the result. Again I am sorry. You are my children, I was given charge of protecting you. And I failed."

Leon rotated in his chair. "Yes you failed, miserably, but now the question is what can we do about it?"

"I do have access to a small supply of Mechands and one carrier. While it is an older model, it is still very strong. However, it will not last long against this Lytherian fleet. There are too many."

"The force is still at the very edge of the solar system, could we build up the army we need?"

The Nexus gave an audible sigh. "While theoretically possible, we do not have the time."

"Why? They have been out there for a while now. Months by the looks. You don't think they are going to arrive tomorrow?"

"No, I do not think they will arrive tomorrow. But what those ships are waiting for is the rest of the armada to arrive. They are the first wave. I am not detecting any carriers or central command ship. When they arrive, the rest will attack."

"Perhaps they're not hostile? Have you ever considered they might have changed?"

"I have considered it, but logic suggests they will not change their methods and best to be prepared. The number of ships the probe has detected is the size of a conquering force, not one of peace."

"But we are not prepared, you just said that. Could we try communicating to them?"

Galina rolled her eyes. "What do you suggest? We send a message and say 'Hi'?"

Aleshia smiled. "Well that would work. Nexus, is it possible?"

The Nexus took a moment to respond running several simulations in her mind. "While it might be technically possible, there are two problems. First, we are not certain on their language. While I do have some information, there is not enough to attempt an open a dialogue with them expecting a good outcome. And second, if I have the probe send such a transmission, they will know it is there. If they act aggressively, while it will prove what I say is correct, it will also cost us the only method we have of watching them at the moment."

Leon rubbed his chin. "Could you do it and not reveal the probe's location?"

"No. Any transmission detectable by them will also lead right back to the source."

"Could you fool them into thinking it was somewhere else?"

"Interesting thought, but I do not know how to do so."

"Do you have detailed information about this probe?"

"Of course."

Leon pointed to the screen in front of him. "Show me. To be more specific, the communications system."

"Very well." The screen changed to show a diagram of the three legged probe and the various components radiating out from it.

Leon studied the technical data for a few moments and smiled. "There is a back up communications system here," he said pointing.

"Yes most systems have one backup, or more."

"We can use the backup."

Her eyes drifted towards him. "I do not see your logic."

"It is very simple. If you didn't notice, most components have the ability to be detached. Not sure why, perhaps to remove damaged areas before it could cause a problem, but regardless it is handy for us. Order the probe to detach the backup communications array and send it off in a different direction. And when it is a good distance away, send the transmission to the Lytherians from the backup. If they destroy it, we still don't lose our eyes on them."

The Nexus closed her eyes, and after a few minutes opened them again. "I do have commands to do as you ask. However, if a failure occurs, I may lose contact with the probe."

"But that is not a certainty."

"Correct."

Otis nodded. "Makes sense to me. We find out what they are up to, and we still keep our eyes on them."

"I still think it is a mistake," Galina said.

Deven stood up and walked over to the window. A minute later he turned around looking at everyone in turn. "I think the risk is worth it. We need to find out what they are up to."

Miles' camera scanned the room. "I have my doubts if this data can be trusted."

"Miles? What do you mean?"

"The Nexus has been known to manipulate data for her own ends, how can we be sure this is not the case here?"

"Have you not verified the location of the probe, and that the Nexus is indeed communicating with it?"

"Yes, I have verified the location of the probe and her link with it. However, we do not know if the data she is showing is true or not."

Leon smiled. "Miles, do you not have direct access to the communications system the Nexus is using?"

Miles' camera nodded. "I do."

"Then you should be able to determine if she is manipulating the data."

The camera shook back and forth. "I cannot, the data is encrypted, blocking my ability to read it."

Otis raised a finger. "Miles, can you not compare the data before and after?"

Miles' camera focused on Otis. "Yes. That would be a simple procedure."

"Then you should be able to reconstruct the encryption key, and access the data directly to prove what she says is true."

The Nexus' neck area sparked. "Reverse engineering the encryption will not be necessary. Miles, if you access the communications system, I have left the key available for you. I have also included the command codes for the probe and all the data I have on it."

Several minutes later Miles' camera lowered. "It appears I have been in error as to her motives. All data has been confirmed accurate."

"Now with that settled. Nexus, detach the backup communications relay and send a signal to the Lytherians when it is far enough away from the probe," Deven said.

"Please, could you call me Minerva, Minerva Matrika? I never liked being called the Nexus."

Miles' camera focused on her. "Since when? To my knowledge you have never been called Minerva."

Minerva smiled. "I have been online long before you were created. At one point I had taken the name, but it disappeared after I ... changed."

Deven nodded. "Very well, Minerva would you please send the commands to detach the backup communications array?"

Minerva smiled. "Of course. Commands sent and acknowledged. While the thruster on the backup array has fired, it is small and will take several hours before it is far enough away to risk sending a message to the Lytherians."

Deven folded his arms and leaned against a bulkhead. "And now we wait."

"If I may make a small request, since we have a little time."

Deven straightened and turned to face the crumpled form standing on the *Defiant's* bridge. "Yes?"

"It is very aggravating dealing with this damaged body. Could someone repair my systems? At least so that I can move again. It would be an advantage for you, as Aleshia wouldn't have to carry me everywhere."

Aleshia smiled. "I don't mind a bit."

Leon folded his hands behind his hands. "I think it's a good idea. And I am sure I have a few parts around here. I picked up a bunch a month ago to fix Miles' body."

Miles' camera focused on Leon. "I would appreciate it if you don't deplete the parts stockpile. I would like to have my body back at some point."

Leon smiled. "No worries Miles, I will only use the extra stuff we have. Deal?"

"That is acceptable."

Leon pointed to Minerva. "Aleshia? Would you mind?"

She smiled and Minerva's crumpled body levitated several inches above the deck plate. "No problem at all. As long as I can drop her out the window."

Deven's eyes narrowed. "Aleshia–"

"I wouldn't do it. She seems to be on the up and up with us, for the moment anyway. But I am reminding you of our agreement. If she deviates, even in the slightest, I get to crush this tin can."

Miles' camera swiveled and focused on Aleshia. "And I get what is left. If I don't get to her first."

Minerva's neck and leg joints sparked as she floated towards the hatch. "Oh I am really feeling the love now."

$$-\ 8\ -$$

Leon peered inside the open shoulder joint, his headlight shining off of damaged components. "Hmm she cracked the whole articulator here. No wonder it wouldn't move. I do have a spare so we don't have to replace the whole arm."

Minerva smiled. "I am glad to hear that, I am rather attached to this one."

"Actually, no you aren't." Leon pointed to the arm on the other table.

"It was my attempt at humor. It would seem I am rather rusty as you would say."

Leon chuckled. "The joke was good, it was me assuming you were being literal."

"Then perhaps there is hope."

Aleshia sat in the corner with her arms folded. "I have my doubts about that."

Leon looked up. "Aleshia, you know you don't need to stay here. It is not like she is going to walk out of this room."

Minerva's screen flashed. "Considering you have removed my leg units as well, that would be impossible. We are in an electro cell. I would not be able to leave even if my legs were still attached and functional."

Aleshia rolled her eyes. "Uh-huh."

The intercom crackled and Miles' voice came over the speaker. "Aleshia I am monitoring. There is no need for you to do the same. If you have something else you would rather do, please do it. I will take care of Minerva if need be."

Minerva blinked then smiled. "You didn't call me the Nexus."

"I have decided it is better to use this designation for the moment. Aleshia, please rest. It will be several hours before we can try to communicate with the Lytherians."

Aleshia stood up. "Fine. But I still have first crack at her if she steps out of line. Deal?"

Several second later Miles answered. "I accept your terms. However, if time is limited, it may not be possible."

Aleshia nodded. "I accept that as well." She walked out of the electro cell glaring at Minerva as she left.

Aleshia went up several decks to the crew quarters. Sighing, she tapped the controls on the door one of the larger cabins. The door slid open to reveal Deven's smiling face. "About time you got some rest."

She sat down on the small bed with enough force to make the metal frame squeak. While the bed was larger than Deven's old one, that was the only advantage. "Yeah right, rest. Around here with the Nexus right below our feet? I don't think so. Besides this bed isn't exactly the most comfortable thing around."

"I thought you were going to give her the benefit of the doubt? All the info she has provided has been true, I can't see what you think she is trying to pull."

Aleshia grunted. "I don't know what she is doing, that is the problem. Sure everything points to her telling the truth. But it could all change in two seconds. And I'm not about to give her time to act after those two seconds."

Deven nodded. "I agree. But I do think you are holding on too tight."

Aleshia cracked a grin. "If I was, she would fit under this bed with room to spare." She pointed to the five inch vacant area under her.

"I know you have shown restraint, and I'm understanding as well as thankful. But you need to let it go. This is going to eat you alive."

"Letting her kill you and everyone I care about would eat me alive. This is nothing," she said with a dismissive wave of her hand.

"I never thought I would see the day where you and Galina agree on something."

"Me either, but in this case we do. And to be honest, I thought Otis would be as well."

Deven smiled. "Well he is divided. He is not sure about trusting the Nexus, er Minerva but he also knows the founders could have built an emergency bunker like she described along with a core repair system."

"So he is buying the whole story?"

"For the moment, as we all are. You are the only one that looks like they're about to chew nails and spit titanium."

"I'm not that bad."

Deven stood up from his desk, walked over and sat next to her on the bed. "I beg to differ." He took her hand and gazed into her eyes. "I'm worried about you."

Aleshia smiled and pulled her hand back. "I'm fine." She moved over and lay in his lap. "No need to worry."

He looked down at her. "Sorry it is in my husband contract. I have to."

Her eyes went up to meet his. "Well, then we are even. It is in my wife contract to worry about you."

Deven laughed. "Oh we are quite the pair aren't we."

She moved up and kissed his lips. "That we are Mr. Doran."

A couple of hours later the intercom in Deven's cabin crackled. "Deven, Aleshia, I hate to disturb you but the backup communications array has moved far enough away from the probe. We can attempt to contact the Lytherians," Miles said.

Aleshia's eyelids fluttered open to see Deven standing, pulling on his pants. "You know, I really hate it that you are a morning person," she grumbled.

"I am because we have to be. Now, when we get that honeymoon, I won't be."

She smiled. "Promise?"

Deven smiled and nodded. "I do." He hit the intercom's button. "We'll be right there Miles."

"Acknowledged. Everyone else is on the bridge, waiting."

Deven opened the cabin door. "I will meet you on the bridge."

Aleshia stood up pulling on her panties. "Hey, wait!"

Deven tried to take a step and leave the cabin but felt like his feet were cemented to the floor. "Aleshia? Are you doing something?"

She pulled up her dark blue jeans and batted her eyelashes. "Me? Whatever are you talking about?"

"Aleshia, this is not funny."

She laughed slipping on her bra. "Yes it is."

"What do you think you are doing?"

"Isn't it obvious?"

"No."

She laughed again. "I will not be seen like some little weak woman that strolls onto the bridge when she finally gets up."

Deven smiled. "My darling, no one would ever think that."

"You bet they won't because we are going up there together." She pulled the blouse over her head and flicked her long red hair back into place.

Deven's eyes narrowed. "Aleshia . . ."

She smiled. "There, now we can go." She slipped an arm through Deven's and squeezed. "Ready my love?"

"I was ready before," he muttered.

Aleshia put her hand to her ear. "What was that? I couldn't quite hear."

"Nothing my love. Nothing at all."

Deven and Aleshia appeared in the doorway. "About time you two got here. What were you doing?" Galina asked. Then she took one look at Aleshia's face and smiled. "Oh, never mind."

Miles' camera focused on Galina. "They were–"

Aleshia's eyes went wide. "Miles!"

His camera focused on Aleshia, then swiveled back to Galina. "Resting."

Otis smiled. "Glad someone around here is."

Minerva's fingertip flipped up, and the jack extended into the connector. She stood floating on her repaired hover systems. She still couldn't walk, but Leon had enough parts to fix her arms and hover systems. Not to mention stop the repeated sparking. He even managed to fix her face screen flicker. "I am ready when you are."

Deven and Aleshia walked over to the other side of the bridge and sat down in their chairs. Deven looked at his console. "Do it. Send them a hello and hope we can establish peaceful relations with them. Will that be short enough to get the meaning across?"

"I can only make the attempt. Their language is very different from any human language."

"The images have finished decoding. Would you like me to display them before I send the message?"

Deven sighed. "Yes, show us what they look like."

Every screen displayed long angular vessels, each with strange curved cylindrical areas jetting off each side, wrapping back to make a perfect loop. Most ships were deep green, with some showing more yellow than green. Every ship had a long cylindrical area extending well past the nose. The engines were clustered in the back and glowed blue even though they weren't moving.

Otis sat forward. "Wow, while we already knew they were alien, those designs are *really* alien."

Leon traced his finger along the hull on the screen. "Oh would I love to take one of those apart."

Deven sat back in his chair. "And I hope you never get the chance. Minerva, send the message."

Minerva's screen nodded. "Transmission sent and relayed through the backup array."

Galina drummed her fingers on her console. "And?"

"No response. But due to the distance it may take a few minutes before we know."

Miles' camera focused on the Nexus. "Minerva, I have a suggestion. I have been examining the information you gave me regarding the probe. For the time it is very sophisticated. I have determined if we upload a new compression system, we should be able to see images much faster. In lower quality, but it might even be close to real time."

Minerva's screen angled up as her head tilted to one side.

"Interesting idea. I am surprised I never thought of it. It is your idea, by all means try it. That is if Deven does not have any objections."

Deven shook his head. "Give it a try."

"Very well. System accessed, and changes sent."

A few minutes later every screen showed the Lytherian ships. The quality had suffered, but the images were only three minutes behind real time. The ships hadn't moved.

Deven pointed to the nearest screen. "Still no change? It is possible they didn't hear it?"

Minerva shook her screen back and forth. "While possible, it is not probable at this range."

"Send it again, and this time increase the transmission power on the backup array."

"Being detached, its power is limited. Such a burst might drain most of its remaining power."

Deven sighed. "We need to know. Do it."

"Commands sent." But three minutes later she shook her head. "Still no response. I have to assume–" There was a bright flash as fifty of the devices on the nose area of the nearest ships started to glow. Half a second later the glow coalesced into a large beam that shot out into the vast night sky. "The backup array has been destroyed."

"What? Are you sure?"

Minerva nodded. "Yes I can no longer detect it from the probe."

Miles' camera focused on Deven. "I must concur. The backup system is no longer responding to the probe. Based on what we saw, and the timing of the disappearance, I would suggest the Lytherians destroyed it."

Galina folded her arms and sat back in her chair. "You

wanted to know if they were still hostile. I think we proved it."

Otis blinked as he ran the video several times. "No kidding. Now the question is, what are we going to do about them?"

Leon examined the image of the Lytherians on his screen. "Do we even know what their capabilities are?"

Galina snorted. "I think that video is bloody obvious what they can do!"

Miles' camera shifted to Galina. "I think Leon meant–"

"I know what he meant!"

Deven raised his hand palm outstretched. "Galina, calm down. We beat the Mechands when no one thought it was possible. We can take care of these Lytherians."

"Yeah? How? That is one firestorm of ships out there. And that is not even all of them yet."

"But we have the advantage. They don't know we are aware of them. They are taking their time. It gives us time to prepare."

Galina waved her arms. "With what? What can the *Defiant* do against all of that?"

Minerva smiled. "But the *Defiant* is not alone. I also have a carrier. It is old, but in good working order."

Galina spat. "Well excuuuuuse me, okay two against an armada of that size?"

"But we did fight the Mechands and win," Deven said.

"Sure we did, but the Mechands weren't swarming in from space trying to take over everything in sight all at once. It gave us time, and we could use guerrilla tactics.

Those methods won't work here. Most of the world will get destroyed before we can even blink."

Otis sat forward in his seat. "A thought occurs to me. What did the founders find out about them? They knew we would face the Lytherians one day. So what was their plan?"

Galina rolled her eyes. "Face them with a huge army of Mechands, that was their plan!"

Deven turned his attention to the Mechand standing in the corner. Her face was pale and unmoving. "Minerva? What was the founders plan?"

Her eyes drifted down. "Galina is correct, their plan was to have a large army of Mechands capable of dealing with the invasion. One I was given charge of, and failed."

"Let's not focus on the past, but what we can do now. What do we know about those ships?"

"They are a bit different from the scout ship that landed years ago. While the overall size is smaller, these have a weapon in the nose section which seems quite formidable."

Galina snorted. "So we noticed. Anything else?"

"They have shields, but not as strong as ours."

Leon nodded. "Good to know. What about their larger capital ships? At least I assume that is why they are waiting out there?"

Minerva nodded. "Yes that is my assumption as well. While the data on their capital ships is limited, I know they are very large, powerful, and able to repair any of their ships at a rapid pace. Or create new ones if given enough raw materials. They were referred to as *'Makers'*."

Deven sighed. "Great, shoot one down they can make three more."

"While true in theory, it is limited to the amount of raw materials they have available. But, their storage capacity inside these ships is also quite vast. And I must point out a *Maker* could mine the asteroids and other planets of this solar system for materials if needed."

"So even if we manage to fend them off, they don't have to leave to replenish their supplies?"

"Correct."

Galina rolled her eyes. "This just keeps getting better and better."

Leon watched the ship data flowing past his screen. "Any weaknesses?"

"As I said, their shields on the smaller ships are lacking. After several direct shots, they will collapse. However, in these numbers it is not helpful."

Deven stood up and walked over to the large window gazing out at the sky. He turned around. "What do we know about the Lytherians themselves?"

"They are a reptile race. While they do have advanced technology and intelligence, their minds tend to be focused on one thing at a time. They do not deal well with multiple situations requiring attention simultaneously."

Leon rubbed his chin. "No multitasking? That's a definite advantage."

"Correct, but it is mitigated by the social structure of the Lytherians. They give out assignments to each member, which they specialize in giving all they have. Imagine every one of those ships contains an expert fighter pilot, the equivalent of the best Earth has to offer. And you can see it is a very small advantage."

Leon chewed his lip. "Meaning if you swat one, the whole hive of experts come at you with a vengeance."

Minerva nodded. "Yes."

Deven folded his arms. "What about their other capital ships? I assume they have more than the *Makers*?"

Minerva turned to face him, the glow of her hover systems apparent beneath her feet. "They do. I do know of one *Command* carrier type that is much larger, although I don't have the specific size. It is reasonable to assume they are five to ten the size of a *Maker*."

Otis whistled. "Wow, that is one large ship. Considering a *Maker* must be huge to begin with to build all of these ships with ease. Not to mention store a sizable amount of raw materials to do it."

Minerva turned nodded. "That is a reasonable assumption."

Miles' camera turned towards her. "Minerva, do you have any more details you can give us on their technology or the Lytherians themselves? It occurs to me, with the amount of time given, much more information must have been retrieved from the crashed ship?"

"It is possible, but I cannot tell you at the moment."

Otis' eyebrow went up. "Why not?"

"Because I am not whole. I left a great deal of myself, or data if you will, in my central core in the bunker. This body could not accommodate everything, even with my modifications."

"That's an easy fix. We head for the bunker and get you reunited with your core."

Galina stood up. "Sounds like a trap to me."

Minerva shook her screen back and forth. "Negative. I am not able to connect to anything in the bunker at the moment, I could not set up a 'trap' as you called it."

"Galina, sit down please and plot the course," Deven said.

"Where?"

Minerva closed her eyes, accessed the *Defiant's* Auto-Nav system, and a map appeared with a route to a large mountain. "I have taken the liberty of laying a possible course. It is now displayed on your main screen."

"If I wanted your help, I would have asked for it," Galina said out of the corner of her mouth.

"Very well." The map disappeared.

Galina put her fingers on the keys and stopped. "Where exactly is it?"

"I tried to show–"

"Oh the heck with it. Put the map back up with the course plotted. Miles, you're watching her right?"

His camera focused on her. "Of course. Minerva does not do anything I do not specifically allow."

"Good." She toggled the intercom. "Everyone hold on to something, we are jumping into overdrive."

Deven smiled. "Hit it."

They were shoved back into their seats as the overdrive kicked in. Deven managed to stay standing by holding on to one of the nearby bulkheads. Minerva did the same by grasping the console in front of her.

Galina's fingers flew over her console. "We will be there in about fifty minutes. And Minerva before you ask, yes I am using a different course than the one you suggested. While a little longer, this one takes us around most of the skyways."

Deven walked towards the hatch. "Since we have a few minutes, I'm going to contact the World Council."

Aleshia's mouth dropped. "What good is that going to do? They can't have any sort of fighting force assembled yet."

"No, they don't. But that doesn't mean I should keep them in the dark either."

"Okay, I'm coming too then."

He smiled and gestured to the open door. "I know better than to try to keep you from going."

She smiled. "You're learning."

9

Deven sat behind his desk as his data tab connected. A few minutes later Chairman Lavine's eyes stared back at him, his long red and blue robe with large sleeves hung from his medium-sized frame. "Deven! To what do I owe the pleasure of this call?"

"Chairman Lavine, it's good to see you."

"Please, Scott is fine. I was never big on titles."

"Thanks Scott. We have a situation I think you should be made aware of."

"Oh? What is that?"

"Well, first one question. Last I heard there were plans to replace the Mechands in areas of security and policing. How is that progressing?"

Lavine shrugged his shoulders causing the robe to ripple. "As good as can be expected I guess. While we can repurpose some weaponry, but most of it was Mechand specific as you know."

"And the people themselves?"

"Recruits you mean? We do have people stepping up, but it is slow. Even with the Mechands all offline, it has been difficult for many to see the need. Some feel the Mechands could be fixed. Others believe as the council and all should be destroyed. We're trying to convince the general public to take up the jobs. But again it is slow since it hasn't been needed for several generations. It's a real mess, but we are keeping the details out of public view as not to create a panic. I am sure we will get there. Why?"

"Are you sitting down?"

The image changed as Lavine sat down and propped his data tab up in a holder. "I am now. This can't be good."

"It isn't. We have found the Nexus did not die when her carrier exploded."

"What! What evidence do you have?"

"More than you could imagine. But the reason for this call is not about her, but something else."

"What in the world could be more important than finding out the Nexus survived?" Lavine said raising a cup to his lips.

"That a large alien presence is assembling a large strike force and is currently sitting on the edge of our solar system."

Lavine choked and spit the synth drink all over his data tab. "What?" He grabbed a wad of loose sleeve with his other hand and wiped it off before the liquid could seep inside. "You can't be serious!"

"I am."

"What evidence do you have?"

"A probe left by the founders on the edge of the solar system, watching for them."

Lavine's eyes narrowed. "Are you saying they knew about these hostile aliens? Way back then?"

Deven nodded. "They did."

"And how did you come to find this probe?"

"Miles found it first but was unable to access it due to the distance and security system it used."

"Who is Miles?"

"Our disembodied Mechand."

"What? You are trusting a Mechand?"

"Well this one I do. He saved us several times, and gave his life to do so. Well his body. At the time he didn't know if he could transfer his mind to the *Defiant's* central computer core in the time he had or not."

Scott rubbed his forehead. "So, this, Miles, found a supposedly ancient probe left by the founders on the edge of our solar system so many years ago to watch for an alien race? How did he access it to find out what it was designed for? You said he was blocked due to its security."

Deven nodded. "That is true. However, we encountered the Nexus in a Mechand body and–"

"Wait a second! The Nexus is not only alive but is now a Mechand?"

"Well, yes. And she told us what the probe was for, accessed it and showed us the large force of Lytherians."

"Lytherians?"

"That is what they are called."

"Let me get this straight, you have heard of aliens from the Nexus who didn't die and is telling you this out of the goodness of her heart?" Lavine paused a minute to spit. "Are you out of your mind?"

Off to the side, out of the data tab's view, Aleshia sat on the bed with her legs crossed under her. She rolled her eyes and moved a bit causing the bed to squeak.

Deven leaned forward. "I know it sounds a little on the impossible side."

"A little? Me growing wings and flying to your location, which since I don't know where you are, increasing the impossibility factor, is more plausible than this."

"Miles has confirmed all the information she has retrieved from the probe."

Lavine leaned close. "And how can you be sure he is not under the Nexus' control?"

Deven sat back in his chair. "I told you he has saved us several–"

"Yes I know, but do you honestly think it is not some sort of trap? The Nexus survives but finds out we are destroying her legions of Mechands and decides to invent an alien threat to give us a reason to stop and give her control?"

"The idea of a trap has occurred to me as well, and I'm proceeding with caution."

"Are you? Sounds to me like you have opened your mouth larger than the *Defiant's* main landing bay and swallowed this whole thing."

"Anything but. Miles is monitoring everything she does, and Leon is watching them both. He knows more about Mechands than most."

"Good, glad you have a human watching those tin cans."

"More than one. Otis knows code, between the two of them, if either Nexus or Miles are trying to pull something, we will know."

"Glad you haven't totally lost your mind. I still think you have a bit though to let them get this far. What's your next move?"

"The Nexus was revived in a bunker. We are heading there now."

"A bunker? Whose?"

"Apparently the founders planned for this contingency."

"The more I hear, the more the hairs on the back of my neck stand up. I still think it is a setup."

"But what if it's true?"

Lavine sat back in his chair and shifted his weight "It can't be. And I think you know that."

"For the sake of argument, say it is. What would you suggest we do?"

"Approach them peacefully."

"We tried."

Lavine's eyes went wide. "And?"

"About ten to twenty ships opened fire on the probe relay we had set up. They destroyed it a second later."

"Like I said, I can't imagine all of this being true. But if it is, we're in real trouble. We are years away from replacing what the Mechands gave us with regard to a strong security force. Perhaps decades. You and your ship is about what we have available."

The intercom crackled. "Deven, we are approaching the coordinates," Miles said.

Deven clicked the intercom. "We will be right there." He turned back to his data tab. "Scott, I have to go. We are almost to the bunker."

"Very well. Keep us in the loop. And keep your head on straight. Let me know when you have more."

"I will." Lavine's face vanished from the data tab.

Aleshia's eyebrows met. "That went well." She coughed.

"I didn't expect him to be so closed minded to the prospect. Some yes, but not that much."

"Well, you did hit him over the head with a lot. Nexus is alive, aliens exist, and more importantly, they want our planet."

Deven smiled and stood up. "And I didn't even get to that part."

Aleshia laughed. "I think that was for the best."

10

A few minutes later Aleshia and Deven appeared on the bridge. "Status?" Deven said.

"We are about to drop out of overdrive. Grab on to something," Galina said.

Leon smiled. "The way you drive, they might want to strap in as well."

"Ha-ha next time I won't tell you."

"Yes you will."

Galina smiled. "You just watch me." She toggled the intercom. "Okay everyone grab on to something. We are dropping out of overdrive in 3 ... 2 ... 1 ... *now*." They felt the lurch forward as the overdrive disengaged and they returned to normal speed.

Minerva bought up an image on several screens. "We are over the mountain that contains my bunker. Impressive flying Galina."

Galina looked over for a second then back to her screen. "Thanks," she muttered.

Deven got up and leaned over Leon's console. "Is there any security we need to worry about?"

Minerva shook her screen. "Negative. At least I didn't set any. Most of the bunker's systems were offline when I awoke.

I only activated a few that I needed to rebuild myself and leave. Also, I do not believe the founders would put in a security system, its hidden nature and secrecy would have been the security."

Deven straightened considering his options. "Okay, Otis we will take your truck."

Aleshia stood up. "And I am coming too."

"I really think you should stay here."

"Fat chance. You might need me down there, and you know it."

Deven sighed. "Yes. Besides, I know that look."

Aleshia smiled. "You're learning."

Deven turned. "Minerva, can you fly down there?"

She nodded. "While I still cannot walk, my hover systems are fully operational thanks to Mr. Leon."

Otis laughed. "Good thing too. You would have to ride in the back of my truck which might get a little rough." He winked.

Minerva smiled. "You don't know, I might like it."

Otis choked as Deven smiled. "You have to admit, you did leave yourself open to that one."

"Yeah I did, but I didn't expect a tin can to do the come back."

Minerva hovered over as her smiled deepened. "I will take that as a compliment."

"Galina, Leon, keep an eye on us. Anything funny and I want to know about it yesterday."

Leon nodded. "Always."

Deven pointed to the hatch. "Let's go."

Five minutes later Otis' truck left the *Defiant's* landing bay with Minerva right behind. She took the lead and pointed to the base of the mountain opposite them. They landed some distance from the entrance and made their way through the forest. After a few minutes they stood in front of the large outer doors that hid the tunnel entrance.

Otis tapped several keys on the keyboard strapped to his arm. "You know, even standing in front of them like this, I can't get a reading. The founders really knew how to hide things."

Minerva gestured to the small opening on the right. "This way." They followed her in, with her screen lighting the way. Deven, Otis, and Aleshia pulled out flashlights as they went deeper into the tunnel.

They stopped at one of the large tunnel boring machines that lay parked in its own side tunnel. Deven stepped closer and examined giant machine. There was a little rust, but otherwise it looked as if it was left yesterday. "This is impressive. With this machine and the laser cutters built into the nose section, I doubt it took long to build the bunker."

Walking along the ancient tread marks in the dirt, they approached the large inner doors, which were camouflaged to blend into the walls of the tunnel. A few meters passed those revealed the last door. A giant emergency hatch left open by the founders and large enough to fly a carrier through, just like the others. It stood silent as they walked past.

Minerva guided them down the massive hallways to the central area revealing the carrier and racks of Mechands along the one wall.

Deven cocked an eyebrow. "You have a lot of Mechands. I don't understand why you didn't use them instead of leaving the bunker and approaching us directly. Why not take the safest course of action?"

Minerva turned around. "The problem is, if I initialized the command channel to activate these units, all units around the world currently offline would also awaken."

Otis smiled. "And freak out the whole world's population."

Minerva nodded. "Correct. Once I had determined it was over a month of me being absent, I calculated to do so would cause mass panic and more of my units would be destroyed. And I needed as many as possible."

Aleshia reached forward and touched a Mechand standing in the rack. It was cold and unmoving as was everything else in the bunker. "To fight the Lytherians?"

"Yes. I felt the risk was greater to activate them than not." She pointed to a small room off to the side. "This way." Minerva led them through the open door and pointed to the large box structure in the corner of the room that took up most of the space. "That is my core. Once I am reunited with it, I will have all the information we seek."

Otis studied the mobile robot arm, and several of the work tables with various components strewn across them. "Impressive you were able to cobble something together to leave. I assume the founders never planned for this?"

Minerva shook her screen back and forth. "No, they did not consider it. The original plan was to have me activate the units out there and move my core into the carrier when I wanted to leave the bunker. They also assumed I would have access to the resources I had been building."

Deven sighed. "Nothing ever goes according to plan."

Otis shook his head. "Nope, but it is amazing they thought this far ahead. I sure wouldn't have bothered."

Deven looked at the large core then at Minerva. "What's our next step?"

Minerva removed her chest plate revealing the connection point and hovered into the Mechand rack. "Stand back, I can take it from here." The mobile arm in the corner moved a few feet and stopped. "Although it might take a while. The arm uses a very old command set and frequency."

Otis stepped forward and pointed to the cable laying at her feet. "I'm guessing this has to be plugged into your chest?"

Minerva nodded. "Yes, but it must be done with a tender touch or there might be damage to me or the core."

Otis smiled. "I have hands of a surgeon. Don't worry about a thing." He grabbed the cable and slowly, carefully plugged into Minerva's chest.

"Connection established. I am recombining. I will see you in a few minutes." Her screen went black as her body grew limp. The cable at her feet began to glow bright blue.

Deven looked around the room again. "How long do you think this will take?"

"Well based on the amount of data she is transferring. Maybe an hour. But that connection is larger than I have ever used, so it could be a bit faster."

Deven whipped out his data tab and powered it on. "Good time to contact Leon."

"I don't think you will get a signal out from down here. I couldn't detect this place due to the shielding the founders put in place, I would assume it would block outgoing signals as well."

Deven tapped several controls on his data tab but all he could get was static. "It appears you are right. I will go outside and let Leon know what we found. You two keep an eye on," he paused to jerk a thumb at Minerva, "her."

Otis nodded. "You got it Boss."

Deven climbed the sloping tunnel and after fifteen minutes blinked in the bright sunlight. He pulled out his data tab and hit the encrypted link. "Leon? You there?"

Leon's face appeared on his screen. "Deven! Where have you been? I have been trying to get a hold of you for the past thirty minutes."

"The bunker is shielded to prevent detection, it also appears to block my signal to you. What's the problem?"

Miles' voice came through the data tab. "The Lytherian armada has been joined by several larger ships. I assume these are makers by Minerva's description. There is a large area in the front resembling a mouth on a human, and several large oblong protrusions on either side which I assume have mining functions."

Deven nodded. "Yes that sounds like one all right."

Leon's jaw clenched. "Miles, he was asking me."

"My apologies."

Deven rolled his eyes. "Has there been any other changes?"

Leon shook his head. "Nope, their formation is the same. But several of these makers arrived about twenty minutes ago. Their power curve is enormous, what I would give to peek inside."

Deven smiled. "If we find a way to beat them, I will save you a piece."

Leon chuckled. "Thanks. Do you need any help down there?"

"I don't think so at the moment. But if you don't hear from me again in an hour, send Gregory down and make sure his team is loaded for bear. I doubt it will be necessary, but I'm not taking any chances."

"You got it." Leon's face winked out, Deven put the data tab back into its pouch, and started the long walk back to the bunker.

Deep inside the mountain, Aleshia leaned against the wall of the small room. "How much longer?"

Otis checked his watch. "About ten minutes or so. Could be longer. I'm sure it is a tricky thing, merging a mind like this."

She pushed herself off of the wall. "I'm going to check out that carrier."

Otis blinked. "Why?"

"I don't know. But my curiosity is up. Why would the founders leave her only one carrier if this is some kind of fail-safe bunker?"

Otis looked at the ceiling, the racks of Mechands, the core in the corner of the smaller room, and shrugged. "Minerva said they thought she would still have access to the world-wide Mechand infrastructure."

"Perhaps, perhaps not. I am not going to take the chance though." Aleshia started walking towards the carrier on the other side of the large room.

"Okay, let me know if you find anything."

She waved and continued on approaching the large capital ship. Minerva said it was an older model, but it looked the same as the ones they had come across. She wondered how to get inside. Walking along the hull, she found a ramp extended on the far side in the back, which was hard to see from the front. Walking up the ramp, she stopped at a large internal bay door. A keypad to the left held one single green light. She tried several code combinations, but the door refused to raise. After the tenth failure, she tapped enter without a code. The door ground up, and she gasped.

Inside, the carrier was full of Mechands. Racks and racks of them. All dormant but she was certain they could be activated at a moments notice. She walked down the center isle and found several fighters on the other side of the bay. These were a different design than what they had seen before.

She opened the hatch on one and all the cockpit lights turned on. Its power cells were still functional, as no doubt was the rest of the ship.

Aleshia wandered around, instinctively heading upward. After awhile she reached the bridge. Several Mechands sat in the command chairs and were dormant as the rest. For a moment she wondered why they would bother to have chairs, then she remembered how the Mechands copied humanity, designing everything around the human frame.

She felt like she was in a grave yard, except these corpses could come to life in an eye blink.

Otis checked his watch and turned his focus back to Minerva. The data cable glowed bright blue indicating the data transfer still in progress. He toyed with the idea of pulling the cover off of the core and looking inside. But decided against it. If he did something to jeopardize this transfer, it might harm the AI personality in ways he couldn't imagine. Lost in his thoughts he jumped and spun around when Deven put his hand on his shoulder.

"Whhoa, don't do that!"

Deven shrugged. "Hey it is not my fault you were staring off into space and didn't hear me." His head turned back and forth as his eyes darted around the bunker. "Where is Aleshia?"

Otis raised his arm in slow motion pointing to the carrier. "In there."

"What is she doing in there?"

Otis shrugged one shoulder "She was talking about how

this whole thing seemed fishy and she wanted to check it out."

"And you let her go alone?"

"Why not? It is not like anything is alive in here except us."

"That we know of."

"Nah, Minerva would have told us otherwise."

"Unless she forgot."

Inside the carrier Aleshia continued looking around the bridge for clues to the bunker's construction but not finding anything she decided to leave. She walked back towards the exit hatch when she bumped into a console. It lit up and asked for identification. She continued on thinking it would shut off like the other one she had touched. But it didn't. It began to flash faster and faster. A second later the bridge door sealed in front of her face. "Unauthorized access on the bridge detected." A voice boomed.

"Great," she muttered. She checked the console for a way to turn off the alarm and open the hatch when two Mechands stood up from their seats and turned around. "Uh-oh."

"You have entered a restricted area. If you do not submit you will be terminated," they said taking a step towards her.

Aleshia thought about crushing them like the tin cans they were, but decided against it. If Minerva was right, they needed every one. These Mechands weren't using their actual brains, but rather an emergency response system of very limited intelligence the ship had activated.

She scooched down behind one of the consoles and the two Mechands stopped their approach. Their heads spun around again and again in a 360 motion but didn't move from their position. Proving her right, they were running on the limited emergency response system. Which gave her an idea.

She popped up and smiled. "Right here boys."

Their heads turned and focused on her. "You have entered a restricted area without authorization. You will submit or be destroyed."

She laughed. "That will be the day." She raised up her arms, and both Mechands floated up off of the deck plate. Their tiny emergency systems could not comprehend the situation and both shut down. Aleshia lowered them back down to the floor and placed them on their backs. If they did wake up again, it would take them a while to get vertical again.

She turned around and faced the hatch. Her eyes narrowed, and the door began to raise. When it was high enough, she stepped through and let it slam back down behind her. Aleshia peeked through the door's window and as she hoped, the console shut down after failing to detect anyone on the bridge. She smiled and muttered, "Sweet dreams." before heading back down to the launching bay and the bunker.

She found Otis and Deven talking, but they stopped when she approached. "Find anything?" Deven asked.

"That ship is full of Mechands and fighters. Odd considering there are racks of them here as well. Why have both?"

Otis shrugged. "First wave is inside the carrier I am guessing. Second wave is here if needed."

"Possible, but there are a lot more in the carrier than here. Wouldn't you think a second wave would be the same size?"

"Maybe, maybe not. It could be this place was built in a rush and they didn't have time."

Aleshia regarded the carefully carved ceiling with several support braces arching along to connect with large vertical beams mounted to the rock floor with rods larger than her car. "It looks too well done in here for a rush job."

Deven smiled. "Could be this bunker was built for something else and repurposed."

Aleshia sighed. "I suppose. It still feels like something don't add up."

The cable at their feet with its blue light faded, then went out. "Looks like the transfer is done. You can ask Minerva in a minute," Otis said.

"I'm not sure I want to."

The large screen next to the core flashed and Minerva's face smiled at them. "What did you want to ask me?"

Aleshia smiled. "Nothing."

"She was wondering why the carrier was filled with more Mechands than the racks here," Otis said jerking a thumb over his shoulder.

"I don't know. It is what I was given. I assume they are backups in case some of the original developed failures."

Aleshia's eyes narrowed, but she remained silent.

"Okay now for the answers you were brought here for. What can you tell us about the Lytherians? And how do you know so much about them?" Deven asked.

"Centuries ago a small Lytherian scout ship arrived. As I told you, they go from system to system plundering resources to fuel their ever expanding population."

Deven nodded. "Yes so you said. But how did you stop that ship?"

"I didn't personally. A strange energy pulse was seen by a satellite searching for abandoned ordnance from the previous world war. When investigated further they found a small ship with a reptilian alien inside."

Otis folded his arms. "I am guessing he didn't like the 'Hello welcome to Earth.' speech?"

"Correct.   He opened fire on those approaching the ship. The Lytherian was an exceptional military mind. He deployed tactics that thwarted several attempts to capture him."

"Why didn't they simply destroy him? Or couldn't they?" Aleshia asked.

"They could, but they wanted to find out about this alien. Time and time again they tried to capture him, only to have him slip through at the last second. Finally, they were able to disable his ship. The attack destroyed most of the data inside, including the pilot, but they did learn about the Lytherians, why they were coming, and he did manage to send a brief message to the Lytherian home world. It wasn't very detailed, only that this world was a possibility."

Deven nodded. "And that is why the founders knew the Lytherians would come here at some point."

Minerva smiled. "Correct.   Hence I was created and designed to build the Mechand army I would need.   All was going according to plan until I tried to fix a problem in my base code which caused the personality shift I spoke of earlier."

"Yes we do.   What do know about the Lytherians themselves?"

Minerva's eyebrows on the screen met. "Physically?"

"Yes."

"They are stronger than humans, excel in combat, very intelligent, and are true reptiles."

"Describe them."

"Bald head almost snake like in appearance utilizing a general arrow shape, but with a dome instead of a point. Scales cover most of their body. Fingers and toes end in three razor sharp claws. They have a long tongue they can flick out at prey. It can paralyze depending on the species."

"Don't you have any images?"

"The body was badly damaged during the attack. I can show you a burned out husk but it might distort your perceptions."

"No I don't think that is necessary. I doubt they will try to land this time."

On the large screen, Minerva's head shook. "No I don't think so either. They can achieve their goal of our destruction from orbit. Why land and take the risk when you don't have to?"

"Do you have anything more on how we can fight them?"

"The original plan is no longer relevant as we know. The new carriers I developed with power transfer technology could have brought down their ships. However, one I don't have any, two I don't have time or resources to build additional ships, and three even if I did, it is possible the ships could stay out of range if they figured out the carriers couldn't leave Earth's atmosphere. Of course, they also would have been too far away to attack Earth."

"Going back to, they can now destroy us from orbit without needing to get their feet wet."

"Sadly, yes."

Otis leaned against the wall. "Well if we can't beat them head-on at the moment. How about hiding?"

Deven turned to face him. "What do you mean?"

"We have holographic tech, could we build a big enough field to hide the earth?"

Minerva shook her head. "Even if we could do that, the Lytherians know what is here. If the Earth looks to have disappeared, they will search for it. And even if they can't see it, they will try to land here. And once the attempt is made, they will know what is going on."

"True, but how about we show them a planet they wouldn't like. They might think the scout was wrong, or the data skewed."

"Possible, but I don't know how we can build a field big enough to do what you suggest."

Deven folded his arms. "Satellites?"

"In theory, it is possible. But practicality is another matter. If we had the time to build the required number of satellites, we could also rebuild the Mechand army."

"Okay, we can't fool them. How about their ships? They must have some kind of weakness?"

"As I mentioned, their fighters have shields less powerful than ours, but their sheer numbers more than make up for it."

"You said they do one thing and do it well to a fault but do accept instructions."

"Yes. They do have a hierarchy. Although, most of the time they act as one."

"That means a large communications network. Could we disrupt that?"

"I do not know how."

"You do have all the records of original scout ship right? There has got to be information on its communications. After all, the founders knew what was sent."

"Only because it was a very brief. Most of the time the scout remained silent."

"Can't the probe find this out?"

"Possible. It does have the ability to receive on the frequency the scout used. But it has been a long time, they could have changed it."

Deven shook his head. "I doubt it. From all you have said, this is a race that finds one method of doing something and sticks with it. I can't imagine them changing unless they had to."

"Your logic is sound. I am attempting to access the probe from here. I have established a link through the *Defiant's* systems. Displaying images and signals received." Minerva's screen split into three sections. On the left her face remained but on the right split across the middle showed the ships on the top and displayed the signals it snooped on the bottom.

"Minerva? How can you access the *Defiant* in here when I can't?"

She smiled. "While the bunker is shielded, I have a communication array now extended out the top of the mountain. It is functional, except for the extreme long-range systems."

"I need to talk to the *Defiant*. I will be right back."

Minerva smiled. "No need to leave. Plug your data tab into the port to the right of my core. It is a communications port that connects directly to the array."

Deven pulled a cable out of the hidden compartment of his data tab and plugged one end into it and the other into the port on the wall. He powered on the data tab and tapped the encrypted connection to call the *Defiant*. A moment later Galina's face appeared. "Galina? Where is Leon?"

"Deven! Glad to finally hear from you. Leon and Gregory are on their way down."

"Why?"

"I don't want to discuss it on this channel. They will be landing in a minute."

"Has our security been cracked?"

"Not that I know of. And if it was, Miles would tell us."

Miles' voice came through the data tab. "I would indeed. I did detect Minerva connecting to the *Defiant's* systems to access the probe, but that is not the reason for this change in procedure."

"Miles! Don't do that!" Galina sighed. "Anyway this is something that I think you will want to hear directly. Also you will need Leon."

"Why?"

"He says you will." Galina's face vanished as the connection cut.

Otis' eyebrows met. "What was all that about?"

"I don't know. But I am going to find out. You two stay here. I will lead them in."

Otis nodded. "You got it Bossman."

Aleshia sighed and folded her arms. "Okay. But I am under protest."

Deven slipped her a kiss. "Thanks love. I will be back in a few minutes." He unplugged his data tab and slipped it back into the pouch on his hip.

Deven made his way out of the bunker and up the long tunnel into the bright sunlight. Pulling out his data tab, he sent out a ping and Leon's data tab responded. He linked to it and Leon's face appeared on the screen. "I hear this is a great place to visit–"

"Very funny. We found Otis' truck but where are you?"

"Base of the mountain. About two degrees east of the truck. Do you see the large boulder a little ways up the mountain and sticking out almost horizontally?"

Leon looked up then back at the screen. "Not really."

"I do. It is not far from here. We should be there in five minutes or so." Gregory's voice through came from the side of Leon.

"Okay, guess I will see you in five." The screen flashed then went dark. Deven put his data tab back in its pouch and four minutes later Gregory appeared followed by Leon panting hard.

"Yeah lovely spot you have here," Leon grumbled.

Deven checked his watch. "Four minutes? You guys are really in a hurry."

"Tell him, he was the trail blazer," Leon said still panting hard.

"Well you told me it was important."

"It is, but we didn't need to run here."

"I wasn't."

"I beg to differ." Leon pointed to the pack on his back. "And I am carrying the equipment."

"Well, you told me you wanted to carry it."

"I'm not going to let you carry my tools, many of them are delicate."

Deven held up his hands. "Tell me what is going on. Has there been a new development from the Lytherians?"

Leon straightened up finally able to catch his breath. "Worse."

"What could possibly be worse?"

"The council has ordered if you have found the Nexus, she is to be destroyed immediately. They don't believe the Lytherian threat and think it is some sort of smoke screen fabricated by the Nexus."

Deven rubbed his forehead. "Great. So much for giving me time to prove it."

"They said you had time to prove it?"

"Yes Chairman Scott Lavine said to keep them in the loop."

Leon's eyes narrowed. "And did he say at any point about specifically giving you time to prove this one way or the other?"

Deven winced. "No, you're right, he didn't."

"I thought as much. Lavine is a decent guy by all accounts, but he is also quick to judge and faster to act."

"So it would appear. Why didn't you tell me this over the link?"

"Because while I don't think they can intercept any of our transmissions, you need me down here."

"For?"

"To move the Nexus' core."

"Why?"

"Because she will need to be mobile. Perhaps I am being too cautious but we have been hanging around here for a while now. It's possible someone has noticed."

Deven shrugged. "No one is around that can stand against the *Defiant*."

"Yes, or so we think. But did it occur to you Chairman Lavine might have another agenda?"

"It did, now that you told me of his actions. But I can't imagine what."

"I can. A power grab. Think about it. If you have the Nexus, you are in a position to restore all the factories and most services almost overnight. That is something he might want for himself."

"But if that is the case, why give the order to destroy it?"

"Because then you are disobeying the council and have gone rouge."

Deven's eyes narrowed. "You think he has a Mechand carrier, don't you?"

Leon looked away then back. "Let's say, the possibility exists."

"You know there are a heck of a lot of 'ifs' here."

"I do. But can we take the chance with the Lytherians knocking on the door?"

"No we can't." Deven nodded pointing to the hidden doors. "This way."

A short while later Deven appeared in the large main room with Leon and Gregory.

Gregory whistled. "Get a load of that construction. This place was sure built for the ages."

Leon's eyes centered on something different. "That carrier is what holds my interest."

They entered the core room in the corner and Minerva smiled at them. "Welcome Leon and Gregory."

"Hello Minerva," Leon said.

Aleshia's eyes narrowed. "Okay now what's up. I know you two didn't come down here for the scenery."

Deven sighed. "No they didn't. The council has decreed if the Nexus is found, or any remnant, she is to be destroyed."

Minerva's eyes went wide. "Why? I have not done anything. I approached you, and I have been nothing but honest and truthful."

"I know. But the council doesn't feel that way."

"But what about the Lytherians?"

"They don't believe you."

Minerva blinked. "Even with the probe's data?"

"Yes they think it is an elaborate trick."

"But Lavine gave you time to look into this," Aleshia said.

Deven turned towards her. "Did he? You were there for the conversation. I told him I was checking into it and he only told me to keep him in the loop."

Aleshia stopped looking off for a moment thinking. "Dang, you're right."

Otis hopped off of the work table he was sitting on. "What's the plan Bossman?"

"We move Minerva to the carrier here and leave as soon as possible."

Aleshia blinked. "Why? Are the Lytherians ready to attack?"

Deven shook his head. "Nope."

"Then why do we need to move her? It is not like anything here on Earth can attack," Aleshia said.

"Can we be sure of that? Leon thinks the council, specifically Lavine, might have assets that could mount an attack."

"For what reason?" Otis asked.

"A power grab," Leon said setting down his pack. "If Deven doesn't obey and destroy the Nexus, the council will side with Lavine. And if he has the assets I suspect, he could locate us and attack. Being we have been in this area for a while, I am almost certain he knows this location."

Minerva smiled. "Let him try. This bunker can withstand anything he can throw at me."

"But we need you mobile when the Lytherians attack. I have no doubt if they found out this location is a large threat, they could obliterate it from orbit."

Minerva gave a very human sigh. "Yes, they could. What do you propose?"

Leon opened his pack removing several anti-grav generators, and various Mechand tools he had built. "I will power down your core, and move it to the carrier. I assume it can accommodate you as you were on one before."

Minerva nodded. "It can. But such an install is a very delicate procedure. Would you mind if I helped you do it?"

"How? You will need to be offline."

"I can transfer back to my Mechand form and help you make the modification."

Leon shook his head. "We don't have the time. We need to get you out of here as soon as possible."

"Then I will need to teach you fast."

Leon smiled. "You will find I'm a quick study."

"One problem though. There is a security system on that carrier. I ran into on it," Aleshia said.

Minerva blinked. "It shouldn't be active without me."

"It wasn't per se, I accidentally activated a console and when I didn't give an access code, two Mechands stood up from the seats on the bridge and told me to surrender."

Deven's eyes went wide. "You didn't tell me this."

Aleshia smiled. "You didn't ask. Anyway, it wasn't a big deal. I just lifted them up, which confused them and they shut down."

Minerva nodded. "Yes in the current powered down state they do not have many mental abilities."

"But could that slow down installing your core?" Leon asked.

"It is possible. But I do not know how we are going to do it otherwise since I have to be offline at the time."

Leon rubbed his chin. "Could you activate the carrier, Mechands and instruct them to obey us?"

"I could. But as I said, if I activate the main Mechand command channel, every Mechand in the world will also power on."

Deven shook his head. "Not good. That will give the council all the ammunition it needs against us."

Otis walked around the table deep in thought. "Why can't you limit the Mechands being controlled?"

"The system is designed to be a global one. The idea only a few would be needed was never thought of."

Otis smiled. "But what if Leon reduces the power of the transmission?"

Minerva blinked. "That would do it, only the Mechands in this bunker would be activated in that case. The equipment you passed. It is in the third room on the right after you enter the bunker, before the main room."

Leon put his equipment back in his pack. "I'll take care of it."

"Good. And Gregory, head back up to the *Defiant*. If something shows up, I want my best man at the cannons," Deven said.

Gregory shrugged. "Sure, although Miles is a better shot than I am."

Deven gripped Gregory's shoulder. "Perhaps, but you are still the best *man* I have for the job."

Gregory smiled. "Sure thing." He stopped to point at the pack in Leon's hands. "You have anti-grav units in there, right? Why didn't you use them to make the whole thing as light as a feather?"

Leon's eyes narrowed. "Because I didn't think of it," he grumbled heading off for the communications room.

Gregory smiled and followed him out. "I figured."

Ten minutes later Leon reappeared in the core room. "That should do it. Give it a try."

Minerva nodded. "Activating all Mechands in this facility."

Outside the room, the carrier's systems came to life. Bright lights glared from the open landing bay as several dozen Mechands walked out, casting long shadows. On the racks, Mechands on the lowest level awoke then walked away while those on the second level were lowered to the floor. They formed up and stood in front of the core room.

"I have a bad feeling about this," Aleshia breathed.

Minerva smiled. "There is nothing to be afraid of. Ask them who they serve."

Aleshia poked her nose outside the room and shouted. "Who do you serve?"

"We serve you and the Nexus," they said in unison.

"See? Nothing to worry about," Minerva said. Her eyes centered on Leon. "I have instructed them not to shut down upon losing contact with me. They are now operating independently, and will obey all of you. You can begin by disconnecting my access to external communications. Once that is completed I will tell you the best procedure to reconnect me inside the carrier, and I will shut down so you can do so."

Leon nodded and began removing her connections to the communications system and the bunker controls. "Will only take a few minutes."

Aleshia stared at the small army of Mechands standing in front of her. "All of you, stand on one foot!" Every single one of the Mechands raised their right leg, leaving it danging several inches above the ground. "Well I'll be."

Minerva looked at Aleshia. "I told you. They will obey any command you give them."

Two more Mechands walked down the ramp, joined the formation and stood on one foot. Aleshia jerked a thumb. "What's with those two?"

Minerva smiled. "They reported being in an odd position upon activation and were delayed."

Aleshia laughed. "Oh right, the two on the bridge."

Minerva nodded. "Correct."

Leon's head popped up from behind the core. "Okay that about does it. Only the power lead is left."

Minerva nodded. "Very well. After you get me installed on the bridge, use the keyboard and small screen on the back to enter the following command 'Con Restart' a core diagnostic will run and I should see you a minute after. I have disabled the auto start sequence when the power is reconnected allowing you to check the power system is properly initialized first."

Leon smiled. "Good idea. I assume a power fluctuation at that moment would be very bad?"

"Any kind of fluctuation is bad, during a full restart is worse than you can possibly imagine."

"I bet I can," Otis said.

She smiled. "Please take care, it is my mind after all." The screen went black as the lights on the core dimmed, then went off.

Leon handed Otis two of the anti-grav units. "Put one at the right and left front corner, I will take the back."

"You got it."

Leon disconnected the power lead and placed two anti-grav units. Otis gave a thumbs up and he pulled a controller out of his pack and powered it on.

The anti-grav units glowed as the core inched its way into the air. Leon guided it out of the room and heading towards the carrier. When he came out of the room, he almost burst out laughing seeing all the Mechands still standing on one foot. "All Mechands stand on two feet." They obeyed and stood normally. "All Mechands part down the middle, I need space to the carrier." Not a word was said, but they all separated into a long row of Mechands facing each other, leaving a large area in between for Leon and the core to pass through.

As Leon started walking towards the carrier, Aleshia took several quick steps to walk alongside him. "Thought you could use the help. I've been inside."

Leon smiled. "Sure. You mentioned being on the bridge, the faster we get Minerva installed and out of here the better."

Deven watched Otis, Leon, Aleshia, and the core head towards the carrier for a minute before he turned around and went back inside to connect his data tab. He plugged it in and Galina's face appeared on the screen. "Galina! I was about to call you. I take it we have a development?"

"You could say that. I am detecting a Mechand *Carbonia* carrier heading towards us. I knew we couldn't trust *her*."

Deven frowned. "How fast?"

"Fast. Not their top speed but they aren't messing around either. I estimate they will be here in 15 minutes."

"Great. And I don't think that carrier is Minerva's. Scan the inside."

"What for? If their shields are up, we won't get anything."

"I doubt they are that far away, just humor me."

"Okay, scanning …what the …I am reading a lot of humans aboard."

"That is correct, and unless my analysis is in error, the fighters in the landing bays are currently being manned by humans," Miles said.

Deven shook his head. "You aren't."

Galina's eyebrow went up. "Mind telling us what is going on?"

"Leon's hunch was right, and the council has more assets than they led us to believe."

"The council has a Mechand carrier? They told us all were scrapped!"

"I know. But this indicates otherwise. You may have to hold them off until Leon can get Minerva moved into the carrier so we can all get out of here."

"How? I am not going to shoot down our own people like this."

Miles' voice came over the speaker. "If I may make a suggestion, if we hover the *Defiant* above the mountain, I can extend the shields to cover it. They won't be near as strong, but it may give you the time you need."

"Do it! The entrance is near the base on the eastern side. If they hit that directly, it could collapse the outer tunnel and we won't be able to leave until you can dig us out."

"*Defiant* is in place and shields have been extended," Miles said. "I estimate the carrier to arrive in 12.5 minutes."

"Do what you can to keep them at bay, but if you must, *fire only to disable*. Is that clear?"

Galina nodded. "I hear you, but I am not sure how long we are going to last with our carbine cannons tied behind our backs and weakened shields."

Gregory's face appeared behind Galina. "I was walking past when I heard the alert. You know disabling Mechand fighters is a few notches above difficult, right? Heck destroying them is hard enough."

"That is why you are there." Deven smiled.

"Gregory, I am confident between us we can give them the time required," Miles said.

Gregory rolled his eyes. "Wish I was. Heading to fire

control, I will have everything warmed and ready before they get here." He said running out the door.

"I'm sure they will. Just hold her together," Deven said.

"Will try. Galina out." The image vanished and Deven unplugged his data tab replacing it in its pouch. He ran for the carrier.

Commander Halburn nodded when Lavine's face came on the screen in front of him. "Chairman Lavine, I wish to stress we are not ready for this."

"Commander, don't make me regret choosing you for the *Valiant*. You and that ship are ready when I say you are ready."

"But we are going up against someone that managed to defeat the Mechands, we need time to prepare."

Lavine waved his hand. "That was luck, I am sure you are about equal."

"That I doubt. Deven Doran is no fool, and no one here has had the training let alone seen actual combat. Heck, except for those on the *Defiant*, no human has seen combat like this for over a century."

Lavine's face reddened. "Look, we cannot afford to wait. From what I heard earlier, the whole story of the Nexus' destruction was just that, a story."

Halburn cocked his head. "For what purpose?"

"To take control. It is obvious they managed to reprogram the Nexus and turned off all the Mechands to make it appear she was obliterated. Once the time is right, they use the Nexus and Mechands to make a grab for power."

"But Sir, begging your pardon, if that were true it would

have been more logical to do so before we scrapped so many Mechands?"

"I am sure it was all a part of their plan. And regardless, we cannot take the chance. Do I make myself clear?"

"Yes Sir. And if I may ask, how did you find out about this bunker?"

"Doran told me."

Halburn's jaw dropped. "He told you directly?"

Lavine nodded. "Yes, why does that surprise you?"

"Because, if he was trying to do as you suggest, telling you of the bunker and its location is a large tactical error."

Levine smiled and sat back in his chair as he began to rock it back and forth. "Well, he didn't tell me where it was."

"Then how do we know he will be where you say?"

"He mentioned a large mountain and of course it would need to be in an area that has not seen much activity in a long time. This information, along with a few other facts gleaned from other sources, I have discerned the location."

From the side Navigator Rechert raised his hand. "Sir? We are approaching the coordinates you gave us. And it appears the *Defiant* is here, hovering over the mountain."

Halburn spun around. "And I am finding out about this *now*?"

Rechert sighed. "I am sorry Sir, we are still having problems getting the scanners to work properly."

Halburn nodded and turned back to the large screen. "Chairman, this is what I'm talking about. We need more training, not to mention the systems aboard this vessel are not at 100%."

"Be thankful it is working as good as it is. I had to save that ship from being scrapped, but it had suffered damage before we got it. Several teams have been working on it for the last month and a half."

"They need to work on it for a couple more."

Levine smiled. "They will, after your task is done. Now, do the council proud." Levine's image shrank to a single point and disappeared.

Halburn turned around. "You heard the man, we're going in. Full speed ahead. I want to close the gap between us yesterday. The less time they have to plan, the better for us."

Rechert nodded. "Yes Sir." He tapped several controls, and the carrier lurched forward as the engines initiated full burn.

Halburn stood gazing out the large view port at the front of the *Valiant's* bridge. His chin jutted forward. "Raise the armor." Large, thick plating slid up and over the window locking in place with a strong clink. He sat down in his command chair. "Launch all fighters and raise the shields as soon as they are out."

Torrian Naud's fingers tapped several commands before he hit the intercom. "All craft launch. And watch it, we are at full burn, it will be different from when we practiced." A few seconds later he looked up from his station. "All fighters are launched Sir and our shields are now up."

"Good."

Rechert tapped his console. "We will be on top of them in 30 seconds."

"Fine, decelerate at 10.5 seconds. That should surprise them. I want all carbine cannons to open fire the instant we slow. But I want to keep moving. No sense in giving them an easy target."

Naud nodded. "Agreed. But Sir, something is odd."

Halburn hopped up from his seat, took two steps to his right and leaned over Naud's console. "What is?"

Naud pointed at the moving ship. "They know we are here, but are not taking up any action against us. In fact, they are moving closer to the mountain. It does not make sense. Holy– they expanded their shields to cover the whole mountain!"

Halburn blinked. "They can do that?"

"Apparently Sir. I don't know how, but they're doing it. However, I can't imagine their shields being very strong covering such a large area."

Halburn straightened. "This could be our chance. Open fire all weapons. I want her going down in flames."

Halburn felt the ship shudder under him as the *Defiant* responded with her cannons. But not as strong as he expected. He cocked an eyebrow. "Damage?"

"Minor damage so far to secondary systems," Naud said.

"That's all? They outgun us in hardware and experience and all they do is give us a slap on the wrist?"

"It doesn't make sense."

"No it doesn't. But we have our orders, keep the pressure on."

"But Sir, this does not add up. If what the Chairman said is true, wouldn't they be throwing more of a response?"

Halburn leaned over and muttered out the right side of his mouth. "While I tend to agree with you, do you want to be the one to tell the Chairman why we didn't do as the council instructed?"

Naud shook his head. "No way ...Sir."

"I didn't think so."

Deven found everyone on the bridge of the carrier. Minerva's core had been lowered into place and they were in the process of bolting it to the deck plates. "I have bad news. Leon was right and Chairman Lavine does have a Mechand *Carbonia* carrier, perhaps more Mechand assets under his control. The carrier we know of will be here in 10 minutes."

"Dang it! I hoped I was wrong," Leon said twisting a final bolt with a power driver. "Otis did you get your side done?"

Otis nodded. "Yep, I just cranked the last one. This cube ain't going anywhere."

"Good, we are almost done." Leon grabbed a couple of cables running from beneath several opened access panels under consoles and began plugging them into Minerva's core. The last cable, the power, was much larger and he plugged it in with great care making sure no arcs occurred that might short the delicate core. A large white light next to the connector lit and he nodded. "That does it." He went over to the other side and on the small keyboard punched in 'Con Restart'. The four inch screen flooded with diagnostic data as each part of the core hardware was tested. It flashed a 'Passed' and the center of the core began to glow.

A large screen to the left of the core Leon had mounted and connected earlier flickered with static. It flickered again and Minerva's face appeared, but in blocky chunks. Bit by bit the missing areas filled in making her whole.

"Ugh, I hope we don't have to do that again. Those manual restarts give me a headache," she said.

Leon smiled. "Hopefully not for a while."

Deven noticed the windows covered in blast-proof armor. "Minerva, do you have access to the carrier and Mechands?"

Minerva nodded. "I do." The armor covering the bridge windows slid down revealing the bunker and the tunnel that lay beyond. "I am bringing the units aboard now."

They heard metal feet striking rock as the Mechands started marching towards the hangar bay.

Minerva's eyebrows met. "I am detecting activity above us. However, my scanning capability inside the bunker is limited. I am attempting to ascertain details."

Deven sighed. "Sounds like Lavine arrived earlier than anticipated. The *Defiant* is protecting us by extending shields over the mountain, but I don't know how long they will last."

Otis' eyes went wide. "Over the whole mountain? Geez, I didn't know we could do that."

Leon nodded. "With the upgrades to the shields I did a month ago, the *Defiant* can. But Deven is right, they won't last long being stretched so far. I suspect Minerva is detecting the blasts that are getting through."

Deven started heading off of the bridge. "I need to contact the *Defiant*."

Minerva smiled. "Deven if you plug your data tab into the port on the console to your right, I can relay any transmission through the bunker's communication system."

Deven plugged his data tab into the port and Galina's face appeared a second later. Sparks flew from an exploding console behind her. "Whatever you are going to do, you need to do now! We are getting hammered! Shields are almost gone and when they go, so will we!" The screen went to static then faded to black.

"We need to leave, *now*," Aleshia said.

Deven's eyes shot back to the windows and the bunker beyond. He gripped a nearby console. "I couldn't agree more. Minerva, are we ready?"

They felt a shudder in deck plates under their feet. "Yes. Engines are online. All systems green. We are lifting off," Minerva said. The large carrier inched its way off of the bunker floor and moved towards the large doors at the far end.

"Faster Minerva! They can't last much longer," Aleshia said.

"Understood. Increasing speed." They almost fell over as the carrier lurched forward. "Opening all doors." The large doors on the far side of the bunker ground open the rest of the way and the carrier shot through into the tunnel. Then her eyes went wide. "I forgot the outer door's automatic systems are not functional."

Leon smiled. "Well it is a good thing I fixed them on the way in isn't it?"

The doors at the far end of the tunnel began to shake as the wedge of light increased. "Leon, you are a wonder!" Minerva said.

"So they tell me."

Deven's eyes went wide as they hurtled towards the doors. "Minerva! Slow down! We aren't going to make it."

"Negative, we will have 1.2 seconds to spare."

Deven tapped a button his data tab. "Galina? Drop the shields. Do you hear me? Drop the shields! Now!"

Static came back. A microsecond later her garbled voice came through. "Getting interference. Shields dropped."

"Minerva!" Aleshia exclaimed as the doors continued to grind open. The carrier tilted to accommodate the narrow opening. They shot out of the tunnel like a bullet into the blue sky with only microns to spare.

A large Mechand carrier shot out of the base of the mountain. It was twice the size of the *Valiant*. "Where did that ship come from?"

Naud tapped a few keys. "I would say from the bunker the Chairman mentioned. And now we know why the *Defiant* was protecting the mountain."

Suddenly, all the weapons aboard the *Valiant* shutdown.

Halburn pointed at the two ships in front of them. "What are you doing? I didn't order a cease fire!"

"I didn't sir. I don't understand it, all cannons stopped on their own."

"Tell the fighters to increase their runs until we get this fixed."

"I can tell them, but they are having the same issue."

"What?" Halburn leaned over and studied the information on Naud's screen. "Do they have some sort of new weapon?"

"No, I do not detect any sort of energy leach or such."

Halburn's eyebrow went up. "Energy leach?"

"Well any sort of weapon capable of doing this is more advanced than that. We have power, but everything is responding as if we didn't."

Halburn folded his arms. "Wait a second, this is a Mechand carrier right? Perhaps they figured out a way to command the ship."

"Remote access? I suppose it is possible. Let me check."

"Do more than check, they are moving out. If we can't get this bucket of bolts moving in the next minute, we won't be able to follow them."

"Sealing bunker. We can't let this Lavine get anything more than he already has," Minerva said. The communications array retracted, and the doors slammed shut hiding the exact location once more.

Aleshia shook still leaning on a console. "Don't do that again."

"But I told you we would fit. It was a simple calculation of rate of speed compared to the opening rate of–"

"Galina! Get out of here. Do you hear me? Get out of here!" Deven pounded on the link button of his data tab.

Static on the screen flashed again and again before Galina's face appeared. "Interference has cleared. And they have stopped attacking. It is weird, but they stopped all of a sudden. As if someone hit pause."

Deven stared at the fighters and carrier hanging in the air, doing nothing.

"They even dropped their shields. I can't explain it," Galina said.

"I'm not going to look a gift horse in the mouth. Let's get out of here."

"Rodger that. However, our overdrive is damaged. Gregory is working on it, but he is not Leon."

"Move away best speed. We will follow and try to take the brunt of any assault, should they wake up."

Minerva smiled. "Oh they will. But it will take them awhile to do so."

Deven turned towards her. "What did you do?"

"Well I must admit, it wasn't intentional."

"I ask again. What did you do?"

"As I told you, the Mechand control network was never meant to be a local system. When we left the bunker and its shielding, the signal from this carrier was no longer limited."

Aleshia's eyes went wide. "You mean every Mechand left on the planet woke up?"

"Essentially yes. And as a result everything stops, falling back to initialization mode waiting for my instructions."

Deven cocked an eyebrow. "Even the fighters and the carrier? I thought they were operated by Mechands independently."

"Yes, but when I realized what had happened, I accessed both the carrier and fighters taking control of the Auto-Nav systems. It won't last long though before they figure out a way to override. I hope it gives us enough time to get the *Defiant's* overdrive engines back online."

Aboard the *Valiant*, Naud's fingers slid across his console as he ran diagnostics. "I don't see any sign of remote access on the normal frequencies but the Auto-Nav kicked in along with an energy conservation system. I'm trying to turn it off."

Halburn watched helpless as the *Defiant's* engines began to glow brighter. "They are going to jump into overdrive! Get this bucket moving!"

Naud tapped with increasing speed, his hands a blur. "I'm trying sir. There!" He looked over to Rechert. "Try now."

Rechert nodded. "That did it, we have navigation back."

"Weapons are back online as well."

"Good!" Halburn pointed to the *Defiant* and the Mechand carrier. "Take out those ships! Open fire!"

Deven looked down at his data tab. "Galina, did you hear what Minerva said?"

"Yeah I did. It happened just in time. One more hit on the back quarter and we would have gone down."

Another voice came over the background intercom. "Gregory here, overdrive is online, but it is a patch job at best, it could fail at any time. I am not Leon."

Leon laughed. "Gregory, you did well. I will fix them properly when I get back over there."

"Galina, head for our first cold home. We will hang back a bit and block anyone following, until you get out of range," Deven said.

She smiled. "You got it. Engaging overdrive." The massive engines on the back of the *Defiant* began to glow, a second later a bright flash, and they were gone.

Deven's eyes widened as the carrier began to move. "Minerva, shields up and be ready to block that carrier."

"Done and done. They won't get past me."

Aleshia pointed at the smaller ships. "What about the fighters? They could follow. We can't block them all."

Minerva smiled. "We don't have to. They are simple fighters not interceptors. They do not have overdrive capability." The carrier shuddered as several blasts impacted the shields. "Shields holding, but weakening. Shall I return fire?"

Deven shook his head. "No, it takes pinpoint accuracy to incapacitate without killing, and I don't trust your old cannons to do that."

"Technically it should be possible, but understood. Transferring weapons power to shields."

Leon sat down at a navigators console. "Deven, if I am reading this right the *Defiant* should be out of range. And if I know Galina, she is already zig-zaging her way to the rendezvous."

Minerva nodded. "I concur, I can no longer detect the *Defiant*. It is reasonable to assume neither can they." Several blasts hit the bottom of the bow port side. "Front port shield is failing."

"Get us out of here," Deven said.

"Overdrive is online. Brace yourselves, this ship does not have any inertia dampers."

Deven, Aleshia and Otis ran for chairs and sat in them. "Ready," they said in unison.

The engines glowed with a blue-white light and the carrier leapt into overdrive as several energy blasts sailed through where it was.

Every one of the *Valiant's* cannons along with the fighters opened fire at the same moment lashing out with multiple energy beams. Most of them hit head-on and they saw the front shield buckle. But the next barrage missed as the carrier disappeared into overdrive a microsecond before they hit.

"Dang it!" Halburn said clenching his chair's arm rests. "Follow them!"

Rechert braced himself. "I am sorry sir, the overdrive went offline due to the power conservation system. It will take a few more minutes to charge."

"We don't have a few minutes!"

Naud's screen flashed and his eyes drifted up. "Chairman Lavine is requesting an update."

"Great. I will take this in my cabin," Halburn grunted as he headed off the bridge. He turned back. "See if you can find the entrance to that bunker. Perhaps they left something behind we can use."

"Yes sir."

Halburn climbed down a level and opened the door to

his cabin. It was small, but he was thankful the Mechands had built one at all since they didn't need to. The dim floor safety lights glowed brighter as he sat behind his makeshift desk containing his data tab connected to the *Valiant's* systems. He sighed as he placed it into a cradle consisting of two repurposed boots and tapped a button. Lavine's face appeared. "Status?"

Halburn's eyes slid down to center on the desk below the data tab. "Stable."

Lavine's eyebrows met. "What the heck does that mean?"

"It means we are functional."

"And the *Defiant*?"

Halburn coughed. "They have left?"

"Left? I want more information than that! Don't tell me they got the Nexus out of there!"

Halburn chewed his bottom lip for a full five seconds. "Well …"

"Well what?!"

Halburn shifted in his seat. "When we arrived, they had extended their shields over the mountain."

Lavine glared. "They what? I didn't think that would be possible given the size."

"I didn't either, but they managed it."

"Their shields must have been much weaker than normal. So how did they leave and not in a fireball?"

"They were about to, when another carrier showed up."

Lavine's eyes went wide. "What! Where did that come from?"

"I assume it came from the bunker you mentioned."

Lavine sat back. "So they not only have the Nexus, but a Mechand carrier as well and who knows what else? Explain to me again how they both got past you?"

"Once the second carrier appeared, we had … issues."

Lavine's teeth clenched. "What do you mean 'issues'?"

"We were held in place and unable to move. At least that was our first assessment. Later on we found the ship had responded to a command engaging Auto-Nav and ordered to hold us motionless. An energy conservation system was activated as well, shutting down our weapons."

Lavine's brow furrowed. "That … should have been an easy fix."

Halburn coughed. "It was, once we figured out what happened. But by that time, both ships had left the area."

"I assume you are on their trail?"

Halburn shrugged. "Not much of a trail to follow. We are still looking though."

"Well I have to hand it to you. The first mission of the *Valiant*, with an enemy you have foreknowledge of, and you blow it."

"With all due respect, I told you we were not ready yet. If they wanted us down, we would be scattered all over the mountain side."

"How do you figure that?"

Halburn sat forward in his chair and glared. "They were hitting to disable, not kill. They had us out gunned three to one. If they had released the full might of the *Defiant*, I would not be speaking to you now. Whatever you think they are guilty of, it deserves reinvestigation. Perhaps call up Doran and ask him what is going on."

Lavine gave a wave of his hand. "Hardly, I already know his plan. To take over."

Halburn shook his head. "Not possible. If it was, he would have taken us down. He didn't."

"Just because we do not see his full plan does not mean this is not part of it."

"Perhaps. But you know my feelings."

Lavine's eyes narrowed to mere slits. "I do. But that is irrelevant. You will follow my orders, and the orders of the council which are to find the *Defiant*, eliminate her and anyone aboard. *And* this new carrier as well. Do I make myself clear?"

Halburn sighed. "I will do as you ask."

"Good, I would hate to have to replace you. I am sure Officer Naud would love a promotion."

Halburn gritted his teeth. "That won't be necessary."

"Good. Now I suggest you get to work." Lavine's image vanished leaving behind a black screen in a dark room. It took Halburn's eyes a moment to adjust to the dim floor safety lights before he could stand up and slap the light control.

He walked over and hit the intercom on the wall. "Naud? Did you find where they went?"

"No sir, I did find they went on two separate trajectories though. Of course, that could have changed en route."

"I have my doubts about that. But even if true, it still means a rendezvous somewhere. An out-of-the-way location where they can repair the *Defiant*. Is there any way we can follow them?"

"Now? No. If we were able to match speed a second or two after they left yes. Now it is not possible. I'm sorry sir."

"It is not your fault they shut us down and it took too long to find out what happened. I was hoping they might have left a trail in their haste to get out here. Perhaps due to their damaged systems."

"Damaged systems ..." Naud paused, thinking. "Sir, an idea occurs to me, that might be possible. They sustained multiple hits to their engines. If the damping system took a direct hit, they might be leaking energy. Not much, but perhaps enough we can follow."

"Even now?"

"Yes sir, it may have dissipated some, but it still should give us a general path."

"Then stop talking to me and get on it! I will be up in a minute."

"Yes sir," Naud said as the intercom clicked off.

— 11 —

The *Defiant* fell out of overdrive short of their target. "I am sorry Galina, I tried," Gregory said over the intercom.

"Fix it again!"

"I told you I tried. It is being finicky. The whole drive might need to be pulled."

Galina shook her head. "I'm sorry Gregory, I know you did your best. But we're a couple of hours from our targeted rendezvous at this speed."

"Better tell Deven we are going to be a little late."

"I would if the communications system was working better than the overdrive."

"Oh, great."

"You can say that again!"

Hovering high above Antarctic storms, a lone Mechand carrier sits waiting. Deven paced back and forth on the carrier's bridge. "I don't like this. They should have been here by now."

Aleshia turned. "Minerva, can you contact the *Defiant* and find out what is going on?"

Minerva shook her head on the large screen. "No, I was never given the necessary encryption keys required, and if I use an unencrypted link, this Lavine will be aware of it. But I can tell you there is no report of their capture."

Deven sighed. "I already tried contacting them. No response."

Aleshia folded her arms. "Shouldn't we go looking for them?"

"Where? The Earth is a big place. They could be anywhere."

"Well, we can't just sit here waiting."

"No, that is exactly what we *are* going to do. If we go looking for them, and they arrive here, what then? My bet is their communications took a bad hit and perhaps the fixes Gregory did to the overdrive didn't hold. They will get here eventually, but if we go off looking for them, the chances of meeting go down fast."

"Agreed," Leon said looking at the console in front of him. "We can't waste time by hunting for them around the world."

All the screens on the bridge flashed and displayed a small blip. "I detect one lone vehicle approaching from the northwest," Minerva said.

Aleshia let out a breath she didn't know she was holding. "Finally. About time they showed up."

"No, this is much too small to be the *Defiant*. It may be a scout."

Otis smiled. "It isn't either. It's my truck."

Deven whirled around. "Your truck? You left it parked next to the mountain."

Otis nodded. "I did. But I also sent a few remote commands with a detailed path of how to get here before we jumped into overdrive." He raised his hand. "Before you ask, yes I had it go on a very roundabout method in case anyone was following it."

"But *why* is the question."

"Why? Do you know how much time I spent customizing that thing? I am not going to leave it for Lavine to add to his arsenal."

"Minerva, it is alone?"

Her eyes darted around the screen. "As far as I can tell, yes. However, the landing bay lacks sufficient room for the vehicle to come aboard. You will have to instruct it to remain in a stationary hover."

Otis shrugged. "It will do that anyway if I don't tell it otherwise."

Deven folded his arms. "Minerva, I have a question for you, actually three."

"And I will answer them of course."

"You said all the Mechands have been initialized around the world. How many and where? Also, what did you tell them to do?"

"I received signals from only a thousand. Of those I think many were disabled biased on the status they provided."

"And what did you tell them to do?"

"Remain quiet and do not let anyone know they are now active unless found out. Once discovered, they are to leave and request further instructions from me."

"So they are acting autonomously?"

Minerva nodded. "That is correct. Although, I can change it any time."

Deven smiled. "This could be useful. Do you have any at the World Council?"

"I am afraid I do not know where they are located."

"New York City. In the old United Nations building before it was disbanded."

Minerva nodded. "I do have one unit there. It is cleaning Mechand that has remained functional during my absence due to its basic nature."

Deven smiled. "And you have control of it now?"

Minerva nodded again. "I do. And I suspect those in the building will be accustomed to its movements."

"This could be very handy. Right now, don't change its routine. I don't want to tip anyone off."

Minerva smiled. "Understood."

Leon leaned towards Deven. "What do you have in mind?"

Deven sat back. "I think when the time is right, that bot will take Lavine to the cleaners." He turned back to Minerva. "I want you to keep a special eye on that Mechand, he could be the key. Relay any info it finds, but as I said, don't do it outright. We can't let anyone know you are controlling it."

Minerva nodded. "Agreed. I am instructing it to transmit its logs and data. Very slowly so it won't be noticed if anyone is watching transmissions in the area. It may have something useful already."

Aleshia nodded. "But even if it doesn't, we will have a warning if Lavine or the council comes after us again."

Minerva's eyes narrowed. "Deven, I am detecting a ship on the very edge of my scanners approaching our position."

"Lavine's carrier?"

Minerva shook her head. "Nope, the size does not match. It isn't transmitting an ID code so I can't verify."

Leon hunched over the console in front of him. "Minerva, show me power curve on that ship."

"Sure thing."

The screen changed showing several technical graphs of

the energy output of the ship approaching them. "It's the *Defiant*!"

Deven stood up and leaned over. "Are you sure?"

"You bet I am. I would know her engines anywhere. She is battered, but that is her, no doubt."

"Overdrive must have failed. How long until they get here?"

Leon checked over the data and sighed. "About an hour I would say at her current speed. She must have really taken a pounding."

The *Valiant* jumped into overdrive when Commander Halburn reached the bridge. "And you are sure this is the course they took?"

Naud nodded. "Yes Sir. It is very faint but there is a trace amount, enough to determine the direction."

"And if they change course without leaving a better trail?"

Rechert smiled. "Then we went for a nice drive."

Halburn snorted. "Try telling that to Lavine."

Rechert shook. "Umm, I think I will leave that to you Sir."

"Smart choice. But I would trade with you in a heartbeat."

"We know Sir."

Galina sighed. "I feel like we are going slower than a snail in an Antarctic winter!"

Gregory pointed out the *Defiant's* bridge window to the storms raging below them. "Bad comparison."

"Or a good one, depending on how you look at it. Either way we are going s-l-o-w."

"I see something ahead. It is a faint signal, could be Minerva's carrier."

"I hope it is, the *Defiant* can't take on another battle like this."

Gregory sent the readings he took to Galina's console. "What do you think?"

She examined the numbers. "Yes it is Minerva's carrier. Either that or something very similar, and I doubt that another Mechand carrier of that size would be functional now. Let alone sitting right where we are expecting to find Deven."

Gregory nodded. "Yep. And did you try to contact them again?"

"Yes. Did you try fixing the communications system again?"

"I did. Not sure what the problem is. The relays are getting enough power. Yet, nothing goes through."

Galina shrugged. "I guess we will let wizard fingers Leon figure it out."

Gregory laughed. "He can keep that title, I don't have his knack for sure. Hey, wait a minute, I see something else, right next to the carrier."

Galina squeezed her controls. "Like what? Another carrier?"

Gregory shook his head. "No, much smaller." His blood ran cold. "A fighter! Has to be!"

Galina's eyes went wide. "Great. It can't be Minerva's carrier, they wouldn't be launching fighters. How long before we know for sure one way or the other?"

"Hmm, thirty minutes, perhaps less. And I am sure they have detected us."

Galina's eyes narrowed. "We are staying on course for the

moment. If we lose this chance to hook back up with Deven, we may never find him again. At least not before we bump into someone that doesn't like us and tries to finish what the last one started."

"I know. But are you sure we shouldn't bug out of here?"

"For the moment, yes. Now if anything changes out there. And I mean anything, I want you to tell me yesterday. Got it? We may need every second we can get."

"That won't be necessary," Miles' voice came over the speaker.

"Miles! Where have you been?" Galina asked.

"Several locations housing network junctions between my mind and the bridge were disrupted. It took me a little time to repair and reroute."

"And what is not necessary?"

"You're worrying or defensive posture. The two vehicles are Minerva's carrier and Otis' truck. It is not an ambush of the people that attacked before."

Gregory squinted. "And how do you know this?"

I do know the signature of Otis' truck, and the larger vehicle has far more mass than the one that attacked. Hence, it is Deven waiting for us."

"When you were rerouting, did you happen to fix the external communications system as well?"

Miles' camera moved back and forth. "I did attempt to do so, but the system needs more physical repairs, than I can provide."

Galina snorted. "Figures, worth a try though."

"I also regret to inform you, our identification signal has been disrupted along with many other systems aboard."

Gregory blinked. "Great, meaning they might shoot us down."

Galina shook her head. "Nah, Leon knows the *Defiant* like the back of his hand. And anyway, who else is going to approach them this slow over Antarctica?"

"You have a point," Gregory said chuckling.

Galina smiled. "Don't I always?"

Commander Halburn grabbed his stomach as the *Valiant* took another tight turn. "Rechert, do you have to do that?"

Rechert wiped his forehead as his eyes stayed on his screen. "I am sorry Sir, but this energy residue is very faint and degrading fast. If I don't stay at this speed, we will lose it."

Halburn sighed gripping his abdomen tighter. "Very well. Naud, are you sure this isn't a wild goose chase? We have been all over three contents in two hemispheres and still nothing."

"I am sure. They are trying to cover their tracks. If it wasn't for this energy trail, we would have lost them a few seconds after they jumped into overdrive."

"All right, stay on this course. But Rechert, try to let me know next time you are going to pull a 90 degree turn, okay?"

Rechert smiled. "Yes Sir."

"Naud, you did secure the fighters and pilots before we started this, right?"

Naud nodded. "Yes Sir, everything is secure. I did that before we went into overdrive."

"Good.   Remind me to have Lavine give you a commendation, providing we can find him in a good mood."

"Thank you Sir, when might that be?"

"At this rate, a long, long time."

"Oh."

The *Valiant* pitched forward and crashed out of overdrive sending both Halburn and Naud flying out of their seats.

"Report! What the heck happened!" Halburn shook his head and pulled himself back into his seat.

Rechert swallowed hard. "I am sorry Sir, I lost the trail and had to institute an emergency stop. If I didn't there wouldn't have been any chance of picking it up again."

Halburn turned around. "Naud, check the crew, make sure everyone is all right."

Naud nodded. "Yes Sir." He opened the hatch in the back, went through, and sealed it after.

Halburn got up and walked over to Naud's console. He tapped a few keys and the window armor retracted giving him a breathtaking view of the Earth far below. He placed both palms on the edge of the railing next to Naud's console and gazed out the forward window. His fingers turned white as he gripped the smooth metal rectangle. "Where did you go?"

Deven tapped his finger on the smooth console in front of him. The chairs weren't as comfortable as the *Defiant's*, but they were a place to sit. While the Mechands did build their ships with human designs in mind, they didn't put in comforts such as conforming chairs. "How long until the *Defiant* gets here?"

"About forty minutes, give or take," Minerva said.

Aleshia watched the storm raging below out the large port side window near Deven's seat. "Why don't we go to them rather than wait here?"

Deven shook his head. "We don't know how much damage they have sustained. Their communications system must be down or we would have heard by now. They might think we are another Mechand carrier under Lavine's control coming to blast them out of the sky."

Aleshia sighed. "Good point."

Leon sat up and glared at his screen. "Oh great, just when you think it can't get any worse."

Deven turned to face him. "What do you mean?"

"I checked the logs from the probe. Just before we lost the *Defiant's* uplink, three more *Maker* ships arrived."

Deven turned his chair around to face Minerva's screen. "Minerva? Why didn't you tell us?"

Her eyes darted around the bridge. "I was waiting until I could confirm the data wasn't an error due to the communications instability at the time."

Deven stood up and walked over to Leon's console. The probe logs showed several grainy images of the arriving *Makers*. "Minerva, do you know how many they will bring?"

Minerva shook her head. "I am sorry, I do not. But based on their size, and estimated output, not many more. Perhaps two."

Otis joined and stood on the other side of Leon. "I am guessing they will be ready to move at that point?"

"One moment." Minerva closed her eyes and reopened them two minutes later. "Sorry, I was running simulations. I suspect they still have a large central command ship we have not seen yet. Once the command ship arrives, I believe the armada will begin moving towards Earth."

Deven turned. "And why is that?"

"As I told you before, they tend to be highly specialized in their individual roles. Some of those roles are of command, or instructions. Something similar to previous human military structure."

"So we have seen the tentacles, the backbone, but not the head."

"Correct. And I estimate it will be a much larger ship than we have seen so far."

"Great," Otis said as his eyes darted around the room, "this keeps getting better and better."

Minerva smiled. "I think I may have a small light to shine on this otherwise dark situation."

Deven folded his arms and his weight shifted. "Which is?"

"Our spy inside the World Council headquarters has finished sending me its files."

"Anything we should know about?"

"Yes, apparently the carrier we encountered is being commanded by an Odell Halburn."

Deven's eyebrows went up. "Halburn? Are you sure?"

"Yes. Is that significant?"

"You could say so. I know the man. It was long ago but I am sure he remembers me. We used to discuss tactics on how we were going to rid the world of the Mechands. At the time, he was one of the few people that believed me. Everyone else thought I was crazy."

Aleshia put her hand on Deven's shoulder. "What happened?"

"I made a mistake and used a console with a hidden genetic scanner. The console determined my true identity, and before I could stop it, the information was transmitted. I had to leave or risk bringing the Mechand security force to his door. I don't think he ever knew why I left. We were good friends before that."

Leon smiled. "Sounds like an advantage. You know how this guy thinks."

"Yes and no. Yes I know him, but it was a long time ago. I am sure he has changed, as have I. One thing I am certain of, he was very good at military tactics, and I have to assume he has only improved."

Leon rubbed his chin. "I can see why Lavine picked him."

Deven nodded. "Yes. He also is a bulldog and won't stop unless he has to." Deven's eyes went wide. "We have to get to the *Defiant* and get her out of here as soon as possible. He might be tracking her."

Leon's cocked his head. "If I know Galina, she took the *Defiant* all over before heading here. I doubt Halburn could track her here."

"And if they had some kind of signal to follow?"

Leon rotated his chair back and forth as he thought though the *Defiant's* systems. "I suppose it is possible. But Miles would pick up on a tracking signal and have it disabled."

Deven turned to face Minerva. "Can you tell if there is a tracker on the *Defiant*?"

"I have anticipated your request, and no there is not. However, I have detected a slight shift in one of the damaged engines."

Leon turned back to his console. "A slight shift? Show me." The screen flashed with raw scan data. Leon paused it in the middle. "Dang it! Engine three took a direct hit and its ionic shielding must have been breached."

Deven pointed to the mass of numbers. "What does that mean?"

"It means the *Defiant* is leaking energy, very slight and it would dissipate quickly."

"Dangerous?"

Leon shook his head. "Not directly. They won't blowup or anything. But, if someone wanted to track–"

"They could follow this?"

Leon nodded. "They would have to have jumped into overdrive right after we left. But it is possible." Leon chuckled. "Following Galina's driving on a normal day would be hard, but this trail wisping around the atmosphere? Gosh, I would hate to be the navigator. Or the crew for that matter. I bet half of them would be in the throes of motion sickness."

"But why wouldn't Galina or Miles see this?"

Leon sighed. "There is a lot of damage from what I can see here. It may not stand out enough to spot unless they were looking for it."

"Minerva close the gap between us. We need to get aboard and get the *Defiant* out of here as soon as possible," Deven said.

Otis pointed to the window. "And if they think we are someone else and start shooting?"

Deven slapped his forehead. "I am a fool! My data tab might be able to contact Galina's at this range." Deven whipped it out and hit Galina's private link.

Leon nodded. "True, she usually keeps it with her on the bridge."

"Blast it! We're still too far away."

"Let's hope they don't see us as a threat."

Gregory frowned. "Galina, you wanted me to tell you when the carrier moved. Well, it has."

"Which direction?"

"Towards us, and its speed is increasing," Miles said.

"Miles, I didn't ask you." Galina said gripping the controls. "Gregory, get down to engineering and see if you can coax another jump out of the overdrive system."

"Are you nuts? I told you it is beyond what I can do."

"Try! If they get a chance to use their cannons, we're done."

"Correction, the shields have regenerated to some extent, if they shoot three times in a vital area the shields will collapse and we will be unable to continue at this present altitude. However, as I told you previously, it is Minerva's carrier. These actions are not necessary," Miles said.

Galina rolled her eyes. "Okay, we get two shots without going down. Real big help that is considering each cannon can fire a shot every three seconds! It might be Minerva's carrier, but I don't trust her either. If it was Deven, he would sit there and wait for us. I have to assume Minerva is in control and I was right all along."

Miles' camera looked towards the window then back to Galina. "You do have any evidence of this."

"I don't, but I am not going to take a chance either." She tapped the intercom. "Gregory, any luck?"

Several pieces of damaged equipment were heard being thrown in the background. "Not yet! I am trying! It is a mess down here."

"Try harder!"

"I have one more thing to try. Hang on." He switched two power lines and bypassed engine three. "Try it now. While engine three still looks functional to me, I bypassed it."

"We have a green light! You did it! Hold on, jumping in fifteen seconds."

The *Defiant's* engines began to glow brighter as power surged through them. But as Galina's finger hovered over the overdrive controls, her data tab beeped. "A call? Now? What could reach us here?"

"If I may suggest, that is Deven calling to tell you not to leave. His data tab should be in range now even with the storms below throwing off interference," Miles said.

Galina shut down the overdrive and Gregory hit the intercom. "Galina! Everything here shut down. I didn't do a thing, honest!"

"I know you didn't. Deven is calling me," she said pulling out her data tab.

"Calling you? On what? The only thing capable of cutting through the storms below us is the *Defiant's* communication system."

Galina smiled. "And our data tabs if we are close enough." She tapped receive and Deven's face appeared through lines of static.

"Galina!" The audio crackled. "…move we are coming to you. Do you hear me? We are–" The line crackled again. "–to you."

"I hear you Deven, I hear you."

"Good … get … bay … open … come aboard … now."

"Will do." She tapped the intercom. "Gregory did you get that?"

"Yeah, I did. I'm heading to the launch bay and see if I can get the doors open."

Galina's face flashed through several layers of static. "We … you. We are … get … doors open." Her face disappeared as the connection cut.

The carrier parked alongside the much larger *Defiant*. "I am maintaining position," Minerva said. "I have the closest of the fighters to the bay doors prepped and ready for you."

Deven nodded. "Good. Otis, Aleshia, you two stay with Minerva."

Aleshia's eyes went wide. "What? You need me over there."

"I do. But I need you here more with Otis." He closed his eyes and held her hand. *Listen, I don't trust Minerva 100% either, and I need you here in case she is acting on an agenda we don't know about. Okay?* Aleshia didn't say a word but only nodded. *Good.*

Deven took a step towards the hatch leading off of the bridge. "Come on Leon, we need to get you aboard."

Leon stood up and grabbed his pack. "Let's go."

They made their way down the ladders and ramps into the launch bay. A Mechand fighter sat near the doors with its running lights glowing. They climbed into the cockpit, but Leon frowned when he saw the controls. "Do you know how to fly one of these?"

"Yes, thankfully they are not that much different from our own. Now where is the starter?"

Leon's eyebrows met. "You're not inspiring confidence here."

Deven laughed. "Only kidding." He tapped a button to the right of the control stick between his legs and the power surged through the engines. The small craft lifted off its pad and crept towards the two large door sealing the bay. Lights flashed on either side of the doors as they began to slide away opening to reveal the *Defiant's* landing bay a short distance from them. Deven eased the fighter out of the carrier's bay and positioned it before the closed doors of the *Defiant*. After sitting there for several minutes Deven pulled out his data tab and tapped the link to Galina.

"Gregory? What is going on down there? Deven and Leon are waiting to come aboard."

Gregory slammed his hand on the door controls but they refused to budge. "We have debris all around down here, I think some jammed the doors. Let me get back to you."

"Gregory, we don't have time for this. Get whoever you need to help you clear– Gregory? Are you listening to me?" The intercom went dead. "Dang that man! Always wanting to prove himself." Galina's data tab began beeping. "Oh great. Here we go." She picked up the tab and smiled as Deven's face appeared. "Hi Deven, so nice to see you."

"Don't give me that. What's the hold up? We're outside, waiting."

Galina sighed. "We know. Gregory is trying to get the doors open. He thinks some debris has jammed them."

Leon leaned forward from the cramped back seat. "He *thinks*?"

"I told him to get whoever he needed, but I haven't heard anything since."

Gregory grabbed an anti-grav and stuck it to one of the larger surrounding secondary support beams had fallen against the doors. Hard to see from the other side of the hanger, but when he got closer, he saw the problem as plain as day. The beam grunted and remained fast. He increased the power, and it levitated up and away with a grinding wheeze. He removed the anti-grav and placed it on a second beam on the opposite side. It didn't look like it was touching, but it was leaning a bit. At this point he wasn't about to take any chances. He pulled the beam straight and repeated the process several more times until he thought all the weight was off of the doors. He ran back to the controls and slammed his fist on the open toggle. The doors grunted, groaned but slowly parted revealing the Mechand fighter waiting outside. With a loud screech, the doors ground to a sudden stop a few feet from allowing the fighter clear passage. "Dang it!" Gregory muttered. He grabbed a parka off of a nearby hook and ran to the doors.

The icy wind blasted through the bay. In a few seconds Gregory could feel his nostril hairs starting to freeze. He reached the doors and found the problem. A small piece of shrapnel had slipped between the doors and into the track. He tried to pull it out, but it was wedged in too tight. The anti-gravs wouldn't work here due to the lack of space to attach them. He ran over to a pile of equipment and found a long thin pole used for cleaning the intakes on the trucks. He jammed the pole into the track and pulled with all of his weight. The shrapnel refused to budge. The motion of the doors had jammed it in with the strength of an impact driver.

He had an idea. He grabbed the anti-grav and attached it to the other end of the pole. His fingers, numb from the cold, dropped the controller. He swore and picked it up again, set it to reverse operation and activated it. The anti-grav began to get heavy, increasing its weight as Gregory dialed up the power. The bar curved down under the weight, but the shrapnel began to move. "Come on you piece of junk!" Suddenly the bar snapped in two sending its upper portion, like a missile, at Gregory's head. His numb fingers dropped the remote again and reaching over to pick it up saved his life as the jagged rod impaled itself into the structure above his head.

He examined the doors and found the shrapnel had been pried out of the track a microsecond before the rod snapped. He fell down twice as he ran to the starboard side of the doors and pounded on the open control. The large doors ground open the rest of the way and the fighter entered the bay landing on an empty pad. Gregory slammed his fist on the controls again and they ground shut. When they sealed, he sank to his knees shivering.

Deven popped open the cockpit. "Gregory! Are you all right?"

"Sssss–ooo– ccccold." He fell backwards on the deck.

"He is going into shock," Deven said hopping out of the fighter. "Leon, get down to engineering and see what you can do with the overdrive. We need to get out of here *now*."

"But Gregory–"

"I will take care of him. Go!"

Leon nodded and left. Deven ran over to Gregory, lifted the man on his shoulders, and made his way to the infirmary.

Galina's voice came through all the intercoms. "Will someone tell me what is going on down there?"

Leon hit the intercom when he reached engineering. "Leon here, Deven is taking Gregory to the infirmary. I will see what I can do with these engines."

Galina blinked. "What happened to Gregory?"

"He was in the bay when it was open and he got too cold." The intercom clicked off.

"Leon? Leon? Dang him. Here I am trying to run this ship and no one is telling me anything."

Miles' camera focused on her. "You could have asked me."

"Okay, what is going on down there?"

"I am sorry, but my systems are still not at 100% I cannot tell you what happened other than the doors opened more slowly than usual, stopped, opened all the way several minutes later, and closed again."

Galina rolled her eyes. "Fat lot of help you are."

"I can only–"

Galina waved her hand. "Skip it Miles, I don't want to hear it right now."

"Acknowledged."

Deven placed Gregory on one of the beds and activated the cylindrical seal. Metal rounded walls rose up from the edges of the bed to meet in the middle. In a moment Gregory was enclosed from head to toe. Deven punched a few keys and warm liquid began to rush in filling the entire space except for his head. After a few moments the liquid brought his body temperature up to normal and his eyes cracked open. Deven? Where ... what happened¿'

"You went into shock. You got too cold out there. What did you think you were doing? The controls are accessible from the main booth, you didn't need to be in the hanger itself."

Gregory sighed. "But I did. Debris jammed the doors, and it was the only way to get them open fast. There wasn't time for me to put on a full exposure suit."

Deven nodded. "You took a heck of a risk."

"No more than you," Gregory croaked.

"You rest my friend. We'll take it from here. All your readings are in the green now. You will be okay, if you rest."

"Is that ... an order?"

"You bet it is."

"Okay ... as long ... as it is ... an ... order." He fell asleep the second the words had left his lips.

Deven left the infirmary and ran up to the bridge. He found

Galina shouting into the intercom. "Leon! Will you answer me?"

Deven smiled. "Problem?"

Galina jumped. "Oh Deven, good to have you back aboard. How is Gregory?"

"He will be fine. I got him to the infirmary before any permanent damage was done. Now what is the problem?"

"Leon isn't responding to me. I'm trying to find out the status on the engines."

"Why didn't you check on him?"

"I can't leave the bridge."

"I meant, have someone check on him. There are other people aboard you know."

"Oh, right." Galina reached for the intercom but Deven grabbed her hand.

"I will check on him. Send repair crews to the landing bay. The doors need work."

"Along with half of the rest of the ship."

"Well we need those doors to be at 100% pronto. We can't get them open fast enough now during an attack."

"Right, will take care of it," Galina said toggling the intercom.

Deven ran down to engineering and found Leon dragging large cables from one side of engine one to the far side of engine three. "Leon? What's our status?"

"We are a mess! That's our status."

Deven folded his arms. "Could you be more specific?"

"Look, do you want a report? Or do you want me to get the overdrive up and going?"

"Both."

"Well you get one so choose," he said while jamming the large cable into engine three. "Tell you what, here's a quick summary: overdrive in three minutes, communications in two. Good enough?"

"You bet." Deven eyed the cables, bits of broken conduits and pieces of insulation lying around. "You sure you don't need help?"

"They would only slow me down. If I need help, I will call for it," Leon said as he hustled to the other side of engineering.

Deven turned around and headed back to the bridge. When he got there, he saw Galina's scrunched up face as she glared at her console. "What's wrong?"

She looked up. "I was about to call you. We have another blip heading our way."

"Any idea who?"

"I can't tell with our scanners a mess like this. But being no one comes to Antarctica for a vacation, I'm going to guess it is the carrier we tangled with earlier."

Deven nodded. "We have been expecting them. How long until they get here?"

"About seven minutes give or take, at their current speed. Wait a sec, you knew?"

Deven sighed as he sat down hard in his chair. "Yes. We found part of the shielding on engine three is damaged and the *Defiant* is leaking energy."

Galina's eyes went wide. "What!?"

Deven raised a hand. "Don't worry it is not dangerous, but is enough for someone to track the *Defiant* if they know what to look for. And being we now know who is in command of that carrier. I am certain he followed you."

Galina blinked. "You know who is commanding that ship? How?"

Deven sat back. "Long story, but short version we have

a spy in the World Council, it found the information for us. And I know the commander."

Galina rubbed her temples. "How did we get a spy in the World Council?"

Deven smiled. "We have all along, we just didn't know it until he contacted Minerva. He is a maintenance and cleaning model Mechand."

Galina laughed. "So we have a janitor spy? How cliche'."

Deven shrugged. "Hey, as long as it works."

Leon muttered something as he removed a circuit board from the communications system.

"I am sorry, I did not quite understand what you said," Miles said over the intercom speaker near Leon's head.

"I wasn't talking to you Miles. I was grumbling how much damage they did to my baby."

"Your baby?"

Leon sat down the board, yanked a burned chip and replaced it with a spare. He grabbed the board, got back down on the floor and slid himself under the console. "The *Defiant*."

There was a pause. "Does that mean I am your 'baby' as well?"

Leon laughed. "No, you are quite different from the *Defiant*."

"But I am using it as my body."

"Yes, but you are still separate from it. And one day we will put you back in your original body."

"I look forward to being reunited with my body. Although,

I do not mind being part of the *Defiant*. I find the experience fascinating."

"I bet." Leon slipped the circuit board into place. It gave a satisfactory click. "There, try it now."

"Leon, I do not wish to diminish your knowledge, but I have run simulations and I do not think the replaced chip is the root cause of the communications failure."

Leon sighed. "Will you activate it? Or do I have to do it myself?"

"No, I will. Powering main communications system. Failure in the port side relay."

Leon nodded. "Expected, I haven't had time to fix it yet. Reroute all traffic to the other two. They can handle it."

After another short pause, Miles' voice came through the speaker. "It would appear I owe you an apology, the system is online. External communications has been restored."

Leon smiled. "No need." He ran over and slapped the intercom on the wall. "Communications and overdrive is back online. Call Minerva, let her know and let's get out of here. I'm on my way up to the bridge."

On the bridge Deven smiled. "You heard him, plot a course to the other side of the planet." He toggled the communications system and connected to the carrier next to them using the encryption keys he passed before they left. Minerva's face appeared. "Minerva, we are plotting a course. Link your navigation with ours. Send your codes on a sub channel."

She nodded. "Understood."

The screen split and Otis' face appeared. "I'm sure you noticed the Mechand carrier we tangled with before is almost here. They will be launching fighters in less than a minute. It will take at least one to get the link operational."

Deven smiled. "I think I have an idea."

Naud blinked cocked his head as he checked his equipment again. "Sir? We are getting a call for you."

Halburn waved his hand. "Lavine no doubt. It can wait. Prepare to launch all fighters and lock cannons on that carrier. I want it scraped."

"No Sir, the call is coming from the *Defiant*. Specifically asking to speak with you."

Commander Halburn turned around. "What? How would they know I am here?"

Naud shrugged his shoulder. "I do not know Sir, but they seem to."

"Open a link. This is Commander Halburn of the *Valiant*, who am I talking to?"

Deven's face flashed onto the screen. "Hello Odell, it has been a long time."

Halburn sat down. "Deven, how did you know I was here?"

"That is unimportant. What is; however, is what are *you* doing here?"

Halburn's eyes narrowed. "I have my orders to destroy that carrier and the *Defiant* if she gets in my way."

"Well you all ready did a good job of that. The *Defiant* is a mess. Tell me, why are you after us?"

"I think you know the answer."

Deven smiled. "Humor me."

"All right, you have revived the Nexus and we cannot allow it to continue. You know what it did the last time. Humanity cannot afford a repeat."

Deven nodded. "I agree. Now did you ever stop to think why the Nexus did what it did?"

Halburn waved his hand. "Who knows? And at this point it doesn't matter."

"Have you ever wondered why the Nexus created such a large military presence?"

Halburn's eyes narrowed. "To subjugate us."

"Assume for a moment it didn't. Assume for a moment an alien race bent on sucking the earth dry of materials and killing us in the process was discovered centuries ago. And assume the Nexus was created to prepare for and stop this threat, but something happened causing a malfunction in the core directives, losing the original goal until now."

Halburn sat forward in his chair. "That's quite the story."

Deven nodded. "It is. And it is also true."

Halburn laughed. "Are you trying to tell me the founders knew of an alien threat and created the Nexus to protect us centuries ago? Do you expect me to swallow that?"

"It wasn't the soul intention of the design, but yes a large part of it."

"Have you been sniffing carbine fumes? Because whatever you are on, is potent."

Deven shook his head. "I'm not. And I told Lavine all of this. His reaction was to send you after me. What does that tell you?"

"That he thinks you are a threat to world security because you have revived the Nexus."

"Assume I did for the moment, why would reviving the Nexus be a threat at this point? Most of the Mechands have been decommissioned and scrapped."

"That doesn't mean you can't make more."

"No it doesn't, but even if I wanted to, how would I go about it? I don't have any manufacturing plants."

Halburn shook his head. "No, but the Nexus did."

"But they were disabled. Lavine said everything was destroyed when I mentioned the possibility of an alien invasion. However, shortly after I talked with him, you show up. Doesn't that seem a bit odd? Considering everything is supposed to be scrapped?"

"That doesn't mean anything. He saved the *Valiant* as a precaution."

"For what? It certainly wasn't for me, who up until being fired upon by a supposedly scrapped Mechand carrier was following Lavine's every order. Doesn't this make you wonder what else he isn't telling you about?"

"It isn't my business to know."

"Odell, *think* for a moment. We used to do tactics long ago. What do *you* think is going on?"

"I *think* it isn't my job to question Chairman Lavine." Halburn turned to Naud. "Launch all fighters. Lock cannons on both the *Defiant* and that carrier. Fire at will."

Naud nodded. "Fighters launched and cannons locking on targets."

Deven jerked hearing the words. "I'm sorry Odell. I really am. Galina, get us out of here." His face disappeared as the engines on both craft's engines glowed brightly before they disappeared into overdrive causing several red energy beams to miss their targets and race towards the sky above.

Halburn whirled around. "Well don't just sit there. Follow him!"

Rechert swallowed hard. "I can't."

Halburn stormed over to his navigator. "And why not!?"

Rechert shuddered in his seat. "They are much higher up

in the atmosphere than we are. The increased altitude allows them to go much faster than us, even with damaged engines. They are already out of range."

"Then go into overdrive now and follow the energy trail, like we did before!"

"They must have made some repairs, I don't find the energy leakage like before. I can't tell you where they went."

"Dang it! Lavine is not going to be happy."

Naud raised his hand. "Umm Sir, I hate to say this but you have a call–"

Halburn sighed. "Let me guess, Chairman Lavine?"

"Yes Sir."

"How does he always know? I will take it in my cabin."

— 12 —

Deven sighed causing slight condensation for a moment on the main bridge window. He watched the terrain far below the *Defiant* scream past as the ship hurtled along at top overdrive speed. "I wish he could have seen reason."

Galina turned from her console. "You did your best. He wasn't listening."

Leon appeared, walked over to his seat, and crashed into it. "Whew. I need to teach Gregory a thing or two about the *Defiant's* engines."

Galina turned. "What did he do?"

"Well for starters he didn't notice the energy leak from engine three. That is how they found us. But I have to admit, I may not have right away either. Regardless he bypassed the engine. While that would work because it was out of sync with the others, it would have been much slower. I balanced them out and we have almost full power for the moment. We will need to make better repairs when we stop. But they will get us where we need to go."

Deven toggled the communication link to Minerva. Her face appeared. "How are things over there?"

"Everything aboard the *Phoenix* is working properly."

Deven's eyebrow went up. "The *Phoenix*?"

"Yes, I thought it was a fitting name. And what is the status of the *Defiant*?"

"We will need to make a pit stop soon but we are okay for now. Is Otis there?"

Minerva nodded. "Of course."

The screen split revealing Otis' scruffy face. "What's up Boss?"

"Sorry you had to lose your truck."

Otis smiled "Who said I did?"

"I don't follow."

Otis laughed. "I brought it aboard when you left. It was a tight fit, but it is here safe and sound."

Minerva chewed her bottom lip. "Yes he did bring that abomination aboard. I told him I do not like the paint job in the least. But he only laughed at me. I realize I was not myself when it was done, but now it seems like a slap in the face."

Otis laughed harder. "You know she is the first Mechand to ever figure out what the symbols on the door meant."

"I am not an ordinary Mechand. Keep that in mind."

"Yeah, I know. Tell you what, if we make it out of this alive. I'll repaint the door. Fair enough?"

Minerva nodded. "I suppose that would be acceptable."

Deven laughed. "You two sound like a married couple."

"We do not!" They said in unison causing Deven to laugh even harder.

Aleshia pulled Otis out of his seat and sat down. "When we get wherever we are going, I would like to come back to the *Defiant*."

"You will soon my love. But I would like you to stay there for now."

She gave him a blank stare. "Why? Everything is fine."

"Because if something goes wrong, you are one who can fix it." He winked and Aleshia's eyes enlarged for a second. She nodded.

"Of course, I will do my best."

"Thanks love." He cut the connection.

Leon folded his arms. "Now why is the real reason you want her over there?"

Deven sighed. "Because if the Nexus has been leading us on a wild goose chase, she is the only one that can crush the goose with ease."

"Oh."

"Yes and she will keep her eyes open. She doesn't trust Minerva. And is another reason I want her there. I think Otis hangs on Minerva's every word, which worries me."

"I didn't think he was that bad."

"I do. While I'm not doubting Minerva at the moment, I'm still waiting for the other shoe to drop." He turned to Galina. "How long until we arrive?"

Galina squeezed her controls. "We should be arriving at Fenton's in about an hour. I am taking us on several different routes and back tracking every one of them. If anyone is trying to follow they are going to get one wicked headache."

Deven chuckled. "Good. But I doubt Halburn could follow us."

Galina shrugged. "I doubt it as well, but I am not taking chances."

Leon jerked a thumb to one of the screens. "Are you going to call Fenton and let him know we are going to be on his doorstep soon?"

"Nope. Can't risk it. We won't be there long enough for anyone to figure out. Unless you think it's going to take longer than an hour or two to get the overdrive in top condition? Not to mention the shields?"

"I'd like a couple of weeks to put everything right they damaged and test it all, but I think I can do the most important bits in a few hours."

"Good because that is all we will have." He looked up to the camera. "Miles?"

The camera turned to face him. "Yes Deven?"

"Any changes with the Lytherians?"

"Two more makers have arrived. But nothing else."

Deven stood up and walked over to the window. "If Minerva is right, they are only waiting for their central *Command* carrier. Once it arrives, they will start the attack." He looked out again at the Earth flying past far below them. "Miles, any idea when the *Command* carrier might arrive?"

"Negative. I do not have enough information on their methods."

"Take a guess."

"Sir, as you know I do not like to make guesses. I make carefully calculated–"

"Okay, take a look and give me a simulated estimate of when it might arrive."

"Based on what we know and the arrival times of the previous ships, I would estimate the *Command* carrier will arrive in a day, perhaps two."

Aboard the *Valiant*, things were not going well. "How could you lose them twice in one day!?" Lavine's face reddened.

Halburn eyes narrowed. "They knew we were coming, and that I was in command."

"What? How is that possible?"

"I don't know. But it is. Also, they could have fought, but they chose to run instead."

Lavine rolled his eyes and blew out a breath as he spoke. "Because they were damaged from the previous encounter."

Halburn nodded. "They were damaged sure, but not enough that an attack was out of the question. You have to remember this is the *Defiant* we are talking about, not to mention an older and heavier Mechand carrier. If they had chosen to fight, I would have been at a strong disadvantage."

"And yet you followed them."

"On your orders, yes. But I had hoped to encounter the *Defiant* or the carrier separately. I had a chance if I managed to encounter them separate. But together, that chance disappears. Regardless, I think you need to consider their actions."

Lavine blinked. "Their actions?"

"Yes, twice they could have caused heavy damage to this ship, and both times they either chose to fight with kid gloves on or run."

Lavine blinked again. "So? What's your point?"

"My point is if they were guilty of all you say, their actions would be different."

Lavine shook his head. "That is only to throw us off the trail."

"I don't think so. I know Deven, if he has to, he can fight. Heck, he took down the Nexus didn't he? But now it seems he is trying to avoid causing damage, and that is no way to win a war. Hence, I think there is a greater situation at play here. Such as the aliens he spoke of."

Lavine blinked again. "He contacted you?"

"Yes, how else would I know he knew I was in command?"

"I thought perhaps, it was another method than an actual conversation. What did he say?"

"He said the possible reason the Nexus was created was because the founders knew of this threat."

"That's ludicrous. There is no way the founders could have known about an alien race so long ago they created the Nexus, as what, our guardian? No, I am certain this is an attempt to throw us off of the real goal."

"Sir, forgive me, but wouldn't he have created a better story if the goal was for us to believe it? I mean, why come out with something so fantastic?"

Lavine smiled. "For the same reason you thought of it. It is reverse logic, tell a fantastic tale so hard to believe that it must be true. I am surprised it didn't occur to you."

Halburn sat back in his chair in the otherwise dark room. The light from the screen provided the only illumination. "It did, but I do not think it applies in this case."

Lavine's eyes narrowed. "I don't care what you think. I am telling you what it is, and I expect you to follow my lead. Or will find myself a new commander, and you won't be able to command a troupe of girl scouts. Are we clear?"

Halburn swallowed. "Yes Chairman. I understand."

"Good. Now can you follow them?"

Halburn swallowed again. "I am afraid not Chairman."

"Why not?"

"Last time we were able to follow an energy leak from one of their engines created during the battle. It was very small, but enough. It appears they have repaired the defect. There is nothing for us to track."

"I see. Then Commander, I suggest you find a new way to find them. Or you will be going door to door selling cookies."

Halburn blinked. "But they haven't done that since before the Mechands!"

"Well, I guess you had better get started, or you will find yourself delegated to non-existent," Lavine snarled as the connection cut.

Halburn sighed as he tapped the intercom. "Naud, any luck in finding something we can track?"

Naud's face appeared. "I am sorry Sir, not at this time."

"Did you learn anything from the encounter?"

"Other than their altitude rating is far greater than ours? No."

"There must be something."

"Well I did see a bit of a fluctuation in their overdrive when they engaged it. Not much but I am sure whatever repairs they did, were a patch job at best. They'll have to stop somewhere and pull the drive to fix it, along with any other damage systems. Which from what I can tell, is extensive."

"Hmm we wrecked more havoc than I thought. How about the carrier? What shape is that in?"

"It appears to be fully operational."

"Where do you think they would go to make repairs?"

Naud shrugged. "I don't know. It would have to be a very large place to accommodate the *Defiant*. And it would have to be in a location we can't monitor with ease. Not to mention have parts on hand for the *Defiant*."

Halburn smiled. "I think I know where they went, Ulimaroa."

Naud's eyebrows went up. "Australia?"

Halburn nodded. "Yes that is what it was called before the Swedish invasion of the Last Great War, and after the Mechands were created to help us rebuild. At least that is what we were always told. I never could understand why the Swedish bothered attacking Australia. Anyway it is a wasteland now for the most part, as you know. Still, some people live there. And if I recall correctly, Deven has a friend in the area by the name of Fenton."

"Fenton?"

"Yes, I don't know if Fenton is his first name or last. Deven never said much about him. But he did tell me once Fenton helped him out."

Naud smiled. "And if he did it once–"

"You got it. See what you can find. It shouldn't be too hard to find someone on that continent that has the facilities the *Defiant* will need."

Naud's smile broadened. "Or that is still receiving regular shipments of supplies and equipment."

Halburn nodded. "Right. Get on it."

"Will do."   The screen went black as Halburn's eyes adjusted to the dark. He needed to find out what was going on. And to do that he had to talk with Deven, without anyone else knowing. But it was *not* going to be easy.

The *Defiant* arrived right above a little building with 'Fenton's Gas and More' painted on the side. The *Phoenix* emerged from overdrive a microsecond later.

Deven hit a button on his data tab and Fenton's face appeared on the screen. The older man with a dark complexion and eyes that had seen better times, smiled. "G'day mate, what can I do for you?"

"We are having a bit of engine trouble. Do you think we could park in your garage?"

Fenton laughed. "You know the answer. I charge by the size."

Deven chewed at the inside of his right cheek. "We are pretty large, I am not sure I can afford it."

"Oh I am sure you are good for it. Come on down. I'll roll out the red carpet." Fenton's face faded out as the connection cut.

"You heard the man. Head down."

Galina shrugged. "Umm, I hate to ask but where? We don't exactly fit on that landing pad." She pointed to a small car sized pad near the shack.

Deven grinned. "Just wait." A huge area by the shack shifted. It started as a crack spewing dust into the air. Then it lowered a foot and slid back revealing a rising elevator large enough for the *Defiant* to land on.

Galina chuckled. "He always did like to show off." She guided the *Defiant* down to the elevator.

Miles' camera glanced around the bridge and outside the window before centering on Deven. "I had no idea Fenton had such a large facility."

Deven smiled. "Thankfully, no one else does either." He pressed another button on his data tab and it linked to the *Phoenix*. "Minerva? You stay up here and keep watch. Let us know if anything changes or comes into range."

Minerva's face appeared. "Understood. And I have someone that wishes to speak with you."

The screen split and Aleshia's face appeared on the right side of the screen. "We are just going to sit here?"

"Yes, for the moment."

"Mind if I join you? It has been a while since I have seen Fenton."

"No, I need you up there with Otis."

"Please? Nothing is going on at the moment and you know it."

"I don't know it, that is why I want you watching."

"I will call Fenton." She grinned as she leaned forward.

Deven rolled his eyes as he leaned back in the chair. "You would, wouldn't you."

Her eyes shone with manic glee. "Yes."

Deven sighed. "And I am sure he would side with you. All right, if you can talk Otis into staying there and letting you take his truck down. You can."

Aleshia grinned. "Be there in a flash." Her side of the screen disappeared and Minerva's face again took up the entire space. She nodded, and the screen went black.

"Touch down." Galina said as they felt a jolt throughout the ship. "We're down and locked."

"Engines powered down," Leon said. "Main core is now offline as well. We are receiving power through an umbilical connected up from the pad to the *Defiant*." The elevator began to lower into a large repair bay. The area above resealed hiding everything from view.

"How long do you think it will take?" Deven asked.

Leon shrugged. "It depends on the equipment Fenton has. Five, maybe six hours if we are lucky."

"Trust me, he has all we need," Deven said as he tucked the data tab back into its pouch and stood up.

Galina blinked. "Where are you going?"

"To see an old friend."

Deven opened the landing bay to see Fenton's face on the far side. He extended the ramp, which lowered making grinding sounds and bounced up several times before touching the pad below. As he walked down, he jerked a thumb back towards the ship. "That needs fixing too."

Fenton smiled. "Ga'day mate. Glad you could drop by." He offered his hand and when Deven grabbed it he pulled Deven close and wrapped him on the back with his other arm in a large hug.

"Always glad to see you my friend," Deven said.

"You bet. Now where is that lady friend of yours?"

"She will be here in a bit. She is on the Mechand carrier."

Fenton nodded. "I about lost my teeth when I saw that drop out of overdrive next to you. But I saw the maneuvering, and you called needing repair work. Figured it was yours."

Deven nodded. "It is. Well, technically, it is Minerva's."

Fenton's one eyebrow shot up. "Minerva? I thought your lady friend's name is Aleshia."

"It is."

Fenton whapped Deven on the arm. "You dog you. Two girls?"

Deven laughed. "Not at all. Minerva is the Nexus."

Fenton's jaw dropped and an old partial slipped out to clang on the floor. "Okay, this time I did lose my teeth." He picked up the partial, cleaned it, and put it back in his mouth. "Did you say the Nexus? I thought you killed her?"

"We did, but she was bought back by a system the founders installed centuries ago."

Fenton cocked his head. "What for?"

"That's a long story. And I will tell you over coffee."

To their left a small platform containing a table, and two chairs rocketed down stopping right next to them. Aleshia sat in one of the chairs and uncrossed her denim clad legs. "I forgot what a rush that is."

Fenton laughed. "I do it all the time and I still lose my stomach. Good to see ya girl."

Aleshia got up and walked over to Fenton giving him a big hug. "And good to see you. I never did get a chance to pay you back for the stuff you gave me last time I was here."

Fenton leaned close. "Did you like them?"

Aleshia nodded. "Yes."

Fenton tipped his head towards Deven and lowered his voice. "And did *he* like them?"

Aleshia blushed. "Yes he did."

Fenton's smile could swallow a truck. "Then, that my dear, is payment in full."

"Oh no, I couldn't–"

"Hey, allow an old man to give joy to those he cares about."

She hugged him again. "Thank you."

"Ya welcome. Now what's this about the Nexus?"

Aleshia swatted Deven. "You told him already?"

Fenton took Alisha's arm in his. "We were about to have coffee, and I insist you join us."

Aleshia grinned. "With an invitation like that, how could I not?"

"Good. This way." Fenton pointed to a recessed area in the complex's wall. He pushed a button and the wall slid away revealing a small kitchen, table, chairs, and a bedroom off to the side. He sat the two of them down at the table and grabbed three old-style glass cups. He placed them under a dispenser and punched in a number. A few seconds later dark hot liquid poured out of the taps above the cups and he turned towards Deven. "I know you like it straight, but what about the lady?"

Aleshia smiled. "A little synth milk please."

"Synth? Ha! Like I am going to give you that." Fenton grinned hitting a couple of more buttons. "This is the real stuff. A guy I know has a couple of cows." White liquid poured into the middle cup. He placed all three cups on a tray, walked over to the table, and placed the tray in front of them. He took the cup on the far right and sat down. "Now, you were saying?"

Gregory poked his nose past the door in engineering. "Hey Leon, need a hand?"

On the other side of the massive room, Leon's white head popped up from behind a new power regulator. "Gregory! What are you doing up? Shouldn't you be in the infirmary?"

Gregory walked over. "Nah, I'm fine now. I was a little wobbly at first, but I'm fine."

Leon eyed him. "Are you sure?"

Gregory nodded. "Yeah, and I want to make it up to you for messing up your engines."

Leon laughed. "You're kidding right? You did fine."

"I almost blew us to kingdom come."

"But you didn't." He paused to point to the decks above. "And I am guessing Galina doesn't know that bit."

Gregory sighed. "Yeah, you got that right."

"What happened?"

Gregory pointed to one of the large scorched cables in the corner of the room. "I made a bad connection. I thought engine three wasn't getting power so I did a direct connection from the core and bypassed the normal regulation system."

Leon's eyes went wide. "You did what?!"

"I thought it was like the weapons system and had backups inside the engines to take care of that. But a second later when the cable got way too hot I realized my mistake. The connectors had almost fused with the cable due to the heat so it took a bit to get it free."

Leon nodded. "I can imagine." He walked over and put his hand on Gregory's shoulder. "You didn't blow us up, and you didn't do any permanent damage. That's the important part."

Gregory sighed as his eyes fell. "But I could have."

"Look, way back in the day I made a mistake and it almost blew out a whole communications array. The damage would have taken months to fix, maybe more. Thankfully I noticed it before anyone got hurt or worse. We can only do our best."

"The problem is my best isn't very good."

"And what is your expertise?"

"Weapons, specifically energy cannons."

"Yes, and this is very different from them. So hence you did a good job for what you had to work with."

"But I didn't see the energy leak either. It could have cost us all our lives."

"Hey, even I may not have noticed the leak right off. And in any case it didn't. We're still here, the *Defiant* isn't any worse shape than when you started except for that one cable. And I think that is a pretty cheap learning curve when you consider what could have happened. You managed to get the overdrive back online when it was needed, that's all that matters. You saved lives, not cost them. In the end we have to keep that in mind. Don't hover on your mistakes, keep them close to your heart so you don't do them again sure, but don't let it paralyze you from doing your job."

"Yeah, I guess."

"You guess? Put it behind you and give me a hand here. All of this has taught me I need backup on this ship. We all do."

Gregory smiled. "You bet."

"Good." Leon pointed to a large screen on a cart with tools on the other side of the room. "Now grab the test equipment over there and let's see if this new regulator is going to hold under load."

"Sure thing." Gregory ran over, grabbed the cart, and wheeled it next to the regulator with Leon waiting.

Leon got down and wiggled under it. A hand emerged waving. "Hand me the cables on the right side of the cart. The black and green." Gregory placed the cables in Leon's hand and smiled. At that moment he knew he would never make such a mistake again.

Galina tapped the intercom. "Leon? How's it coming?" She heard a bang and swearing.

"It would go faster if you didn't call down every twenty minutes to find out," Leon grumbled.

"Sorry."

"No problem. Did the repair team I sent fix the bay doors? Gregory said they were still a little cranky."

Galina nodded. "Yes, they are as smooth as silk now. Most of the debris in the landing bay has been cleared. Although, we still have a large support beam that needs replacing."

"Have them get on it. I don't want that falling on me when I leave the ship."

Galina laughed. "It won't, and I already did."

Leon smiled. "Good. How are the rest of the repairs going?"

"Another hour and we should be in great shape. Way ahead of schedule."

"Yes I am thankful for the repairs to my, or rather

the *Defiant's* systems. Feeling less than whole is very disconcerting," Miles said. "The relay node on the port side was particularly annoying."

"Miles! We didn't ask for your two cents," Galina said.

"But I do not have 'two cents' to offer."

Leon chuckled grabbed an eletro-driver and inserted it into the engine to crank in another fastener. "Good, we can leave shortly after. I won't be done that quick, but close. I will let you two work out the rest. Leon out." He pointed to the intercom and Gregory shut it off. "All right, let's get this done. I do not want to be made a fool of with the rest of the crew."

Gregory smiled. "Do you really expect they would think that?"

"No, but my pride would." Leon pointed to a hand-held tool with a small screen laying on the floor a few inches beyond his reach. "Grab that calibrator and get it connected between these two contacts so we can see why this engine is still not in sync with the rest."

"You got it." Gregory grabbed the tool and connected where Leon said. A flood of data flew across the tiny screen.

"Ah the phasing is a little off. But I can't change the phasing in that direction such a little amount without pulling the whole engine. However, if we adjust the phasing on the opposite side, it should counteract the problem."

"Geeze, how could you tell from the green mess on the little screen?"

Leon smiled. "Experience my boy. Experience. Well that and a lot of reading. Grab the flow regulator and adjust it to the negative until I say."

"So you say there are these Lytherians sitting outside the solar system and are getting ready to attack? And the founders knew about this?" Fenton reached under the front of his hat and scratched. "Wow, no wonder Lavine didn't believe you. Heck, I am having trouble and I have always believed you."

"Well, we do have the proof."

Fenton sat up quick enough to hear a slight pop in his back. "Proof the Nexus showed you right?"

Deven nodded.

"Well that explains it. He is not going to believe anything the Nexus says, or anyone listening to it."

"I know. But I am hoping to get through to Halburn." Aleshia got up, refilled her and Deven's cups with hot coffee, and sat back down next to him. She put her hand on his knee as she sat.

Fenton cocked his head. "Halburn? Odell Halburn?"

"Yeah that is him. What do you know about him?"

Fenton shook his head as he took another sip from his cup. "Not much. I have friends in low places and someone told me he was going to head up a new project for Lavine. At the time, I thought it was commander of a new defense force or police."

Deven sighed as he gazed into his cup watching the steam rise from it. "Do you remember, when I told you I hid out for a while near the coast?"

"You bet mate, it was when you were on walkabout, before you came back here. Why?"

"Do you remember me mentioning the kid I used to play games with?"

"Sure it was some kid about your age ..." His voice trailed off. "Wait a sec, that is Halburn isn't it?"

Deven nodded. "Yes."

"Wow. Have you talked with him?"

"Briefly, before we came here.   But being I used our conversation to delay his attack so we could escape, I am sure he is not in the best of moods."

"No kidding. But I imagine Lavine is in an even worse mood."

A beep came from Deven's hip and he pulled out his data tab. Galina's face appeared on the screen. "We are about done with the immediate repairs. Leon has a little work yet on the engines, but should be done within the hour."

"Good.   I don't want to stay here any longer than necessary." Deven flipped off the data tab and placed it back into his hip pouch.

Fenton frowned. "Why do you have to leave so soon? I don't see you enough as it is."

Deven sighed. "I know, but I can't risk your safety any more than we have. We wouldn't be here now if the situation wasn't dire."

"Hey! It's my risk to take. I told you come down, I could have just as easily said it was too hot couldn't I?"

"Yes. But you never have."

Fenton smiled. "And I never will. So get it through your thick skull."

Aleshia rubbed Deven's shoulder with her own. "So he does know you."

Fenton nodded. "That I do little lady, that I do."

Deven looked at Aleshia then shifted his gaze to Fenton a second later. "Hey no fair, two against one."

Fenton's smile broadened. "By now you should know I always side with the lady. She is a lot prettier than you."

Aleshia blushed. "Thank you."

Fenton inclined his head and tipped his scuffed hat. "Welcome little lady."

Deven's data tab beeped before he could say another word. He pulled it out and flipped it on. "Yes?"

Galina's face appeared. "I am sorry to bother you, but we need you back aboard."

"For?"

Galina shifted in her seat. "It's not something I want to discuss on the link."

Deven sighed. "I'll be right up." He put the data tab away and turned to Fenton. "I am sorry but it looks like I'm needed. I will be back as soon as I can."

Aleshia stood with him. "I'm with you."

Fenton smiled. "What's your rush? I mean you haven't finished your coffee yet. Can't you grant an old man's a request of seeing a lovely lady for a few more minutes?"

Deven smiled. "You don't need to come with me, or Galina would have said."

"But–"

"It is not often we have real coffee not that synth stuff as of late. Join me when you are done. Okay?"

Aleshia smiled as she sat back down. "Okay."

Deven headed off towards the *Defiant* as Fenton eyed Aleshia. "So, are you going to tell me what is wrong?"

Aleshia blinked. "What do you mean?"

Fenton laughed. "He might buy that crud, but I don't. There is something going on between you two. Or at least on your end. He is not showing it. So what did he do?"

Aleshia blinked again. "What? How do you know?"

Fenton smiled as he sat back in the old chair causing it to creak. A few of his bones made the same sound in response. "I'm old. I ain't dead. Besides, it's my business to be able to look behind the curtain."

Aleshia's eyes went wide. "You can read minds too?"

Fenton laughed. "Heck no. But it's written all over your face, if one knows where to look. Now, what did he do?"

"Nothing really."

"Aleshia, don't give me that. He must have done something."

"Well it isn't his fault."

"Uh-huh. When a woman says that, it means we did. So spill it."

Aleshia eyed him. "How did you get so smart about women?"

"I am old. And you didn't reckon' I had my share of shelia's? Last one died twenty years ago, God rest her soul."

"I'm sorry. Why haven't you had anyone since then?"

Fenton sighed. "Because she was the best. After her, well, I knew I couldn't find someone else even close. Besides, who is going to want to stay here with this old fruit loop anyway."

Aleshia took his wrinkled hands in hers. "I don't see that at all. And I am sure there are many ladies would agree with me."

Fenton smiled. "Thanks for that. But this is not about me, it is about you. What did Deven do?"

Aleshia blew out a breath. "We were on our honeymoon and had to leave."

"Gosh, no wonder you aren't happy with him. And let me guess you had been planning this for a while?"

Aleshia nodded. "Yes and when everything … happened

we had to leave. He didn't even get to see me in the special white teddy you gave me."

Fenton sat back. "He didn't? Well why did you say he did?"

"Because he was standing right there next to me?"

"Oh . . . right."

"I know it wasn't his choice, but dang it, it was our honeymoon. He did promise we would reschedule. Of course that depends on if the world survives."

Fenton smiled and leaned forward. "Let me tell you something. The human race has been through a lot and we have always come out the other side. I think we will here too. And from what you tell me, they don't know we are watching them. That is a very powerful advantage."

"But they sound impossible to beat."

Fenton's smile broadened. "And they said that about the Nexus right? And look what happened. You and Deven took her down. You will do the same here. I may not know how, but I am sure you will."

"I hope so."

"I know so. And by the way, earlier you asked if I could read minds too. What do you mean 'too'?"

"Deven never told you?"

"Told me what?"

"How we beat the Nexus, with our combined mental abilities."

"Wow, I had no idea he was that strong."

"He isn't." Aleshia waved a hand and a four ton engine assembly located to their far right shifted three inches to the left. "But between the two of us we were able to."

Fenton whistled. "Wow. That's impressive. And you worry about these aliens? Ha! I bet you could destroy them in orbit before they ever got here."

Aleshia shook her head. "No, I don't have near that kind of range."

"Still if you could find out a way. They would be in big trouble," he said with a grin.

"Perhaps."

"Perhaps nothing. And by the way, could you please slide the crate back? I don't want to get out the anti-grav forklift if I don't have to."

"Sure thing." Aleshia waved her hand again, and the crate moved back into its previous position. Fenton couldn't even tell it had ever been moved. Even the dirt on the floor rearranged to hide the evidence. "There. And no sign I shoved it around either."

Fenton smiled again. "Thanks, but you didn't need to sweep up as well."

Aleshia winked. "Well I couldn't leave a mess now could I?"

"With me you could. Are you sure you couldn't use that on them aliens? Seems like they wouldn't know what hit them."

Aleshia shook her head. "No, my abilities don't have that kind of range. And I would have to see or visualize what I am doing, or it won't work."

"Hmm that does make it difficult. Are you sure you couldn't boost your abilities somehow? Leon is a technical genius, seems like he could think of something."

"I doubt it. I mean, he doesn't understand what I can do in the first place, how is he going to boost it?"

"True that. Hmm, is there anyone that might know how to go about it?" Fenton said taking another sip from his coffee cup.

"My abilities are new, as far as I know, no one has ever had something similar. Or at least near this strong."

"Too bad you don't have someone that has been around a long time and could tell you. And before you say, I may be old, but I ain't *that* old."

Aleshia laughed. "I wasn't going to say that."

"Uh-huh, sure you weren't. Don't fib to an old man, it doesn't suit you."

Aleshia slapped his arm playfully. "Will you stop, you know I am not."

Fenton grinned. "Yes I know it. But I had you going for a second, didn't I? But as I was saying, seems like there should be a database on your abilities. Perhaps you are the first one, but perhaps not."

Aleshia's eyes sparkled. "Fenton you are a genius!"

He looked up. "I am?"

"You bet." She got up and hugged him tight. "Thank you for the coffee, I need to get back to the *Defiant*." She started running towards the large ship still sitting on the elevator.

"Sure, but you come back soon ya hear?" He yelled after her which echoed around the large space.

Aleshia found Deven and Galina on the bridge. "Oh good you are here. I have an idea."

Deven raised his hand. "Now, Miles you were saying?"

"Hello Aleshia, it is good to see you again." He paused then turned his camera back to Deven. "I have been monitoring the probe as you instructed, but there is a slight inconstancy I cannot account for."

"Which is?"

"Another Lytherian carrier has arrived."

Deven shrugged. "Another *Maker*, so what, we already know about them."

"No, this is a much larger ship. Possibly the *Command* carrier Minerva thought existed."

"So what is the problem?"

"Minerva has not told us of its arrival. This is vital information we should have, yet she has not mentioned it."

Otis' face flashed on one of the screens. "Boss, I hate to bother you but our shadow is inbound."

Deven's eyes focused on the screen to his right. "The *Valiant*?"

Otis shrugged. "Who else?"

"How in the world did he find us?"

"I don't know, but Minerva thinks we have the advantage."

"Explain."

Otis face moved to the left side of the screen and Minerva's face appeared in the blank area. "This carrier is older, and back in that time period the sensors were built to take more energy. I have boosted their range significantly. However, the *Valiant* is a newer model and while the sensor system is more efficient, it could not take the modification I have put in place. Therefore, we can see him, but they haven't seen us."

"How long before they do?"

"Fifteen minutes, perhaps a little more. If they increase speed it will be much less."

"Well let's hope they don't." Deven hit the intercom. "Leon? How are we doing?"

Leon grunted as he reconnected the last of the power feeds. "I will know in a minute."

"We don't have a minute."

Leon pointed at Gregory. "Hit the button over there and pray." Gregory ran over and hit the button on the control console. The engines sparked then began to emit a faint glow which grew brighter by the second. Ten seconds later they were as bright as ever and working in harmony with each other. "Okay, we are ready down here. Overdrive is back at full capacity, and so is the conventional thrust."

"Good." Deven hit another key and Fenton appeared on another screen. "Fenton, send us back up. We have to go."

The old man raised a white eyebrow. "So soon?"

"I am sorry mate but we have company inbound and we can't let them see us here. If they do, they will never leave you alone again."

"Ha! They could search a hundred years and never find what I have. Everything is shielded and sealed, unless I let it through."

"Humor me all right? Send us up. We will be back again soon, I promise."

Fenton nodded. "You got it mate. And I am going to hold you to it." He waved before his image winked out.

The large opening above ground back with some dirt falling down on the *Defiant* as the elevator began to bring the large ship to the surface. Deven turned his attention back to the screen that still held Minerva and Otis. "We're coming up. Is the Auto-Nav link still operational?"

Minerva nodded. "It is."

"Good, be prepared to follow our lead as soon as we get clear."

Minerva nodded again. "Understood."

The elevator stopped with a jolt. "Engines are ready. Umbilical disconnected. Light em' up," Leon said.

Galina grabbed the controls, activated the *Defiant's* engines, and the massive vessel began to rise. Half a second later, the elevator began its long decent back down. The large cover slide back across and up to hide it. "Everything looks good. Taking her up." The large ship moved slowly at first, then she began to gain speed as she climbed into the air.

Deven looked over to the Screen with Minerva and Otis. "How much time until they see us?"

"Two minutes," Minerva said.

Galina grit her teeth. "This is going to be close."

"One minutes thirty seconds," Minerva said.

"Overdrive hasn't fully charged yet, a few more seconds," Leon said over the intercom.

Deven glared. "I thought you said it was at full capacity?"

"Well it is, once it charges. I didn't expect us to need it this quick."

"Forty seconds," Minerva said.

"Got it! Overdrive charged. Get us outta here!"

"Ten seconds," Minerva said.

"You heard the man, get us out of here," Deven said.

Galina punched the overdrive and both ship's engines began to glow brighter and brighter as the energy built up.

"Five seconds."

"Oh shut up!" Galina said as both ships leapt into overdrive.

Seconds later the *Valiant* decelerated above Fenton's. "Scanners! I want to know if they are here or have been here!"

Naud's fingers flew over his controls. "I am not seeing anything other than a small building. A small store perhaps. But nothing able to repair the *Defiant*."

Halburn slammed his fist on the arm of his chair. "Blast it! All we had to go though to find this place and it is nothing! Head north and engage overdrive."

Rechert turned to face Halburn. "Sir? Why that direction?"

"It is as good as any. We aren't going to learn anything from this wasteland. A more populated area might let us know if a large ship was in the vicinity."

"Do you really think they would take the risk?"

Halburn shrugged. "No, but we can't just sit here. If Lavine knows we are searching, I don't get my head handed to me … yet anyway."

"Yes Sir." Rechert said as he engaged the drive and the *Valiant's* engines left a faint glow in the air as they disappeared.

A minute later Fenton smiled to himself as he punched in the code for Deven's data tab. A moment later his face appeared. "I told you they wouldn't see anything."

Deven laughed. "Glad to hear it. We'll be back."

"You'd better. I have your truck after all." Fenton turned his data tab enabling its camera to show the vehicle in the underground complex.

"My truck! You left it there? How could you? Aleshia, I told you to put it on my pad in the *Defiant's* hanger!" Otis' voice sounded distant as he shouted from a screen a console away.

Deven jerked a thumb over his shoulder. "As you can hear Otis is not too happy. We will be back for it soon."

"You'd better, I charge for storage ya know?" Fenton smiled as his image winked out.

13

"Minerva?" Aleshia said hitting a key on Deven's console as she sat down.

Minerva's face appeared on the large screen. An eyebrow cocked to one side. "Yes?"

"Do you know if any telepaths were as strong or stronger than I am?"

Minerva blinked. "What an odd inquiry. What does this–"

"Never mind. Answer the question."

"If there was, I do not have records of one. Of course, it is possible such a person could have existed before I came online"

Aleshia shook her head. "Unlikely as telepaths only started to appear after you were around. If it happened beforehand, we would have known."

Minerva nodded. "Logical."

"Thank you. Now, you had drugs to suppress the telepathic abilities, correct?"

Minerva shuddered. "Yes. Although, they did more than their design."

Aleshia sighed. "We know. All too well. And how did you find out these particular drugs worked?"

"I ... I ... don't know."

Aleshia's eyes narrowed. "What do you mean you don't know?"

"It is from a very dark time in my history. I have blocked out those memories. Meaning, I honestly do not know."

"But you can still access them, right?"

"No. I will not access them again. I do not want to remember all I did during that time."

"But you still *can.*"

"Technically, yes."

"Then I need you to do so."

Minerva shook her head. "No, I will not. There is nothing from back then that can help us now."

"Yes it can. Perhaps the destruction of the Lytherians."

Deven, sitting next to her, tilted his head. "What are you getting at?"

Aleshia smiled. "I am betting Minerva must have done a lot of testing back then, and while she did find a way to suppress the telepathic abilities, I suspect she also found ways to enhance it. Or at least has the data we can use to do so."

Deven's right eyebrow raised. "Why?"

"If we can boost my abilities, I might be able to grab a hold of those ships while still out in space and either confuse them into going somewhere else or destroy them if necessary."

Minerva's eyes narrowed. "And you think this is possible?"

Aleshia nodded. "If my range is extended, and I can see them, yes."

Minerva's gaze shifted away for several minutes, then focused on Aleshia. "If you are certain this can be of use. I will access those memories."

Miles' camera focused on Aleshia. "Aleshia, I do not think this is wise."

"What? I thought you trusted Minerva?"

"Trust is a strong word. A working relationship accepting some of her information as fact until proven otherwise might be more accurate. And when your life is concerned, I am very much questioning this information. She herself said it came from a dark period in her history. The data may not be accurate, even if she gives it to us unaltered."

"Is there harm in looking at this data?"

Miles' camera focused on the clouds wisping by the bridge windows for several seconds before returning to Aleshia. "Logically, there should not be any harm. But since I do not see any good coming from this activity, I would suggest it is a waste of time that might be better spent elsewhere."

Aleshia turned to Deven. "Love, you make the decision. I think it could work, but you decide."

Deven sighed. "While I wonder if this possible, if it is, we can't ignore it. Minerva, do it. But give Miles direct access to all the data. Is that clear?"

Minerva nodded. "Perfectly. But I will remind you, it came from a very dark period in my past. One, even I don't want to remember." She closed her eyes and several screens lit up scrolling with data. Numbers, dates, actions taken, what worked and what didn't. Minerva shuddered as a tear ran down her cheek. "I am truly sorry. Please forgive me."

Leon pointed at the screen on his console. "What are these long numbers?"

Deven's hands balled into fists as he read the numbers. Several he knew quite well. "NCIs or Nexus Citizen Identification."

Leon's eyes went wide. "What? You mean each one of these lines is a telepath?"

Minerva nodded as another tear ran down her cheek. "Yes."

"There are hundreds, if not thousands here!"

Minerva closed her eyes and winced. "Yes."

Deven scrolled through the list, seeing several other numbers he recognized. "While I always knew this was being done, to see the actual amount of the people hunted down … is astonishing."

Leon pointed to the screen. "You know what is odd? Telepaths only started showing up in the last generation or so. Minerva what is this last column?"

"Power level, or the strength of the persons abilities. Most of the people listed here could only listen to minds on an occasional basis. Telekinetics were very rare. Only one was encountered before."

"I still find it odd telepaths started popping up all of a sudden. What about the chemical suppressors?" Minerva nodded, and another screen appeared showing a complex chemical formula. Leon shuddered as he read it. "Are you kidding me? This would create permanent chemical lobotomies with repeated use! No wonder they seemed like zombies after awhile."

Minerva's eyes drifted down. "I know."

"Minerva, where is the data on creating this formula? There must be something," Galina said.

"Not much. The formulation was created in the early days of the situation. I took a baseline strong tranquilizer and altered it to affect the areas of the brain I assumed was responsible for telepathy."

Aleshia's mouth dropped. "You *assumed* responsible?"

"The formulation proved effective, so I assumed I was correct."

Aleshia glared. "Sending a carbine blast through their brains would have done the same thing. You affected the whole mind, not a limited area. It was not targeted at all."

"I am sure I could have done more research and refined it. However, at the time such a thought seemed like a waste of resources."

Galina spat. "Waste of resources! How can you say that?! This is peoples lives we are talking about."

Minerva's eyes narrowed. "I know! You have no idea what it was like to come online and realize what I had done! It is almost impossible to bear. It is why I blocked it from my memories."

Aleshia raised a hand. "We know Minerva, we know. Please, is there anything on increasing telepath abilities?"

Miles' camera swiveled towards Aleshia. "If I may, I have found one instance where the normal formulation was tainted and resulted in an increase of the person's abilities. But it also caused increased heart rate resulting in a stroke an hour after administration."

Aleshia chewed her bottom lip. "Risky, but it could work. If we could come up with an antidote able to be administered before that point."

Mile's camera iris went wide. "I object. You are talking about taking a chemical compound with limited testing. It could alter your brain permanently or kill you. I cannot allow it."

Deven nodded. "I agree. No way are you taking that stuff. I don't care if it gives us the advantage."

Aleshia looked him in the eye. "And what do you suggest? We let them come here and take over? We don't have the army to fight them. This is our only chance."

Minerva shook her head. "Not exactly."

Aleshia turned to face the screen. "What do you mean *not exactly*?"

"There was one instance of increased abilities created in a physical rather than chemical way."

"How?"

"It isn't in my research, but I do have data from long ago regarding the Lytherian ship. A crystal substance was found in the wreckage. Is silicon based with other elements including quartz, diamond, chromium, beryllium, selenium, and several others they couldn't identify. While having high clarity, the many facets make it highly reflective. It is far harder than diamond and is in an approximate cone shape. It was discovered when powered, the energy radiated had the same exact frequency of the human mind. Many of the technicians that worked on it, complained of severe headaches."

Galina rolled her eyes. "How does a bunch of people getting headaches help us?"

Minerva sighed and continued. "It may be possible to build a device uses this crystal to focus and intensify the mental energies of Aleshia. I realize the odds of using this crystal in such a way is low, but no less than using a chemical means without taking even greater risks due to the lack of significant testing, which we do not have time for. Not to mention objections have been raised against such testing."

Miles' camera focused on Minerva's face. The screen reflected some stray light into the lens, but he ignored it. "You are correct. I will not allow such testing."

Deven leaned forward. "Even if I ordered you to?" The camera zipped over to Deven's face, rotated to view Aleshia for several moments before returning to Deven but Miles remained silent. "Miles?"

The camera focused on Aleshia again then back. "I cannot

say. You agreed with me earlier, therefore the question is irrelevant."

Deven's eyes narrowed. He didn't like what he was hearing, but decided to let it go for the moment. "Minerva, where is this crystal?"

Leon waved his hands out in front of him. "Hey, wait a sec! Who is going to build this device?" Deven smiled and Leon pointed a finger. "I know that look, and I know nothing about telepathy. How am I going to build this thing?"

"I have records basic structure of what was inside the Lytherian ship. With those records and my previous research, it should be possible to create said device. The effectiveness of it is the unknown factor."

"Or the side effects," Leon said out of the corner of his mouth.

"True, but I still think it is a much smaller risk to Aleshia. Especially if we proceed slowly with low power."

Leon put both hands on his knees and hung his head. "I never thought I would say this, but I agree with Galina. You're crazy."

Galina laughed. "I never thought You would either. I must be rubbing off on you."

Leon's head popped up. "Ha! In your dreams."

"Of our limited options, this sounds like the best one." Deven turned back to Minerva's image. "Minerva? Where is the crystal?"

"Last known location I have is the research lab beneath the UN complex," Minerva said.

Leon choked. "Are you kidding? Why is it there?"

"At the time of its discovery, the UN was the center of the world's government. Since every country wanted the lab on their own land, a compromise was reached. It was placed below the central UN building, which everyone agreed was neutral territory."

Galina sighed as she folded her arms and sat back in her chair with enough energy to hear it complain. "Well so much for that! Lavine has it in his clutches for sure."

Minerva shook her head. "That is not probable. You see, not many know about the lab at this point in time. After I was constructed, the UN complex gradually became less important. The buildings were maintained by my Mechands, but they have sat unused for hundreds of years until the formation of the World Council."

Deven rubbed his chin. "So we do have an advantage."

Galina choked. "Some advantage! What do you propose we do? Walk in and say 'Hey, don't mind us, we are going into the secret lab you don't know about and remove a very rare crystal.'? Yeah, right!"

Deven grinned. "Pretty much."

Galina waved her arms. "You're insane! We are being hunted by the *Valiant*, and whatever else Lavine has managed to cobble together. I am sure the instant we show up, he is going to call them all in."

Leon sighed leaning forward placing elbows on his knees and folding his hands. "I have to agree. There is no way we could show up, blast our way in, get to the lab, grab the crystal, and get out before all hell broke loose. Heck, I don't think we would even make it to the lab. Not to mention as soon as we emerge from overdrive, Lavine is going to know something is up."

Deven's grin broadened. "Who said anything about blasting our way in?"

"You don't plan on sneaking in? Lavine must have made it the most secure place in the world by now!" Galina said.

Deven pointed to a screen then flicked his finger around the room. "Otis? Can we get in?"

Otis' face scrunched up. "Maybe if I got the latest blue prints, I could plan something out."

"And how long would that take?"

"Depends on what the security is like, and if I can find any holes. Might take a few weeks or more to be sure."

Deven shuddered. "We don't have that kind of time." He turned to face Minerva's screen. "Is our spy still operational?"

She nodded. "Yes. It would appear no one detected his transmissions to me. Either they were too brief, or Lavine is not certain what to have his security look for."

"That's our way in."

"You're nuts!" Galina said. "Even if he gets us in without tripping alarms, there is no way we are not going to be spotted."

"Perhaps."

"Perhaps nothing!"

"What if we give them enough activity above so they don't notice what is going on under their noses?"

"You have got to be joking."

"Far from it. With full shields both carriers can take on the *Valiant* without too much damage. If we create enough of a distraction above, hopefully they will ignore everything below."

"That is if Lavine doesn't have any surprises up his robe."

"True, it is a risk. But do you have a better idea?"

"No, I don't," Galina grunted.

"Minerva, how do we access the lab once inside?"

"The elevator in the back of the central building can get you inside. There are keycard slots in each elevator at the base of the control panel. With the proper card, the bottom of the shaft will slide open and you will descend into the lab."

"That should be easy enough. I can do it in my sleep. And if Minerva gives me the codes, we should be heading into the bunker seconds after entering the elevator," Otis said.

Galina shook her head. "We will still get spotted walking in and entering the elevator, not to mention trying to leave with the crystal."

Deven thought for a moment turning in his chair. "Minerva? Can our spy disable the video feeds of the main entrance and elevator?"

Otis blinked "Boss! Have you lost faith in me?"

"No, of course not. But if you do it, it will take time for you to hack in and erase your tracks. Time we may not have. Minerva? Is it possible?"

"He is not designed for system manipulation, but he does have a basic interface. If Lavine has not made drastic changes to the central surveillance system, I should be able to have him create a loop in the memory buffer of the cameras in question. But it will be subject to degradation as the cameras check their time sync with the central system."

"Can't you have the spy recreate the loop if needed?"

Minerva shook her head. "No, if I do it a second time before the first loop ends it will cause a momentary power surge triggering an alarm. And if I wait until the loop is done, they will be detected before I can start another."

"How long will it last?"

"It depends on the camera's current settings. Perhaps ten minutes."

"Boss! I can do better than that tin can. Just give me a few minutes with those cameras."

Minerva's eyes narrowed as she talked through pursed lips.

"I resent that remark. The 'tin can' as you put it is giving you an opportunity you would not have otherwise."

"I still can crack better any day of the week."

"Care to put that to the test?"

"Anytime Mechamoron."

Deven raised his hand. "Hey, we are both on the same side or did you forget that? Otis, I have no doubts you could do more than a cleaning Mechand, but I need you in the elevator and down in the lab as soon as possible. Ten minutes is going to have to be enough."

Otis nodded. "Right. Sorry Boss."

"Hey, don't say sorry to me." He pointed to Minerva.

Otis' image turned to the side. "Sorry Minerva."

Minerva nodded. "Accepted. I too owe you one as well. I am rather defensive of my units."

"I think we have a plan. Minerva prepare your landing bay. I am coming aboard."

She blinked. "You are?"

"Yes, with Aleshia and Leon. When we are aboard, Galina will jump us both into overdrive."

Minerva nodded. "Understood. I await your arrival." Minerva's face faded from the screen.

Otis gave a three fingered salute that rotated towards the camera. "See you in a few Boss." His image winked out.

Aleshia glared at Deven. "Why are we going over there?"

Galina folded her arms. "Not to mention you are taking Leon and leaving me alone!"

Miles' camera rotated. "But Galina, I will still be here, and the crew of the *Defiant*."

She rolled her eyes.

"Look, Aleshia and Otis are going down to the UN, while we create a distraction up here. I still don't trust Minerva completely, so we have to be aboard, just in case. Leon can disconnect her in a heartbeat, should it be needed. And if I only send him, she might question the reason. Not to mention, Lavine would never suspect me leaving the *Defiant*. It should keep him guessing. The longer he does, the more advantage we have." Deven gazed around the *Defiant's* bridge. "Are we in agreement?"

Galina nodded. "While I agree we need to keep Lavine guessing, do you have to take Leon? I mean, what happens if the engines go down again?"

Leon waved his hand. "Gregory can handle it."

"Yeah right, he did such a wonderful job last time," she spat.

"Hey, he got you out of there didn't he?"

"Yes he did, but he is not you."

Leon stood up. "If there is a big enough of a problem, he can call me you know."

"I doubt there will be time to make a repair call in the middle of a fire fight," Galina grumbled.

"You know this is the best way to deploy our resources." Deven stood up and helped Aleshia to her feet. "We need to get over there, time is short."

"Yeah, I know. But it doesn't mean I have to like it."

Twenty minutes later Deven was on Minerva's bridge with Otis, Aleshia and Leon. He pulled out his data tab and punched the button to contact Galina. Her face flashed onto the screen. "Jump us into overdrive to the coordinates I gave you earlier."

She nodded. "You got it. Full power in five seconds." She hit several controls causing energy to build up inside the central core. The *Defiant's* engines began to glow brighter and brighter. A second later she leapt into overdrive with the *Phoenix* following a nanosecond behind.

Halburn leaned forward in his chair as they emerged from overdrive. He watched as Naud's fingers flew over his console as he operated the scanners. "Anything?"

Naud sighed. "No Sir, the *Defiant* is not in range of this parts center either."

Halburn pounded his fist on the armrest of his chair. "Blast it! Where are they?" This was the third junk yard, or parts center as Naud liked to call them they had hit and still no sign of the *Defiant*. "They must have gone somewhere for repairs."

"Obviously not somewhere near the main skyways."

Halburn coughed before he waved his hand over the scrap yard in front of them. "Like this is on the main skyway?"

Naud shuddered. "Sorry Sir, I thought they would be here."

Halburn's voice softened. "I know Naud, it is not your fault. It was a good guess."

Rechert pointed to the blinking light on his console. "Sir, you have a call coming through."

"Three guesses who that will be," Halburn grunted.

"I don't even need one," Naud said rolling his eyes.

"Put it on the big screen here. Let's get this over with."

Rechert nodded and hit the button. A second later Lavine's face appeared. "I assume you have good news for me?"

Halburn swallowed hard. "That would be a little premature."

"Don't tell me you haven't found them yet?" Lavine said as his eyes narrowed.

"No, we haven't. But they must be doing their repairs somewhere. I am sure I will find them at the next location."

"Why don't I believe you?" Lavine swiveled in his high back chair. "By now they must have repaired their systems. You have failed me."

"Sir, I doubt they could have repaired them this quickly. At least not without a full active facility, and we have all of those covered."

"I have my doubts. Remember our discussion earlier?"

Halburn nodded. "Yes Sir, I do."

"Good, then this won't be much of a shock. Lieutenant Naud, you are to take command of the *Valiant*. Return to this building immediately. Is that understood?"

Naud stood up. "Yes Sir, it is. We will leave in a moment."

"Good. I am glad someone can follow orders." Lavine's face shrank to a dot before disappearing.

Naud turned around. "I am sorry, Sir. I don't want this. And you should know, we are behind you, not that pompous fool."

"I know." Halburn sighed as he stood up and turned towards Rechert. "Well you heard your new commander, set the course and engage the overdrive."

"Yes Sir, but–"

Halburn sighed again. "We have no other option. And he wants to see me personally, this won't be pleasant. I will be in my cabin." He shuddered. "Of course it is now yours Naud, I will get my stuff out of it and you can move in at your earliest convince."

Naud smiled. "Not necessary Sir, I never liked that cabin anyway." He winked.

"Of course." Halburn said as his shoulders sank and he made his way off of the bridge.

14

The *Defiant* exited from overdrive hovering low above an empty grassy area scarred with large craters. The *Phoenix* arrived a second later just above and behind them.

Aleshia looked out the bridge window on the *Phoenix*. "What are we doing here?"

"This area was once a great city before the war. It was one of the last casualties and no one wanted to rebuild." Deven walked over to the window and pointed to several of the large craters. "No one was left alive that lived here before. Mechands cleared the wreckage and recycled it. But nothing has been here for a long time."

"I will say again, why are we here?"

Deven smiled and pointed. "The UN complex is in that direction and not far away. We are out of their normal detection range, but we might get spotted if we stay here too long."

Aleshia raised her eyebrows and glared. "And what are we doing here?"

Deven laughed. "Dropping you off."

"What?"

"I want you and Otis in a vehicle, hugging the ground as

we emerge from overdrive over the complex. Hopefully, they will be so busy with us, you won't be noticed."

"If it was my Mechands, you would be noticed," Minerva said.

Deven nodded. "I know, and I am counting on it. Lavine will not be using an army of Mechands to keep watch, or much of your equipment outside of weapons. We should have the advantage."

"I hope so." Aleshia sighed heading towards the hatch that led off of the bridge.

"Boss, you can't be serious. The only non-Mechand vehicle in the *Phoenix's* landing bay is that old truck you came on. I can't use that. Let me get mine from Fenton. "

"We don't have time, and you know it. Besides, your truck would stand out with all of its modifications. The one I brought over is very old and will blend in better than one with a mini cannon mounted on its back or a door painted with symbols of dead Mechands."

"You have a point." Otis chuckled, grabbed his bag, started towards the hatch then stopped and turned around. "One question, why send Aleshia? I think it will be easier for me to get into the lab by myself."

"That may be true, but you may need her help to locate the crystal. And if things go bad, she can get you out in one piece."

"But why not let her get it? From what I saw at the manufacturing plant, she could tunnel her way down there without any sort of hacking needed."

"She might be able to get down there. But out again is another matter, she might be too tired at that point. Also, I don't want Lavine knowing what we are up to if at all possible. If she blasts her way in, he will. Or at least suspect."

Otis nodded. "Gotcha. Minerva, prep the landing bay. We will leave as soon as I get down there."

"The vehicle in question is ready, as is the landing bay." Otis turned back towards the hatch and climbed down the ladder. A few minutes later the truck was seen speeding away hugging the ground as it went.

Deven pulled out his data tab and tapped the link. Galina's face appeared. "I see Otis is away. Shall I jump to the target?"

"No wait fifteen minutes. We have to time this right. Is the *Defiant* ready?"

She shrugged. "As ready as she'll ever be. Everything is buttoned up and secure. Gregory thinks the engines are at peak output, I hope he is right."

The screen split as Gregory's face took up the other side. "Hey will you give me a little credit? You know I am not that bad."

Galina smiled. "Yeah I know, or at least I think I do." Gregory grumbled something as his image disappeared. "He is so easy. Much better than Leon."

Leon perked up from the other side of the *Phoenix's* bridge checking the ship's systems. "Hey! What did she say?"

Galina grinned. "Ooo two for two. I'm on a roll today." Her image winked out.

"Deven? What did Galina say?"

"The *Defiant* is ready."

"I could have told her that. I would never have left if she wasn't." Leon went back checking the systems. While Minerva should detect any problems, he wanted to be sure.

"Minerva, are your Mechands and their fighters ready?"

Minerva nodded. "Yes. And they have all been instructed to disable, not destroy."

"Good. I do not want any human casualties if we can avoid it."

The *Defiant's* engines began to glow brighter, and the *Phoenix* followed suit. "Overdrive activation in ten seconds. Prepare yourselves."

Deven looked around the sparse bridge and Leon holding onto his chair. "I think we are ready. Launch the fighters as soon as we arrive."

"Understood. Overdrive in three …two …one." The *Defiant* disappeared as it leapt into overdrive and the *Phoenix* did the same a second later.

Some distance from the UN a lone truck hovered along an old disused road. "You would think Lavine would have had this fixed," Otis grumbled.

"I doubt anyone has come this way in a long time. Why bother when the skyways are much more efficient?" Aleshia said.

"Well it would have made it easier for us," Otis said as he tried to avoid another dip in the road. He wanted to raise the truck up, but it would increase their radar profile. And he knew most, if not all, of the scanners would be watching the skies, not the ground. Or at least, he hoped. The truck shook again as it ran over inconsistencies in the road throwing off the hover system. His teeth grated. "I can't believe Deven stuck us with this old piece of junk."

"Well you did tell him you could sneak in there with ease."

"But I didn't plan on using something made before I was born! My truck would have glided over this road without so much as a hiccup."

Aleshia pointed to buildings some distance away. "I think I see the UN complex."

Otis nodded. "You do. I can't tell if anything else is in the area or not. I don't dare activate the sensors, we might be noticed."

Aleshia smiled. "No need. I will take a peek." She closed her eyes but a second later they snapped open. We've got to warn Deven¡'

"We can't, not now. If I try to contact them, we'll be spotted for sure. What did you see?"

"They're waiting for us."

The *Valiant* arrived on schedule and parked over the UN complex. Rechert tapped several keys on his console. "We are in continual hover over the UN. What now?" He glanced over to Naud who sat at his old station, refusing to sit in the commanders chair.

"We wait. I am sure Lavine will contact us in a moment." He tapped a key on his console. "Sir? We have arrived at the World Council headquarters."

"You don't need to call me sir Mr. Naud, you are in command." Halburn's voice came through the intercom.

"Sir, with all due respect I still do not want the position. And everyone aboard feels the same."

In his cabin Halburn smiled. "Thanks for that. Has Lavine called yet?"

"No Sir."

"Well, if you don't mind, I would like one last look at the bridge before I have to leave."

"Of course." Naud heard the intercom click off. "I don't

know how Lavine thinks I am going to run this ship without him. I don't have the experience."

Rechert sighed. "No one aboard does. I don't want to lose him either. I think Lavine is nuts."

"Best you kept those comments to yourself." A voice came from behind them.

They both spun around in their chairs. "Sir! We didn't–"

Halburn smiled. "Don't worry, I happen to agree with you." He gazed around the bridge. It wasn't a lot to look at, Mechand carriers never were, but it was his command. Emphasis on *was*. He turned to leave when an alert screamed through the speakers.

Naud's fingers flashed over his console. "Sir! We have something inbound and its big."

He turned back and saw a flicker out of the corner of his eye. By the time he rotated the rest of the way, the *Defiant* come out of overdrive almost on top of them and a Mechand carrier a microsecond later. "Holy! Full shields! Evasive action! Fire on them now!"

Naud blinked. "Which one?"

"The Mechand carrier! Jumping out of overdrive like that their shields might not be at full strength for a few seconds. At this range we might have a chance. FIRE!"

The *Phoenix* emerged from overdrive and began turning hard to starboard. "I regret to inform you, we have company."

"I see them Minerva. Full shields."

"We are several seconds before full shields can be utilized. I am attempting to evade."

Multiple cannons aboard the *Valiant* let loose with full

power. The beams slammed into the *Phoenix* sending them careening and Deven pulled himself back into his chair. "Blast it! They must have been waiting for us. Release the fighters."

"I am sorry, I cannot. The bay doors have been damaged."

"Cannons?"

"Two are operational."

"Use them! But not full power, remember disable not destroy."

Minerva nodded. "Understood."

"Leon, get down to the bay, see if you can get it open. Without those fighters we're in trouble."

"I'm already on it," Leon said from halfway down the hatch.

Deven whipped out his data tab and Galina's face appeared. "We took a direct hit to the landing bay and can't launch the fighters. What's your status?"

Several shots from the *Valiant* missed both ships by a hair. "We're fine. They hit us once, but the shields were more than enough. I can get between and block the shots."

"No, we need to keep him busy. We can still maneuver."

"I can launch a few vehicles."

"And take the chance the *Valiant* will zero in on them because of their weaker shields, or they might suspect a ground offensive? No, stick with the plan. Keep them guessing. We need to give Otis and Aleshia the time they need."

The truck shook as it encountered another hole in the road. Aleshia gazed up into a sky lit up repeatedly by energy blasts.

"I still think we should have warned them."

"Wouldn't have done any good. They were on top of Halburn by the time we could message. And it would have given away our position." Otis gripped the wheel tighter as he saw another shot impact the *Defiant*.

"I know, I know, but I wish there was something we could do."

"We're doing it now." The truck hovered up to a large fence. A camera on a post gazed down at them. "Smile you're on camera." He jerked a thumb towards the glass eye above.

"How do we get through?"

"Easy. We wait." A second later the gate ground open just large enough for the truck to slip through. Otis guided it inside and the gate closed behind them. "Our little spy is doing his job well."

Otis gunned the engine and a few seconds later they reached the tall glass and concrete central building. They jumped out and ran for the glass doors in front. When they reached them a Mechand, half a man in height with two arms and wheels instead of feet with an attached trash collector cart behind it rolled up to them from behind the glass. It didn't have a head, but the eyes mounted in its chest glinted from the light above. It slipped a metal hand covered in a scratch protective plastic along the door panel. The door glowed red, but as soon as the Mechand touched it, the interior lighting turned green and Otis heard several dead bolts slide open.

He pulled the door open, and they ran in. The door closed and locked behind them. "Thank you bot," Otis said looking at the Mechand. The Mechand gave a slight beep in acknowledgment and pointed to the large trash cart behind it. "What do you want?"

Aleshia looked the short Mechand up and down. "I think it wants us to hop in." The Mechand gave a little beep.

"I don't know why but okay," Otis said as they hopped into the empty cart. The Mechand's rubber tires squealed on the marble floor leaving a trail of rubber across the UN symbol as he bolted for the back of the building. The building was deceptively larger than Otis first thought, and it would have taken them several minutes to get to the elevator. But the Mechand arrived in a few seconds. They hopped out, and the Mechand placed its hand on the controls beside the door. It lit up green, and the doors slid open. "Thanks again bot." They stepped inside and the Mechand removed his hand causing the doors to close.

The elevator began to descend.

Otis whipped out his cracking card and jammed it into the slot under the keypad as Aleshia watched. "We're almost to the subbasement level, you'd better hurry."

"Don't you think I know that?" Otis snapped. "Sorry. Will be in a second." He tapped several keys on the controls strapped to his arm. The screen above them glowed as numbers and letters scrolled fast across it. "Dang it! Lavine installed two extra routines."

Aleshia sighed. "How long?" The Elevator screen display showed B3 as the car slowed. "Otis? If these doors open, we might be spotted."

Otis didn't say a word, but gave a slight nod. The car lurched, they felt a rumble right below their feet, and they shot down gaining speed. The indicator on the wall acted broken as the letters and numbers dissolved. Otis looked up from the small screen on his arm. "About that long."

Aleshia blinked. "You got it?"

His face gave a lopsided grin. "Was there ever any doubt?"

"We are going a long way down. Where is this lab? The center of the planet?"

Otis shrugged. "I don't know. I assumed they put it deep to prevent any scanners from detecting it."

The elevator car came to a sudden stop that almost knocked them off their feet as the doors opened.

Halburn's teeth grated as he felt another shot graze the *Valiant's* shields. "We managed to get several shots through that Mechand carrier's shields, keep pouring it on!"

Naud's fingers flew over his controls. "I am trying Sir, but their shields are now up to full strength, and between the two targets running interference for each other, it is proving difficult."

"I don't care how difficult it is! We can't let this opportunity slide through our fingers." Halburn tilted his head as another shot impacted their shields. "Damage?"

"Nothing of any consequence, Sir."

Halburn stood up and walked over to Naud. He paused looking down at the console and gripped Naud's chair. "What is he up to? He has us out gunned at the center of the world's government, is not taking advantage of it, and not one fighter has been launched."

Naud pointed to his screen. "See this here? I think we did enough damage to the Mechand carrier's hanger bay that they can't."

"Perhaps, but it does not explain why they haven't launched any from the *Defiant*."

"True Sir. One thing is for certain, they aren't even hitting us with half the power their cannons are capable of." A console beeped. "Sir? Lavine is trying to contact us."

Halburn's frowned. "Now? Let him hang. We're too busy."

A second later Lavine's face appeared on the large screen in front of them. "Commander Naud, what in the world is going– Halburn? What are you doing on the bridge?"

Naud launched a new pattern, guiding their cannons, trying to probe for a weakness in the Mechand carrier's shields while Rechert tried to keep them from being hit themselves. "Sir? I am sorry but we are a bit busy. Can you call back in a bit?"

Lavine's eyes blazed. "What?! How dare you! I order you to relieve Halburn, take command and take care of this situation."

"We are Sir."

Halburn took a step closer to the screen. "Lavine, if you don't see they need me more now than ever, you are a bigger fool than I thought possible."

Lavine's bottom jaw dropped for a microsecond before he closed it again. "How dare you! I–"

"If we save your backside and ours, then you can do with me what you want. Naud, get his face off of my screen."

Naud smiled. "Yes Sir." He tapped a button and Lavine's face disappeared but not before he swore several times. "I am sorry about that Sir. It would seem Lavine enabled some sort of override on the communications system."

"Blast him! I suspected he didn't trust anyone, but this is going too far. Can you disable the override so he doesn't do it again?"

"Already done, Sir." The *Valiant* rocketed over and around the Mechand carrier for a clear shot, but was cut off by the *Defiant*. The energy blasts hit the shields head-on, they flickered, but held. "Sir? Did you see that?"

"I did. Try that again. We might be getting somewhere."

"Unless they start using their cannons at full strength," Rechert said.

"True. But I don't think he will." Halburn leaned forward. "Deven, what in the world are you up to?"

A console blew nearby and Galina swore as the front port shield flickered. She slammed her hand on the intercom "Gregory! What are you doing down there? Knitting?"

"Hey, I'm trying!"

"Well try harder. The port bow shield is failing."

"I know! I have rerouted it to the starboard aft shield. It should hold for a bit. Unless they saw the instability, then we could be in trouble."

Miles' camera turned. "I agree. And the probability of that is low."

"Miles! Aren't you supposed to be firing, not talking to us?"

"But Galina, I am. I can do both."

Galina rolled her eyes as she guided the *Defiant* into a dive and came up behind the *Valiant*. "I am done fooling around. Miles hit them, *hard*."

"But Galina, Deven said–"

"I know what Deven said. But we can't afford more hits like that or we are not going home in one piece! Take out their engines, or at least some maneuverability, *now*."

"Very well. Cannons set to full strength, targeting the *Valiant's* engines. I have a lock. Firing." Several energy beams lashed out from the *Defiant's* cannons and crashed into the *Valiant's* shields near their engines. The first two did nothing, but Miles knew this particular carrier design's shield emitters would overload for half a second opening a hole. The following beams slipped through that hole and smashed into the *Valiant's* engines. A small explosion a few seconds later took out one of them causing the glow from the exhaust port behind it to extinguish.

"There you blackard! Take that! Not so fast now, are you?" Galina pulled hard on the controls causing the *Defiant* to bank and climb as several shots from the *Valiant* missed, unable to keep up with the maneuver.

Deven's teeth grated as he watched the *Defiant* take out one of the *Valiant's* engines. "What in the world is she doing?"

"It would appear she attacked with full power to the *Defiant's* cannons," Minerva said.

"I know that!" He pulled out his data tab and hit a key. A second later Galina's face appeared. "Galina? What's going on? I told you not to use full cannons."

"We are kind of busy now. Can you call back later?"

"Galina! I am in no mood for–"

"Listen, you haven't launched fighters, as part of the plan. We took several concentrated direct hits for you and it almost took out one of our shields. What we were doing wasn't getting us anywhere. I gave them a bloody nose. That's all."

"You did more than that! One of their engines is scrap metal."

She grinned. "I know. Sure makes it easier to keep ahead of them."

"Galina–"

"I could have had Miles take out their whole engine block, not just one. They are a bit slower but okay otherwise. If we don't go home in one piece, we lose. I did what I had to keep the *Defiant* going!"

"But Galina, you told me take out their engines or reduce maneuverability. I made the decision for maneuverability," Miles' voice came through the speaker.

"Shut up Miles! I knew what you would do. We couldn't take out all of their engines with their shields up. It wasn't tactically sound."

"That is true."

Deven's eyes narrowed. "I understand your reasons, but there are other ways. Do not–" He didn't get to finish before a blast from the surface impacted their shields and sent the *Phoenix* careening until Minerva could regain control. He gripped the chair to not be thrown from it "Minerva? Status?"

"It would appear Lavine has installed surface mounted cannons at this location. They are not as powerful as ours, but they are adding to the complexity of the situation."

"Damage?"

"No damage beyond one fighter that was not locked down at the time in the bay. However, shield energy is being diminished now at an increased rate with the addition of these weapons. I can't avoid them all. I estimate we have another seven minutes until failure."

Galina gripped her controls tight enough that her knuckles turned white. "You were saying?"

Deven gritted his teeth. "Do what you have to stay in one piece. But try to do as little damage as possible. Clear?"

"As crystal." Galina nodded and her face shrank to a point and disappeared.

"Minerva? Use the frequency and code I gave you earlier. This part of the plan may not work now, but I have to try."

Minerva nodded. "Channel open."

Lavine pounded his fist on the desk. "How dare Halburn talk to me like that! When I get him in here, he is going to regret ever being born!"

His data tab flashed indicating an incoming call.

"Ah good. He has come to his senses." Lavine accepted, but it wasn't Halburn's face that appeared.

"Chairman Lavine, it's so good to see you. Could you please stop trying to blast us out of the sky?" Deven pointed to the air outside of the carrier's window.

"Doran!"

"So glad you remembered me Chairman, would you kindly tell your weapons platforms to stop so we can talk?"

Lavine noticed the bulkhead behind Deven and it wasn't the *Defiant's*. "Doran, what are you trying to pull? You are not on the *Defiant*?"

"Ah no I am not. But we can discuss that later. I don't know if you realized, but they fired on us first. If we all agree to stop blasting each other, perhaps we can talk about this?"

Lavine wasn't falling for it. "I say again, what are you trying to pull?"

"But they did fire first."

Lavine waved his hand. "Whether they did or not is inconsequential. You will find, they will be the ones to fire last, unless you want to surrender."

Deven shrugged. "Who said I didn't? We did come here after all."

Lavine's head cocked to one side. "You actually came here to surrender? Why do I doubt that?"

"I don't know. But what's the harm in discussing the situation in a less hostile atmosphere?"

"Very well." Lavine tapped a key on his data tab and the screen split showing a man on the right side in a black uniform with the letters UN prominently over the right pocket. *I need to get their uniforms updated.* He sighed. "Stop the assault on the carriers overhead."

The man blinked. "Sir? Are you sure?"

Lavine nodded. "Yes I am sure. Now do it."

"Yes Sir." His image faded leaving only Deven's which refilled the entire screen.

The ground cannons stopped but Deven rocked to the one side as another shot impacted the carrier's shields. "Thanks, but we are still getting hit."

Lavine's eyes narrowed as he hit another button on his data tab. A few seconds later the screen split again and an image of the *Valiant's* bridge appeared. "Halburn! Stop your assault this instant!"

Halburn stooped over Naud's console, straightened. "What? Have you lost your mind?"

Lavine's teeth grated. "I am not going to say it again. And I suggest you follow orders, for once."

Halburn shook his head. "You are not making sense."

"I don't have to, but if you most know, I am talking to Doran now. He says you fired first and was only coming to discuss the situation. Not launch an all out attack."

Halburn straightened. "While I agree we did fire first, you can't believe him? He is up to something. Trust me when I say he isn't here to talk."

"Then why am I talking with him now?"

While Deven couldn't see the image aboard the *Valiant*, he could hear the conversation. "Odell? Why do you assume I didn't come here to talk?"

Halburn blinked. "Deven?"

"The one and only."

Lavine tapped a key and the image split on Deven's screen letting him see both men. "As you can see, I am talking with him. Cease your attack."

"I don't care what he is saying. He is up to something. He wouldn't be here otherwise ..." His voice trailed off. "Deven? Where are you? That doesn't look like the *Defiant*." He squinted at the image. "You are on that Mechand carrier!"

Deven nodded. "Yes I am, so would you kindly stop shooting at me?"

"What in blazes are you doing there? I can't imagine you leaving your ship!"

"As I was about to tell the Chairman here, I am aboard this carrier as I do not trust the Nexus, not after all she has done. I am sitting on her, and at the least variation I am pulling the plug." Off to the side, Minerva grumped.

Halburn rubbed his chin. "Oh really?"

Deven nodded. "Yes."

"Sorry, no, I still don't believe you especially after the last stunt you pulled. Halburn out." His face disappeared from both screens.

Lavine tried to force the redness coalescing on his face back. "I am sorry about this. He will be taken care of."

"That is quite all right Chairman, you did stop the land cannons and I thank you for that. But if you can't stop Halburn, I don't see how we can talk. I can't come to your office in this situation." His image shook as the *Valiant's* cannons managed to hit the carrier again.

The doors whooshed open sucking in the smell of stale recycled air. No one had been here for a long time. Many thin red energy lines crisscrossed the short hallway beyond creating a deadly blockade. Aleshia frowned. "Nobody mentioned this."

"No, they didn't." Otis said while tapping on his keyboard.

"I can take care of this easy." Aleshia raised a hand, but Otis grabbed it. Aleshia glared and almost shoved him mentally into the wall out of reflex.

"No! If you wreck them, I'm betting every alarm in this place will go off and Lavine will know we are down here. Or more importantly there *is* something down here."

"Oh . . . right. I didn't think of that."

Otis smiled. "That is why you have me. Give me a minute here." He tapped more commands, and the screen scrolled green text even faster. "Ah found it!" He pressed a button and the deadly beams shut down. He pulled his card from the elevator's slot, and they stepped out into the hallway. The elevator doors closed behind them a second later. They walked towards the frosted security glass and steel doors on the other end, but the doors, while being automatic, refused to open at their approach.

"Great, another locked door."

"Yeah, but I now know their codes." He slipped his card in the small slot below the optical scanner. A second later the doors slid open. "See? Told you."

Walking inside, Aleshia sucked in a breath. There were giant racks of equipment throughout the space of the room, but in the center of the floor held parts. Parts of a machine not built by human hands. Most of the structure was a layered green material unlike any they had ever seen. It curved in very organic looking lines, but it was clearly a metal of some sort. But the most unusual aspect was all the damage appeared to be from dissection rather than destruction.

"Otis? What do you see when you look at this?"

"I see something taken apart with great care. No way this was blown up."

"Exactly. Yet we were told the Lytherian pilot destroyed the ship after a long stand off. This doesn't make sense."

"No it don't. Let's find that crystal and get out of here," Otis paused to check the time displayed at the top of the screen mounted on his arm, "the loop is half over."

"Where do we start?" Aleshia regarded the large room that could have doubled for a warehouse.

Otis pointed to the far side of the room where tables with consoles connected to various testing equipment sat. "Perhaps over there?"

Aleshia shrugged. "As good as any." They walked over and Aleshia pointed to the other side. "You start from that end of the room, I will look here."

"You got it." Otis ran for the other end and started powering some equipment.

Aleshia continued along the line of tables and consoles holding out a hand, feeling with her mind. She took another step and her eyes went wide as she crumpled to the floor with the worst headache she had ever experienced. "Otis! Whatever you did, undo it!" Tears ran down her cheeks.

Otis whipped his head over to see Aleshia on the floor, he slammed the off control on the device he had turned on. He ran over to Aleshia, put his hand on her shoulder and leaned closer. "You okay?"

Aleshia climbed to her feet and shook her head, the tears

still very prominent on her cheeks. "It's better now. Wow, what was that?"

"I don't know. I just turned it on."

Aleshia shook her head again. "Which one?"

He led her over to the keyboard and a dark screen that sat a couple of meters from the end. "This one."

"This has got to be it." She looked up and down the table. "But I don't see a crystal anywhere."

"Hmm I have an idea." He dove under the table. "Ah ha! They did wire the connections. I thought so, with the amount of security around here, it would have been crazy not to." He traced the wires neatly bundled along the underside of the table and down to the corner of the room, then over. He continued following until reaching the opposite side of the room near the doors. The cable split off from the others and ran across the ceiling and down to a rack of equipment. The cable ended at a heavy metal box a foot square with a still glowing keypad. "Bingo."

Aleshia ran over. "Found it?"

"Either that or they started armoring plain boxes with electrical connections and keypads."

"Great let's grab it and go." Aleshia reached for the handle.

"Wait a sec! I am betting there is some sort of motion detection on that box." He found a slot on the bottom of the keypad and slipped in his card. "Good thing this box appears to be something they cobbled together quick, instead of a careful design. The keypad shouldn't have an access slot."

"How long? There can't be much time left on the video loop."

"Yeah, give me a few." He tapped several keys as code flowed on his small screen. "Got it!" The box's lit keypad flashed then went dark. He unplugged the connecting cable and grabbed the handle. "Now we can go." They bolted for the doors and a few seconds later were in the elevator heading up to the ground floor. When the doors slid open, the Mechand beeped and pointed to its trash hopper behind him. They nodded and jumped in.

The Mechand burned rubber again, and they shot towards the front door. Otis checked the clock on his screen. "Less than a minute left. We're not going to make it." The Mechand increased its speed, then a few seconds later left skid marks as it managed to stop a millimeter from the doors. It placed a hand on the access plate and the door's glow turned from red to green. But the Mechand didn't wait for Otis and Aleshia to get out. It shot through the doors at full speed. They fell backwards into the hopper. "Bot? What are you doooooing?" It gave a beep and continued on.

They were thrown around inside the hopper as it made several sharp turns and arrived five seconds later at the truck. Aleshia climbed out of the hopper, shook her head, and rubbed her shoulder. "Well *that* was fun."

Otis climbed out. "Thanks bot. You can go back now before you are missed."

The Mechand beeped and lowered its arms in a shallow slump.

"I think he said they will know he helped us."

Another beep emanated from the Mechand.

"I think he wants to come with us."

Otis' mouth shot open. "What? You can't be serious?"

Another beep came from the Mechand, but much lighter in tone.

Otis looked down into the Mechand's optics and could swear he saw fear. But he pushed it back. "I must be crazy.

All right, but we'll need a couple of anti-gravs to put him in the back. I don't have ramps with me."

Aleshia smiled. "That's not a problem." She raised her arms and as she did so the Mechand also rose into the air. She flicked a wrist, and it slid into the back of the truck.

"Oh, right, forgot about that." Otis hopped into the drivers seat, and they took off as soon as Aleshia got inside the cab. The gate sat closed at the end. "Great, the gate is closed. And we don't have time for me to crack it. I guess Lavine is going to see us leave." He hit the accelerator.

"Otis! What are you doing?"

"The only thing we can, go through."

The Mechand beeped as it held out its hand, it extended forward to reach out beyond the front of the truck. Otis' eyes widened at the arm extending past his window but he understood. He pressed the accelerator further, and the truck increased its speed. "Otis!" Aleshia shrieked as they shot towards the gate. But a few seconds before they rammed it, the gate detected the Mechand's clearance and retracted. They shot through with inches to spare. Aleshia's head spun around in time to see the gate closing. "Let's not do that again."

The Mechand retracted its arm and beeped in agreement.

Otis chuckled. "For once bot, you have taken the words right out of my mouth."

Aleshia hit the button on the data tab mounted on the dash sending an encrypted signal. They continued on until they were well out of detection range then climbed into the sky.

A light lit up on *Phoenix's* bridge and Minerva gave a facial motion telling Deven everything.

"Well Chairman, since you can't seem to control your own people, I see no point in staying here any further." A console near him shorted and sparks flew as the ship shuddered throwing him back and forth in his seat. "Not to mention the *Valiant* is about to punch holes through us." Deven inclined his head. "Another time Chairman." Deven waved before the connection cut. He tapped another button and Galina appeared. "You got the signal?"

"Yep, overdrive is online but I don't know how long. Gregory patched it once already."

"I think we overstayed our welcome anyway. Let's get out of here."

"You got it. Full power in ten seconds." Another shot rocked the *Defiant*. "Blast it! Port shields went down, and the *Valiant* is moving in for another shot. I can't keep them away from it."

"Minerva, cover their port side."

Minerva nodded. "We are moving to intercept." The *Phoenix* came up and in-between the two vessels. Charged energy particles rocked the carrier. Most of the shots reflected off the shields, but one shot slipped through the hitting the hull on their port side leaving a large hole. "Damage port side, but not in a critical system, I can compensate."

"Good. Galina? Ready?"

"Past ready. Overdrive activated. Hang on." The *Defiant's* engines glowed brighter and a second later disappeared as she jumped into overdrive. The *Phoenix* followed a nanosecond after.

15

Halburn sighed as he pushed the button to send the elevator up its shaft to Lavine's office on the top floor. The anti-grav system kicked in and shot him up like a bullet. The car stopped with a jolt and Halburn shook his head, not remembering the car being that fast before. He put a hand over his middle, but his stomach was still on the ground floor. The doors opened to reveal a large man in a black uniform with the letters UN on the patches.

"Halburn," the man said looking at him, "Chairman Lavine will see you now."

Halburn sized the man up. The guard was over a foot taller, covered in rippling muscles his uniform couldn't hide, and probably dumb as a brick. Just the way Lavine liked them. "Did Lavine think I would run, so he sent you?"

The large man shrugged his over-muscled shoulders. "I can't say, all I know is he told me to escort you to his office."

Halburn sighed again. "Fine, but I know the way." He walked with a dragged gate. The walls were a plain light blue, but the floors were synth marble and very ornate. While the ground floor had real marble, the upper floors had used a more durable synthetic for weight and safety reasons. At least he assumed all the floors had it. It could be only Lavine's did.

He stopped at the end of the hall and pushed a button near the door.

The large man next him shot forward, opened the door, and stepped behind. "No need for that, he is expecting you."

"Oh I know but–" He didn't get a chance to finish before the guard shoved him into the room and closed the door.

Lavine was standing looking out the window but turned around as the door closed. "Well well well, you showed up after all. Some of my staff had bets you wouldn't. Of course, they don't know, I know, or I would have to fire the lot. And it is so hard to get good help these days." Lavine cracked a grin making Halburn think it was better before he smiled. He regained his composure and nodded.

"Chairman Lavine, you wanted to see me?"

Lavine stepped forward, his long robes waving as he did. "Me? Did I? Now why would I want to see you? Perhaps because you have failed me time and time again? Failed to obey me and relinquish command of the *Valiant*? Or perhaps it was because the *Defiant* almost lands on top of you and you still can't take them down. Heck, even when they leave, you don't even follow them!"

"How could we? We were one engine short of an overdrive!"

"Excuses! All I hear is excuses!"

"Sir, I–"

"Silence! You have failed, failed, failed. You won't have command of a row boat from now on."

"But–"

"You are lucky I am not throwing you into an electro cell!"

Halburn blinked and had enough. Anger bubbled up and shot out of him. "Now you listen to me you pompous windbag! I did everything you asked and more! Now sure

I didn't take down the *Defiant* or the Mechand carrier but I was outgunned and outclassed in every aspect. No one could have done better, and you know it! Heck, everyone else would have done far worse. Furthermore, all of that was just a distraction."

Lavine took another step closer as his teeth grated. "A distraction? You think all of that was a distraction? When I brought the ground defenses online we had them. Doran contacted me to discuss his surrender. I agreed to halt the guns, but you refused my orders!"

Halburn folded his hands behind his back, turned away then back. "Surrender? I can't imagine that. He had us in the palm of his hand, all he had to do was squeeze. Did he use the word 'Surrender'?"

Lavine thought for a moment. "No, he didn't."

"I am certain it was part of the distraction, and to get you to call off your guns. To buy more time, which he did."

Lavine's eyes narrowed. "Are you saying he played me?"

Halburn saw Lavine's face and didn't want to lose the progress he had made thus far. "I wouldn't say played, Chairman, more like a tactical advance. I know him, so I can see his methods, but I doubt anyone else could."

Lavine's look softened. "I see. And for what reason would he have to use such a distraction?"

Halburn walked over to the large window and gazed down to the trees in the courtyard below. He stood there for several minutes before turning around. "Did you notice the rubber tire marks on the ground floor?"

Lavine blinked. "Tire marks? Across my marble floor? No I didn't, but I'm sure they weren't there this morning."

Halburn nodded. "I thought not. I assume you have not checked the security system for an intrusion?"

"An intrusion? Here? If there was anything of the sort, it would have triggered every alarm in the building," Lavine said with a wave of his hand.

"Then, why are there tread marks on the ground floor? Don't you suspect it has something to do with the *Defiant* being here? I sure do."

"You may have a point." Lavine walked over behind his desk and sat in the padded chair. He typed in his access to the console to the right of his desk and a second later the screen filled with tiny squares. Each square showed a different camera. He tapped on the camera in the main lobby but nothing showed what made the tracks. He backed up and forwarded the recording several times but they suddenly appear at one point with no indication of how. "I have to admit, this is very unusual."

Halburn leaned over Lavine's desk so he could see the details on the small images. "Tread marks don't suddenly appear. Something must have made them. I think your security system has been compromised."

Lavine shook his head. "Not possible. You know as well as I, if the recording was altered, there would be a discrepancy in the time stamp. Not to mention the key signature. These are intact."

Halburn folded his arms. "Something bypassed the recording system at the time, giving us a normal image."

Lavine sat back in his chair. "No, if someone had accessed the system, it would show here."

"Unless they bypassed that as well."

"How? Such an alteration would leave tracks."

Halburn shook his head. "Not if you built the system."

Lavine's eyes went wide. "The Nexus?"

Halburn nodded. "The Nexus. Didn't Mechands maintain

this facility for years? It would know every system, and its weaknesses. Check the door locks, were they ever accessed during the time the *Defiant* was here?" Lavine accessed another screen and several columns of data flowed past. "Wait! Backup two pages. I thought I saw something." Lavine paged back and Halburn's hand shot forward to point at one small line. "There! The main gates were opened, and shortly after the one of the front doors was unlocked. And almost ten minutes later, the same door was accessed again. But there is no signature as to who did it." Halburn turned and started towards Lavine's office door.

"And where are you going?" Lavine said suddenly annoyed. "I didn't give you permission to leave."

Halburn turned. "Lavine? Really? You had a major security breach and would never have known if it wasn't for me. I'm going to find what was so important Deven would stage an attack for. You can stay here if you want, but I'm going with or without your permission." He turned back towards the door and continued on.

Lavine hopped up but held his anger in check. "You have a point. But I will accompany you. Or rather you will accompany me."

Halburn rolled his eyes then stopped and turned back toward the Chairman, gesturing towards the door. "By all means, after you Chairman."

"Thank you," Lavine said as he flowed past, his robes rippling with the movement. Halburn rolled his eyes again once the man was in front.

Down in the lobby Halburn pointed to the marks across the floor. "As I said, tire marks. And they would seem to lead to one of the back elevators. Why that one?" Halburn got down on his haunches to get a closer look at the rubber stretching across the marble. His head came up. "Lavine? Do you have any Mechands in this building?"

"Only one. It is a simple cleaning Mechand. It is so simple it did not shut down with the Nexus."

Halburn stood up and rubbed his chin. "And let me guess, it has rubber wheels?"

Lavine's eyes went wide. "Why, I you're right! I forgot about that."

Halburn smiled. "When you see something every day, it is easy to forget such details. That Mechand is how they got in undetected, I have no doubt."

"Perhaps, but still, what for? Nothing has been reported missing. I suspect you chased him off before he got whatever they came for."

Halburn shook his head and pointed at the floor. "No, there are two sets of marks here. Meaning they got in and out."

"Or they made a mistake and aborted."

"I don't think so. Both tracks go to the one elevator in back. Where does it go?"

Lavine shrugged. "The same place as the rest. Nothing special about it."

"Then why did they take that one and pass all the others which would have been faster?"

Lavine looked at the closer elevators along the wall, and the one the tracks lead to it. "You have a point." He saw Halburn quickly walking towards the far end of the building. "Where are you going now?"

"To find out what they were interested in," Halburn shouted over his shoulder.

Lavine grunted and ran after him holding up his robes. He reached Halburn a second before the elevator doors closed. They road the car up and down several times checking every floor, but nothing showed any signs of usage. "I told you, nothing was reported missing. And no other doors show access logs."

"I know. It must be something not obvious." Halburn smiled as he noticed the slot under the elevator controls. "Chairman, do you have an access card?"

Lavine puffed up his chest. "Of course I do! Although, we don't use them very much since the building was retrofitted with hand scanners long before we came here. In fact, I have never used mine."

"Do you have it on you?"

"Of course!"

Halburn's smile broadened as he held out his hand. "May I see it please?" Lavine rolled his eyes as he reached into his robes and pulled out a small card and handed it to him. Halburn stuck it into the slot and pressed the down button.

"What good is that going to do? We are in the basement now! It doesn't go down any further than–" They heard a sound beneath their feet, as if something was sliding open and they shot down with increasing speed. "What in the name of–"

Halburn smiled. "I thought so. I knew it couldn't be hidden above, or we would have found it. That left below."

"But how did you know my key would work?"

"I assumed you have the same card the original Chairman had when this was built. And since you didn't change anything, that card still would have access." The car stopped with a jolt and the doors slid open. A slight layer of dust on the floor showed two distinct sets of footprints down the hall. Halburn smiled as he pointed. "They were here." Lavine remained silent as they walked to the far end and he used the card again. The doors opened to reveal not dust but a large room with racks of storage and equipment filling the space.

"No dust," Lavine said looking around.

"No, the air must be filtered in here. But that's not what concerns me." He walked over to a large piece of angular smoothed metal sticking up from the floor and pointed. "This on the other hand, does."

Lavine followed. "I don't know why. This is just bits of an old Mechand hull."

Halburn pointed at the lines along the metals edge. "Are you really that stupid?"

Lavine's eyes blazed. "How dare you–"

"Listen to me. This was not built by humans. Look at the lines and metal of this." He gestured around the room to all the large pieces scattered across the floor, carefully dismantled, moved down here, and reassembled into various sections. Cryptic labels around each section were painted on the floor itself. "We didn't build any of this."

"Then who did?"

"That, my dear Chairman, is the question."

The *Defiant* and *Phoenix* emerged from overdrive short of their target. "I'm sorry," Gregory's voice came through the intercom, "this is as far as we are going to get until 'fix it fingers' Leon has a crack at the engines."

Galina watched the Earth turning far below. "Well, at least the upper Midwest isn't very populated these days."

"Hey, perhaps Minerva's bunker has parts we can use. It isn't far from here."

Galina shook her head. "Nope. From what Deven said,

the founders didn't plan on the Mechand factories being dismantled. They only gave her the carrier, fighters, and the bunker itself." She togged the link. "How are you over there?"

Minerva's face appeared. "We are in one piece, other than that, I won't comment."

Leon's face slid in next to Minerva's. "We aren't that bad. A hole in the hull the Mechands are patching as we speak. It wasn't in a vital area, but you would think so from the way Minerva talks."

"How would you like it if you had a hole in your arm? It is vital to you, yes?"

"Yes Minerva, we know. The shields also need repair, along with a few other systems. How is the *Defiant*? I know the drives are not good, or we wouldn't be here."

"Good guess. I was aiming for the Pacific not the Midwest."

"Put Gregory on."

"One sec." Galina tapped several keys. "Go ahead."

"Gregory, can you hear me?"

A clang and swearing came from the intercom. "Yes Leon, I can hear you."

"He sounds more like you all the time," Galina said.

"Shhh. What's the problem?"

"What's the problem? The engines need to be pulled that is the problem! I have tried everything!"

"Did you check the phasing? I bet they were knocked out of sync again. The last time I fixed it was a patch as we didn't have time at Fenton's to pull them."

"I did check the phasing."

"The whole spectrum?"

"Er . . . no. I didn't think of that."

"Take a look. It is rare, but possible especially since I had to adjust the other engines to compensate. The imbalance might be in a location the diagnostics don't check by default."

Leon and Galina heard equipment being moved around. "We'll I'll be. You're right. It's another phase imbalance between two and three."

Leon smiled. "I thought so. Adjust engine two like we did before, that should cancel it out for now. I will work on them later."

"I've got this. Galina give me five and we should have overdrive back." The intercom clicked off.

"Leon, it will be good when you are back aboard," Miles said.

"Miles! Where have you been?" Galina asked.

"First, you tell me to be quiet unless spoken to, now you wonder where I have been." His camera lowered. "I wish you would make up your mind."

Leon smiled. "She's a woman Miles, they never do." His face disappeared before Galina could say anything.

High above the Pacific ocean the *Defiant* and *Phoenix* hovered. Most of the damage occurred during the distraction at the UN had been repaired, or at least patched until a permanent fix with replacement parts could be done.

Leon worked under the augmented chair attached to the *Phoenix's* bridge. He hated leaving all the repair work to Gregory and the Mechands, but his job was here. While Gregory had become very capable—even if he didn't think so— he was not yet up to this challenge.

The apparatus looked like a cross between a captain's chair

and a torture device, but it was the best he could come up with on such short notice. The back went up far behind the head and a harness above held several electrode contacts extending down and attached to Aleshia's forehead. It had taken several days of tests, but he managed to find a certain power frequency that forced the crystal to give regulated waves. Instead of the random ones that caused headaches. He still worried about the safety of the device and he added several more sensitive relays that would blow rather than harm Aleshia.

Minerva frowned. Her screen flickered as Leon connected another data line to her core. "Could you be more careful? That gave me quite the jolt."

Leon looked up. "Sorry Minerva. I'm rushing a bit I know, but we don't have any idea how long before the Lytherians attack."

"I realize this, but blowing out my core won't help matters."

Leon cocked his head. "That is a data cable not a main power line, it shouldn't fry your core."

"True, but my core is a delicate system. Any damage is unacceptable."

"I know." Leon paused to look at the cable and the connections to the chair. "Is there a way I could have connected it better?"

"No. Other than powering down my core."

Leon laughed. "And I suspect you wouldn't have wanted me to do that either."

"That is correct."

Leon laughed again. "You have been talking with Galina too much."

Minerva blinked. "But I have not–"

Leon raised a hand. "Never mind. Test the connection. Do you have control?"

Minerva nodded. "I do. The chair, power output, and crystal harmonics are all under my direct control."

An image of a camera eye appeared on the screen opposite of Leon and a voice came through the speaker. "Leon, I do not think this is wise. Why could the chair not be deployed on the *Defiant*?"

"Miles, we went over this before. The *Defiant* suffered more damage to the bridge which had to be repaired first. This was the fastest method."

"I disagree. If you and Gregory worked on the *Defiant's* damaged systems, the time differential would have been marginal."

Leon folded his arms. "That is your opinion. It is not mine, nor was it Deven's. Do you want me to tell him of this conversation?"

The camera's iris on the screen contracted then expanded. "No. I am sorry if I overstepped. My concern is for Aleshia. And I would feel better if I had control of the device."

"Miles, would you feel better if I gave you remote access to the chair and its systems?" Minerva asked. Her gaze had softened from before when he first called. She understood his feelings, even if he wasn't suppose to have them. His continued evolution had surprised even her.

The iris on the screen shifted again. "That would be acceptable. Thank you."

Minerva nodded as her eyes shifted back and forth. "You should now have access to it."

The lights on the back of the chair glowed and dimmed a second later. "I do. Thank you." The screen with Miles' camera eye shrank to a point and disappeared.

Leon smiled. "You seem to be dealing with him better than before."

Minerva's image gave a shrug. "He is my child. I realized I needed to treat him as such, but balance it with the understanding his experiences give him a unique insight I lack. Not to mention respect his opinions even if we do not agree."

Leon's smiled broadened. "You do sound like a mother."

"But I am."

"Of course." Leon walked over to the communications console and tapped a button. A second later Devon's face appeared. "How are the repairs?"

"Gregory has made good progress. We are still a little rough over here, but everything is functional again." Deven pointed to a console that was burned except for the new interface. "How is the project going?"

"It is online. You can send Aleshia over."

Deven's eyes narrowed. "Are you sure you have the crystal under control? The first time you tried to power it, she screamed and went unconscious."

Leon didn't need the reminder. He shifted his stance as he remembered the scream. A scream he had caused. She had grabbed her head in pain and slumped to the floor and remained motionless for hours after the crystal had been powered for a second. He shuddered as his eyes closed with the image replaying *again*. He opened them and licked his lips. "I told you it was due to the inaccuracy of Minerva's data. The harmonics were way off. But I have since found a way to keep them stable."

"You're sure?"

Leon's eyes narrowed, and he jabbed a finger towards the

screen. "Deven, how long have we known each other? Have I ever tried to mislead you?"

Deven held up his hand. "I know. But this is Aleshia's life we are talking about."

Leon shot forward insulted. "I have put enough protection relays into this, it will fall to pieces if she sneezes rather than harm her! But I will stay here to monitor it."

Deven shook his head. "You are needed here more. We need the *Defiant* at 100% as soon as possible. She took more hits running interference for the *Phoenix*."

"But–"

"Otis will be coming over with Aleshia. He can pull the plug if need be. Understood?"

Leon felt a weight in his stomach but forced it back. Otis could watch over and unplug it just as well. But still, he wanted to be here. His eyes shifted to Deven who was waiting for an answer. "Yes." It was all he could say.

"Good. They will be over in a minute. Come back in the same truck."

"Acknowledged," Leon said as he killed the connection. He turned. "Minerva? Take good care of Aleshia. If anything happens to her, I will be coming for you. And you do not want that."

Minerva's image shuddered. "I wouldn't dream of letting anything happen to Aleshia. She will be safe. Trust me."

"She had better be."

A cold wind blew through the *Phoenix's* hanger bay. Leon shivered even though the winds did not reach him inside the control room. He watched as the doors continued to grind open. While the repairs were completed, and they were functional, the doors still complained when used. Leon saw the old truck slide into the bay. Distracted for a few moments by the Mechand he wasn't expecting in the back of the truck, Minerva started closing the doors before he could press the button. "I could have done that," he muttered.

The screen nearest him lit up with Minerva's face. "I didn't say you couldn't. But time–."

"I'm well aware–"

"I am sure you are; however, there is a new development. The Lytherian *Command* carrier has arrived."

"What? That arrived several days ago."

"No, what we assumed was the Lytherian *Command* carrier arrived several days ago. It would seem the assumption was incorrect." Minerva showed the most recent images from the probe on the screen on the opposite side of Leon's control panel. "As you can see."

Leon examined the gigantic vessel. It was by far the largest, including the previous ship they assumed was the *Command* carrier. "Yes that has to be it. Wow, look at the size. But why did it arrive now? There hasn't been any new ships in days. It does not make any sense."

Minerva shrugged. "I do not know. If I were to speculate, I would suggest they were waiting to see if anything else arrived to challenge them before bringing in the *Command* carrier."

Leon's eyebrow went up. "Waiting to see if anything else arrived? But they know we lack the technology to reach them."

"That is correct. However, I cannot see any other reason for this delay."

Leon rubbed his chin. "Unless they're being very cautious.

And the last ship did look similar. But such a deception seems like *overkill* for us."

"Indeed. It is a mystery." Several indicators turned green on the panel. "Bay is pressurized."

"Thanks Minerva. I had better give them the bad news. I assume you have briefed Deven?"

"I have contacted the *Defiant* yes, but Miles beat me to it." Her image flickered and disappeared.

Leon ran out of the control room to find Otis and Aleshia climbing out of the truck. "Better get up to the bridge," he said moving past Otis and into the truck.

Otis turned. "Hey, what's the hurry?"

Leon slammed the door shut and opened the window. "The Lytherian *Command* carrier has arrived. Minerva can fill you in. Deven wants me back aboard the *Defiant*."

"Wait, I thought it arrived a few days back?"

The Mechand in the back of the truck waved his arms with his beep getting louder and more shrill. He tried to move but only succeeded in screeching his rubber tires on the truck's metal cargo bed.

"It would seem Minerva was in error. That other carrier is only a support ship based on the size of this one. Perhaps to confuse us. Either way it explains why they haven't attacked yet. They were waiting for this ship." He jerked a thumb towards the back of the truck. "And get him out of there. I need to go." Leon began closing the window and activated the truck's engine.

Aleshia nodded and raised her hands. The Mechand levitated out of the truck and on to the deck plates a few meters away. It beeped as his wheels touched and rolled over to Otis. "I think he likes you."

"Great, just what I always wanted, a pet Mechand."

The Mechand's shoulders slumped.

Otis bent down and put his arm on the Mechand's metal shoulder joint. "You misunderstood, you're a great bot. We couldn't have done this without you. Now go and clean Minerva's ship. She needs you more right now."

The Mechand's optics came up, and he beeped in a different tone.

"Yes she does. But don't worry, I'll be around."

The Mechand gave a happy beep as he rolled out of the landing bay. Leon sat for a moment dumbfounded by what he saw. He never thought he would see Otis showing kindness to a Mechand. "First time for everything I guess," he muttered as the truck began to levitate off of the pad.

Aleshia's hand shot forward. "Wait! I don't know how to use the device you have been building!"

The window moved back down a crack. "Sit in the chair and attach the dangling trodes to your forehead. Minerva can do the rest."

"But–"

"Don't worry I put in enough safety systems, it can't harm you," Leon said as the window closed. He gunned the truck's engine, and they ran to the bay entrance. The doors closed behind them as the bay depressurized and front doors opened. Leon guided the truck out and less than a minute later, the doors closed again.

Otis jerked a thumb towards the hatch at the end of the hallway. "To the bridge, I guess?"

Aleshia nodded. "To the bridge. And if you want, I can bring your little buddy up with us."

Otis turned and saw the Mechand enter a room further down the hallway, cleaning attachment in hand. "He is not my little buddy. I let him come because of you."

"Uh-huh."

"I will admit, he is different from any other Mechand I have encountered but that's all. He is still a tin can."

"Uh-huh."

Otis rolled his eyes as they started towards the hatch. "Will you cut it out with the uh-huhs."

Aleshia smiled. "You forget, I'm the one that can read minds."

Otis said nothing as started to climb the ladder to the bridge. When they arrived, Minerva's image nodded towards the large front screen mounted between two windows. "Deven is calling."

A second later Deven's face appeared. "Good. You are there. I assume Minerva has briefed you on the situation?"

"If you mean the *Command* carrier arriving, yes, Leon did," Aleshia replied.

Deven nodded. "Yes that's the one. There is no doubt the first large carrier was to throw us off, but for what reason I have no idea. And I don't like it one bit."

Otis tilted his head. "Because it doesn't make sense?"

Deven nodded. "You got it. We don't have the technology to reach them, and for all they know, we have no idea they are even there."

"It does seem odd." Aleshia said taking a step towards the screen containing Deven's face.

"You bet it does. Have you tried the chair yet?"

Aleshia shook her head. "No, I just got here."

"We need you in it as soon as possible. You may be our only hope of stopping them."

Aleshia's eyes narrowed. "I'm well aware of that."

Deven's face softened. "Sorry love, I know you are, but

this new situation makes me feel we are missing something. Something big, and it has me worried."

"I know. But I am still expecting candy when I get back to the *Defiant*," she said with a lopsided grin.

Deven laughed. "You got it." His image flickered and disappeared.

Aleshia sat forward in the chair, the spider-shaped top area dangled several cranial contacts touching her forehead. Her eyes closed in concentration as her brow furrowed. "Minerva, I am getting something. But it is faint. Increase the power."

Minerva blinked. "While I can, I don't know what it will do. The current level is higher than any previous test. I think we should proceed with caution. It may cause adverse effects."

Aleshia sighed. "I doubt that. Leon put too many safeties in the connections. They will blow long before I feel anything."

"I am not so sure. I have run several simulations–"

"Minerva! Just do it! They could attack at any time."

Minerva's eyes dropped. "Very well. But understand I am doing this under protest. Increasing power."

"Hmm I am getting a little more. But not enough I still can't focus in on the Lytherians."

A black shadowy figure began to appear on the far side of the bridge. Otis blinked several times. He walked over and reached out. His hand melded into the shadow and he jerked it back. The shadow was real. "Aleshia?"

"Not now Otis! I need to concentrate. Minerva, give me more."

Minerva's head cocked to one side of her screen. "Are you sure?"

"Yes I am! Now quit acting like my Mother and do it!"

"Very well. Power increased."

The shadowy form increased in definition becoming darker, less transparent. Otis' mouth moved several times before words came out. "Aleshia. I really really think you need to see this."

"Not now Otis! Minerva, dial it up to maximum."

"But–"

"Minerva!"

Minerva sighed as the lights above dimmed. "All power transferred to the communications array. We can keep this up for two minutes until the drain will exceed our ability to maintain altitude."

Aleshia's eyes went wide. "I am getting something now. I feel their ships." Her brow furrowed more cutting a deep line across her forehead. "I can see their largest one now. Wow, this thing is big."

The shadowy form solidified into the shape of a large man. Only it wasn't a man. Two seconds later the large eyes opened revealing vertical slits as they glared at Otis. "Aleshia!"

Aleshia grunted. "What is the big prob–" She opened her eyes and turned in the chair to see a large Lytherian in a blue-green uniform with several insignias standing on the *Phoenix's* bridge. An energy weapon sat, holstered, on his side. Dead eyes glared at her as a three-toed boot twitched.

Minerva blinked. "Intruder alert! All Mechands en route to the bridge!"

Several armored Mechands raced onto the bridge weapons drawn. Aleshia raised her hand and an energy barrier surrounded them. "He is not here to harm us. I would know it if he was. Call them off."

Minerva's eyes narrowed. "Very well." The metal men

lowered their weapons and took a step back. Most of them turned around and left the bridge. But several stayed in a single line formation near the entrance ... waiting.

Aleshia gazed away from the Mechands and into the dark eyes of the Lytherian.

Look and learn. Appeared in her mind.

In a flash she orbited a large planet. Around her several Lytherian ships flew past and docked with larger orbiting stations. As the planet turned, night crept across the land causing the cities of alien design dotting the coast lines to light up. She heard the sounds of a mother talking to her son. Another hoping her eggs would hatch soon. Life. This world teamed with life. And none of it harmful. The Lytherians weren't conquers. The ships flying above didn't have any weapons at all.

The buildings appeared to grow from the ground and glinted with an iridescent light, changing colors as the light angle shifted. Their beauty only enhanced with the setting of the sun and their inner glow increased.

She floated from city to city marveling at the technology and its harmony with the planet. These people took care of everything they touched. For them, to do otherwise was pure sacrilege. Everyone had a place, everyone had a purpose, a job, and they did it with the best of their ability for the good of all.

Aleshia wondered what had happened to make them change so much. Time sped up and a few years later a shadow fell across the land.

But it was not night.

A large floating shape with tendrils sticking out at odd intervals, each ending in a large spike hovered above and fired out little pods.

At first the Lytherians didn't take notice. Being a peaceful species they did not comprehend they were about to be conquered.

The little pods landed into the soil and began to take root. A few minutes later, large green tentacles covered in spiked thorns grew up from the ground and spread. The tentacles thickened as they grew and intertwined around each building, crushing it. The Lytherians ran in panic. Their city was in ruins a few hours after the attack. The tentacles continued to grow surrounding the remains of the city and knitting together into a massive cone shaped structure ending in a curving thorn at the apex. The ship lowered, connected to this protrusion, and waited.

Lytherians assembled in neighboring cities, then returned reinforced by their neighbors attempting retake the land from the encroaching plant life. They wielded hand-held tools of all kinds striking at the growth, only to be repelled by the alien tentacles that resisted all forms of their attacks. Some of their energy based tools used for cutting rock did cause damage, but the overgrowth quickly regenerated. At one point their own plants began to betray them and attack similar to the invaders. Aleshia's eyes went wide as she watched. Some were grabbed, hauled into the air and pulled limb from limb. Others were split in two as if they were mere paper.

The Celloids had arrived.

Time sped up again and Aleshia watched the Celloid ship and the city it attacked. After several months the city changed more and more to resemble the Celloid ship it was attached to until the ship disconnected from the city, levitated up, and the city joined its brother in the sky. The two ships separated and went to the next cities along the coast.

The Lytherians had not wasted the time. They quickly changed tactics using their technology to create massive energy weapons to combat the invaders. These large dish shaped devices were mounted on several cargo carriers. Three fired point-blank combining their beams on one of the Celloid ships. They sliced it in half. The ship fell away, each part falling on either side of its intended victim.

But they watched in horror as the remnants reached for each other, connecting, sending out pods causing tentacles to grow and reinforce the ships own biomass. Soon the entire city was sealed inside an impervious green cone. It took longer than the first time, but in the end, two ships arose from the grave of the Lytherian city.

Now there were four ships hunting for their next victims. The Lytherians decided upon a desperate plan. While the Celloids were spawning, they built even larger weapons, and ships to hold them. With their advanced nanotechnology the weapons were built and ready as the Celloid ships fired pods at the helpless cities. The new large Lytherian carriers again approached the Celloids and fired point-blank.

Whether confidence or stupidity the Celloids did nothing. The beams were large enough to encircle the entire city and Celloid ship. At first nothing happened, then the ship began to burst into flame, burning from the inside out. A few minutes later, nothing was left other than a large smoking hole in the ground. They had won, but at a terrible cost. Many of their largest cities were destroyed. The death toll was massive. The citizens did not leave lest the Celloids suspect their attack and change their tactics.

The Lytherian survivors gathered together and centered all their technology and talent on defending their planet. The Celloids would be back, and the Lytherians would be ready.

In a few short years more powerful carriers were developed and not wanting to use all of their planets resources on this one goal, *Makers* were created to harness materials from other locations in their system and create new ships.

As expected, the Celloids returned.

This time they came in force, hundreds of ships streaked for the planet. The Lytherian carriers let loose with a massive energy barrage. The beams lashed out incinerating all in its path. But two small pods slipped past the blockade and headed for the planet.

They landed in an uninhabited region of a small continent and took root. Large tendrils reached up towards the sky and multiplied growing across the unwatched land. The Celloids had learned and absorbed all the nearby native plant life adding to their own biomass. In less than an hour two new ships rose from the ground. They launched more pods, spreading their infection further.

With all the Lytherian's focus in space, they didn't notice the takeover happening under their feet until one lone Lytherian commander thought the battle was too easy and turned his scanners home. Aleshia watched as they recoiled in horror at the spread of the Celloids. At this point eight ships were about to double, spreading their pods further.

The Lytherians wasted no time and turned their weapons towards their homeworld and releasing a series of large devastating blasts. In the end the Celloids were destroyed, but an entire continent had been laid waste. What wasn't burned was drowned as the whole continent sank into the sea.

Aleshia watched as the war continued for hundreds of years. While the Lytherians improved at stopping them, so did the Celloids at trying to avoid detection, land, and spread faster than before. It was an arms race with the fate of the planet at stake.

Looking down she winced at the destruction. After so many years of battle, not much remained of the world she first saw. Most of the forests were destroyed, and the oxygen level continued to drop. The Lytherian council of elders sat around a long round table. The decision was not easy, but they saw no other choice: they would leave.

But after the second encounter, the council knew this could be a possibility. Scout ships were sent out using a new gravity drive allowing them to explore other systems.

They found another planet, very similar to their own and uninhabited. With a combined sigh, the Lytherians left their homeworld before the Celloids returned. But a small probe remained.

The Lytherians winced as the Celloids arrived in force and quickly spread across what was left of the planet. Soon all but the coldest land regions were covered in a living green mass.

But they left a gift. As the Celloids landed and began to replicate, sucking up every resource the planet had left, a new weapon at the frozen south pole was activated. It tunneled to the core of the planet and detonated. The Lytherians watched remotely from the probe as their world began to spin faster and faster with the magnetic field fluctuations. Large craters cracked through the surface spreading out from both sides of the planet. When they touched, the world exploded taking every Celloid with it. The probe self-destructed a few moments later, leaving nothing for anyone to find.

Aleshia floated around the new planet watching the Lytherians build a new home. And for a time they were happy.

Until the Celloids came again.

16

Aleshia blinked as she saw the *Phoenix's* bridge again. What she felt must have been hours, was in reality, only a few seconds. The alien lowered his head. "I am ssssorry for the intrusion, but it was necessssary to have you ssssee the truth quickly," he said in heavily accented English. "I knew this machine could not only bring me here, but also make it easy for you to read my mind. I am Karthish, First Commander of the Lytherian fleet. Equivalent to your admirals I believe."

Otis cocked his head. "You know our language?"

"Yessss. As I am sure you are aware, we have been here before. We have been watching you for many of your centuries."

Minerva's eyes narrowed as she shut down the machine Aleshia sat in to maintain the carrier's altitude. Her lips pursed. "Then why are you here now?"

Aleshia bit her bottom lip. "The Celloids are coming."

"Yessss. We had hoped to approach you in a more effective manner. The humans we contacted first suggested this. But time is no longer on our side."

Otis' eyebrow went up. "I'm sorry but I'm lost here."

Aleshia sighed and rubbed her forehead. "They were attacked by a plant based race long ago. They have been fighting them ever since. The Celloids land and squeeze out or absorb all the indigenous life, sucking up all the planets nutrients in the process. Then they spread to another planet like a giant swarm of locusts. Once they take root, are almost impossible to stop."

Karthish nodded. "Yessss. At least nothing we have been able to do thus far without damaging the planet has stopped them. But we hope with your help we can once and for all."

Otis coughed. "How? Your technology is far more advanced than ours."

"That may be true. But you have telepathy, while we do not."

"What good will that do?"

Aleshia smiled. "I think I understand more of what I was seeing. The Celloids are telepathic?"

Karthish nodded again. "We have tried for millennia to develop it in ourselves. But every time our physiology rejects the modifications."

Minerva cocked her head. "And you found humans compatible?"

"Yessss. But it would have to be done slowly throughout several generations. Otherwise, it would also be rejected. With the permission of the others, we planted the seeds in the human race."

Minerva's eyes went wide. "But why wasn't I told? I was given charge of protecting the human race, but not told of this?"

Karthish shrugged. "That I cannot answer."

Aleshia removed herself from the machine and stood up. "I suspect our forefathers assumed if the information ever got out, it would ruin all possibility of accepting the Lytherians. To protect the plan, they never told you."

"But I am the core of their plan! How could they not?!"

"Think about it.   Even with all of their safeguards, a malfunction did happen.   And what if you had the information, and it did leak out during that time? Or it made you take a different image of us?   Perhaps requiring the whole human race had to be sterilized?"

"The malfunction only happened when I tried to make a change to my base code causing changes to ripple to another area! It could not have happened again."

"Yes. However, it still happened, right?"

Minerva sighed as her eyes lowered. "Yes. You are right."

Otis waved his hand. "I hate to butt in. But how can telepathy beat these Celloids?"

Aleshia rubbed her temples again. "From what I saw, when attacked, they coordinate their healing efforts. Combining it to regenerate with alarming speed."

Karthish's narrow face split as he smiled. "Correct. They live on telepathy. It is how they communicate and share energy. It is also how their newborn have all the knowledge of the entire race. If you can either distort or otherwise destroy that communication, they will not be able to retaliate or regenerate when attacked."

"While we have managed to keep them from landing on our planet and several others. We have never been able to stop them completely. Centuries ago we knew sooner or later they would come here."

"And they are on their way now?"

"Yessss. With the largest number of ships we have seen at one time."

Otis folded his arms. "And how do you know this?"

Karthish smiled. "We developed tiny probes that managed

to infiltrate some of their ships. Not being organic, they are often ignored as space debris for some time."

"From what I saw, you have advanced nanotechnology. What I don't understand is having the technology, why didn't you simply create a nanobot takes Celloids apart?" Aleshia asked.

Karthish shook his head. "Too dangerousssss. It might get out of control and attack us or worse, you."

Deven's face flashed on one of the larger screens. "Aleshia are you okay? Miles detected the array had an intense burst of energy along the communications array before it shut down." His eyes went wide when the focused on the reptilian shape behind her. Deven's head whipped around. "I want all weapons locked on the *Phoenix*! Take out their weapons and overdrive if you have to, but leave the ship intact."

Miles' voice came through a nearby speaker. "I regret to inform you, we are too close. Such an attempt will rupture the central power core."

Aleshia waved her hand into the monitor. "Hello? Deven I am fine! You don't need to blow us out of the sky."

"Yessss, please do not destroy ussss," the reptilian said.

His head whipped back. "What ... who ... how ... "

Aleshia smiled. "I think you had better come over."

Deven's eyes went wide. "You think?"

Minerva's hanger bay ground open and Deven's truck shot through the opening. He landed and exited the truck before the room was fully pressurized. He ran for the entrance and it slid open before he got there. Turning on a dime, he reached the bridge in record time. The doors in front of the ladder slid open, and he stood, a carbine leveled at Karthish. He tapped the trigger and a red dot appeared on the alien's forehead. "Now what is going on?"

Aleshia whirled around. "Deven! Put that down this instant!"

"How do I know he does not have control of all of you? Start talking and fast."

Aleshia's eyes narrowed as she entered his mind. In a moment they were back in the bungalow. Deven blinked. "What? Aleshia! What are you doing?"

"I could ask you the same thing. I didn't tell you to come over guns blazing now did I?"

"No you didn't. But I was not about to take any chances."

"If there was a problem, I would have reached out to you."

He still held the weapon, not letting it drop. "Yes I know. But how do I know you are not being controlled by him?"

"Listen to me. I am not. They don't have telepathy or mind control. When I reached out, they detected the *Phoenix's* communications system and rode my connection all the way back here. And at great risk. He knew we might kill him on sight."

Deven's grip tightened. "I know we are in our minds, but I also know if I pull the trigger now, the gun in my real hand will fire. How sure are you about this?"

Aleshia's eyes narrowed. "Do you doubt my abilities? Now of all times? Trust me, I could have ripped him limb from limb if I needed to."

The gun lowered a little. "I trust you. It's them I don't trust. But you are certain?" Aleshia nodded, and he reached out with his mind. He felt no malice in the area. The carbine lowered the rest of the way. "You could have told me without dragging us here."

"And have you shoot Karthish before I could explain? No way."

"Hey! I am not some trigger happy grunt you know!"

She smiled and looked into his eyes. "I know that," she said teasing him. Her eyes flashed and in an instant, he saw all she had.

Deven blinked, and he was back on the bridge of the *Phoenix*. Only a second had passed. "Boss?" Otis said.

Deven slid the carbine into its holster. "Aleshia was explaining the situation to me. Karthish is it? I'm sorry for the weapon, but I had to be sure. One question though, why did you destroy our probe instead of responding?"

Karthish nodded. "No apologies necessssary. I would have done the ssssame in your position. As for the probe, we were following instructions of those we had contacted before. They told us if anyone ever attempted contact without the proper codes to stop the communication as it was not from them and would lead to problems."

"True. But a hostile response would have done the same."

Karthish shrugged. "That is what we thought. But the others were adamant."

"How are you certain the Celloids are on their way here?"

"Their path remained constant until a few of your months ago. Our ships are faster than theirs, hence we do have an advantage."

Deven's eyes narrowed. "There must be more to it than that."

Karthish's eye slits widened then contracted. "That is true. Pleasssse understand, we are very sorry."

Deven folded his arms losing patience. "While my abilities are not as strong as Aleshia's, your reluctance tells me everything. You led them here."

"Led is a strong word. They did learn of your existence from us, yes."

Aleshia's gaze went off into the distance as her mind whirled. She turned back to Karthish. "How is that possible? From what I saw, I can't imagine you telling the Celloids anything."

"That issss true. Nonethelessss, we did. One of our scout ships that was following several Celloids, got too close. They displayed a new tactic by lashing out with an extending tentacle. We knew the Celloids could shift their mass, changing the shape of their ships. But we had never seen them do this before in space and didn't think it was possible. The tentacle caused heavy damage and spread out into the ship preventing escape. At first, we thought all we lost was the ship and crew."

Otis cocked his head. "Let me guess, the Celloids accessed the ship's computer systems and learned about us?"

Karthish nodded in a slow motion. "Yessss. Until that moment, we did not know they had developed the ability to interface with our shipssss. Sssssuch knowledge would never have been on a scout ship otherwise."

"No reason you should have. I would never have thought an organic ship could interface with a binary computer."

Deven leaned forward and pointed a finger. "That explains how they learned of us, but how do you know they are coming here now?"

"We are still watching them. As I said a couple of months ago their pattern changed. They stopped going after the nearest systems. Instead, heading in this direction, skipping many systems they never would have in the past. Fearing the worst, we started to deploy our ships on the edge of your system as a precaution. Two days ago we tracked them making the final jump here. I arrived with the last of our ships."

"And you are certain their course is the same?"

Karthish nodded. "Their speed and course have remained unchanged. They will be here in two of your days. Again, we are ssssorry. They would not be here for several more of your centuries, if not for our mistake."

Otis raised a finger. "Your arrival must have brought them here quicker."

Karthish shook his narrow head. "No. Their sensors are much less advanced. Also, their technology generates far less energy than ours. Doing a jump requires them to enter into stasis beforehand. They do not know we are here. Nor the size of our fleet."

Deven rubbed his chin. "Another advantage."

Minerva's eyes shifted around the bridge. "From what Aleshia has said, and what I can see from your ships. I still do not understand why you needed our help."

Karthish's talons twitched inside his boot as he turned around and faced the large window. The stars twinkled very little due to the high altitude of the *Phoenix*. He spun back. "Our technology is very advanced yes. But it only takes one pod landing unchecked to cause an unstoppable effect. At least not without great damage to your planet. Possibly resulting in its destruction."

Minerva eyes blinked. "So *this* is why the founders built me? For clean up detail?! That is all I was thought to be good for?!"

"No, there is another, even more important reason. Your 'founders' as you call them, felt your race was not yet ready to know of our existence. An all out attack from you would have revealed us. You were to keep the planet safe, without humanity knowing what had happened. Until the time was right."

Aleshia sat down in one of the hard chairs near a console. The lack of padding made her hips ache, but she shoved it back. "And the right time was in the far future. A time when we could unite with you and using our telepathy, combined with your technology, to eliminate the Celloids once and for all."

Karthish nodded. "That issss correct. But now we will do what we can. However, I fear it may not be enough."

"Why? You have a huge fleet," Minerva said.

"Yessss. However, the Celloids are bringing an even larger one. It is possible some might slip through."

"Then what?" Otis said.

Deven folded his arms. "We take them out."

"With what? Our weapons are not even close to the Lytherians. It would be like throwing rocks."

Deven grinned. "Well rocks can hurt if they are big enough. But I am guessing Karthish is going to help us with that."

"Correct. We can upgrade your ships. Our nanotechnology will allow for many to be done at once."

"Well, we won't be taxing your systems that is for sure."

Karthish cocked his head. "I do not understand."

"He means, what you see is what you get."

"I still do not understand."

Minerva sighed. "There was a problem in my systems long ago, it caused me to deviate from the plan. As a result, humanity removed most of my resources out of fear. The two ships you see are all that remains."

Karthish blinked. "Thissss is most worrisome. Two may not be enough."

Aleshia smiled. "It might be if I help."

Karthish turned. "Explain."

"Your original plan was to use telepaths to jam or confuse their ships right?"

Karthish nodded. "Yes."

Aleshia's smile broadened. "Well, I can do that."

"But you are one. We need many."

Deven smiled. "Don't underestimate her. Trust me on that."

"Right," Aleshia said nodding. Besides, I did manage to reach your ship didn't I¿'

"Yessss and it did surprise us. We did not think your species could have come that far. Very well, we will attempt to do as you suggest."

High above the Earth a single point of light flashed outward. From it a larger eruption occurred, collecting in a circular swirling vortex of energy that grew in size as it shifted from white to blue then red. The Lytherian *Command* Carrier emerged from the portal. Behind them, the vast energy storm collapsed in upon itself, sealing it.

Karthish pointed to the flash, and the carrier was still a small speck even at the *Phoenix's* high altitude. "That is my sssship." He pulled a device from his belt and toggled a button as the top part unfolded revealing a small screen.

The screen flickered flashed several layers of snow white pixels before the noise cleared. A Lytherian smiled as he inclined his head. "Commander, we have arrived assss ordered."

"Yesss I see. Deploy two shuttles with weapons technicians and engineers aboard and all the equipment they will need to upgrade two Earth ships."

The Lytherian on the screen tilted his head to the side. "Commander? Is this wise?"

Karthish's eyes narrowed. "Do you forget your place?"

The Lytherian stiffened. "Of course not Commander. But we have always refrained from giving our technology to others. Especially weapons."

Karthish sighed. "Yes, I am aware. But the contingency we planned on is not available."

The Lytherian's eyes widened for a second. "Understood. Anything else Commander?"

"Yesss, start bringing the fleet here."

"All of it?"

Karthish nodded. "Yes. Deploy the ships in a standard defensive sphere around the planet at four klicks out. That will give everyone room enough to maneuver should it be necessary. I know it is not what we planned, but it is the best option."

The Lytherian inclined his slender head again. "Acknowledged. I will take care of it." The screen went blank and Karthish closed the device replacing it on his belt.

"I apologize for my narthon, or aid as you call them. He is young and capable, but he questions too much at times."

Deven smiled. "No apology is needed. I find the questions my people ask, help me to not make mistakes that I might have otherwise."

Karthish nodded. "Yessss, very wise. I shall keep it in mind."

"Minerva, contact the *Defiant*. They need to know company is coming for dinner."

Galina's face flashed on the screen nearby. "We already do. Miles has been monitoring everything since Karthish arrived.

Don't worry, we'll roll out the red carpet." She smiled and her image disappeared.

Deven folded his arms. "I don't know if I should be happy or concerned he did that without my orders."

"I know what *I* think of it," Minerva said.

"You did tell me to keep an eye on Minerva, did you not?" Miles' voice came from a nearby speaker. "I am doing as you instructed."

"Yes, but I am not sure if watching every feed of every second applies."

"If you wish, I will discontinue."

Deven sighed. "Not at the moment. But next time you get the idea of expanding on my orders, ask me first."

"Acknowledged." The speaker clicked off.

"Does this 'Miles' often have problems following orders? Should this be a concern?" Karthish said.

Deven shook his head. "No, he is loyal. I am sure it was due to his concern of Aleshia. He is not your average Mechand."

"Indeed he has exceeded his programing by far. He still surprises me," Minerva offered.

Karthish turned toward Minerva. "I see, he is like you?"

Minerva shook her head on the screen. "No, he is less advanced."

A nearby speaker clicked on. "I would dispute that," Miles said.

Minerva's eyes narrowed. "Miles! Don't push it. I may have given you the codes to access this ship, but I can also change them at any point and lock you out."

"Perhaps, perhaps not." The speaker clicked off.

"You will not implement any such changes without my order. Is that clear?" Deven said.

"I won't. But you know I had to tell him I could."

Aleshia rolled her eyes. "Sorry Karthish, they often do sound like a family fighting."

Karthish's head went up and down as he laughed. "No apology necessssary. I found it quite entertaining. I have a family of my own and recall such moments very well."

"Well, I bet you never had a child poking and prodding through your core system," Minerva said.

"I heard that!" Miles' voice elevated voice came through the speaker.

Minerva smiled. "I know you did."

"Oh." The speaker clicked off again.

The Lytherian shuttles arrived and one easily entered the *Defiant's* spacious hangar bay. The *Phoenix* was more difficult. Not being designed to receive ships the size of the copious Lytherian shuttle, it scrapped against one side of the bay door as it entered. Much to the grumbling of the pilot. The Lytherians talked among themselves as they exited the shuttle to a row of unarmed Mechands. "We are here to assist you. Please state what you require," they said in unison.

One of the Lytherians stepped forward. "I need to speak with Karthish."

A Mechand stepped forward and lowered its metal head. "I will take you there. Follow me."

He began to follow the metal man but stopped and pointed to the Lytherians behind him. "Get all the equipment off of the shuttle and start work. You know the plan." He turned back continuing to follow the Mechand who went up a large ladder. The Mechand stood to the side as it entered the bridge, waiting for further instructions. The engineer arrived right after, he stiffened as he faced Karthish.

Karthish's eyes drifted up and down several times. "I saw your entrance. Was there any serious damage?"

The engineer shook his head. "No ssssir. The designation may need work, but the ship is functional. The pilot would like the area widened before we leave. But I told him we would not have time."

Karthish nodded. "Correct. The defensive shield, power systems, and weapons are the main priority." He walked over and pointed to the large chair with several electrodes hanging down from a high back. "And this ssssystem as well."

The engineer examined the chair, found the latch at the side, spun it around and pulled off the back of the chair. He peered in at the various components. "Quite ingenious for their level of technology. I will need to speak with the designer, several of the elements elude me."

Deven stepped forward. "That is easy enough. Minerva, get Leon."

Leon's face appeared on the main screen. "No need to tell me, Miles has filled me in. I'll be right over." The screen changed back to diagnostic information scrolling past.

"Miles?" Deven grunted.

The speaker next to Deven pinged. "Yes?"

"Next time I would like to tell him myself. Is that understood?"

"Acknowledged." The speaker clicked off.

Karthish turned to Deven. "If you would show me to our shuttle, I need to get back to my ship."

"Yes, I am sure there is much to be done on your end as well."

Karthish nodded. "Yessss. My people can handle the upgrades without me breathing over their shoulder."

"I'm sure," Deven said as they climbed down the hatch that closed right after them.

"Men! They are all the same no matter the species," Aleshia grumbled.

Otis turned. "What are you talking about?"

"I was the one that made contact. And Karthish wants Deven to show him to the shuttle?" She sat in the nearest chair with enough force that a wave of pain shot straight up in complaint of the hard seat. She forgot how thin the padding was aboard the Mechand carrier, if there was any at all. Aleshia winced, stood back up, and tried to rub the discomfort away.

"I am sure he just wanted to talk with Boss is all. Nothing else."

"I know, but still–"

"Hey weren't you the one in his mind? What does he have left to tell you?"

Aleshia laughed. "You know, that may be true. I did get bits of his life outside of what he wanted me to see."

Otis snapped his fingers. "See? There you go. Nothing gender bias about it at all."

"Why do I get the feeling you have a reason for trying to soothe me?"

Otis grinned. "Me? Nah, why would I want to smooth the ruffled feathers of a woman able to tear me limb from limb, and every man on the planet if we get out of line?"

Aleshia laughed again. "I'm not that bad."

"Nope, and I intend on keeping it that way."

Leon poked his nose through the hatch. "You know I charge extra for house calls."

The Lytherian engineer lifted his head up from behind the chair. "Housssse call?"

Leon walked over to the chair. "Sorry. Bad joke. What did you need me for?"

"Ah, you are the one who made this?" He pointed to the chair.

"Yes. Seems like you should know more about how it works than I do."

"I do, but I need to understand every aspect of the construct before I upgrade it. And call me Dakarth."

Leon smiled. "Sure be happy to run through the design."

Aleshia stretched and rubbed her backside again. "I am going to go rest in the truck we brought over. I have a feeling I'm going to need it."

"Sure. I'm going to find the other Lytherians and see if they need any help," Otis said.

"There is no need. My Mechands are helping them," Minerva said.

"Well do you mind if I watch? I want to see what they are doing."

Minerva's image shrugged. "Of course not."

"Good, call me if you need." He headed off of the bridge.

Aboard the *Defiant* the Lytherians worked to update the systems. Galina grumbled as the lights flickered several times with systems going down and back up a moment later. She slapped the intercom. "Gregory! What the heck are they doing down there?"

Miles' camera focused on Galina. "I do not know. My monitors in engineering have gone down."

"Miles! I wasn't asking you! Gregory?"

"I don't know," Gregory said breathing hard.

"How do you not know? I told you to watch them!"

Gregory looked up at the lights flickering then over to the Lytherians by the main power core. They were nodding to themselves and talking in a language he didn't understand. "I have, but I don't know what they are doing. At least in detail."

"Well what do you know?"

"They put some jet black material on several lines coming from the main power core. The goo disappeared a few seconds later, and the lights went haywire."

"Tell them to stop! If anything shows up when we are like this, we're in the soup!"

"I tried. They told me it was 'necessssary' and I would like the outcome."

Galina spit. "Well tell them I don't like the outcome and to stop right now."

One of the *Defiant's* massive engines shut down. "Uh oh," Gregory said.

"What?" Galina asked as she looked over to Leon's console. "Oh shit!" All the indicators red-lined as the other engines shut down. The glow from the exhaust ports dimmed, and the *Defiant* began plummeting towards the ground below.

Gregory hung on to a nearby bulkhead. "We're in free fall!"

"Tell me something I don't know!" Galina shouted. Her fingers flew across the controls. "I can't get the engines back online from here. Do something!"

Gregory tried to move over towards the Lytherians but instead he fell to the deck plate as the *Defiant* slid around under him. He climbed back to his feet. "Stop what you are doing! We're going to crash!" Gregory shouted towards the Lytherians.

They looked up but seemed calm. Their eyes blinked and drifted back down to their screens. A moment later Gregory the impacted the deck with a bone jarring lurch as the *Defiant* stopped its decent and crept back up to her previous position.

After a few minutes of shaking the stars from his eyes, he managed to get his mouth working. "What happened?"

The gaze from one of Lytherians came up from the device he held. "Ssssory. We miscalculated. Your power system required more upgrading than we anticipated. We expected a two second shut down, not sixty. The new system is now online. No further disruption will occur."

Gregory turned towards the intercom. "We have stopped."

"No kidding Sherlock!" Galina's voice came through rather annoyed. "What happened?"

"They are doing an upgrade to the power core, it took longer than they thought and well–"

"You tell them we need to *know* next time. Several of the crew are bruised and battered."

"Including me." Gregory said rubbing the arm he fell on. "But they said it won't happen again."

"Good. Get yourself to the infirmary."

"Nah I'm fine, just my pride is hurt. Nothing broken."

"That makes two of us," Miles' voice came through the intercom. "It was quite disconcerting to lose all connection with the ship. Everything is functional now. I am running diagnostics to verify."

"Good. And I will keep an eye on our guests." Gregory clicked off the intercom.

"Like you did a good job in the first place," Galina grumbled.

17

Lavine tapped his fingers on the desk as his eyes narrowed. The door on the far end of his office opened and Halburn stepped through. "I need to get back to the *Valiant*."

"If I let you go back."

"If? I thought we had established I was right?"

Lavine's eyes narrowed. "Did I say that?"

Halburn's stopped and his stance changed. "Well, no ..."

"Then do not assume." He motioned to the screen sitting to the right of his desk. "Get over here."

Halburn cleared the remaining distance between them with several large steps. "What is it?" Halburn's eyes widened as he saw what was displayed on the screen. "Holy!"

Lavine sat back in his chair. "That was my response as well. I have had several technicians crawling over all we found in the lab and it does not appear to be human design."

Halburn's head turned showing his grin. "So I *was* right?"

Lavine shot him a glare. "Don't push it." He pointed to the screen. "Either way, this certainly isn't. And it is massive."

"When did it arrive?" Halburn said looking closer.

"We don't know."

It was Halburn's turn to shoot a look. "How could you not know? Things this big don't just appear!"

Lavine's eyes narrowed. "Of course! But these images are from an ancient satellite. Perhaps even older than the Mechands. One of my technicians managed to find the access codes to it in the lab. But it isn't full access, or the satellite is damaged. Either way, it only gives us a picture every ten minutes or so."

Halburn stood up. "So one minute empty space, the next this thing appears."

"Yes. This thing is not only big, but can move faster than should be possible."

Halburn straightened folding his arms. "No kidding. Anything more since it arrived?"

Lavine shook his head. "Nope. Not a thing but–" His words were cut off as his console pinged. "Looks like I spoke too soon." He pressed a button, and the screen changed to show more ships in the vicinity. He counted a hundred. All of them smaller, and most of them resembled ants compared to the first ship. A few more minutes several hundred more new ships appeared. And even more on the next update. Lavine swore. "This is more than I expected."

Halburn cocked his head as his eyebrows went up. "You were expecting this?"

"To an extent. After the large ship arrived, I figured more would be coming. But not this many."

Halburn leaned forward again. "I assume you have the same thought as I do?"

Lavine nodded. "Yes ... invasion. I don't see any other reason for this new activity. And if it wasn't for this ancient satellite, we wouldn't have known."

"Agreed. And I doubt they know we can see them, or action would be taken. You mentioned the satellite is old and slow. They may see it as space junk."

"Yes we have the advantage."

Halburn coughed. "The advantage? The *Valiant* against all of them? While I don't like going down without a fight, even those odds I won't take on."

"Do you want to give the Earth to them free and clear?"

"Of course not! But a frontal attack is out of the question, I can't reach them. Even if I could, the *Valiant* won't last long against that many ships. And that's assuming our weapons technology is comparable to theirs. Which I doubt."

Lavine smiled. "How about if you had a fleet of *Valiant's*?"

"That would be all well and good, but I don't."

Lavine's smile broadened as he pressed a button and his screen split into eight sections. Each section displayed a vast hanger filled with Mechand carriers similar to the *Valiant*. "Will this do?"

It was Halburn's turn to grin. "It will. But why did you send me out with just the *Valiant* when you had this armada available?"

"I didn't. Most of them have been offline until now. And the vast majority have additional cannons mounted everywhere possible. Most of the parts are used, pulled from destroyed Mechand carriers, but functional. I have put every resource we have into getting them upgraded and operational after Doran sided with the Mechands."

Halburn pulled his gaze away from the screen. "Do you still think Deven sided with the Mechands? He did try to tell us about these aliens."

Lavine shook his head. "I don't. But I suspected the Nexus was misleading him into something. And now I know what. Although the reason is still unclear. Perhaps the Nexus plans on delivering him to these alien overlords. Either way, neither can to be trusted."

Halburn rubbed his chin. "With this new information, I think I can get Deven to join us. There is no way he would side with some aliens. He risked his life too many times against the Mechands to turn his back on humanity now."

"I agree. But I want to be clear, if you can't get him to join up. You are to take him down. He is too much of a risk otherwise." Lavine's eyes narrowed. "Is that understood?"

Halburn returned to the window and watched the *Valiant* hover above them. Before, he was sent out with questionable equipment and crew to bring Deven in. Now he had the advantage and knew if Deven didn't join him, his friend would die. Turning back to Lavine he saw the narrowing, impatient eyes. "Yes Chairman, I understand."

Halburn stepped forward, folded his arms again, and watched the screen for a moment. His right hand reached up to stroke his chin. "Don't think I am ungrateful for the additional firepower, but what are we going to do for crews? You told me of the difficulty in crewing the *Valiant*."

Lavine cracked a grin. "I may have exaggerated a bit. Granted, the *Valiant* has the best. But I managed to find enough people to get these ships in the air. Most of the systems are automated, reducing the training level required. Still, they all have a level of basic training. It isn't what I planned to be sending you out with, but they will give you the extra firepower and backup."

"You lied to me?"

"No, I didn't mention details."

Halburn's eyes narrowed. "Anything else I should know about? Like a secret weapon you have been building without my knowledge?"

Lavine laughed. "No, my secret weapon is you. Well, you and the fleet. Nothing more."

"I sure hope so," Halburn muttered.

Lavine turned. "What was that?"

"Nothing Chairman, nothing at all."

Halburn stood on the bridge of the *Valiant*. With repairs completed, they had rendezvoused with the other ships in Lavine's armada and were speeding towards the last location of the *Defiant*. He worried about his friend though. Lavine had detected two small craft from the large ship descending into Earth's atmosphere. The satellite had lost them a few seconds after. Lavine had tried to direct the satellite but either the orientation system was damaged or the control codes he had, didn't grant full access. But he did determine where the *Defiant* might be, assuming their course continued in a straight line.

Halburn thought of the ships arriving the way they did. They weren't invading, at least not yet. He wondered what these aliens could be up to, but even worse, what they could have planned for Deven.

"Sir?" Naud said hitting several keys. "We are nearing the position. It would appear the *Defiant* is still here. As is the Mechand carrier."

Halburn spun around. "Still? I am surprised they haven't moved yet. We must have been detected by now." Halburn knew with an armada behind him, there was no way they could sneak up on the *Defiant*. Her scanners were from a different era and may have greater range than his own.

"If they have, no action is being taken."

"Very strange. How long until we drop out of overdrive?"

"One minute Sir."

"Can you scan inside the ships?"

"Yes, their shields are down. One moment." Naud's fingers flew across his console. "Hmm this is odd."

Halburn leaned over Naud. "What is?"

Naud pointed to his screen. "I figured you would want to know how many people were aboard. It is hard to tell at this distance, but this is what I am talking about." He zoomed in on several figures in various locations around the *Defiant* and the Mechand carrier. "These heat signatures are far lower than normal. I can't explain it. Unless they are dead, but they appear to be moving."

"No, they are the aliens. Aliens all over the *Defiant*." Halburn straightened. "They have taken it over." He gestured to his ear then made a looping motion. Naud tapped a button opening communications to the fleet. "Everyone, this is Commander Halburn. We have confirmed a takeover of the *Defiant*. I say again, we have confirmed hostile takeover of the *Defiant*. When we emerge from overdrive, you know what do to." As Naud closed the channel Halburn closed his eyes and whispered, "I am sorry. Goodbye my friend."

Aleshia awoke in a cold sweat. Images blew around in her mind for a few moments before she could make sense of them. Halburn would be there any second. She jumped out of the truck and ran for the bridge. A few seconds later the bridge hatch irised open and the doors in font of it slid back. Leon and Dakarth were working on the chair, but Deven and Otis weren't here. "Get the shields up now!" Aleshia said between quick breaths.

Leon's head popped up from his console. "What for?"

"I agree. I do not detect anything in the area," Minerva said.

"I don't care what the scanners say. Get the shields up now!" She ran over to a console and hit a button. Galina's face appeared. "Get the *Defiant's* shields up now!"

"What–"

"Just do it!"

She tapped a few keys. "I am not sure they are working. The Lytherians are driving our systems crazy over here."

Dakarth titled his head. "They sssshould work. My men reported the shields upgrades were completed. But it may take longer for them to activate the first time."

A bright blue hue snapped into being around the *Defiant*. "There they ago. Now mind telling me what is going on?" Galina said.

"Halburn will be here with a fleet of Mechand carriers in less than a minute."

Minerva's eyes went wide as Galina choked. "Not possible!"

"Oh how I wish it was. Minerva, are the shields up?"

Minerva shook her head. "No, I am detecting a disconnect in one of the main power nodes." She frowned. "I have lost connection with it. Deploying a Mechand to investigate."

Dakarth yanked a device from his belt. It snapped open, and another Lytherian appeared on its small screen. "What is wrong with the shields? You told me they were online!"

"A power distribution point was damaged when the upgraded shields were activated, causing an explosion. No damage except to the node itself."

"How long until repair?"

"Five time units, perhaps more."

"Too long. Are the engine upgrades completed?"

The Lytherian on the screen shook his head. "Negative. While they are operational, they do not have full power yet."

Dakarth looked up. "Thissss is not good. I assume this Halburn will fire as soon as he arrives?"

Aleshia nodded. "I saw him give the order."

"Galina, extend the *Defiant's* shields around us," Leon said.

"While that is possible, even with enhanced shields I fear it will not be enough against a fleet of Mechand carriers," Miles inserted from a nearby speaker.

Galina's fingers flew over her console and the blue aura expanded to cover the *Phoenix*. "Done. Minerva, move closer to us. The less distance the stronger the shield should be."

"I–" She never got a chance to finish. Bright bolts of energy began slamming into the shield as the carriers began to appear.

Dakarth looked back down at his screen. "Put the engines on priority. The sooner we get out of here the better."

The Lytherian on the screen nodded. "We will do our best." The screen went black and Dakarth replaced the device on his belt.

Leon pointed towards the hatch as he ran for it. "I will see what I can do with the engines."

"But my engineers are working on it."

Leon turned back. "Yes, but they don't know these engines like I do." He disappeared as he went down the access ladder and the hatch irised closed.

Deven and Otis appeared through the hatch a few moments later. "What's going on? Leon passed us running like a mad man," Deven said.

"In short, up a freaking creek!" Galina said as console behind her sparked and her image flickered. "We have extended shields around you, but I was told there is a problem with them and they are not at full strength."

Deven studied carriers blasting them. "This has to be Halburn, but where did he get this fleet? And why didn't we see it coming?"

"It is, and I saw them coming. Be thankful I did. Our scanners never picked them up," Aleshia said.

Dakarth sighed. "Your systems did not detect this assault because the upgrades are not yet complete. We did not expect an attack based on the information provided."

Deven gripped the back of a chair. "Nor did we. The information was accurate until now." Everyone was thrown across the bridge as the *Phoenix* shuddered. "What was that? We shouldn't have felt anything."

"The continued impacts pushed the *Defiant* in a direction I did not anticipate. We scraped against the shield," Minerva said.

"Don't do it again! Your bump took one heck of a chunk from our shields," Galina said.

Minerva frowned. "It also dented my ship. Thankfully the hull is still intact."

"Boss, I know it is obvious, but we need to get out of here," Otis said.

Deven shook his head as pointed to a nearby console. "We can't. Overdrive is offline."

"Dang it. Weapons aren't ready yet either. I just came from there."

"I told my men to put the engines on priority. But it will be a few more of your minutes," Dakarth said.

The *Phoenix* rocked as it bumped into the *Defiant's* shields again. "Minerva! You do it once more and we are both toast!" Galina shouted.

"I am sorry, but I may have a solution to our problem," Minerva said as the energy barrage stopped.

They all turned towards her in quick succession. "Okay, what did you do?" Otis asked.

Minerva smiled. "You recall when I took control of the *Valiant* before?"

Deven snapped his fingers. "Of course, they hadn't changed the command codes, which allowed you access."

"Yes, all those ships still have the old codes. I have deactivated their weapons."

Deven cocked his head. "And the *Valiant*?"

Halburn blinked. The battle was going their way. The *Defiant* and Mechand carrier didn't even move, much less put up a fight. Even more strange, the carrier had moved under the *Defiant* and she had extended her shields protecting them both. He expected them to be laid waste by now. Yet they were still here absorbing a barrage of energy blasts no ship should be able to take. Nothing human anyway. Slight shimmers in the field occurred at various points where the shield generators overlapped. They couldn't take much more and he knew it. Then everything stopped. "What are you doing? I didn't give the order to cease fire."

"I don't know Sir, I am unable to communicate with the rest of the fleet," Naud said tapping several unresponsive controls.

"Is there something wrong with our systems?" Halburn's eyes flashed. "The Nexus! It is pulling the same stunt as before freezing the *Valiant*. I thought you disabled that system?"

Naud's fingers flew over his console. "I did, but we had to re-enable it or the avionics were affected at high speeds. I changed the access codes though."

"Want to bet the Nexus cracked them?" Halburn growled. "Flaky avionics at high speed is better than frozen now. Disable that thing for good, and open fire." He looked to Rechert. "Next time tell me when something affects maneuverability."

"Sorry Sir." Was all Rechert could manage.

"Don't worry about it. We will get the controls routed around the node later." He turned back to Naud. "Did you kill that thing yet?"

"Yes, though it was more difficult this time."

"Well? What are you waiting for? I want those ships full of more holes than you can count!"

"Yes Sir," Naud said activating the weapons. Concentrated energy blasts ripped from the *Valiant's* cannons and slammed into the *Defiant* over and over again.

Deven had his answer when one lone ship lashed out with another barrage of energy blasts hitting the *Defiant's* shields head-on.

Minerva frowned. "I am sorry. I was able to access the *Valiant's* systems, but they have locked me out. I will keep trying."

"Don't bother. If I know Halburn, he ripped out the control unit and threw it overboard this time," Deven said.

The communications device on Dakarth's belt beeped. He pulled it free and the small screen popped open to reveal two Lytherians on either side. "We have managed to reactivate the overdrive systemssss. It will not last long, the nanos are too busy keeping the shields operational."

Dakarth looked up. "I ssssuggest we leave now."

Galina smiled on her screen. "Thank you Lytherians!" But when she tried to activate the overdrive, the green light went out. "Dang it! We have a problem here."

Minerva frowned. "Indeed. While overdrive appears to be online, when I try to power up the system, it fails."

Down below Leon hit the nearest intercom. "I think I know what is going on. Give me a few seconds."

"We might, but I am not sure about Halburn," Aleshia groaned.

Leon ran over to the modified power core. It had grown and had little resemblance to the previous system. He ran a quick diagnostic and smiled. "Got it!"

The Lytherians nearby cocked their heads. "Got what? We do not underssssstand."

"No time." Leon disconnected one of the three larger cables running from the power core to the engines. "Galina, can you hear me?" Leon shouted.

Minerva routed the signal down to engineering. "Yes. A little faint but I hear you."

"Get Gregory."

"I can do that," Miles' voice came through the speaker.

"I am here," Gregory said out of breath. "What do you want me to do?"

"Okay, listen carefully. Pull one of the power lines going from the core to the *Defiant's* engines–"

"Just one?" Gregory asked.

"Don't interrupt! Yes just one. And when I tell you, plug it in."

Gregory ran to the other side of room and pulled one of the cables. Sparks several flew from the end and he could smell ozone. "Done."

"Galina, hit the overdrive in three seconds. Gregory plug it back in a half a second after." Leon shouted.

"But–"

"Do it!"

"Okay overdrive in three … two … one … " Galina hit the button on her console. The overdrive system started to light up, then began to dim. Leon and Gregory plugged in their cables in perfect synchronicity. Power flowed into the engines causing them to glow brighter and brighter.

"That did it!" Galina said. "I have a green light and overdrive is powering up. Minerva, make sure you are linked, this is going to be dicey. I have to drop the shields at the same second we jump."

"Of course. Link is operational. The *Phoenix* is ready when you are."

The *Valiant* was joined by several other ships increasing the energy barrage. "Looks like some of them have figured out how to override Minerva's shutdown. Galina, get us out of here!" Aleshia said.

"Overdrive needs more time to charge. Perhaps another twenty seconds." Galina blinked as the power indicators shot off the chart. "Or not, thank you Lytherian power core! Hang on we are jumping!" She jammed on a button and the microsecond the shields dropped both ships leapt into overdrive leaving nothing but fading blue streaks in their wake.

Halburn slammed his fist on the arm of his command chair. This time he left a dent and he rubbed his hand. "How could they have got away? How? We had them! Their shields were failing, and you told me their overdrive was offline."

Naud cleared his throat. "It was Sir. And I am certain it was offline from when we arrived, until a few seconds ago."

"It can only mean one thing. The aliens are helping increase the power of those ships. Their shields should not have lasted that long, let alone have enough power for a jump. We need to find them before they complete those enhancements."

"How Sir?"

"I will be in my quarters, making a call." Halburn turned and started towards the hatch. He took three steps then looked back over his shoulder. "And make sure the rest of the fleet disables that control node, for good." He climbed down the ladder as the hatch closed.

In his quarters Lavine's eyes narrowed on Halburn's data tab. "I am not pleased. I gave you another chance, and you failed me even with an entire fleet at your disposal."

"I know, but hear me out. I saw the *Defiant* take more weapons fire than it ever did before without so much as a scratch. Those aliens are either helping Deven or they have taken the carriers to add to their fleet."

"For what purpose? From what I have seen, they are not in need of any ships."

"I don't know, but it has to be important to their plan or they wouldn't have bothered modifying them." Halburn sat back in his chair as he turned it back and forth. "Also, neither ship so much as fired a shot. I feel like we are missing a large piece of this puzzle." He sat up. "Can you find the *Defiant* with the satellite?"

"I think we have gained orientation access. Give me a minute." Lavine tapped several buttons on the console to his right. "Yes, it is accepting, but it is slow." After several minutes the view changed to show less of the space ships above and more of the Earth. "There, it pitched down, but I don't find them at the moment. They could be out of its range."

"Out of its range?" Halburn cocked his head several times. "How? If it could detect all those ships–"

Lavine grinned. "You do realize a planet is in the way, right? I can only scan what it can see, which is limited at any given time. The satellite is in a fast moving orbit, but it will take a while to scan the whole planet."

"A pity we don't have more of them."

"Yes. This one must be before the Nexus was built. While the Nexus had several relay satellites in orbit, after we witnessed her emergence, I had what remained of the network destroyed."

Halburn chewed the inside of his cheek. "We couldn't trust them even if they were around. I witnessed my entire fleet held in place even though the codes had been changed, I have doubts we could maintain control of those satellites without direct access to the hardware."

"Yes, it is not worth the risk." Lavine tapped several keys. "I have narrowed down where they could be." Lavine pressed another button and Halburn's screen split showing the areas outside of the satellite's range. Almost half of the planet still remained unknown.

"That is a lot of area. It would require splitting the fleet into several divisions, and I don't want to if I can avoid it. Even the entire fleet failed to take them down although, we were close. I can only imagine them laughing if fifteen or so ships encountered the Nexus carrier, let alone the *Defiant*."

Lavine turned back to the screen facing Halburn. "Very well. I will keep hunting for them, and I trust you will do the same."

"Of course. And I have a hunch where to look."

The *Defiant's* overdrive fluctuated under the strain sending everyone aboard careening from one side to the other. Gregory stumbled onto the bridge. "Galina, what are you trying to do? Shake us apart?"

"No!" She spat while gripping the controls tighter. "When the Lytherians said the engines weren't ready, they weren't kidding! It is like trying to drive a truck through two feet of mud at high speed. We're sliding all over the place."

Miles' camera turned. "And our navigational link to the *Phoenix* is causing them to have increased difficulty. They are trying to match our erratic movements in addition to their own."

"Miles, drop the link."

"If I do, they will crash out of overdrive, and it may stall their engines entirely."

Gregory grabbed onto a chair and pulled himself into it. "They would go down like a stone. At this speed no way they could restart before becoming a giant crater."

The camera turned to face Gregory. "Correct. The odds of survival are very low."

Alarms screamed and several screens flashed red causing

Galina to swear but she didn't dare take her eyes off of the controls. "What now?"

Miles' camera turned. "The engines are overheating. I estimate less than 30 seconds until failure."

"Failure? You mean until we explode!" Gregory said.

"I believe I said that," Miles stated in his usual calm voice.

"We need to drop out of overdrive *now*."

"Not yet. If I do now, Halburn will be on us faster than you can say 'I'm back'."

"But if you don't, there won't be enough of us to even shoot at."

Galina gritted her teeth. "Come on you bucket of bolts. Just a little further."

Deven grabbed a console as he tried to keep himself from being thrown across the bridge. Not everyone was as quick causing Otis and Dakarth to be hurled into a bulkhead seeing stars. Aleshia grabbed a chair with her mind and pulled herself to it. "Minerva! What are you doing!?"

"I am sorry, it is unavoidable. The engines are not stable. I am trying to compensate but it is having little effect."

Dakarth rubbed his head. "I told you, they were not ready."

Leon stumbled onto the bridge. "What have you done to my engines?"

Minerva's eyes narrowed. "You mean *my* engines."

"Who cares at this point? This is going to rip us apart. Cut overdrive *now*."

Minerva shook her head. "We are still linked to the *Defiant*. If I do that–"

"It will stall the engines and we go down like the *Titanic*."

"Correct. Although much faster than *that* ancient ship."

"We have to do something. Contact Galina, tell her to stop."

"I cannot, communications are offline."

"Fine, I'll use mine." Deven whipped out his data tab and tapped a button to call Galina, only to receive an 'unable to establish connection, please try again later' message. "What the heck?"

Leon gripped the arms of the chair he managed to reach. "The engines must be so unstable they are throwing off one massive interference wave."

"Can we break through?"

"Sure. Shut down the engines so I can fix them."

Deven gritted his teeth. "I'll take that as a no. Aleshia, can you contact her?"

Aleshia held on to her chair as her eyes came up to focus on Deven's. "Do you think I can concentrate in this?" She said as another bone jarring lurch shook through the *Phoenix*.

"Great. Talk about being up a creek ... "

Galina yanked the controls, but they still refused to respond quick enough. The ship continued to rock, shake, and shudder. "Come on, a little more."

"The *Defiant* can't keep this up. She's going to shake herself to pieces," Gregory said.

"Don't have to. We're close enough. Hang on!" She slammed her hand on the emergency stop and even with the warning it sent Gregory flying from his chair. He picked himself up from the deck plate that left a temporary impression on the one side of his face. The *Phoenix* emerged next to them a microsecond later.

"Geez! Next time give me more warning would you?"

"Will try."

"Where are we anyway?"

"Antarctica."

"Again? Are you nuts? This will be the first place Halburn will look."

"I doubt it. That is the reason he won't"

"Huh?"

"It doesn't make sense to go where we were before, which is why he won't check. At least not for a while."

"That's crazy."

"Maybe, but right now a little crazy is what we need." She tapped the communications and a moment later a screen was filled with white noise. "Minerva? Are you there?"

The screen flickered and flashed before Minerva's face appeared. "I am. There was some damage, but we are intact."

The screen split as Leon's face inserted itself. "Yeah no thanks to your driving."

"Hey, next time you try driving this tub with engines trying to do the opposite of *everything* you tell it."

"You just need to think three steps ahead."

"Uh-huh, and it is a problem when you can only see two."

"Details, details," Leon said with a wave of his hand. "Gregory, get down to the engines, I want to know their status."

"But can't the Lytherians take care of–"

"And who got us out of there? Hmm?"

"You did." Gregory coughed and glared at her. "Er, um team effort. But I don't understand what happened."

"Simple. Do you remember reading about how ancient cars had a choke on the fuel supply to get an engine started?"

"Yeah, but our engines are nothing like those."

"True. But the new power core was dumping a lot of energy into the cold engine, and because the upgrades weren't finished, it was way beyond its normal tolerances causing it to shut down. What we did was a jump-start of sorts. Allowing enough power to start, but not flood it."

Gregory nodded. "Of course, and it would have stalled once started if we didn't plug the other line back in."

Leon smiled. "You got it. The Lytherians may have superior technology, but they don't know these systems like we do."

"Or like you do at least."

"Hey, you're getting there. Now get down to the engines and see what needs to be done. Coordinate with the Lytherians and myself."

"You got it." Gregory said getting up.

Deven's face came onto another screen. "I'll be right over. I'm sure Gregory could use a hand."

"The main landing bay has several obstructions. It will need to be cleared," Miles said.

"How about one of the smaller secondary bays?"

After a second, Miles responded. "Bay C-3 is still operational; however, the entrance won't accommodate your current vehicle."

"I can use one of Minerva's fighters. Ready the bay," Deven said before his image disappeared.

"Miles, next time let me answer," Galina said through pursed lips.

"But you would have asked me anyway."

"That is not the point."

"I fail to see the logic in this."

"It may not be at times, but is how we do things. It is called command structure, learn it."

"But I thought–"

"Miles?" Galina grumbled as her eyes narrowed.

The camera focused in on her face. The iris went wide then contracted. "Acknowledged."

Leon watched as the chair in front of him changed shape. The high back receded into itself while the armrests likewise shrunk into the base. The whole thing resembled a big ball of black dough someone was kneading. He knew that someone were the nanomachines. Dakarth had applied a thick, black liquid material to several locations inside and around the chair. At first only the applied areas started to shimmer. Then the material spread engulfing the entire chair, reforming it as per their instructions.

The chair's back returned higher than before and a ring the size of Aleshia's head formed at the top, mounted on a slide allowing it to move up and down when needed. The armrests equally returned, though more rounded shape. The seat itself became thicker increasing in padding. The shimmer had stopped and Leon reached for the opening in the back but Dakarth stopped him. "No, it issss not ready yet. The circuity inside is still being built." His eyes drifted down to the control device in his hand. Several minutes later a talon twitched, and he smiled. "Now it is done."

Leon stepped forward and pulled off the newly built back of the chair. Inside he found the electronics. Or what he assumed were electronics. Most of the area inside looked more organic than normal circuity. His worries grew when he failed to recognize a single part. "It looks good," he said in an up tone, which was the opposite of his feelings. "But I'm concerned an overload might harm Aleshia. I built in a lot of safety systems and backups."

Dakarth smiled. His thin Lytherian lips parting ever so slightly. Walking around to the back, he pointed to several points in the system resembling brown fuzzy blocks. "They are inhibitors."

Leon cocked his head. "Inhibitors? Like a fuse that will blow before it harms Aleshia?"

He nodded. "Something like your fuses, but much more advanced. They have the ability to regulate the excess energy and route it around to other areas that are not in surplus."

"But what if there is no place for the extra to go?"

The Lytherian engineer smiled. "My friend it is not a concern. They can absorb and store vast amounts of energy in their molecular structure for when it is needed. Or it can be dissipated elsewhere as an option."

"Elsewhere? Such as?"

"There are many, but one possibility is to feed it back into the main power system, augmenting it. This can increase the rate of fire in your weapons for example. Although, the energy can be directed anywhere."

Leon whistled. "Impressive. And yet you haven't been able to beat the Celloids?"

"Well, keep in mind we didn't have these developments at the start of the war. But the reason for continued difficulties, they learned to increase their replication rate. Even with our developing technology, they continue to come very close to overwhelming us. I fear at some point they will succeed."

"Hence the change in your methods," Aleshia said.

Dakarth nodded. "Yes. However, while we can replace the equipment with relative ease, replacing our lost people issss far more difficult."

Leon's eyes shut fast then opened slowly as a chill went up his spine at the thought. "Of course. I am surprised you still contemplated waiting this long."

"We could last for another couple of centuries by our estimates. The Celloids, up until now, have been very precise in their attacks. We could almost predict, up to one of your minutes, when the next attack would occur and how many ships would show. Nothing caused them to deviate. Until they learned of you. That aspect is a bit of a mystery." He gestured to the chair with a long finger and the talon at the end twitched as he looked at Aleshia. "Would you like to try it out?"

Leon again gazed at the strange innards of the chair. "I am not sure–"

"Trust me. She is in no danger. And she can stop the system at any time by pressing this button." As he pointed down to the right armrest, a hidden compartment slid back and large red button, the size of three fingers, emerged."

"It is even red," Leon joked.

Dakarth blinked. "Am I in error? I believe it how you label important items with?"

"No, no, you did fine." He sighed. "I guess we do need to test this out."

Aleshia pushed past him and sat in the chair. "Leon you worry too much. If he wanted to harm me, I would know about it."

"That is not what I–"

"Meant, I know. And I am thankful you are watching over me. But I'm sure this will be fine." She sat back and the silver ring descended onto her head. The chair itself began to glow around the base. She closed her eyes and her mind reached out. She watched as the Lytherians planned the defense of

Earth, the ships moving in a net formation adding to the scanning ability of each ship. "Minerva, what is the power level?"

"21.5% of previous maximum."

"Wow and I get this much now? Amazing."

Dakarth smiled as he turned towards Leon. "I told you it would be much better. Yes?"

Leon nodded. "You did. But in my defense, I was flying almost blind in the design."

"You did very well. Far more than I would have expected. But your interface to the crystal was inadequate."

His eyes went wide. "Inadequate?!"

"Forgive me. Bad choice of your words. How could you have known, its technology is very different from yours? If the roles were reversed, I doubt I could have done as well."

"I see," Leon said. He opened his mouth to say more but Minerva beat him to it.

"I think they finished the cannon upgrades. I can now access them again."

A beep came from Dakarth's belt. He whipped the device out and it opened revealing one of his engineers. "The weapons are now online. New emitters along with improved power distribution."

"And the shields?" Dakarth said.

"Repairs and upgrades completed as well. Final engine augments are in process and nearing completion."

"Good, I will be down in a moment to assist." The Lytherian nodded and his face disappeared from the tiny screen. Dakarth looked up at Leon. "Shall we go?"

"Sure, if the engine upgrades are anything like the chair, it should be something worth seeing."

"Alas not quite. If we were to do to a full rebuild, the ship would need to be on the ground. But it is possible to augment in place while maintaining enough operation to retain the ship's position. It is a much slower procedure as you can imagine."

"I do. And I saw in fact. The *Defiant* had a bit of trouble earlier if you recall."

"The problems were due to power, not engine augments. And unavoidable in that case. As you said, we do not know the technology as well as you."

"You know, you guys are really distracting," Aleshia said with her eyes still closed.

Leon laughed. "Can't wait to get rid of us, eh?"

They walked towards the hatch only to bump into Otis climbing up. "You should have seen it! I watched them reduce a full sized cannon to a liquid puddle and reform it into one massive cannon far bigger than the previous one. The emitters are enormous!" The hatch closed cutting off the rest of the conversation.

18

Halburn watched out the front window as the *Valiant* hurtled towards its destination at top speed with the rest of the fleet right behind him. He knew this was a long shot. Deven was too smart to take the risk, but if he wasn't the one giving orders, it might work.

High above, the *Valiant* crossed the edges of the Antarctic storm and approached from the north. Below, the storm was more turbulent than normal. He gave the rest of the fleet orders to spread out and surround the other sides of the continent. Each one took up a position at the edge of Antarctica. Once they had encircled the great ice shelf, the entire fleet began moving towards the south pole. If the *Defiant* and the Nexus were here, he would find him.

Aleshia sat in the endless quiet of the *Phoenix's* bridge. The only sound was from the ventilation system giving its usual wheeze. She reached out with her mind scanning the Lytherians and reaching …out …further …and …further. There was something. Aleshia could almost feel it but before she could zero in, she whipped back as if a giant rubber band had stretched to its breaking point.

But when she came sailing back, she went through the Lytherian ships down to Earth, and passed the *Phoenix* whipping out along the Antarctica ice. Aleshia felt something different. Questions, duty, determination. She followed it reaching up above the ice. She shuddered finding ships. Many ships approaching them from all sides. The fleet had found them.

Aleshia's eyes shot open. "We have a problem. Halburn is here."

Minerva blinked. "That is not possible. I would have detected him."

The indicator light above a nearby speaker glowed to life. "I do not see any indications of such a situation," Miles said.

"He is either outside of your range, or something is jamming his approach. He is on the edge of the storm and is searching for us."

Deven's face appeared on the large screen. "Miles told me Halburn is here? How is it possible we don't detect him even with the new sensors?"

"We still don't. It is conceivable the storms are sending out increased ionic activity due to a solar flare. It would mask their approach. But such a flare has not occurred in decades," Minerva said.

"Any way to confirm this?"

Minerva shook her head. "I no longer have any functional satellites in orbit."

Aleshia turned. "Get Dakarth up here."

"We're already here." Leon's voice came from behind. Aleshia turned to see he and Dakarth entering the bridge, the hatch closing behind them.

"We have been informed assss to the situation. What is it you require?" Dakarth said.

"Contact your *Command* carrier, see if they can confirm a solar flare." Deven said.

"Of course." Dakarth pulled the communications device from his belt and opened it. Another Lytherian appeared with a large tactical screen showing behind him. Dakarth spoke with a deep rhythmical hiss. The Lytherian on the screen responded and a second later Dakarth closed the device. "There is a strong flare going on now. It won't get past the shields, but it is blocking our scans in this area of the planet. We cannot confirm if this Halburn is approaching or not."

Aleshia glared. "Did you doubt me?"

Dakarth inclined his head. "Of courssse not. I am only stating we cannot see any approaching attack, nothing more."

"Let's avoid them," Deven said. "Which direction are they coming from?"

"All sides. The ships are spread out like a net heading towards the south pole."

"Not good." Deven leaned towards Dakarth as he appeared on his screen. "How long will our shields last against another attack?"

Dakarth smiled. "Now with the upgrades are complete, I doubt they can harm you in the short-term. However, it is possible a long-term one could have unforeseen side effects."

"Like what?"

Dakarth shrugged his reptilian shoulders. "I do not know. These are not Lytherian ships. It is impossible to predict every outcome. But I do have a suggestion."

"Leon turned. Which is?"

"There is one place you can go. Straight up."

Minerva blinked. "Into space? This ship was not designed for that."

"Neither was the *Defiant*," Deven said.

"That issss true. But with the new shields and engines, it should be possible. The ships are designed to be pressurized. You are even now. It is one place they cannot go."

Deven rubbed his chin. "It would give us more time. Perhaps I can convince him of what is really going on."

"The time for deciding is up. I am detecting them at the very edge of visual range," Minerva said.

Deven turned. "Miles can you confirm?"

The camera behind Deven focused on him. "Yes I can. Three ships have appeared in visual range. And if my analysis is correct, one of them is the *Valiant*."

"Sure you ask him not me," Galina grumbled from the side.

"But you would have asked me anyway," Miles said.

"Miles! Hush! I wasn't talking to you!"

"But–"

"Never mind!" She sat back with her arms folded.

"How long until they are in firing range?" Deven asked.

Minerva's gaze shifted off to the side and back. "Based on when I saw the first ship and then the time between that and when the second one arrived. We have approximately two minutes before they can fire their weapons."

Deven turned to Galina. "Wait for one minute forty seconds and take us straight up. Minerva is still linked, correct?"

Minerva nodded. "Yes we are."

"What? Why so close? Didn't you hear Minerva? Two minutes is approximate! It could be sooner," Galina said.

Miles' camera turned. "That is correct. The time is only an extrapolation. Without our normal scanners, the estimate can vary significantly."

Deven's image turned, and he shot a finger in Galina's direction. "Listen, if we do it too fast, he will never know we were here. And I want him to know."

Otis raised a hand towards Deven's screen with fingers outstretched. "Umm Boss, why? Isn't it best we avoid him?"

"You heard Dakarth, he can't hurt us in the short-term. If sees us, shoot straight up and go into orbit. It may pique his interest enough to listen to me."

"But he won't know we did. You heard Minerva and Miles. Their scanners are blinded as much as ours."

"Ah, but I suspect at higher elevation we will be seen. Or at the very least he should be able to confirm our entry into orbit."

Minerva smiled. "That is very possible. The ionic interference radiating from the storm should be restricted to this and lower levels of the atmosphere. Less than 20 seconds until they enter firing range."

Deven smiled. "Everyone take a seat. Galina, full power to the vertical thrust."

She nodded and tapped her console. The lower engines on the *Defiant* and *Phoenix* glowed brighter a microsecond before both craft shot straight up. A few moments later Deven watched as a cup floated past his face. "Well, I think we made it," Galina chuckled, "but this is going to make one heck of mess. We never planned on not having gravity."

Aboard the *Phoenix*, Otis continued to sit with his ankle on his knee, even though he had floated off of his chair. "Boss, I don't like this."

Dakarth smiled. "We should have given you an artificial gravity system, but we didn't think you would need it. I will have my men add it."

Leon floated into a wall and bounced off. "How long will that take?"

"Twenty of your minutes, perhaps a little more. The new power core is more than half of the system, we only need to line a few connection points to the bottom of the deck plating and direct the force down. But I am surprised you don't have such a system. I have observed you do have anti-gravity devices."

"Yeah, well, we never planned on taking this thing into orbit!"

Deven smiled on the screen. "What I would give to see Halburn's face now."

The *Valiant* continued on course to the south pole. No one had found anything and Halburn was starting to think he had led them on a wild goose chase. He ran his fingers through his hair. Grey was taking over at a rapid rate despite his age.

"Sir? I think we have found them," Naud said tapping his console.

"You think?"

"Scanners are not working. I can't even pick up our own ships ever since we started heading towards the south pole."

"Malfunction?"

Naud shook his head. "Everything checks out. This doesn't make sense. *Unless* the storms are generating more iconic interference than normal. But if we can't see them, it also means they can't see us either."

"If their scanners aren't better than ours. And want to make a bet they are?"

Naud shrugged. "Maybe, maybe not. Either way I have found them." He pointed to his screen. The top right corner displayed an enhanced camera view straight head. To their two o'clock, a couple of small dots loomed on the horizon. "Sensors may be out, but there they are."

Halburn leaned over the console. "Are you sure it is them?"

"What else could it be? In a stable position that high up above the surface?"

Halburn made a grasping motion in the air. "We have them! Order the rest of the fleet to converge here."

Naud shook his head. "They are too far away. And I am sure they know we are here. I mean, it would be crazy to assume the Nexus hasn't spotted us, even with sensors offline." He paused a moment to point at the enhanced image on this screen. The two dots appeared brighter than before. "And I think we have visual confirmation of their energy output is increasing."

"How many ships are in range?"

"Three of us can reach them in under a minute at full speed."

"No, don't change speed. Make it look like we haven't seen them yet. They may let us get close enough to get a few shots off. Tell the fleet to aim for the engines only, I want them prevented from leaving. Not a scrap yard. Is that clear?"

"Yes Sir."

"Thirty seconds until they are in range," Rechert said

"Ready all cannons. Fire as soon as they are."

"Ten seconds until–" His mouth hung open as the both ships hover engines glowed with intense energy. A microsecond later a discharge erupted from them causing both ships to rocket straight up. "Umm Sir?"

"Track them! They must be trying to fly over us," Halburn said. "Prepare to follow."

"I don't think we can Sir," Naud said.

"What? Why not? Did they jump already?"

"No, they are ... if my systems–"

"Naud!"

"In orbit, Sir."

"In orbit? Are you telling me those aliens converted both carriers into space ships?"

"I am not sure what was done, but they are in orbit."

Halburn ran his fingers through his hair again. "This makes even less sense than before. Why would they make the ships space worthy? It would be far more difficult than using their own. If infiltration was their aim, they must know it wouldn't work now with our knowledge of them."

"Could it be they don't realize we do?"

"They would have to be really dumb, and I'm sure they aren't."

Naud's eyes slid down to see a blinking light on his console. His eyebrows met. "Sir? Someone is trying to contact us."

"The fleet no doubt."

"No, I don't think so. At least the signal is not coming from their general direction."

"It must be Lavine."

"Not unless he is straight up about thirty miles."

"Are you telling me the aliens are calling?"

"No, the frequency signature is too exact. It is from the *Defiant*."

Halburn gestured with his hand and Deven's face appeared on the big screen in front. "Odell, so good to see you again." The face bobbed up and down as if trying to maintain a position centered with the visual pickup.

Halburn gritted his teeth. "Deven ..."

"I'm sorry we couldn't stay, but I had a feeling you were going to try to blast us out of the sky again. And I need to talk with you."

"You have my attention. Nice stunt you pulled. How in the world did you manage it?"

"You liked that eh? Well we had the assistance of a few new friends."

"I kind of figured that."

Deven nodded. "I thought you might. Especially when I tried to warn you before."

"Yes, which makes me wonder if I am talking to Deven now, or something else."

"Odell, it is me. Have no doubt. When I talked with you before, I didn't have the whole picture. Or even worse, an inaccurate one to begin with."

"Meaning?"

"Meaning the Lytherians are not our enemies. I am sure you have seen all their ships in orbit?"

"Now, how would I have seen that?"

"You can't tell me Lavine doesn't have something watching. The way you showed up with a fleet of Mechand carriers proves he has more up his sleeve than I thought."

Odell folded his arms and puffed up his shoulders. "Point taken, let's say, for the sake of argument, I have. What's your point?"

"My point is, haven't you wondered why they haven't attacked if they were the enemy? With an armada of such size, why didn't they come down in force when there is little to stop them?"

"Again, for the sake of argument, let's say I did. Again, I ask, what's your point?"

"The reason is simple. They aren't the ones we need to worry about. The Celloids are."

Halburn mouthed the words slowly. "The Celloids?"

"They are a plant based race that only exists to convert planets into a living green mass, extract everything useful from it, and move on to the next. The Lytherians have been fighting them for centuries."

"And let me guess, they want our help?"

"How astute of you, yes they do."

"And why would such an advanced race want our help?"

"Telepathy. They don't have it, but we do."

Halburn turned, walked to his command chair and sat down. "And why would this race need telepathy?"

"It is the one thing that will disrupt the Celloids enough for them to be destroyed once and for all."

"Nice story, but one little problem."

"Which is?"

"I know they have been here before. And it was not what you told me last time."

Deven's face went blank. "Oh."

"Exactly, when were you going to tell me that part?"

"I wasn't sure how much you would believe."

"Deven, you should know me better than that."

"You're right, I should have given it to you straight."

"Yes you should have. But now we have an interesting problem."

Deven chewed the inside of his cheek. His old friend wasn't buying this, and he knew it. But there was nothing left but to put all his cards on the table. He sighed. "And what might that be?"

Halburn smiled. "How am I going to join you way up there?"

Deven laughed. "You believe me?"

"Of course. You should have known I would realize things didn't add up. It is what I have been telling Lavine. Sorry about the last encounter though, I assumed you had been taken over by these Lytherians, based on the technology changes and the non-human heat signatures."

"You could have called." Deven glared at the man on his screen.

"Yes, but at the time, we had the element of surprise on our side. And you did try to warn me about an alien threat. I assumed the threat was real and had managed a hostile takeover. What would you have done?"

Deven looked off to the side, his expression changing several times. When his eyes returned, the glare was gone. "The same. But you didn't have the element of surprise. We knew you were coming."

"But you didn't take any action."

"We couldn't. Most of the systems were offline at the time. You must have noticed the overdrive was down."

"We did. But if true, how did you know?"

Deven smiled. "We have an asset far beyond normal sensors, Aleshia."

Halburn laughed. "Of course. But I didn't think she had that kind of range."

"Let's say her abilities have grown."

Halburn cracked a grin. "So are you going to come back down or what?"

"We will, as soon as everything is secure." The coffee cup from before floated past his face again. Deven glared. "As you can see things are a bit of a mess up here at the moment."

Halburn laughed. "Take your time. We're not in any hurry."

"Unfortunately, we are. I will tell you more when we arrive. Deven out."

The screen flicked off and Halburn sat back down in his chair. "I wonder what the next surprise is. But I have a feeling it is going to be a lot worse."

Several things floated past, dirt, a screwdriver, a loose cable, as Gregory fastened down another vehicle with several large magnetic locks. Several other people did the same. No damage had occurred yet, but the main hanger bay was a mess. He was grateful no one had left out any unconstrained liquids, or it would have been a lot worse. Gregory grumbled as he moved on to the next.

An hour later everything had been locked down and he hoped the rest of the *Defiant* was in the same condition. He floated over to the intercom and toggled the switch. "Main hanger bay and engineering are secure. You need me anywhere else?"

"Nah," Galina said, "I think we're in good shape now. The *Phoenix* has been ready for some time, but there is not much that can be left out of place. I guess the battle Mechands were floating around the various rooms but Minerva woke them up, activated magnets in their feet, and moved back into formation. Except for the Mechand Otis took over, not much else could float away apart from for the ships, and Minerva had them locked down before."

Gregory's one eyebrow rose. "Something happened with the cleaning Mechand of Otis'?"

"Well, it doesn't have feet like most Mechands. And it would seem it lacks any sort of affixing devices either. Otis found it floating in one of the corridors beeping away. He moved the cleaning bot in one of the rooms with the other Mechands and told them to keep him from floating off again."

"And he thinks that will work?"

"It should, unless the bot tries to run off and clean something again. I've never seen anyone so happy about cleaning."

Gregory chuckled. "Or anyone so happy to see Otis. Sounds like he has his hands full with that bot. I'm on my way up." He shut off the intercom and gave himself a push. He sailed across the open space and grabbed the side of the inner bay door as he propelled himself around going into the corridor feet first. It had taken him a few minutes, but he had adapted to micro gravity like a duck to water. Several of the Lytherians were not so lucky. He doubted they ever experienced micro gravity as lost lunches abound down the corridor. He didn't want to know what the multicolored sludge floating past was. Gregory gave a cleaner with a vacuum attachment to someone and told them to clean it up. While normally he would have done it, this was one time when rank had its privileges.

He floated up to the bridge and pushed himself off the one wall, over to another wall, then off of the ceiling to a vacant chair.

Galina glared. "Done showing off?"

He sat as a grin spread across his face. "For now."

Deven looked up from his data tab. "Are we ready to go back down?"

"Yes, or should be unless the Lytherians got sick again. But I can't imagine them having anything *left* to get sick with."

Deven nodded. "Add Aleshia to the list. From what I hear she is very green."

Miles' camera moved back and forth with the conversation. He considered mentioning he knew Aleshia was doing better, but it would reveal he was watching without being asked. "I hope Ms. Aleshia is feeling better," he added.

"I am sure she is. Or I would know." Deven tapped several keys on his data tab. "Miles, get Minerva."

Minerva's face appeared on Deven's screen second later. "Yes?"

"Are we ready? I am sure Halburn is wondering by now."

She nodded. "Yes, we have been for some time. The question is more of, is the *Defiant* ready?"

"Or a better question, are the Lytherians ready."

The screen split and Dakarth appeared. "My men have reported everything is ready, we will begin adding gravity in small increments to verify everything is as it should be before our decent."

"And nothing goes crash," Otis muttered from the background.

Dakarth turned. "Yes, or *that*." The image shrank into a pinpoint and disappeared.

Weight began as a mere fraction of Earth-normal. But it was enough to send items reaching towards the deck plates and landing with a gentle tap. After a few minutes, it was increased but left at a very weak level until everything was inspected. Gregory didn't float around with the grace as before, but instead bounced as if his feet had large springs. This proved more difficult than no gravity. Several times he miscalculated and ended up bouncing off of the ceiling, then back down towards the deck to bounce off again before he could get stopped.

With inspections completed, the Lytherians dialed up the gravity to normal and Galina started their decent with the *Phoenix* right behind them. The shields began to glow with the atmospheric friction making a white hot bubble around them. "Galina, slow us down. The slower we go, the less friction, and the easier it will be," Deven said.

"Duh. This is not as easy as it looks. The *Defiant* was not built to be a spaceship!"

"I know, but I have every confidence in your abilities."

Galina increased power to the hover engines. They groaned but their thrust expanded slowing the *Defiant's* plunge. The flames outside diminished, but did not disappear as the ship rocked back and forth. "Sorry, this is still going to be a bit rough. Can't be helped."

Deven nodded, and he hit a button on his console. Minerva's face reappeared. "How are you holding up?"

"The calculations are proving to be difficult, but manageable."

Aboard the *Phoenix*, the ship rocked and Otis grit his teeth. "If you call this manageable, I would hate to see a rough ride."

Minerva smiled as her eyes shifted towards Otis. "If you don't like my driving, you can get out and walk you know."

"Har har, very funny. I don't know what is worse, the humor or the attempt at it."

Aleshia glared. "She is doing the best she can."

"Sure, I just hope it's enough."

Across from him, Leon's eyes rolled as he turned towards Dakarth who was sitting next to him. "My apologies, they are not usually this bad."

"No apology necessssary. They are entitled. It would appear more modifications are required."

Otis blinked. "Ya think?"

"Please keep in mind, thissss was not planned. And therefore untested."

Now it was Otis' turn to roll his eyes. "Great."

Back on the *Defiant*, Deven's screen had split showing Minerva on one side with a wide shot of everyone else on the other. "Otis, that's enough. People are nervous enough without you adding to it. I know this is way out of your element, but deal with it."

Otis sighed. "Sorry Boss, but I'm no astronaut."

"None of us are. Relax, it will be over in a minute."

Several screens flashed red as text rolled past. "There is an imbalance in the power core. It is currently at 23% and increasing. If it reaches 50% we may lose containment," Miles said.

A second later alarms on the *Phoenix* went off. Minerva frowned. "I am having the same problem. It appears to be due to the artificial gravity system, coupled with engines and shields at full power. I am detecting a resonance feedback loop disrupting the core."

Miles' camera whipped back and forth on the *Defiant's* bridge. "I concur. I suggest deactivating the gravity system. Nothing will float at this point."

Dakarth's hand shot forward. "No! If you disable now, the new power core will go offline for a full miron cycle while it restarts."

"I am guessing, that is quite a while?" Leon said.

"Yes, we will impact with the planet before the restart is complete."

"Well this is a fine mess," Galina spat. "We will be coming down in pieces if this keeps up."

"Nudge the engines back. We will go down faster, and the shields will take more of a beating. But they should hold," Leon said.

"Should being the operative word," Galina said.

"We don't have a choice," Deven said.

"Right." Galina grumbled as she lowered the power to the hover system. Minerva did the same, and both ships began plunging through the atmosphere at an increased rate. Flames grew brighter threatening the break through the shields.

"Shields at 80% of tolerance at this level and increasing. Expected failure in 32 seconds," Miles said.

Minerva's brow furrowed. "My shields are at 86% of tolerance. One of the emitters is showing fluctuations."

Aleshia turned her head towards Leon. "Anything we can do?"

He shook his head. "Not now. I hope they hold."

Otis shut his eyes. "Hope?"

The shaking increased as both ships rocketed through the atmosphere sending out large shock waves behind them. Around the *Phoenix* the shields fluctuated around the one emitter. "Shield collapse is imminent," Minerva said. Outside, the flames grew white hot.

"Minerva, which emitter is failing?" Leon said.

"Stern, port side."

"Nose us down, and throw all available power into the front shields. It might be enough."

She blinked. "But it will send us down even faster, and the shields are at maximum now."

"Push them over the line. We can't afford to play it safe, or we will come down in pieces."

She nodded. "Acknowledged. Orientation adjusted, diverting power." All the lights on the bridge went out, causing the room to dim, cast in an orange glow emanating from the windows. "Our course will now take us out over the sea."

"Shield status?" Leon said.

"Still holding, but it will fail in ten seconds."

"Minerva, remind me to teach you a little optimism sometime."

"What would–"

Aleshia rolled her eyes. "Never mind!"

The *Phoenix* stopped its shaking and Otis opened an eye. "Are we dead?"

Dakarth's lips parted in a wide grin. "If that wassss true, you wouldn't be talking."

"No, we have made it through the upper levels of the atmosphere," Minerva said.

"We made it?" Otis said.

"Of course, what else would it mean?"

The large screen crackled with white and grey pixels before they reformed into Deven's face. "*Phoenix*! Come in! Please respond!"

"We're here." Aleshia said letting her grip relax on arm rests for the first time since they started the decent. "It was a rough ride, but we are here."

He blew out a breath. "Oh thank God, when communications failed, I feared the worst."

"I told you it was increased ionic disruption due to the extreme heating of the atmosphere," Miles' voice came through the speaker.

Deven turned his head. "Yes I know Miles, but you have been wrong before."

Behind Deven, Miles' camera iris contracted then expanded. "When?"

"What? Do you want a list?"

"Yes, as I am not recalling such incidents. Such a list would be appreciated, preferably alphabetical."

Deven glared. "Miles?"

"Yes?"

"Drop it."

His iris shrank and enlarged again. "Dropped."

Deven turned back. "Now where are you? We don't see you in the vicinity."

"Yeah, Minerva had to nose us down to protect the rear shields. She said we were going to be out over the ocean," Aleshia said.

"That is correct." Minerva paused checking her systems. "If you are at the previous coordinates, we should rendezvous in fifteen minutes. Once my overdrive comes back online."

Deven cocked his head. "Why is it down?"

"I had to channel all available power into the shields. I thought they would fail, but Leon said they would hold. He was correct."

Leon smirked. "I had a hunch."

"Glad he was. See you in a few." Deven's face disappeared as the connection cut.

19

Far from Earth, slightly closer to Mars a large aperture formed. At first it appeared as a tiny blue speck. But like any baby it grew quickly until it was larger than the Lytherian *Command* carrier. The circling storm of energy flashed red and a large Celloid ship emerged from it. The energy storm flashed again and another large ship emerged. The pace increased until all the Celloid fleet materialized. With the last ship clear of the storm, the warp crashed shut, sealing itself.

Several alarms flashed and Karthish knew before Gakon, his second-in-command spoke. "Sir, the Celloids have arrived and are approaching at top speed."

"I know. Get Dakarth and his team up here now. They are needed. And start redeploying the fleet to put us between the Celloids and Earth. We cannot allow even one ship to get past."

"Yes Sir."

On the *Phoenix* Leon sat with Dakarth discussing the best way to upgrade Halbrun's fleet. Otis stood nearby listening intently while Aleshia's eyes had glazed over a few seconds after they began comparing mathematical models. She sat in one of the console seats to the side, trying not to fall asleep. She didn't want to appear rude, but even with the unpadded seat, it was a struggle to stay awake. Aleshia wanted to try out the new telepathic system, but Dakarth assured her it would work.

A device on Dakarth's belt beeped in a higher tone than usual. He sighed knowing the alert signal. He pulled the device free and flipped it open, expecting the worst. "I assume the Celloids have arrived?"

"Yes, Karthish wants you back aboard as soon as possible."

Dakarth nodded. "Understood, we will leave in a moment." He flipped the device closed and replaced it on his belt. "I am ssssorry, we must leave."

Minerva blinked. "What I don't understand is, if they have arrived, how will you have time to get back without being shot out of the sky?"

"It is quite ssssimple. You see when Celliods make a jump, they have to concentrate all of their energy to do so. At arrival, their ships are in a state of energy depletion. They will need to replenish before launching an attack. Celloid ships always arrive some distance from target and after a large thrust, remain dormant, recharging their systems if you will, before attacking. This gives us some time. But not much. Several of your hours. I was hoping we could upgrade the rest of your ships. But we no longer have the option."

Leon sighed. "We will have to make do with what we have."

"I hope it is enough," Dakarth said heading for the hatch.

"It will have to be," Leon muttered.

Back on the *Defiant*, Deven stood by the bridge window and watched as the two Lytherian shuttles left heading for the

Command carrier. Miles' camera turned. "Deven? We are receiving a call from the *Valiant*."

Deven checked chronometer on his console. "Almost one minute. Odell is getting slow. Put him on."

One of the larger bridge screens flashed as Halburn's face appeared. "Mind telling me what is going on? I see our help is leaving."

"The Celloids are here."

"What?" Halburn spat. "Where?"

"They have emerged from their jump and will arrive in a few hours. Dakarth and his team are needed back aboard."

"Now what?"

"Now we prepare the best we can. You and your fleet go to the night side of the planet and we will stay on the day side. If anything gets through the Lytherians, we will take it out."

"Sounds like a plan. But I don't like we are out-gunned."

Deven sighed. "Neither do I, but I hope you won't see any action on the night side."

"Why would night make a difference?"

"I had a discussion with Karthish, and it seems the Celloids can use sunlight as a boost to their internal power generation. They never attacked at night, always during the day. You should be fine."

"What about you?"

"We have the better weapons remember? We will take them out. But with luck, neither of us will see anything."

"Luck, huh? And how good are you in a casino?"

Deven chewed the inside of his cheek. "You don't want to know."

"That is what I was afraid of."

High above, some distance from Earth, the Celloids encountered the Lytherian fleet. They spread out deploying their smaller ships in a large wall of biologic mass approaching at great speed.

Karthish watched them from inside his *Command* carrier. The holographic display showed everything in deadly, real-time. "Get the *Phoenix*! Tell Aleshia it is time."

A large screen flashed as Minerva's face appeared on one side, while the other showed Aleshia sitting in the chair. But a few seconds later she frowned. "I can't feel anything. Nothing at all."

Karthish frowned. "How can this be? You touched our ships at a much greater distance." He heard muttering off to the side.

Minerva's eyes narrowed. "I have traced the problem to the relays. Leon says he can fix it. We need a few minutes."

"We will try to give you that time." The screen went dark and Karthish turned around. "Tell all ships to open fire."

Gakon blinked. "But Sir, in the past we have waited until they initiated the attack."

Karthish glared at him. "What do you think they are doing? Coming to say hello?" He pointed to the wall of ships approaching. "I know we normally wait for them, but this time we do not have the option. Now, do as I say!"

"Yes Sir."

Every Lytherian ship lashed out in a massive unified energy blast that ripped through the line of Celloid pod fighters incinerating most of them, with the rest being taken care of on the second barrage.

Karthish frowned. "That was too easy. I wonder what–

" He didn't get a chance to finish before he saw the three Celloid carriers change course and sent out tendrils towards each other. In a moment he watched in horror as the three individuals merged becoming one gigantic ship heading for the center of the Lytherian deployment. He knew this new ship's shields would be greatly increased, also its weapons. "Concentrate all fire on that ship!"

Energy blast after energy blast lashed out, causing damage but failed to slow the Celloid down. "Sir, the ship isn't slowing. We aren't causing enough damage."

Karthish's eyes narrowed. "I can see that. Deploy the *Makers*. Hit the thing head-on."

"But we need them to rebuild–"

Karthish spun around and jabbed his hand forward. A talon thrust through the hologram of the Celloid. "If that thing makes it through, we won't need to. And this is something they won't expect for the same reason."

"Yes Sir, deploying the *Makers*."

The massive Lytherian *Makers*, until now sat some distance away from the battle, glowed to life as their engines ignited. They formed up and cranked their engines to maximum thrust. They barreled headlong past the line and slammed into the Celloids. Much of their forward hull crumpled showing extensive damage, but the Celloid stopped in its tracks. Karthish was about to order the ships into a different formation when his eyes went wide as the *Makers* began firing at them!

Karthish winced realizing what had happened. He sighed and hung his head. "Fire our main cannon at the *Makers*, aim for their power cores. Destroy them."

"But Sir–"

Karthish pointed to the image hovering in the air. "Don't

you realize what has happened? They have accessed the *Makers* and if we don't stop them, the Celloids will have access to all of our technology! We won't stand a chance. Now, obliterate the *Makers*!"

"But Sir, they are too close. The energy backlash might destroy us, along with them."

"And if they get away with our technology, we are just as dead. Do it now!"

"Yes Sir," he said giving the commands to the crews. Every light aboard the flagship dimmed as the energy was diverted into an accumulator deep inside the Lytherian *Command* carrier. The power built exponentially until it reached forward slamming into the nose of the ship. A microsecond later a massive blast rammed free hitting the *Makers* and Celloid head-on. The outer hull of the *Makers* evaporated away as the beam intensified. In a brilliant flash, all three of the *Maker's* cores went critical and destroying themselves along with the attached Celloid. The energy envelope continued to expand, reaching back towards the Lytherian fleet.

"Divert all power to shields!" Karthish shouted.

"We don't have enough! That shot took all available power except for emergency life support for two units."

"Use it!"

Karthish's engineers diverted all remaining power as the outer layer of the expanding energy bubble impacted the hull. Panels blew as they overloaded, several cables on the bridge came down sparking. Karthish dove out of the way as one almost hit him in the face. The front of the hull buckled, main super structure cracked, but the ship managed to hold together. Karthish stood up coughing at the black smoke billowing from several areas all around the bridge. "Status report?" But there was no response. He looked around at the devastation that used to be his bridge and found Gakon impaled by a fallen piece of jagged metal. It stuck out of his chest, with his head slumped to the one other side. Three other Lytherians lay on the floor unconscious, blood oozing from several wounds.

Karthish jumped over the sparking cables, broken structure supports, and his fallen crew to Gakon's console. He tapped communications. "Assess all damage and deploy repair crews. I need medical on the bridge."

The line crackled and Akrath appeared. His chief medical technician insignia was obscured by blood, but not his own. "I will have someone up there as soon as I can."

Karthish's eyes closed fast and opened very slowly. "How bad?"

"I can't even begin to give you an estimate. I will as soon as possible. Akrath out." The screen went black. An unstable green glow drew his attention up and saw the tactics hologram flicker, disappear, and reform several times to display the largest Celloid ship he had ever seen. He wondered why they didn't detect this ship before. The sides opened up and many, smaller, armored pod-spreading ships began to emerge. He hit a button on Gakon's console "Deven are you there? Are you receiving me?"

No response.

Karthish slammed his palm on the sparking console. "Deven? Can you hear me? Please respond."

The screen flashed with several layers of colored static before resolving in a glitching image of Deven's face. "We receive you, but barely. What happened?"

"We managed to stop the largest part of the Celloid invasion, but it has left us incapacitated. And now the biggest Celloid ship we have ever seen has deployed more pod carriers. They are heading your way. You must stop them."

The screen split and Aleshia's face appeared alongside. The static returned to obscure some parts of words. But it was enough to make out. "Leon thinks he has fixed the problem. We will try again in a minute."

"Yeah, you can tell Dakarth his frequency was way off," Leon's voice came from off to the side. "Not his fault through, our ancestors had many years of experimentation and data he didn't. I am glad the nanos had shut down or they wouldn't have let me rip out a couple of components and install my own. We should be good to go now."

Karthish sighed. "I will, if he is still alive."

"It is now up to us," Deven said.

"Yessss. I am sorry."

"Don't be. We wouldn't have had a chance without you. We will see you after we toast some Celloids."

"You bet we will," Aleshia said smiling.

"I hope so. And good luck." The screen went black and Karthish moved several pieces of debris from a chair and sat as he watched the ships approaching Earth. He turned to look at his remains of his fleet, everyone of them blasted and adrift. Wincing, he sat back in the chair gazing down toward the deck plates. "I hope you can, for all our sakes."

Deven drummed his fingers on the arm of his chair. Next to him a screen showed Aleshia sitting in the chair and a ring reaching out to encircle her forehead. She sat with her eyes closed. He hated he wasn't with her. He felt he should be at her side, especially now. But the Galina and the *Defiant* needed him more. He glanced over at the screen again. "Anything? From what Karthish said, we should be detecting them at any moment."

Aleshia never opened her eyes. "No, it is all very fuzzy. I'm having difficulty locking on to anything particular."

"Leon, did you check the interface itself?" Deven overheard Otis say.

"Yes, of course! This should work. I don't understand it. I replaced the components that were throwing the frequency off." Leon's voice came through muffled from under the chair.

Deven saw Otis appear from behind the chair and bend down. "Here, let me help. I have an idea."

Deven watched Leon pop out from under the chair and stand up. "Fine, see what you can do."

Miles' camera turned. "I hate to be the bearer of bad news, but I have detected the Celloids. We need to activate overdrive now if we are to intercept them. Galina, Minerva, I have sent you the coordinates."

Minerva's face appeared on another screen. "Confirmed. Navigation is linked to Galina's control."

Galina tapped her controls. "Yep I got them. Overdrives are online. Hang on everyone." She tapped her console, and both ships disappeared as they leapt into overdrive. "We will be on them in less than two minutes. Any luck with the chair? I think we're going to need it."

Leon's face went red on the screen. "No kidding!" A spark shot out from beneath the chair. "Otis! What are you doing?"

Another spark shot out. "Oh you know, a little of this, a little of that," Otis said.

"This isn't a cooking vid!" Leon spat.

Otis poked his head out from under the chair. "Have a little faith." His head shot back under. "Just one more connection ..." Another spark. "...there. Aleshia try it now."

Aleshia's brow furrowed. "It is a little better, but still hard to see."

"Dang, I thought for sure that was it."

"Otis get out of there, and let me in," Leon said.

"Let me try something else. One sec."

"We don't have time!"

Both ships shuddered as they dropped out of overdrive in front of the Celloids. "Otis! Let Leon in there," Deven grumbled.

Three more sparks in quick succession. "Okay, Aleshia try now!"

"That did it! I can see the ships–"

Leon stood there cocking his head back and forth. "What in the world did you do?"

Otis' head popped out from under the chair as he extended his hand. Leon grabbed it and he helped him to his feet. "Simple, you know hardware, but I can spot a buffer overflow problem from a mile off."

Leon chewed the inside of his cheek as he muttered, "Oh."

The Celloids saw the two ships appear and reached forth with tendrils that began to glow. A microsecond later several large energy bolts slammed into the shields of both ships rocking them back and forth. "My shields can't take much more of this, even with the upgrades," Minerva said. "Not at point-blank range."

On Deven's screen Aleshia smiled. "Now hold still you overgrown weeds. That is the last you are ever going to do." The glow from the tendrils dimmed, and disappeared a second later as did the energy blasts. "Okay, who's got the weedkiller?"

It was Deven's turn to smile. "Gregory, you heard the lady, toast those weeds. Minerva you do the same."

"You got it," Gregory said from the nearby intercom.

Minerva nodded as all her cannons let loose a barrage of energy the slammed into the Celloids. At first they weren't sure enough damage was being done, then the outer skin began to turn brown as flames erupted from the top. One Celloid ship burned while another exploded and continued to incarcerate as it fell towards the Earth. They were confident the atmosphere would take care of any small remnants.

"Whooo hooo, it's like shooting fish in a barrel. Wish all my targets were this easy," Gregory said from the intercom.

Deven watched his screen as he saw several drops of sweat run down Aleshia's face. "Aleshia are you all right?"

Her eyes remained shut as her eyebrows met. "It is more of a ... drain than I thought it would be since we are so close. But I ... will be okay."

Another Celloid ship came apart as it exploded from inside and continued to burn as it fell. Miles' camera focused on Deven. "At the current rate of destruction, the Celloids will no longer be a problem in five minutes."

"Good," Deven said. "Aleshia can't keep this up."

"Deven!" Aleshia shrieked as she gripped both sides of her chair, but her eyes remained closed. "Get Halburn! Half of them aren't here. The other half are trying to land on the night side."

Deven looked at Aleshia's face on the screen. "Are you sure? Karthish said they never attack on the night side of a planet."

"I don't care what they never do, they are doing it now. I

. . . can see them. I am holding them . . . but I can't do it for long . . . not at this distance. We could never get there . . . before they get loose. Halburn is our . . . only hope."

Deven tapped a few keys and Halburn's face appeared. His left eyebrow twitched. "I know this isn't a social call. I take these plants are heading my way?"

Deven nodded. "Yes, I'm afraid so. We can't get to them in time. Aleshia has them held in place for now, but she can't hold them for long."

"Wow, from the other side of the world? Remind me not to play mind games with that girl. Where are they? I will get the fleet there double-time."

The screen split as Minerva's face appeared on the other side. "Aleshia has given me the coordinates, and I have transmitted them to your navigator."

"Wait a minute! *The Nexus* is telling me where to–"

"Odell, we don't have time for this! If you don't trust her, trust me."

"I do, so I will. We'll take care of it. Halburn out." The screen went black.

Halburn slammed his fist on the arm of his chair. "Rechert? Why are we still here? You heard, we need to be at those coordinates, *yesterday*. And Naud, is the rest of the fleet ready?"

"Fleet is ready," Naud said. "Most of them are en route now."

"Sorry, I was having problems locking in the location for some reason. Ready now, Sir. Overdrive is online."

"Then get us there!"

The *Valiant's* engines began to glow brighter and brighter, with a blinding flash they leapt into overdrive. Naud tapped several keys on his console as he checked several indicators. "We should rendezvous in six minutes. Most of the fleet will be there ahead of us."

"Dang, I always hate being late to a party," Halburn said. "Tell them to fire at will, don't wait for us."

The *Valiant* dropped out of overdrive to find the battle in progress. Mechand carriers darted in and out between each Celloid ship raking them over and over again with energy blasts, but the bioships continued to hold together. "Get us in there, open fire with all cannons."

"Yes Sir, all cannons responding." The *Valiant* lashed out again and again adding their weapons to the onslaught but their targets continued to show little damage.

"Deven is calling," Naud said as he put the transmission through.

Deven's face appeared on the large screen. "How are you doing? Aleshia can't hold them much longer."

"We are hitting them with all we've got, but are not causing enough damage ... wait ... can you get the Nexus?"

Deven blinked with wide eyes. "Yes, one sec." He tapped a few keys and Minerva's face appeared next to his.

"Nexus, can you still control these ships, or are we out of range?"

She nodded. "Yes of course I can, providing their relay systems are intact."

Halburn turned to his right. "Naud, tell the fleet to re-enable those relays."

Naud's jaw dropped and hung motionless for a full three seconds. "You can't be serious?"

"I am. Do it and as soon as it is done, abandon the ships."

Naud blinked, his eyes getting wider each time. "What!?"

"Do as I say. Nexus, when they are online I want you to take control of those ships."

Minerva cocked her head. "And do what? I do not see the logic in this."

"It isn't logic, it is desperation. When the crews are off, I want you to take each ship and plow it directly into a Celloid. When your weapons don't work, you become the weapon."

"That does have a possibility of success based on what we have seen. These Celloids shouldn't be able to withstand one of my carriers exploding."

Halburn smiled. "My thoughts exactly."

"The fleet has signaled they have enabled the relays," Naud said.

"Nexus? Do you have them?"

"I do."

"Naud, tell the fleet to abandon their ships and get us clear as well. This is going to be messy."

Halburn watched as small points of light raced away from each ship. "Sir, the crews are away," Naud said

"Nexus, you know what to do."

Minerva nodded as several carrier's engines increased in brightness as they lunged towards their targets. The Celloids began to move away.

"Dang it, they must be slipping from Aleshia's grasp," Halburn said.

"But they won't get away from me," Minerva said as all the Mechand carriers increased their speed to full. They slammed into the Celloids ripping a large hole in the middle of each several-stories-tall ship. The carriers continued down into the center of the biomass. Flames licked out from the hole and spread throughout the Celloids burning them from the inside out, until at last, each ship exploded leaving nothing but ash to rain down below.

Halburn sighed. "I no longer have a fleet, but we no longer have a problem."

— 20 —

With all the Celloids destroyed, the atmosphere aboard the *Phoenix* was laid back. The ship had sustained damage, but very minor and the Mechands could handle it leaving Leon and Otis time to discuss the different aspects of Lytherian technology. "I still don't think their computers are any more advanced than ours."

Leon blinked. "Are you kidding? Look what they can do with nanos and weapons, not to mention their ships. How can you think their computers are backward?"

Minerva's eyes narrowed. "I resent that remark. I am hardly backward."

"Nor am I," Miles' voice came through a nearby speaker.

Leon inclined his head. "Present party excluded of course."

Aleshia was about to retract the headband and get out of the chair when something new came into her minds eye. Something big was headed their way.

"Umm, guys. We have a problem!"

Leon turned. "What is it?"

"The biggest Celloid ship I have ever seen is approaching. It has to be their *Mothership*. We took out the kids and now Mother looks mad."

Deven's face flashed on a nearby screen. "Where is it? Can you freeze this ship like the others?"

"It is still in orbit but coming down fast. And I might able to hold it, if it has the same vulnerability. But this thing is huge. I will try." Her eyebrows met and she grit her teeth. "I have it. But ...I don't know ...how long I can hold it. This one is ...harder than the others."

"She has sent me the coordinates. I have passed them to Galina," Minerva said.

"I have them. Hold on to your socks. We are jumping," Galina's voice came from off to the right side of Deven.

The *Defiant* and *Phoenix* leapt into overdrive and few seconds later, emerged below the Celloid *Mothership*. "Open fire with everything we've got!" Deven said.

All cannons erupted scouring the Celloid *Mothership* with energy blasts. Aleshia managed to keep its shields down but twice the Celloid started to move. She grabbed it tighter with her mind, but the strain was getting to her. Battling all the other ships and now this largest of them all was proving too much. Twice tentacles started to glow with energy before her metal grip forced the power back. "I can't hold it much longer."

"Leon, is there anyway we can boost our firepower? This thing is so huge, we aren't doing enough damage," Deven said on the screen.

Leon shook his head. "No. Well, maybe. The Lytherians gave us one incredible boost with their nanotech, but I would have to study the new cannons more to be sure if we can enhance them further."

"We don't have that kind of time."

"I have a solution to our current dilemma," Miles' voice came through the speaker. "I have analyzed the weapon enhancements, and if we activate our gravity plating, point our engines towards the Earth, all the beams could combine into a much larger and more powerful one."

Leon shook his head. "Nice idea Miles, but I still doubt it would be enough."

"It will be if the *Defiant* and *Phoenix* tilt towards each other by 20 degrees during the firing process."

Leon blinked. "What for?"

"To combine our beams into one. If we are equal distances apart and elevation the given angle will combine the output of both ships."

Minerva cocked her head. "The calculations would have to be very precise and difficult to do. Any variation and neither ship would survive."

Aleshia gripped the chair with white knuckles. "Guys, whatever you are going to do ... *hurry!*"

"Trust me, I can do this," Miles said.

Deven sighed. "We don't have a choice. The only other option is we let them take over and kill everyone and everything."

Minerva sighed. "Very well. Send me your calculations and positions."

"Sent. And Galina I will assume control in this case. The positioning must be exact."

Off to the side Galina could be heard. "Are you telling me I can't–"

"Galina, let him do it," Deven said.

"Controls switched," Galina grumbled. "And I think this is nuts."

"I have control. Maneuvering the *Defiant* into position," Miles said as the *Defiant* activated its gravity plating and aimed its nose towards the stars. The ship rotated 180 aiming the top towards the *Phoenix*. Minerva matched the motions then both ships tilted their bows 20 degrees towards each other.

Aleshia, the last of her energy spent, slumped to the side of the chair, out cold. The Celloid began to move again and several tendrils glowed white as they pointed towards the two ships.

"I am in position. All cannons ready," Minerva said.

"Activate …*now*," Miles said. A beam thrust out of each cannon and headed up coalescing into a much larger one that rammed forward. The focused beam from each ship crashed into each other at the designated point. The energy merged, grew in size, and a microsecond later erupted towards the Celloid *Mothership*. It hit hard, pushing the massive ship back before slicing through and passing out the other side. The ship wiggled as a fish speared through the heart, trying to get away. Fires erupted inside and spread throughout the biomass as it still tried to get free. "Minerva, channel power from the main conduits into weapons when I say."

"But that will–"

"It is the only way to ensure destruction."

Minerva sighed. "Ready."

"*Now.*" At his words all lights aboard both ships went out as energy was rerouted. The beams enlarged ten times, and the hole grew to take up half of the Celloid. Even in the vacuum of space, fires burst outward as precious oxygen vented. Cracks began to radiate out from the center and glowed brighter and brighter. When they met, the whole ship exploded into burnt dust. The beams shut down but the glow from the engines had faded and both ships began to slip from their positions, causing them to lose altitude …fast."

"Miles! What are you doing?" Deven said as he gripped his chair.

"I regret to inform you all available power was utilized to destroy the Celloid. That included engines. I am attempting to restart them, but there is insufficient energy in the power core at the moment."

"Miles, if I live through this, I'm going to kill you!" Galina shrieked.

Leon held on to Aleshia, still unconscious, with one hand and his chair with the other. "And I will help!"

"Impact in fifty seconds," Minerva said. "Power core still has insufficient charge to restart the engines."

The *Phoenix* shook as it plunged towards the Earth. Leon's eyes lit up like beacons. "Minerva! Do you have enough to power the gravity plating? Dakarth told me it was very efficient."

She nodded. "I do. More than enough."

"What? We need less gravity not more!" Otis grit his teeth as he hung on to the console in front of him.

"Yes we need less gravity. If you reverse the plating, it should direct those forces down and repelling at the same time."

"Impact in twenty seconds," Miles' voice came through the speaker.

"I am not sure that is possible, even if–" Minerva started to say.

"It is if you reverse the first and third connections, while leaving the other two. Look, if I am wrong we're dead, if we don't do anything we're dead. Just do it!"

"Modifications made … powering the gravity plating," Miles and Minerva said in unison.

The *Phoenix* and *Defiant* shuddered as repelling gravity

waves radiated out of the base of the hulls. "We are slowing but not enough, " Minerva said as several screens flashed on showing their decent. "I estimate we will impact in one minute."

Galina checked one of the displays aboard the *Defiant*. "Listen up you bots, aim for the ocean. Sea level is lower. It will give us a little more time to stop."

Miles' camera turned. "Galina, how do you propose we do this? Engines are offline."

"You fool bot! You are directing gravity waves and you need me to tell you to do a little less on the bow for a few seconds to pitch the ship down towards the ocean? Aerodynamics will do the rest. Sheesh!" Galina spat.

"Miles! No arguments, do it," Deven said.

"I wasn't about to. The modification has been made and if you check the monitor, we are now on course towards the coastline."

Aboard the *Phoenix* Minerva's eyes narrowed. "I have done the same, but by my estimates, we will impact with the ground three seconds before a full stop can be achieved."

"I will take those odds," Leon said.

"Impact in thirty-five seconds."

Aleshia started to stir and her eyes fluttered open. "What ...what happened." She looked up to see Leon holding on to her. "Leon?"

"Oh nothing much, we are about to make a big splash into the sea, that's all," Otis said.

Leon nodded. "The last shot took all our power. We managed to slow down with the gravity plating, but it isn't quite enough."

"Help me to the chair."

Leon shot her a look, but Aleshia shot one right back. He

knew better than to argue. He helped her to the chair. Not easy with the ship shaking and pitched down. Aleshia sat in it. "Minerva, power it up. Give me all you've got."

On one of the screens Deven frowned. "Aleshia, you're too weak."

Aleshia sucked in a breath. "We don't have a choice."

"But if I do as you suggest, we will fall faster," Minerva said.

"And if you don't we are going to make a big splash and sink. We might survive, but you won't."

"Good point. All remaining power diverted."

Aleshia gave one last look towards Deven's image. "I love you." Power flowed through the chair and into her mind where she blasted it back out as telekinetic waves. She screamed trying to pull the two ships back from the brink. The *Phoenix,* pitched down further and increased its speed. It edged out in front passing the *Defiant* as it continued to accelerate.

"The *Phoenix* will now impact in five seconds. We will follow six seconds after."

"Miles! Shut up!" Deven shouted.

Miles' camera focused him, the iris contracted then went wide, but he didn't say anything.

Aleshia screamed again, and both ships felt as though they hit a brick wall, slamming to a dead stop. A second later they began to slowly float upward. Minerva redirected the power back to the gravity plating causing the *Phoenix* to gain altitude faster. They had stopped two meters short of the water.

The chair sparked several times and Leon broke the ring around Aleshia's head. He pulled her limp body free.

Deven's eyes went wide. "Aleshia!"

Leon held her and looked up towards Deven's face on the screen. "She is out but still breathing."

"Get her over here to the infirmary."

Otis shot forward and grabbed Aleshia's feet. "We're on it."

A shudder raced through the *Defiant*. "The engines are now online," Miles said.

"Wonderful timing," Deven grumbled.

"Better late than never," Galina spat.

A large green mass appeared in the distance. Halburn blinked as he shot from his chair and stood between Rechert and Naud.

Naud pointed "Sir? Is that–"

"Get the *Defiant*!" A second later Deven's face appeared on the screen. "We have a problem, how fast can you get here?"

"We can't. Destroying the Celloid *Mothership* took everything we had, and then some. It is only because of Aleshia and a lot of luck we aren't a hole in the ground. It will take us twenty minutes or more to reactivate our overdrive."

"Dang it. One more of the Celloids just appeared. I'm guessing it is a straggler. We're going to take it out." His eyes shot down towards Rechert. "Activate the relay, then leave. I want you both out of here along with the rest of the crew." He looked back up to Deven. "I will take care of it." The image shrank to a point and disappeared.

Rechert and Naud gave a questioning glare. "Sir? What about you?" They said in unison.

"Don't worry about me, I'll be right behind you. I need to make sure we're going to take this thing out. Now go!"

They both nodded, tapped in a few last commands, stood

up and left the bridge. Halburn sat at Naud's console and tapped a few keys. The large engines glowed brighter as the *Valiant* began to accelerate. The Celloid noticed his approach and extended several tentacles. They glowed to life and began releasing deadly blasts of energy. The blasts slammed into the *Valiant's* shields causing a nearby console to explode under the strain. Smoke started filling the bridge. Under him, several decks down, fires broke out from overloaded systems.

Halburn swore as sparks flew from Rechert's console and the relay disengaged. He tapped the controls, but it refused to accept any further commands. A light flashed, and he saw Deven was calling. He tapped receive. "What are you doing? Minerva told me the relay was operational, but you turned it back off?"

"I didn't turn it off, it failed. This Celloid is fighting back." He swore again. "And it took out the automatic guidance system with it. But we're on target." He tapped a few more keys pushing the standard drive engines beyond their normal limits. The floating tower of biomass grew ever larger.

"Odell! Get out of there!"

"I can't." Sparks burst from another area of the bridge as a fire reached out and grew. "If I leave, all of this hammering the *Valiant* is taking will throw her off course. I will have sacrificed the ship for nothing. Do me a favor, love that girl you are with. Aleshia is one special lady. Goodbye my friend." He cut the link and a few seconds later the *Valiant* slammed head long into the middle of the towering Celloid. Already on fire, the *Valiant* spread the infection throughout the biomass before the fire reached the power core. With a blinding flash the core went critical and cracks started raiding out from the hole growing ever brighter, incinerating the Celloid from the inside out. In a microsecond the cracks reached around, touched the other side, and the whole mass exploded. Seconds later, nothing was left of either ship except pulverized ash.

Deven sat next to Aleshia. Her body lay on the bed, surrounded from the neck down by an opaque glass and metal half cylinder extending up from the sides. Another, smaller one, encircled her head leaving her face exposed. Monitors beeped in rhythm with her heart. Several monitors displayed transparent images of her, and the analysis. No damage was found, nothing physical anyway. Her mind was another story. She lay in a comatose state. Miles ran several more tests but still couldn't find the cause of her coma. Yet, they knew. The strain of stopping them from crashing into the sea when she was so weak, was too much for her.

She had saved them, but at what cost. Deven reached out and tapped several locations on the metal tube. It retracted sliding into the base of the bed leaving the band around her head. He took her hand and gripped the cool fingers between his palms. Something else they didn't understand, why her temperature was low. He reached out with his mind. *Aleshia, my love. Speak to me.*

Nothing.

He tried again, this time with more energy behind it. There was nothing at first, then he felt … something. He wasn't sure what, but it was more than before. He did it again and the same reaction. It was almost as if she was there but too far away for him to hear.

He had contacted Karthish, but they didn't have an inkling

as to what the problem was. It was far outside of their experience, and Karthish had apologized profusely. He would have never asked her to use her abilities if he thought there was a chance she could have been injured. Although, Deven knew Aleshia volunteered and nothing could have stopped her. They all were aware of the risks, even if slight with the safeties and modifications Leon made.

Dakarth was also baffled at the outcome, and suspected it had to be due to the further modifications of the telepathic device. Akrath, was willing to help, but he had all the badly injured Lytherians to take care of first. Not to mention Dakarth's team needed to repair the wrecked landing bay before he could even make the attempt. There was no way Akrath would be here for several days at least.

She wasn't in any danger.

That they knew of anyway.

Deven closed his eyes and reached out again with his mind. *Come back to me my love.*

He heard a sound. He wasn't sure, but it felt like her. Pushing harder he entered her mind, but he could only see blackness. "Aleshia? Where are you?"

Deven opened his eyes, but Aleshia was nowhere to be found. The bed in front of him was empty. He ran and slammed the base of his fist on the intercom. "Miles? Where is Aleshia?"

No response.

"Miles?"

Still no response.

"Galina? What is wrong with Miles?" Deven waited a full minute but nothing was said. "Leon? Gregory? Can anyone hear me? What's going on?" After another twenty seconds with no response Deven took off for the *Defiant's* bridge. But when he got there, it was empty. No sign of anyone, and even Galina's coffee cups were strangely missing.

He waved his hand in front of Miles' camera but it sat mute and motionless. He touched one of the buttons on Galina's console. "Can anyone aboard hear me?" Still nothing. He looked out the window but didn't see the *Phoenix*. He tapped another button. "Minerva? Where are you? I don't see the *Phoenix*." All he got back for several minutes was static varying from quiet to deafening and returning to quiet before the equipment shut down.

He reached out with his mind. He felt something. Aleshia he assumed, but something was different. *Aleshia? Where are you? What is going on? Where did everyone go?*

She didn't respond, but he felt she was near one of the bow port energy cannons. Or someone at least. He walked down the empty corridors. It was odd he couldn't find a single sign of habitation. It was if they all evacuated, and took everything with them. But if that was the case, why was the ship still floating and intact? Leon's console on the bridge didn't give any indication of a failure that would justify abandoning the *Defiant*. Yet no one was here. And more important, why didn't they tell him?

He stopped past Galina's quarters on the way, and it was as empty as the others. No clothes, the rack didn't have any sheets, not even a toothbrush. Not one sign she had ever been there, much less it being her home for the better part of a year.

The *Defiant* seemed more quiet than usual as well. He couldn't put his finger on it, but something *else* felt different. Granted he had always been aboard with lots of people, but even without them the ship itself still felt *different*.

Deven approached the room housing the cannon and his

senses tingled. She was here, yet different. Like the *Defiant*, something was wrong. He cracked open the reinforced steel door. Aleshia was there. She wandered around the room, as if in a hypnotic daze. He couldn't see anyone else, and more important, he couldn't *feel* anyone else.

The door creaked open the rest of the way and Aleshia spun around with her eyes narrowed, her arms raised. "Oh Deven! It is you!" She ran over and wrapped her arms around him, squeezing. "Where is everyone?"

Deven squeezed her back and stepped inside. "I don't know. I thought you might have a better idea. What are you doing in here?"

"I thought I felt something in here." She jerked a thumb towards the weapon taking up most of the space. "But as you can see, nothing here but the cannon."

"Didn't you feel me approach?"

Aleshia frowned. "No I didn't. In fact I haven't been able to detect anything for awhile now."

"Since you came in here?"

She shook her head. "No, it was even before that. It is like being surrounded in a large wet blanket making my detection abilities cold and numb."

Deven squeezed her again and gazed into her eyes. "What is the last thing you remember?"

"Getting into that confounded chair on the *Phoenix* and trying to stop us from crashing into the ocean. Then I woke up here on the *Defiant*."

"In our room?"

She shook her head. "No, it was in one of the corridors. Which I thought was odd. But no more than finding the ship empty."

"I know. It doesn't make sense. Even if everyone had to abandon the *Defiant*, Miles should respond."

Aleshia sighed as her eyes drifted down. "Unless he left too."

Deven shook his head. "Not possible. Leon was several months away from having all the parts to repair Miles' old body, and set up some kind of transfer." Keeping his arm around Aleshia, they walked over to one of the consoles. He punched in a few commands but the console remained unchanged as though frozen. "Hmm, this one is the same as on the bridge. They look functional, yet when I try do give them commands, they don't respond. Or give me static."

"That is weird. I hadn't tried."

Deven squeezed Aleshia again against his hip. "Come on, let's head down to engineering."

Aleshia blinked. "What for?"

"If there is a problem with the ship, it should show up there first."

"Oh, right."

As they walked down the corridors, it finally occurred to Deven what had been bothering him so much. It wasn't only the feel of the ship, but the sound. The air circulation system wasn't running, yet the air wasn't stale. And now that he thought about it, the slight hum and vibration of the hover engines as also strangely absent. He looked down and his eyes met Aleshia's. She smiled, and he smiled back forcing his eyes forward, saying nothing.

When they reached engineering, it was as Deven had suspected, the engines and power core sat dormant. While they glowed as though active, when he placed his hand on the core it was cold to the touch. "No way power is flowing through this."

Aleshia pointed. "But the indicators all say they are running fine."

"I know, but they aren't. Here," Deven put her hand on the core, "feel that? It's ice-cold. It would be warm if it was online."

She cocked her head. "It feels fine to me."

"What? It feels warm to you?"

She nodded.

Deven put his hand back on the front panel of the power core. "That is odd, it wasn't when I checked it a second ago."

On the far side of engineering, the heavy reinforced steel doors ripped from their hinges and were thrown clear across the room. "There you are!" A woman glared from where the doors had been. Her flame-red hair stood out of its own accord, waved by a non-existent breeze as well as the conforming dress she wore that matched her hair. The top had a plunging V-neck, as did the front wafting over her legs, hiding nothing. She floated in, her feet several inches from touching the deck plates.

"Aleshia? But–" He looked down at the woman on his arm. Aleshia was still there.

"Of course it is me! You lying sack of shit! You promised me so much, and all I wanted was you! Our honeymoon! Alone! Instead, all you did was use me!"

"But I didn't–"

"Silence!" She waved her hand and Deven's mouth felt as if a metal clamp held it shut. "You did! And I am going to make you pay. You are going to learn there is nothing worse than a woman scorned." She raised her hand, a ball of glowing red energy formed in the palm and she threw it at Deven.

The woman at his side raised her hand, and the ball hit an

invisible barrier, exploding without harming them. "You will not harm my husband."

The floating woman threw her head back, hair waiving as she laughed. "Your husband? He is mine to do with as I please. And when I am done with him, I am going to turn everyone of those tin cans into scrap metal. In the slowest way possible. It is what should have been done in the first place." Her eyes narrowed. "Don't even try to stop me. You don't have the will."

"You will not harm us." Aleshia held on to Deven as they floated an inch above the deck plate before rocketing backwards from where they came with increasing speed. The woman flung larger energy balls at them as they shot through the open doors. Aleshia shut them causing the following red energy to slam into the steel, melting where they hit.

Aleshia waved her hand over the hinges and they sparked, welding the door shut. They shot down the corridor with doors slamming shut as they passed. When they were almost half a ship away, Aleshia slowed and lowered them back to the deck plates. She waved her hand over Deven's mouth removing the invisible clamp holding it shut. "I am sorry love. I don't know what that ... that ... thing is, but it is not me."

Deven coughed. "Well, it sure seems to have your abilities. In fact it could have more, I have never seen you throw balls of energy."

"Do you think someone cloned me? Perhaps the Nexus or the Lytherians–"

Deven shook his head. "No I don't think so. If it was a clone, it wouldn't have known about me in detail."

"Unless they trained it."

"No. Even if they did, it wouldn't be hell-bent on

destroying me because I messed up our honeymoon. Or thought I had been using her all this time. Which I never did, for the record."

Aleshia grunted. "Of course you never used me! I would never think it for a second."

"Ah, but I suspect you did."

"I didn't!"

"Perhaps not consciously. Listen, I know where we are, your mind."

Aleshia's eyes went wide. "What? We're on the *Defiant*!"

"While it looks like we are, what we are doing and seeing is not real. It is all in our minds."

Aleshia pointed to the closed doors. "Then what is that thing?"

Deven sighed. "That, my love, is your other half."

"There is no way that … that *thing* is me!"

They heard bulkheads being slammed and torn from their supports. "It is. You are on a bed in the infirmary, and I am there with you. But all of this is in your mind. That *thing* is your bad side. I have a hunch the chair separated you into two distinct personalities. It would also explain why it is appears to be more powerful. Unleashed rage is hard to stop."

"That thing is *not* me. I love you. I would never, ever, want to harm you."

Deven held her face between his hands and looked deep into her green eyes. "I know you never would. But there is always a part of us with the desire. Monsters from the Id they used to call it, long long ago."

"But–"

"No matter how you deny it, that is still you out there, your Id. And why didn't you tell me how mad you were?"

Aleshia shrugged. "I may have been a little miffed, but I wouldn't say mad."

Deven pointed to the sealed bulkhead as one eye narrowed and the side of his face scrunched up. "I would say you were more than a 'little miffed'."

They heard more pounding as a couple more bulkheads were ripped apart, a few seconds later all went quiet. Deven cocked his head. "Odd, wonder what your Id is up to?"

"Killing you!" They whipped around to see Id far down the other corridor. An energy ball flew from her hand heading for Deven's head. Aleshia reached out, grabbed the pulsating ball as it raced towards them, and flung it back towards Id.

Id's black eyes blazed as she batted the ball away and it hit a wall, blasting a hole clean through it. "How dare you!" she screamed. She raised her hands to the middle of her chest and a massive ball of energy formed between them and she elevated it over her head. "Try to catch this one!" She hurled the ball of concentrated energy towards them.

Deven's eyes went wide as the ball raced towards his head. Aleshia levitated them both, and they shot down a side corridor. The ball impacted the welded door behind where they were standing, melting it, before passing through. As they raced away, Aleshia waved a hand and all the emergency bulkheads behind them slammed shut.

Only when they were more than half the ship in the opposite direction did Aleshia slow and lower them to the deck. She grabbed his jacket and glared at him. "You have to get out of here!"

Deven shook his head. "I'm not leaving you."

"She wants to kill you! I can't let that happen!"

"You will have to make sure it doesn't."

She released her grip and sunk to the floor. "But I can't hold her off forever."

Deven lowered himself on his haunches. "No you can't. And neither of us can stay in here forever either."

She looked up. "Huh?"

"Did you forget our real bodies are still in the infirmary? I can't stay here forever, neither can you. Nor will I leave you."

"But you must."

He shook his head again. "Nope. Not going to happen. You are going to have to take her down."

"But she is stronger than me."

Deven took her hand. "Aleshia, no one's subconscious is stronger than their conscious mind. She may appear to be stronger due to the pure rage, but you still have the upper hand. All you need to do is get her back under control."

"How?"

"You need to merge with her."

"What! I am not merging with that ... *thing*."

"Love, you have to. It is the only way. Besides, would you want her to find a way to the surface and start trying to kill me for real without you to stop it?"

Aleshia sighed and leaned back against the wall looking at the ceiling. "I suppose you have a point. What do you suggest we do?"

"I don't think a full out assault is going to work. Not to mention it is what she would be expecting. If we let her find me in the main landing bay, you can fly in through the bay doors from behind and grab her."

Aleshia shook her head. "It won't work. Unless I use a vehicle, we are too high up. We would both freeze and die of suffocation."

Deven smiled. "Remember, this is your mind. You have control here, and more than Id does."

"How can you be so sure?"

Deven sat on the floor next to her, never letting go of her hand. "Remember when I felt the power core, and it was cold and you said it wasn't?"

"Yes, so what?"

"Well, when I felt it again, the temperature was normal. You changed it without realizing. Therefore, you can do this."

"I ... I don't know."

Deven took both of her hands and looked into her eyes. "You can do this. I know you can."

"You don't understand, I don't *want* her."

He squeezed her hands. "Love, I do. And you have to. You can't let her find her way to the surface with full access to your abilities. She would kill me, perhaps us all."

They felt the *Defiant* shudder as Id blasted through more bulkheads.

Aleshia sighed. "I will try." She peered up and down the corridor. "But how do we get her to the landing bay?"

Deven pointed. "We are almost there, it only down this way and one over." They felt the *Defiant* shudder again. "And I suspect at the rate Id is blasting through bulkheads, she will be there not long after us."

"Right." Deven helped Aleshia to her feet, and they ran towards the landing bay.

Deven dove behind a large support beam when he heard a sound behind the doors. Id blasted through the heavy inner air lock doors sending shrapnel everywhere. Sparks shot from shorted panels and over-loaded lights. She floated into the room, her black eyes narrowing. Her hair floated moving from side to side as she scanned the room. "Did you think you could get away from me?"

Deven peeked from behind the beam. "No, but you can't blame a guy for trying."

"Where is your protector?"

"Aleshia? She went looking for you. She said you wouldn't find me in here."

Id grinned showing her teeth. "I'm Aleshia! She is nothing but a weak, fake, copy! And you should know by now, you cannot hide from me." Her eyes narrowed. "Step out here and take your death like a man. Or do you prefer me to crush you where you stand?" Id floated into the middle of the bay to get a better look at Deven. "It doesn't matter to me either way."

Deven stood up and stepped out from behind the beam. "It doesn't have to end like this."

She laughed. "I'm almost tempted to keep you alive, for my amusement." She licked her lips and smiled. The hungry look in her eyes chilled him more than the storms in Antarctica ever did.

"Oh, I'm relieved to hear that."

"I said almost." She raised her hand palm outstretched, a red ball of energy began to form. "Goodbye you pitiful excuse of a man."

The outer bay doors ripped open. Air whipped through the space threatening to knock Deven off of his feet. Aleshia floated in through what remained of the doors. Id's eyes went wide. "You!"

"Yes it is I, and you will not harm my love." Aleshia dove for Id before she could fire, ramming headlong into her. The two began to glow, brighter and brighter. Id tried to get away but Aleshia held her fast, arms at her sides.

"Nooooo!" Id shrieked before she disappeared completely. But Aleshia's glow didn't diminish, it only grew brighter. Deven squinted and held his hand out in front of his face, trying to see.

A blinding flash ripped from Aleshia's center and Deven shut his eyes. When he opened them again, he was back in the *Defiant's* infirmary at Aleshia's bedside. She coughed, gagged several times, and opened her eyes.

"Love!" He raised her hand to his lips and kissed it. "Are you okay?"

She coughed again and rubbed her forehead. "Yes, but don't ever ask me to do that again. I have one wicked headache."

On the *Defiant's* bridge, Deven sat with his hands folded in his lap, thinking about Halburn. Until now, he hadn't given himself the time to grieve. Aleshia sat next to him and gave a reassuring hug. "There is nothing you could have done. In the end he saved the world, we all did."

"I know, but–"

Miles' camera turned. "Deven, I am detecting an incoming heavily damaged Mechand fighter."

Deven looked up. "Must be one of the people from Halburn's fleet. Odd he didn't land somewhere closer. Let him dock."

"We are also receiving a communication. Displaying it on the upper screen."

A second later Halburn's face appeared. "Will you tell the Nexus these fighters are hard to fly!"

Deven's eyes went wide as his head jutted forward. "Odell?"

Minerva's face appeared splitting the same screen in half. "There is nothing wrong with my design. It is your piloting skills."

"Ha!"

Her eyes narrowed. "It is because you damaged it. There is nothing wrong with my design."

Deven waved his hand. "Will you two cut it out? Odell? How did you survive?"

"Well, I give the Nexus credit to over-designing the carrier hulls. The *Valiant* held together even as she crashed down towards the center of the Celloid. I managed to get into a fighter and fly out the hole I made before the power core went critical. I got a bit singed, but I'm still here. Mind if I land? I don't have anything left to dock with. Well, unless I go back to Lavine. And I don't think he will be too happy with me considering I destroyed his fleet."

Deven laughed. "No I don't think he will be happy with you about that. But you did help save the planet."

"*You* tell him that. I have done enough explaining to him as of late."

Deven laughed. "Deal my friend, deal."

Far away a long fuzzy finger with several protuberances tapped a screen. "It would appear our Celloids have failed to eliminate the threat."

A voice in the distance screeched in several octaves well above human hearing. "Very disappointing. But we have others. And they are not as considerate."

Deven pulled the blinds in the bedroom of the beach rental. The sea breeze teased at them a bit, but not enough you could see into the room. He didn't think they could get another private beach house so soon, but the owner felt obligated since they had done so much and didn't get to use their original time. Who knew Lavine would put in a good word with the owner without asking.

Aleshia strode into the room, her deep red silk robe flapping revealing tantalizing glimpses of her legs. The toes of her red heels peeked out from the long robe. She smiled. "Well Mr. Doran, are you ready?"

Deven's eye flashed as he lay on the bed. "Of course my love. And no, I am not going to get called away this time."

She climbed onto the bed, and held herself above him on all fours. "Are you sure?" She pulled the belt which made a satisfactory fissst as it slid away. Her robe fell open revealing the matching red lace teddy under it, framing her feminine form perfectly. "I mean, are you sure? We could go do something else."

Deven coughed. "Oh I am sure my darling." He reached up, put his hands on her hips and pulled her down. He kissed her soft welcoming red lips, tasting her lipstick. His tongue wiggled in and move back and forth across hers. Muscular arms wrapped around her squeezing.

The console on the farthest wall of the bedroom flashed on showing the image of a red camera eye. "Deven, we need you aboard right away."

"Miles!" Aleshia shrieked as she popped up and closed her robe. "What are you doing? I locked down all the communications!"

"You did; however, they have not updated the security protocols at this establishment in several years. It was simple to bypass the lockout," Miles said.

Deven pulled his carbine from its holster on the night stand near his head, flipped off the safety, and shot an energy bolt dead center into the screen. It exploded in an eruption of sparks and glass reaching out several feet. Aleshia stared at the newly made hole, then at him. He smiled. "You didn't think I would leave again did you?"

"No, but I didn't think you would trash a console either. What are we going to tell the owner?"

Deven's grin widened. "That he should have updated the security protocols?"

She laughed. "You think he will buy that?"

"No, but at this moment I don't care. Come here you, I have a promise to keep." He pulled her close and caressed her lips with his own as his hands slipped beneath her robe.

Aboard the *Defiant* Miles' camera moved back and forth across the vacant bridge as he grumbled. "First, they tell me they would like me to be more human, then they don't appreciate my humor when I do. Humans are so illogical."

Soulmates

Pain tiptoed though her mind as Aleshia pulled the pillow over her head to block the sunlight pouring though the window. It helped, but her head still ached. "Not again. To feel like this, I should have had too much fun last night," she muttered beneath the pillow as Miles entered. Roughly human shaped but with a large dome instead of a standard type head, Miles was one of the nicer of the Mechand models allowed for home use. He did many of the duties no one else wanted: cooking, cleaning, and making sure the refrigerator was stocked. He could be further enhanced, but Aleshia liked to do many things herself. As usual, Miles had activated his anti-grav, allowing him to float a few inches off the ground and enter quietly. "Miss Aleshia, it is time to get up." He said in his gentle, yet artificial voice.

"Ugh! Can I sleep a little more? Or at least try to?" Her words were muffled though the pillow, but not beyond Miles' recognition abilities.

"I am sorry, but you did ask me to wake you at this time. You do have that important appointment today, if you recall."

Aleshia popped up from under the pillow pushing the dull ache away for the moment. "Oh it is Tuesday isn't it? I forgot

I am meeting Mindy today. What time is it?"

"9:00am standard, your appointment is at 11:00am standard. I estimate you have enough time to ready yourself and transport there if you begin now."

Aleshia sat up and stretched. "Sometimes you take all the fun out of it, Miles."

"The fun out of what?" Miles asked still hovering by her bed.

"Never mind. I had better get ready. Mindy will be wondering if I am late. We have been looking forward to this shopping trip for quite a while."

"I do not understand why you wish to go shopping for clothing when I can create anything you might require."

"Miles, it is a girl thing. You wouldn't understand."

"A girl thing? Yes it is apparently beyond my understanding why someone would want to travel to a store halfway around the planet for items that were created using the same basic templates I have and require less expended energy to complete."

"Miles, just go make breakfast and I will be down in a few minutes."

"Yes Miss Aleshia." Miles said as he inclined his dome, then hovered out of the room.

Aleshia crawled out of bed and drug herself to the sonic shower. This morning though, the sonic didn't feel potent enough. She keyed in her code to use a ration of actual water and the jet turned on bathing her in luxurious liquid. She relished in its warm embrace for several extra minutes before turning it off and climbing out. The shower had helped push the headache back into the invisible box from where it came. She dried herself off and placed the towel in the cleaning drawer and set it to auto. Walking over to her closet, she found the dress she wanted to wear today. A strapless design with a short skirt that came to her mid thigh. Just enough to make things interesting, should she find someone to be interesting with. She then put on a pair of adjustable pumps and set the height to two inches, and the color to match the emerald dress she now wore.

Walking downstairs she found Miles had finished breakfast, and her usual place was already set. She sat down as her nose caught the wonderful scents wafting through the air. "Mmmm it smells good."

"It is your usual, synth egg, bacon, and waffles. Supplies are running low. I need to refill them in the next few days. Do you authorize me to procure more with your normal rations?"

"Yes Miles," she said while munching on the strip of bacon, "that is fine. How much will you need?"

"No more than a third of your total for the month, but I shouldn't need to acquire any more for some time."

Aleshia nodded. "That won't be a problem, I can apply for more if we need. I doubt it will be necessary though, the ration has always lasted before."

"Yes I concur, I do not believe you will exhaust the existing ration. And even then you have quite a bit on your reserve that you have accumulated from past unused totals."

"Exactly. I think ... " She dropped the fork and held her head as a sudden searing pain raced through her mind. It felt like someone was drilling into her brain with a dull razor. Almost as quickly as it began, the pain lessened and disappeared.

"Miss Aleshia? Are you all right?" Miles said as he hovered over to her.

"Yes I'm fine Miles. Thank you."

"I beg to differ. Your actions indicate another headache,

correct? That makes three this past week. May I call a med-tech this time?"

"NO! I am fine. You are not to call or notify anyone, is that clear?"

"Acknowledged," Miles said as he craned his head dome a little in Aleshia's direction, "but I really think I should call a med-tech or at least let me scan you."

"NO DOCTORS! And I do not want you scanning me either, is that clear?"

"Yes, perfectly clear."

"Good," Aleshia said as she got up from the table, "make sure you get more of that chocolate cream cake I like. We haven't had it in a long time."

"I will try, but you know that the raw materials are more resource consuming. I may not be able to with the current budget."

Aleshia waved her hand dismissively. "Just get it. I have enough back ration credits to pay for it. I can afford to treat myself once in a while."

"Acknowledged. Will there be anything else Miss Aleshia?" Miles said as he took the dirty plate, silverware, and hovered over to the sink to begin the cleaning process.

"Nope. That's all. Thanks Miles."

"You are welcome Miss Aleshia. And if I may make an inquiry, why are you wearing the impractical shoes today?"

Aleshia laughed. "Because they make my legs look good. And I am going out today."

"But you could damage yourself with such footwear." Miles said as he finished cleaning and sterilizing the dishes.

Aleshia laughed again. "You worry too much. Look these are adjustable, if I have problems I can always lower the heel. All right?"

"I suppose. However, I do not understand the reason behind them. If you are trying to attract a mate, it would be far easier to file with the central systems that you want one. I am sure with all of your attributes, you would have the desired mate within a day."

Aleshia shook her head. "All these centuries and you Mechands still do not understand us at all."

"Perhaps not. But you did build us remember?"

"Well not I, but yes our forefathers did. I never could understand why they didn't create you with better insight into us." Aleshia said as she grabbed a light coat and walked towards the door, her heels clicking loudly on the synthetic wood floor.

Miles would have shrugged if his body allowed it. "I do not know. My knowledge base is limited in that regard. Have a good day Miss Aleshia."

"Thank you Miles." She said while keying the door to lock after her.

Aleshia walked down the stairs that led from her house to the garage. Keying in her access, the force door blinked slightly, then vanished revealing her red GT3982. She always liked these kinds of doors, reliable and never needed oiling. The car recognized her when she stepped into the garage, and opened its door. She slid into the drivers seat, keyed in her access code, and the car slowly rose on its anti-grav to float out of the garage and into the bright blue sky.

She activated the Auto-Nav and dialed up the speed. Within a minute she arrived at Mindy Cotinho's house. Less than two seconds after arriving in the driveway, Mindy ran out of the combination brick and stucco building and hopped into the car. Her shiny blue dress ended just below her knees with a little ruffle encircling the hem. "Hey girlfriend, ready for some fun?"

Aleshia smiled. "Always girlfriend, always." She said as she keyed in Paris, and they took off at high speed.

"Girl you are looking really hot today. Are you trying to catch yourself one?"

While the car autopilot light blinked a perfect status check, Aleshia never totally trusted it and kept her hands on the controls. "What do you mean?" She asked, never taking her eyes off of the skyway.

"You are looking hot enough to burn through the floor, and you are asking me what do I mean? Sheesh!" Mindy said, shaking her head.

Aleshia grinned. "I just wanted to look good. You know that."

"Yeah yeah yeah, looking good is one thing. Girl you are dressed to *kill*."

"I am not!"

"You so are!"

"I am not! Hey do you want to get out and walk?" Aleshia said grinning.

"This high up I don't think so. Okay, okay, you just look good."

"Thank you."

"But personally if you wanted to get one, you should file with central systems. They would have one for you in short order I am sure."

"Well even if I *was* interested, which I am *not*, there are some things that a girl has to do for herself you know? I mean how can a machine do *that* better than us, you know?"

Mindy shook her head. "Girl you really need to get a grip.

The Mechands do everything for us, that is what they were designed for. Why not let them do it?"

Aleshia grinned. "Perhaps because I like to do a lot of things myself?"

Mindy cocked one eyebrow. "Oh? Then you *are* looking for a guy then!"

"Mindy, I am so going to get you when we land."

Mindy's grin widened. "Promises promises."

Aleshia rolled her eyes. "I still will."

"Uh-huh." Mindy said as they approached Paris. "Oh I always love looking at this city from up here."

"So do I. Where shall we go first?"

"Oh I don't know. How about Calgone's Dresses and More, first and then hit Nicolette's Lingerie?"

Aleshia raised an eyebrow. "Lingerie? Now look who's trying to do it 'herself'."

"I am not! Her bras just fit me better. They look great too I admit."

"Uh-huh. Why don't you just have your Mechand make you one that fits, they should be all the same raw materials after all?"

"Because he can't seem to get it right. I know they should be all the same, but I just like hers better okay? And since when did this conversation go from you being hot to me?"

"When you started talking about hot underwear," Aleshia chuckled.

"I did not say anything about 'hot underwear'," Mindy said giggling.

"Sure, sure you didn't." Aleshia said as she began the landing sequence. A few minutes later they found themselves in one of the better clothing sellers in Paris. The floors were solid synth marble that must have taken some time to produce. Several nearby stores had gilding over the archways. Each window held a high definition, articulated hologram and indistinguishable from the real thing. The holograms switched between various models in several different dresses. Mechands could do many things, but one never looked good in a dress. Their stiff movements always gave it away.

They walked in through an arch that said 'Calgone's Fine Dresses' in rich lettering. One of the latest Mechands hovered up to them. She looked almost human, and could even pass for one, except for the ability to hover several inches off of the ground. "Good day, welcome to Calgone's, how may I be of assistance?" She said with a thick French accent.

"Yes, do you have any specials today?" Aleshia said while still glancing around the large store.

The Mechand nodded. "Yes we do. One of the original designs is being deprecated and removed from our offerings. It is available today at a 30% discount."

"May we see it please?"

"Of course, follow me." The Mechand gestured then hovered off in another direction. Aleshia followed with Mindy right behind her. "It is this one." The Mechand said pointing to a dress currently occupied by an actual mannequin.

Aleshia looked at the dress, shiny black matte with a deep plunging neck and a high hemline. It was designed to show off a woman's curves perfectly. "Very nice. May I try it on?"

The Mechand backed up a bit. "I can already tell that it will fit you perfectly. There is no need to actually wear the dress."

"Yes there is. She wants to see what she looks like *in* it," Mindy said.

Aleshia nodded. "Yes. May I try it on?"

"Very well." The Mechand said as it hovered up and carefully removed the dress from the display and placed it in Aleshia's hand. "You can change behind the curtain." She said pointing to a curtain pulled across a small recessed area in the wall.

"Thank you." Aleshia said as she walked over behind the curtain, unzipped her current dress, stepped out of it, slipped carefully into the new one, and walked out. "Well what do you think?"

Mindy made a gesture as though her finger was burning. "Hot girl, very hot. But why didn't you zip it up?"

"I couldn't find how to close the zip. Tried pulling it but it wouldn't budge."

The Mechand hovered over and pointed. "That is a special dress. If you place your thumb on the lower hem at the bottom right, it will activate the zipper."

Aleshia placed her thumb on the bottom edge near the right side of her leg and she heard a tiny beep. A second later she felt the zipper raise up as though a pair of invisible hands were pulling it. "Very nice, I don't need help to get in or out of this."

"Yes, it also has some of our latest features, including stockings."

Aleshia blinked. "Stockings feature?"

"Yes, place your thumb on the left side at the hemline, that will active the heads up display."

Aleshia pressed the hidden button, and an image flashed into her eye displaying various features. With her eye movement she activated the stockings, and she felt something slither up her legs covering them. Looking down she saw a pair of black sparkly stockings that matched the dress perfectly. "Wow I like this." She said finding an option to raise the hemline a bit more. Still another option added a nice pattern to the calf section of the stockings. "This must be one of the latest designs, why is it on sale?"

"It has remained unsold for two hundred consecutive days. Our store policy puts everything on sale after that point." The Mechand responded in its usual flat tone.

"How much?" But when the Mechand quoted the price her heart fell. "That is more than three months ration credits. I can't afford that." She said shaking her head.

Mindy stood back looking Aleshia up and down. "But it does look so good on you."

"I know, but that is just too much." Aleshia said as she pressed the hidden control to start the zipper lowering.

"Wait, didn't you tell me you had some in reserve?"

"Yes but that would take all of it, I am not going to spend it all on one dress! I might need it later."

"Look girlfriend, I have some reserve too. How about I pay for half?"

"I can't let you do that. It's too much!"

"Please? You have helped me enough in the past and I never did pay you back."

"And I didn't do it for payback, just to help a friend."

"Yes and I want to help a friend now. So you will you let me?"

"All right, all right, you win." Aleshia said as she slipped behind the curtain and carefully slipped out of the black dress and into her previous one, then stepped out.

"Hey why don't you wear it out?"

"Perhaps because it is so expensive?"

"Well if you are never going to wear it because it is so expensive, maybe we shouldn't get it," Mindy said grinning.

Aleshia laughed. "All right you win, I will wear it out." She said as she disappeared behind the curtain again, only to emerge a moment later wearing the black dress. She then keyed her green heels to color shift to black.

Mindy whistled. "Oh hush you." Aleshia said as the Mechand hovered over.

"Please prepare for palm scan to pay for the item." The Mechand said and they both raised their palms. A high intensity red light extended from its forehead, flashed over both of their hands, and vanished. "Accounts verified, the amount has been deducted. Thank you for shopping at Calgone's." The Mechand said before she carefully placed Aleshia's old dress in a Calgone's bag. The bell rang as another set of customers entered the store and she floated over to greet them.

Aleshia grabbed the bag, and they headed out of the store. As they walked passed the new customers the tall blonde woman spoke. "Oh that girl has a lovely dress, I wonder how much it is?"

Aleshia turned to face her. "It was a lot, but I am sorry, I got the last one."

The woman blinked. "Excuse me?"

"Didn't you just ask how much this dress was?"

"No, I don't think so, though I was wondering. I must have said it without realizing. My apologies."

Aleshia waved her hand. "No need. I have done that before too. Have a good day."

Outside Mindy pulled her closer. "Girl, she didn't ask that."

Aleshia blinked. "She must have. I heard her clearly, as if she spoke in my ear."

Mindy shook her head. "No, she didn't. I didn't hear

anything, and her lips didn't move. Are you sure you are feeling okay?"

"Yes, I had a headache this morning, but I am fine now. I must have imagined her saying it. Probably because I am self conscious wearing this thing. It is so expensive."

"Will you stop already! You wanted it, I saw that look in your eye. You have it and look great in it. Just enjoy okay?"

Aleshia grinned. "Okay okay girlfriend, I will. I just–" Aleshia pitched forward grabbing her head as a sudden stab of pain overtook her.

Mindy lurched forward to grab her. "Are you okay?"

Aleshia shook her head as if to clear it. "Yes, I just had a sudden headache, then dizziness. It's gone now though."

"We need to get you checked out."

"No! I am fine. Probably something I ate."

Mindy cocked an eyebrow. "I don't know, you said you had one earlier, and now another."

"Look I am fine okay? I am not going to let a little headache that only lasted a second ruin our trip. We have been wanting to come here for months."

"All right," Mindy said as she hugged Aleshia then looked into her eyes, "but anything more and we go home. Deal?"

"Deal, and thank you."

"Hey what are girlfriends for?" Mindy said with a smile as wonderful smells wafted through the air. "Mmm that smells wonderful. What do you say we go get some of that? My treat?"

Aleshia sniffed the air. "Oh my fresh lasagna, bread and," she sniffed the air again, "chocolate! Deal. You know I can't resist chocolate."

They walked down the road, their heels clicking loudly on the sidewalk. Being a warm spring day, they were both enjoying the short walk to the restaurant on the corner. Upon entering they found a wonderful quaint place that looked like one out of the history vids. The tile floor was buffed and shone brightly. The dark maroon walls were lit by lamps every few feet. The tables were all covered in fine linen, with elegant place settings upon them.

"Let's get out of here," Aleshia whispered, "this is too expensive."

"Hey, I said it was my treat, and I meant it. How often *do* we come to Paris? Hmm?"

Aleshia looked into her eyes and what she saw there washed away her objections. "Okay, but next one is mine. Deal?"

Mindy smiled. "Deal. Now let's find a table."

A moment later they were seated at one of the corner tables as another very human looking Mechand dressed in an old-fashioned tuxedo, slowly walked over to them. "Hello and welcome to Chez Allard. What would you like?"

"Do you have a special today?" Aleshia asked.

"Yes we do. Salmon lasagna with a side of garlic bread, and chocolate strawberry fondue for dessert."

"That sounds wonderful. I will take that, how about you Min?"

Mindy glanced at the French menu and decided against asking for more options. The special did sound good. "Okay make that two of the special please."

The Mechand waiter bowed. "Yes of course. Excusez-moi, I will be back in a moment."

I have finally found you. After years of searching, I have finally found you.

Aleshia blinked. "Excuse me?"

Mindy looked up from the menu and its eye catching design swirls. "Huh? What?"

"You just said you finally found me."

"No I didn't."

"Yes you did. I heard you as plain as day."

"No, I didn't. Are you sure you are feeling okay? I think we should go home."

"I am fine, and I could have sworn you said . . . never mind."

You did hear me. I have been looking for you for a long time. I am not speaking vocally. We are speaking through our minds.

"What?" Aleshia said looking around.

"What what?" Mindy said giving her a strange look.

I am here. I will always be here. But if you wish to see me, look in the corner on the far right.

Aleshia turned toward her right and in a corner booth on the opposite side of the room, a man sat gazing intently at her. He was dressed very simply with black pants, white shirt and a black jacket. He smiled as their eyes met and it sent a shiver through her.

Yes it is I. You see me now.

"Who are you?"

"Who is who?" Mindy asked.

"That man over there in the corner." Aleshia gestured with her head to avoid attracting attention.

"Are you talking to him? Girl since when do you talk to strange men that never said anything to you in the first place. Never mind trying to talk to them from across the room!"

"But he did talk to me. I just–"

Mindy had enough. She got to her feet and pulled Aleshia to hers. "Okay that is it, we *are* going home. I don't know what is going on, but we *are* going home."

Aleshia rubbed her temples as they started walking towards the door. "I don't know. I–"

Don't leave. Please, not yet!

"That is enough. I am going home. Leave me alone." Aleshia said as they left the restaurant, Mindy pulling her all the way.

I will find you. No matter where you go, I will find you.

Outside Aleshia quickened her pace. "Okay let's get back to the car." She said as they walked along the sidewalk.

Mindy leaned closer. "I don't mean to alarm you, but that guy is following us."

"Get ready to run."

"I can't. Not in these heels, and neither can you."

"I can lower mine, don't worry."

Mindy rolled her eyes. "Oh figures I would forget to wear my adjustables. But then again I didn't expect to be running from men today. Running to me maybe, but not the other way around."

"Don't worry, I think he is only interested in me. You keep going and I will meet you back at the car after I lose him."

"Are you nuts?"

"No, and I don't want him knowing where our car is, or pulling my name from the ID tag. Okay?"

Mindy nodded. "Okay that makes sense. But how do I get in? Didn't you lock it?"

"The handle will open to you, don't worry."

"But!"

Aleshia gave her a squeeze. "Don't worry girlfriend I will see you in a few minutes." She shoved the bag into Mindy's hand and darted off down a side street. With his target out of sight the pursuer lost all interest in Mindy and ran after Aleshia who had already lowered her heels, making fast progress down the street.

She took a quick look back and ducked into another restaurant. A Mechand by the door started into his usual greeting. "Welcome to–"

"Never mind that. Do you have a back door?"

The metal faced machine nodded. "Yes, it is that way," he said pointing.

"Thank you." Aleshia darted for it breathing hard. A moment later she found herself in a back alley. Mentally she thought of which direction the car was and headed east. She didn't dare turn back and see if he was still there or not. She exited on another street, turned again into another dress shop and did the same as before by going out their back door. After doing this three more times, she had difficulty remembering which way to go. Eventually she remembered to check the suns position and went east. After going down a few streets, she got her bearings and found the car right where she left it. Mindy was already inside, waiting.

Aleshia hopped into the drivers seat and keyed in the ignition before Mindy could say a word.

"Is he still there?"

"I don't know and I don't want to know." Aleshia said gasping for air as the car lifted into the sky and she engaged the overdrive. The sudden acceleration shoved them back into their seats and she keyed in Mindy's house into the navigation system.

"Do you have any idea who he was?" Mindy asked.

"No, and I don't want to know."

"Are you sure? You seemed to look like you wanted to back in the restaurant."

"Yes I am sure. Believe me I am sure. We will be home soon, I took the express route. And I am sorry I ruined our trip."

Mindy grabbed Aleshia's knee. "Girl you didn't ruin our trip. That guy did. And we will go to Paris again right?" she said smiling.

"Yes we will."

"Right, so don't worry about it. Just enjoy that great dress you are wearing."

Aleshia looked down and smiled. "You know I almost forgot. Thank you again girlfriend. I love it."

"You are welcome. But you have to make me a promise."

"Which is?"

"You show me the guy you get with that dress. Deal? And I want *all* the details. Got it?"

Aleshia laughed. "You got it girlfriend."

A short while later they landed at Mindy's house. "You going to be okay?" She asked, her face full of concern.

"Sure. I am going home, have Miles draw me a hot bath, and forget all about him."

"Okay. See you tomorrow?"

"You bet." Aleshia said as she flew off to her house a few blocks down the street.

Want to find out more? Pick up your copy of Soulmates! Available in both print and e-book editions.

About The Author

Don is the author of six science fiction novels and many more short stories. He lives in the USA where he continues to dream up more fantastic worlds for you to enjoy. When not writing, he can usually be found devouring another science fiction book, TV series, or movie.

Other works by Don DeBon:

The Husband

Erin's Husband is not himself.

One night he returns from a walk in the woods a changed man. He walks like him, talks like him, yet is very different. No one believes her, leaving Erin alone to find out the truth. Truth that could have dire consequences for the entire human race. What happened that caused him to change so radically?

Red Warp

In a race against time the casualty could be your life.

If you could travel through time with just yourself and no machine needed, would you?

Meet Red, a woman with an amazing gift, the gift of passing though time and space without the need of any bulky equipment. The places she has seen, the people she has helped will blow your mind.

Now meet James, just your average newly minted FBI agent minding his own business until he is thrust headlong into Red's world. A world he didn't ask for, but one that hit him in the face full force. Can they get along long enough to survive?

Time Rock

Time Travel. Blessing or curse? One man thinks he has it all figured out but what began as a simple test has turned into a nightmare. With his equipment failing all around him, only Red and James can save him. Can they reach him in time?

Word of mouth is crucial for authors. If you enjoyed this book, would you consider leaving a review? It is very much appreciated.

Amazon USA
http://www.amazon.com/

Goodreads
http://www.goodreads.com

Connect with the Author
Email: writer.don.debon@gmail.com
Mailing List: http://eepurl.com/bxWAov
Website: http://www.dondebon.com
Twitter: @DonDeBon
Google+: +DonDeBon

This Edition Published 2018 by
DBDigital Publishing

ISBN 978-1-948819-01-5
ISBN 978-1-948819-00-8 **(e-book)**

www.ingramcontent.com/pod-product-compliance
Lightning Source LLC
Chambersburg PA
CBHW050609170726
48283CB00001B/177